LOLTH'S
WARRIOR

FORGOTTEN REALMS

LOLTH'S
WARRIOR

A NOVEL
THE WAY OF THE DROW, BOOK 3
R. A. Salvatore

HARPER Voyager
An Imprint of HarperCollins*Publishers*

To Diane, who's been beside me throughout this wonderful journey, whose sacrifices and contributions in allowing me to pursue this dream in the same years we were raising our family cannot be underestimated.

CONTENTS

It was a long while before they were able to close their slack jaws.

ARDEN

SCELLOBEL

CATTISOLA

CASCATTE

CALLIDAE

Below and before them lay a valley within the glacier. Callidae.

B'SHETT

MONA CHESS

River Callidae
the only way out without climbing

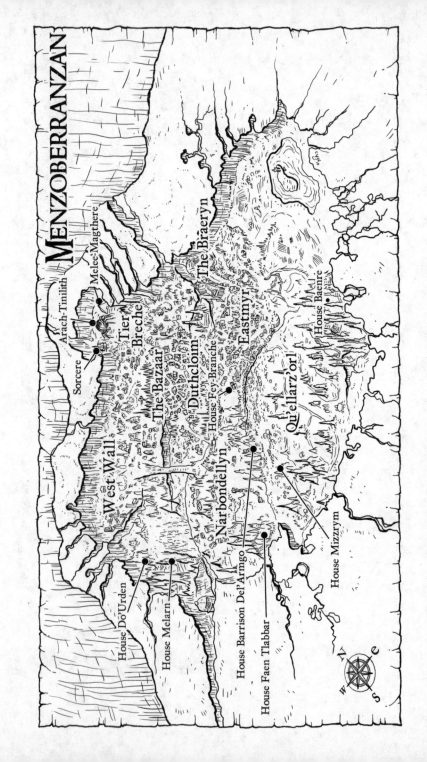

PROLOGUE

Let it play," the lump of yochlol mud who was Yiccardaria said to her co-conspirator Eskavidne.

"Like the sludge swirling at our feet," the other hand-maiden of Lolth agreed. "As it will, without prediction, chaotic and wonderful. How beautiful it is."

"Truly marvelous," Yiccardaria agreed. "It tickles because it flows upon me at unexpected angles. These fools who seek patterns . . ." She shook her head, which, in this particular form, meant that the entire upper half of her half-melted candle-shaped form swayed left and right.

"They need order to make sense of the senseless."

"They need control. But they can never have control. Not truly."

"Lolth is chaos and chaos is truth," said Eskavidne.

"Shall we wager on the outcome?"

"Yes, of course. We mustn't waste such an enjoyable opportunity."

"The winner gets to properly train the newest drider when she is sent to us, as surely will happen in the war up above."

"And the loser?" Eskavidne asked, and she gurgled with laughter—

they both did, for there were no losers to be found among them. Just a winner.

"Training that one would be enjoyable, yes," Eskavidne agreed, knowing exactly the drow Yiccardaria referenced. "She gave her all to Lady Lolth for centuries. Everything. All of it. And to what end? Such a pity. She heads one of the oldest and most loyal houses in the city. For so long, so very long, that one and those around her were strong with Lolth. And now she is not and her fall is complete."

"No pity," Yiccardaria corrected. "That is the beauty, the *surprise* of chaos."

"So true. And now I wish to win this wager. You choose, my sister, Baenre or Melarn?"

"Zhindia Melarn has much on her side."

"Including us!"

"For the moment."

"True, true."

There came a gurgle of laughter from both yochlols, muddy burps in rapid cadence.

"The Baenres and their allies will win," Eskavidne decided. "Matron Mother Quenthel or one of her nobles will see the truth before it is too late for their house."

"No, they are weak now and possessed of mercy. Matron Zhindia is not. She will torture all she can capture, make of them driders. The Blaspheme will turn on the heretics if Zhindia promises them redemption."

"Some, but not all."

"But enough. And Zhindia's alliance is the stronger, for fear of our Spider Queen," Yiccardaria added. "The Baenre allies may well hide in their holes or desert altogether before long."

"They are the Baenres," Eskavidne countered. "They have ruled Menzoberranzan since the beginning. They understand the way of things."

"They have ruled?" came another voice, melodic and beautiful—to the handmaidens, the most beautiful voice ever spoken. It wasn't clear if it emphasized "they" or "ruled," but there was certainly amusement in the tone.

Both turned to see the approach of Lolth, a gigantic spider and drow combination of a being that evoked so many emotions, from love and terror to everything in between.

"Ruled for you, of course," Eskavidne clarified. "Until the heresy."

"Ah, yes, the heresy. And a beautiful thing, was it not?" Lolth said with a continual background of hissing laughter filtering across every word. "When the namesake of Yvonnel the Eternal was first given a taste of stealing back from me the rogue who had been turned into a drider, she simply could not resist."

"Pure chaos," said Yiccardaria. "And no more confused and disjointed than in the minds of those driders who rushed through the web she wove with the Matron Mother."

"A masterstroke. I commend your play these last months," Lolth told the two. "I expected no less of you and am not disappointed."

"Your praise is all," the two recited together.

"Your part is done, then," Lolth explained. "You have rolled the stones from the mountaintop, and now we must just watch and enjoy where the trails and valleys take them."

Few could recognize the face of a yochlol in its true form, and fewer still could understand the expressions on those muddied gobs. Lolth was one of the few non-yochlol beings who could decipher those strange facial tics.

"Why do you appear disappointed?" Lolth asked. "You have rolled the stones perfectly, and the damage is done. Your chaotic child is free to bounce and destroy as it will."

"It was so much fun, though," said Eskavidne.

"Yes," Yiccardaria reasoned, realizing Lolth's will, "but if we continue, then how might we wager without interfering in the outcome?"

"True. But I do so enjoy prompting the zealots and frightening the heretics," Eskavidne said.

"There *are* no heretics," Lolth reminded them.

If it was possible for yochlols to nod, they both did so. "From how afar do we watch?" Yiccardaria asked. "The fires burn bright and there is no limit to their fuel."

"All the better," Lolth said. "Watch from afar or play as you will. There are few rules for you here."

"How many of your children in Menzoberranzan will you allow to die?" Yiccardaria bluntly asked.

"Does it matter in the end?" The spider queen shrugged, ten arms and legs conveying her indifference. "Half may die, but the city will survive. The society may change, but the chaos I've bred there will remain."

"The Baenres could lose control," Eskavidne warned.

"They already have, and it is a beautiful thing," Lolth assured them. "Whichever house, if indeed it is a different house, that ascends when the blood has dried will have earned the right to claim the city . . . until the next conflict, of course."

"And if it is House Baenre, and the heret . . . the upstarts?" Yiccardaria asked.

"Then you two will begin a new play."

"We will rebuild the City of Shimmering Webs," Eskavidne offered. "And fill it with any who survive and prefer the old ways, and find for them many more allies, drow and duergar, or any others who would rush to claim Ched Nasad as a home. A rival city to Menzoberranzan until the Baenres are toppled."

"They will be toppled from within," Yiccardaria insisted.

"From without," Eskavidne insisted.

"I see that you are already on to your next game," said Lolth approvingly.

"A competition this time," Eskavidne agreed. "I think the Baenres will win, and then I will work to defeat them—from without."

"While I work to defeat them from within," said Yiccardaria.

"And if Zhindia Melarn and her allies prove victorious?" Lolth asked. "Then the city will be secure in its devotion, so does the play end?'"

That gave the two yochlols pause, and they slurped about to look at each other and gurgled in unison, the yochlol version of "hmm."

"Then we will have to find division within," said Eskavidne.

"And new enemies without!" Yiccardaria added.

"Perhaps our play is not quite done," Eskavidne offered. "Our play in this initial game, yes, but there are those on the side of Zhindia who are too ambitious to bow to her."

"Mez'Barris Armgo," Yiccardaria purred, and the two gurgled and giggled.

"So if Zhindia should win . . ."

"You see? That is why my word is the truth," said Lolth. "Chaos is easy. It is the natural way."

"So we are done now in letting the sides sort, except to watch and enjoy?" Yiccardaria said.

"And to try not to get ourselves banished in the chaos of battle," Eskavidne added.

"As you will," Lolth offered them. "There is always enjoyment to be found, and you have earned that."

"But are there any we must protect?" Yiccardaria asked.

"Who might there be?"

"The young Yvonnel, who has been given so much," said Eskavidne.

"And Drizzt Do'Urden," the other handmaiden added. "You have long desired to break him to your side. In death, he may be beyond even your long grasp."

"Protect *none*," Lolth instructed with firm resolve. "If Yvonnel cannot find her way out of this danger, then she is not worth the effort. She has served her purpose in this grand play, and so much sooner than I ever believed possible."

"And Drizzt Do'Urden?" Yiccardaria pressed when Lolth hesitated.

"He is no longer of any real importance," Lolth told them. "His actions have helped to bring the city to this needed time of cleansing, this beautiful time of carnage and chaos. But this is the expected and anticipated culmination of his journey. His use to us will be greater if he is killed, for he will become then true legend, a martyr for the foolish, and forever a whisper of false hope and heresy.

"An unwitting symbol of what devotion to my chaos can bring.

"Protect none," the godlike Spider Queen finished. "You have rolled the stones from the mountaintop. Enjoy their paths of destruction."

PART 1

MALAISE

My previous malaise embarrasses me. When I returned to this life, I did so without the proper appreciation of . . . this life! And with that shortcoming, so, too, did I pass that malaise on to those around me. Not intentionally, no, but my actions and words, my detachment from the very responsibilities of friendship, of partnership, of parenting, could not be ignored, even as I worked harder to cover them up.

That which I had witnessed in what I believe is the next existence had brought upon me a great despair, and an almost overwhelming sense of the smallness of our current state of being. Not outwardly, but within my own consciousness.

I could not have been more wrong.

How could I have allowed myself to be so tempted by that which might come next, to ignore that which is here and now? It took a ferocious battle, a great victory, a great personal loss, and a moment of shared exultation to show me my errors.

Callidae was more than I could have ever hoped for—for all of us who were born and raised in Menzoberranzan, the journey through that city among the aevendrow was the fulfillment of our (almost always secret) hopes and visions and lamentations of what Menzoberranzan might have been.

For me, it also ended a personal debate that, from the beginning, seemed to have an obvious answer—yet still, it was immensely satisfying to see my beliefs proven so dramatically:

It was Lolth. Always Lolth.

Not the religion of her worshippers—for how can anyone rightly call it a religion, after all, since the "divine being" for whom you're supposed to take on as a matter of faith is, in fact, a dictatorial menace who's often meddling directly with her "flock," and surely doling out extreme punishments directly? Worshipping Lolth in Menzoberranzan isn't a matter of faith—hardly! It's not even obeisance, or any expression of deserved respect or gratitude or any such thing. No, it is blind obedience, a subjugation of one's own will stemming from either a hunger for power—such as with many of the ruling matrons—or simple, logical terror for almost everyone else.

I will shake my head until it clears, until I somehow come to understand this notion of fear as a great motivation.

But while that has always been a compelling issue for me—and will continue to plague my thoughts and drive my actions—I also must take time to examine my own thoughts and feelings regarding Callidae, my here and now.

That is the most pressing thing, and another important realization: the need to live in the present.

And here I must admit my foolishness in allowing the beauty of transcendence to almost steal so much from me. For if the journey from this life to the next is what I now believe it to be, then yes, had I remained in that higher state, outside of this mortal body, dead to this life and alive in the next, I would have learned of Callidae and of all the other drow cities and clans the aevendrow told me existed throughout the surface world of Faerun. I would have known them in that oneness, in that complete and beautiful understanding.

But would I have felt them? Would I have felt Callidae with the living sensations that overwhelmed me up there on the icy shelf when first I looked over the city? Would I have held Catti-brie for support, and kissed her so dearly for bringing me to that place? Would my joy have multiplied by the look on her face in sharing this discovery she and the others had made with me? And would my joy grow even more in seeing Jarlaxle's smile, Zaknafein's nod, and even the glow that emanated so clearly from Artemis Entreri? By the look on the face of Jarlaxle as he, at long last, found what he had spent much of his life seeking?

We shared a lot on that high ledge when he nodded knowingly to me.

Would I have found wonder in the sublime calm of Kimmuriel, who at long last had found a measure of value and caring that he before could only hope existed?

Or in the sobs of Gromph (though he did well to hide them), the great and powerful Archmage at long last humbled into admitting his own feelings, overwhelmed as he had never before allowed, by something beyond his control, by something that had brought him such joy that was not of his own making?

As much as the sight of Callidae had meant to me—and I cannot understate the importance of realizing that place and those aevendrow—sharing that moment with the others, absorbing their myriad expressions and emotions and taking them as my own and giving to them my own, made it all the more wonderful.

And that is the rub of transcendence. That is the fear I hold of losing something this special if, indeed, there is no individuality. And since this is an answer I cannot yet know, then this is a fear I cannot yet dismiss.

But so be it.

Because, now, finally, I understand.

I am in this moment of my journey, in this forming word of my story.

The present will not be a prisoner of the past.

The present will not be a servant for the future.

In the weight of it all, it is the journey that matters, the moment, the forming word.

I will continue to speak it until I'm ready for that new, different conversation.

—Drizzt Do'Urden

CHAPTER 1

Lines Drawn and
Legs Quartered

I had great hopes for her," Yvonnel Baenre admitted to Matron Mother Quenthel. The powerful drow was frustrated. She had thought that Kyrnill Melarn—who had once been Matron Kyrnill Kenafin and was not thrilled at the current arrangement that had put her into the family and service of the zealous Zhindia—would be her informant in her designs for defeating Zhindia and her Lolthian minions.

But Kyrnill had steered them wrong by indicating that House Melarn would attack the Baenres' allied forces at the lake of Donigarten, when instead the Lolthian forces and their demonic allies had swept into and through House Fey-Branche.

"I will kill her," said Minolin Fey Baenre, who was standing beside Matron Mother Quenthel's throne.

"Let us not be quick to presume—" Quenthel started, but Minolin Fey's huff stopped her short.

The outburst was understandable to the other two women. Minolin was the daughter of Matron Byrtyn Fey, after all, who had been taken in the raid on House Fey-Branche, and was now held prisoner in the city's formidable Second House, Barrison Del'Armgo.

"I have information that Kyrnill's daughter, the priestess Ash'ala, was not murdered by Matron Zhindia," Quenthel explained. "She was tortured most horribly in the milk bath of maggots, but she remains alive."

"What is left of her remains alive," Minolin Fey remarked sourly.

"Enough to make her mother rethink her espionage?" Quenthel asked.

"None of the Kenafin line within House Melarn is loyal to Zhindia," said Yvonnel. "But they are rightfully afraid of her, and of the power that supports her. Whatever the case, our informant is lost to us. We are well beyond that stage of the war now anyway. Only two of the most powerful houses are undeclared now—three, if we consider House Hunzrin truly out of the conflict."

"Four if House Fey-Branche is likewise sidelined," Minolin Fey said.

Yvonnel nodded, but only for her mother's sake. She hadn't even been thinking of House Fey-Branche when she had made her remark. Byrtyn sat on the Ruling Council, for what that was now worth, of course, but that was more a matter of legacy than the current power of House Fey-Branche. And after the successful and brutal raid by Zhindia's allies, House Fey-Branche was even less significant in any material way.

The symbolism, however, remained critical.

"We will know of House Fey-Branche soon enough," Quenthel assured them. "The Ruling Council is called and our demands for Matron Byrtyn and the other captured Fey-Branche nobles have been made quite clear to Matron Mez'Barris Armgo and all else who would side with Zhindia."

"Faen Tlabbar is the only house left undeclared of the noble eight," Yvonnel said. "Their actions at that Ruling Council will be critical, as will those of First Priestess Sos'Umptu."

"Sos'Umptu," Quenthel echoed with disgust. "She will no longer walk on the edge of a knife. My dear sister will fall to the side of Zhindia Melarn or she will step to our side in this fight."

"She will wish to remain above the battle, to serve her demon god when the blood dries," said Minolin Fey.

"There is no neutral position," Quenthel reiterated.

"Oh, but there is," Yvonnel corrected. "And we will see it often among the houseless drow of the Stenchstreets—and who can blame them? And among the lesser houses, who know that to choose wrong in this war will be their utter demise when, as you said, the blood dries. But for Sos'Umptu, you are right: there is no edge to walk, not now that the knife is blooded."

"I should have killed Zhindia Melarn when I had the chance those years ago," Yvonnel remarked.

"The handmaiden stopped you," Quenthel reminded.

"The handmaiden *asked* me to stop. Yiccardaria could not have stopped me had I denied her request." She shook her head. "In that same time, I removed the Curse of Abomination from one of Jarlaxle's associates, a prelude to the great event you and I created on the surface."

"What does that tell you?" Quenthel asked.

Yvonnel shook her head, trying to process it all. She had known she could reverse the curse, but it was not something commonly done, of course, even if the one who had been turned into a drider had later been found to be innocent of whatever insult to Lolth had doomed them in the first place. Yet she had known then that she could remove the state of drider from the Bregan D'aerthe scout, and she had done so with handmaidens in the city.

Was it all a tease by Lolth?

"This all occurred before," Minolin Fey offered then, putting her hand on Yvonnel's forearm.

"Before?" Quenthel asked.

"Before we knew. Before we came to see the truth. Before we came to understand the great deception that Lolth long ago placed upon our ancestors and the devastating march to this present place in Menzoberranzan. For those of us here in House Baenre now, or siding with House Baenre in this fight, can any hold less blame for following the edicts of Lolth's handmaidens than Yvonnel? If we are damned by our actions before we came to see the truth, then we are all damned."

"But we do not believe that," said Matron Mother Quenthel. "Because if we did, then what reason for this war? Because if we did, then what play was our web to steal the Curse of Abomination from the Blaspheme?

"Because if we did, then what is the point?"

"To any of it," Yvonnel finished and agreed. "I only wish I had been more prescient in that moment and finished off the zealot Zhindia."

"You said that already—it's in the past, and your regrets do us no good now. Besides, Lolth would have found one to replace her," Quenthel said with a shrug and a sigh.

Yvonnel couldn't really argue with that.

"At least Zhindia is stupid," offered Minolin Fey, drawing astonished looks from the other two. Minolin Fey took their surprise as a compliment. She rather liked being underestimated by all around her, ally and foe alike. "Well, she is."

HE FROZE WHEN HE HEARD HER VOICE DOWN THE NATU-ral tunnel from his dungeon door. The part of Dinin that just wanted to get it over with could not stand up to the reality that this might *be* the moment. For all the dread of waiting for Matron Zhindia to fulfill her promise, the execution of that threat meant that this would be his last day as a living drow.

He began shaking his head, trembling, his eyes darting all about, looking for some escape, though he knew of course that there was none.

Still he searched, forced himself from his paralyzing fear, when he saw the glimmer of light down the uneven and broken tunnel up here in the great cavern's ceiling above House Melarn.

She was coming.

She was coming for him.

He was going to be a drider again.

No more looking for a way out; Dinin began searching for some way to kill himself. He had held out hope that maybe a reprieve—a rescue—might be coming, but he knew that to be futile now and hoped he had enough agency to go out on his own terms. To end the nightmare before he lived it . . . again. He felt along the walls for the most jagged bit of stone he could find, then backpedaled as far as his small cell would allow.

He bent low, put his arms back behind him, leaned his forehead and face before him. He told himself to go, to rush into the wall. But still, he wasn't moving!

"Matron Zhindia!" he heard a guard say, not far away.

Dinin sprinted into the wall. He managed to hold his arms back just long enough for his forehead to take the brunt of the impact.

He staggered backward, knees wobbling, blood dripping down over one eye.

But he didn't fall.

So he ran again, then a third time, then stood right before the jag of stone, beating his head against it.

The world blurred. The dim light became darkness.

The sweet release of death, he thought fleetingly as he fell, fell, and kept falling. He suffered no pain, felt nothing at all except for the sensation of falling.

He heard laughter. He hoped it wasn't Lolth or one of her handmaidens, hoped that he had somehow escaped the Abyss this time.

Then, so suddenly, he did indeed feel the pain! Burning across his forehead, throbbing in his mind as he returned to consciousness.

He blinked his eyes open to see Matron Zhindia standing over him, laughing at him.

"What fool runs face-first into a wall?" she chided.

Another spell of healing fell over him—not from Zhindia, but from one of the priestesses standing beside her.

"One who knows that the Curse of Abomination is about to befall him," that priestess answered the matron.

"He wasn't even strong enough to kill himself," added a man standing in the back, one Dinin recognized as Narl'dorltyrr Melarn, the house weapon master. Naldorl, as he was called, like his aunt Zhindia had been a Horlbar noble son back in the days before the houses Horlbar and Kenafin had joined to become House Melarn. Dinin knew this one, or had known him long ago, when he had attended the Academy of Melee-Magthere in the same class as Dinin.

Despite his fears at that moment, Dinin managed a scowl at Naldorl. How many times in Melee-Magthere had Dinin bested this one? And that was before Dinin had returned home for even better training under the tutelage of Zaknafein. Yes, this current situation must be an enjoyable moment for that pathetic warrior.

The attempt to bury his fear under rage only lasted until Matron Zhindia began to speak once more.

"Is this true, son of House Do'Urden?" she purred, moving closer to her prisoner. "Did you not think your time as a true servant of Lolth was exhilarating? Do you fear returning to her service now?"

Dinin didn't answer. He was quite sure that he didn't have to answer, given the expression he knew to be on his face, given the way he couldn't stop darting his gaze about, searching for some way out, and given the warm wetness he felt down his leg.

His legs gave out beneath him. He heard the priestess and Naldorl laughing and tried in vain to turn that mockery and embarrassment into the strength to fight back against his weakness.

But he could not. Nothing could be worse than this. No torture, no pain, no loss whether physical or emotional could come near to the dread of what he knew was about to befall him: the exquisite and unending agony of the Curse of Abomination. He could almost feel his legs splitting and then splitting again, his bones breaking and reshaping, and that interminable, ceaseless, and stinging ringing in his ears.

He felt his captors pick him back up and hold him upright, for his legs could not.

"Perhaps I will stay the verdict, Dinin Do'Urden," Zhindia said, but he didn't react, because he was certain that this was just her way of trying to make it even worse—which was impossible, for nothing could be worse!

"Sit him down against the wall," he heard her order, and a moment later, he crashed hard against the stone and heard a groan escape his lips.

A bucket of water was dumped over him, shocking him back to

clarity. He shook his head and opened his eyes wide, and a flash of possibility came to him—perhaps he could leap up and attack Zhindia and force them to kill him before the transformation.

That thought flew away as soon as the scene before him registered clearly, for now two others were standing beside the matron. They were beautiful and they were fully naked, a pair of drow women, or so they seemed for just a few eyeblinks until they transformed into their true yochlol forms, like towering half-melted candles of mud.

Handmaidens of Lolth.

The notion staggered Dinin. Why were they here? He was nothing to them.

"In this one instance, perhaps I was wrong," Zhindia said to him. "You see, that is why we have the guidance of Lolth, here in the form of Eskavidne and Yiccardaria. They have counseled me differently, and so as much as I would enjoy watching you break apart and bloat and become again a drider, that may not be your fate. Not now, at least, and on this promise of mine and of these two beautiful creatures beside me, perhaps not ever.

"It remains up to you, though.

"Are you willing to do a service for the Spider Queen, Dinin Do'Urden? Are you willing to serve Lolth in an important task?"

"Anything. Please." His voice surprised him, the fear and pleading choking out of him. But he did not regret those words, or the speed in which he spat them out.

Zhindia laughed at him and looked to the yochlols in turn, their bubbling chuckles echoing her own.

"You will enjoy this task, I am sure. You do like revenge?"

He nodded slightly, not sure what to make of any of this.

"Then this is something you are well suited to." She looked at him intently, then said with venomous conviction, "Your brother did all of this to you and to your house. Is it not time for you to repay him?"

"Drizzt?"

"Of course Drizzt, idiot," Zhindia snapped. "He is coming here, to Menzoberranzan. This is assured. Who better to deliver Lolth's message to him than the brother he so terribly wronged?"

"He would not know me, and would not trust me," Dinin heard himself stupidly admit.

"Then what use are you to me?" Zhindia asked, and to the priestess standing over Dinin, she said, "Priestess Calstraa, the scroll."

"No," Dinin begged. "No!"

"Who are you to command me?"

"I—"

"You will make Drizzt trust you?" Zhindia asked, although it sounded as much like an order as a question. "And he will know you. Of course, he will."

"I know you, weakling," Naldorl said from the other side of Dinin. "Surely he will, too."

"I cannot defeat Drizzt," Dinin told Zhindia, and again, the words were simply too stupid to be spoken aloud.

He was under a magical spell of truth, he realized.

"A boy with a knife can kill a great warrior if he stabs him unexpectedly, perhaps while sleeping. But no, Dinin, Lady Lolth does not want you to kill Drizzt. Why would she? He has brought her great enjoyment through the centuries. No, no, she wants you to wound him, more profoundly than any blade ever could."

Dinin licked his lips, trying to find the obvious next question and failing.

"Drizzt is married to a human woman, and together, they have brought an abomination of their own into the world," Zhindia explained. "Kill that abomination. Kill Catti-brie if you find the chance, but only after you murder the one fathered by Drizzt. That alone is your quest. Even one as pathetic as you can find the strength to murder a toddler, yes?

"Then, the worst you can expect is that you will feel the wrath of Drizzt, of Catti-brie, of King Bruenor Battlehammer, of Zaknafein—all of them! They will destroy you if they catch you, of course. But they cannot and will not do to you what I can do—what I surely will do, if you fail. They will kill you, perhaps after some torture, though that is not the way of those particular weaklings. No, they will simply kill you cleanly and swiftly and you will be taken into the arms of Lolth once more, but this time, redeemed."

Dinin didn't know how to react or what to do or say.

"We will know if you are lying," the yochlol to Zhindia's right said in a gurgling voice.

"Will you do this?" asked the other.

"Or will you be cursed here and now?" Zhindia asked.

"Yes," Dinin blurted, and it was all pouring out of him now, and it was, of course, very true. Anything, he would do anything, to avoid the Curse of Abomination. He would kill a hundred children, a million children, of any species so condemned. "I will kill the child, and the human woman if I can. I will find a way to kill Drizzt—"

"No!" Zhindia and both handmaidens said together. "Not Drizzt."

"Drizzt will face Lolth again when you have completed your task," one of the yochlols explained.

"Okay—I will leave him alone. But how will I find her?" Dinin asked. "The child? Surely he won't bring her here."

"With patience," Zhindia explained. "Perhaps it will take you a year, perhaps ten. It matters not. You will kill the child and Lolth will arrive to inform Drizzt of his loss. And it will be glorious!"

"Glorious" wasn't the word Dinin would put on such an act, but he would do it.

He would do anything, anything at all, anything and everything, to escape his fate.

IN THE SOUTHWESTERN CORNER OF THE QU'ELLARZ'ORL, the raised region of Menzoberranzan where most of the greatest houses were located, sat a set of large ironbound doors, guarded by powerful magic in the arch that surrounded them and by an honor guard contingent from the school of Melee-Magthere.

Whatever bickering or even open fighting going on in the city at any time, it could not pass these doors.

For this was the entrance to the chamber of the Ruling Council, a small natural cavern sparingly adorned and lit by scores of everburning candles. A rather unremarkable altar to Lolth stood at the far end of the chamber, left as it had been in the earliest days of the city's founding. The room was dominated by a spider-shaped table and eight splendid chairs adorned with jewels. Until recently, the only other piece of furniture within the natural cave was a plain chair reserved for an invited guest, but now a tenth chair had been added—this one as fabulous as those for the eight ruling matrons.

It had been added for the priestess now sitting in it, the First Priestess of the Fane of the Quarvelsharess, also known as the Fane of the Goddess. Like the matrons who would be arriving, she was allowed two bodyguards, and Sos'Umptu's escorts this day were quite unexpected, quite remarkable, and quite telling. She had been the first to arrive to the council, followed soon after by Matron Mother Quenthel.

Quenthel and her escorting bodyguards, Yvonnel and the House Baenre weapon master Andzrel, said nothing as they entered, although both Quenthel and Yvonnel, recognizing the handmaidens Eskavidne and Yiccardaria flanking Sos'Umptu's chair, did raise their eyebrows a bit.

The Matron Mother spoke not a word to her sister, nor looked at her with more than a fleeting glance, as she took her seat at the end of the table's left foreleg, with Yvonnel and Andzrel, who were not permitted to speak in any event, moving to the wall behind her.

The six sat there quietly as the minutes passed.

Quenthel looked at the seat across the spider table's pedipalps, to the empty chair of Matron Mez'Barris Armgo of the Second House. She had feared that Mez'Barris wouldn't show up to the meeting, as that would be a statement greater than any the matron might make here. She held out hope that the woman would soon make a grand entrance, an unharmed Matron Byrtyn Fey at her side.

She wiped all expression from her face, stoically watching; despite her desperate hopes, held her breath in hope when the door opened again.

In walked Matron Vadalma Tlabbar of the city's Fourth House, Faen Tlabbar, long an ally of House Baenre—but now?

Without a word, Vadalma took her assigned seat next to the chair of Mez'Barris.

Quenthel was pleased that Vadalma had come. She glanced at Sos'Umptu, and couldn't read the look on her sister's face as Sos'Umptu, too, considered the latest arrival. On the surface and in normal times, Vadalma seemed an obvious ally of Quenthel's. But these were not normal times. House Faen Tlabbar was among the most devout Lolthian houses in the city, perhaps second only to the insanely cruel Zhindia Melarn and her brood. Those two houses had long been vicious rivals, ever vying for the favor of the Spider Queen. But if the favor of Lolth was firmly on Melarn, would Vadalma be proud enough to reject Lolth's will?

The door opened again, but it was not Mez'Barris escorting an unharmed Byrtyn Fey—had it been, Quenthel might have dared to hope that the war was nearing an end with the obvious defeat of Zhindia Melarn.

But no, it was Zeerith Xorlarrin Do'Urden, escorted by her two children, Priestess Saribel and the wizard Ravel.

Quenthel thought that strange, for she had never seen Zeerith's children serving as house bodyguards at the Ruling Council before.

Old Zeerith wasn't walking, but rather, floating on a magical disc of blue-white light. It drifted up to her chair, at Quenthel's side, and there her children helped the ancient matron into her proper seat.

She looked frail, Quenthel saw. Battered and very fretful.

"I feared I was late," Zeerith said to Quenthel, but loud enough for the others at the table to hear.

"You are," Sos'Umptu replied.

"And yet I'm not the only one. What word on Matron Byrtyn?" Zeerith asked specifically to Quenthel.

"That is why we are here. To learn of her fate most of all, and to see where the alliances have fallen."

"If I am late to the council, it would seem we have our answer to the latter question," said Zeerith.

"Do we?" Sos'Umptu interjected.

"Soon," Quenthel snapped back at her. "Five of the houses are notably absent, and is it really a surprise? The fourth house would be here, and are here in spirit, and certainly we know House Fey-Branche's position in the matter before us."

Across the table, Matron Vadalma cleared her throat, surprising the others and turning all eyes her way.

"I came here to listen, not to speak," Vadalma said. "But it would seem that there is little you wish to say."

"What do you mean?" Quenthel asked her.

"I want to know why," Vadalma explained. "You turned against her!"

"Zhindia? You have no love for Zhindi—"

"Of course not Zhindia. Lady Lolth!" Vadalma clarified. "The heresy . . . how could you—you and that child who now stands behind you in the body of a woman—how could you defy our goddess? Yes, Matron Mother, I have no love for Matron Zhindia Melarn, and less still for her closest ally, House Mizzrym and that double-dealing Matron Miz'ri."

"Long have our houses been allied," Quenthel reminded.

"And longer have I and my house been loyal to the Spider Queen," she snapped. "That web you and your—is she your grandniece?—wove to steal the Curse of Abomination from eight hundred driders . . ." She stopped and shook her head in disgust.

"It worked!" Quenthel argued.

"It worked *against* Lolth, you mean. Blasphemy," spat Vadalma, and Sos'Umptu gave a mocking little chuckle that had Quenthel turning a scowl her way.

"You say it yourself, then."

"Say what?" Vadalma asked.

"By *whose* laws is what we did blasphemy? Lolth's?" Quenthel said, never taking her withering stare off her devout sister, Sos'Umptu. "In that event, by Lolth's laws, can the attack on House Fey-Branche go unpunished? Can the abduction of Matron Byrtyn go unpunished?"

"A minor squabble by comparison," Vadalma replied, incredulous. "What you did has broken a covenant of four millennia!"

"Two millennia," Quenthel corrected. "And a covenant based on lies and false history."

"Do you hear yourself? In this chamber! *You* say these are lies and false history. But can you *prove* that?"

Before Quenthel could answer, the door opened again, and her heart leaped for a moment with hope.

Matron Byrtyn Fey walked into the room, and that hope dropped along with Quenthel's heart.

For she didn't really walk into the room. She skittered.

On eight legs.

Behind Sos'Umptu, the two bodyguards began to laugh, something strictly forbidden and punishable by death—except, of course, these two were demon yochlols, the handmaidens of Lolth.

"You knew of this?" Quenthel accused Sos'Umptu, but she didn't need her sister to answer any more than by the look on her face to realize that Byrtyn's fate had caught Sos'Umptu as much by surprise as it had Quenthel and all the others in the room who were not named Eskavidne and Yiccardaria.

"We will kill you, Quenthel Baenre!" the drider shrieked. "You have lost your way. There is no repentance for you and yours, only war." Eight legs clacking and tapping on the stone floor, Byrtyn the drider spun about and rushed away.

"It is not a fate I wish to suffer," Zeerith said blandly.

Across the way, Vadalma hopped up and waved to her bodyguards.

"Where does House Faen Tlabbar stand?" Quenthel demanded of her.

"In the shadows," was Vadalma's answer. "Watching from afar."

Vadalma and her escorts rushed out of the room, slowing only because she certainly did not wish to catch up to the drider.

"What have you left?" Sos'Umptu asked Quenthel. "House Fey-Branche is an empty shell. Without House Faen Tlabbar, there is House Baenre and House Do'Urden, that is all. And yet, is this really a surprise to you? Matron Vadalma has been Lolth's most devout matron for as long as either of us can remember. Did you really think she and hers would simply throw it all aside because of your circus trick on that field up above?"

"A trick that gave me the Blaspheme, sister," Quenthel growled back.

"And cost you the city, sister. It would appear that House Melarn stands with the Houses Barrison Del'Armgo, Mizzrym, and Vandree."

"The rogues of the Stenchstreets will fight to escape the corruption of Lolth," Quenthel countered.

"Will they? They are assailed by demon hordes even now, being reminded that Lolth is watching."

"Oh, the Spider Queen is indeed," said Yiccardaria from the wall behind Sos'Umptu, her voice full of eagerness.

"Consider your place well, Matron Zeerith," Sos'Umptu went on. "Once you led the proud Xorlarrins, now you are reduced to holding the name of the discredited and discarded Do'Urdens. The blasphemy on that field above is unforgiveable for the two priestesses who initiated it. But what of Zeerith?"

"Come, First Priestess of the Fane," Eskavidne said to Sos'Umptu. "Let us go and retrieve Matron Abomination so we can find her a proper role in Lady Lolth's grand plan."

Sos'Umptu rose slowly, her gaze locked with Zeerith's.

"There must be another way," Zeerith implored Quenthel, and Yvonnel, who moved up to join them when Sos'Umptu had gone. Saribel and Ravel rushed to their mother's side and helped her back up onto her floating disc, which started away immediately. "I cannot believe Matron Mez'Barris would do such a thing to Matron Byrtyn Fey," her voice trailed behind her.

"It wasn't Mez'Barris," Quenthel replied to the departing Do'Urdens, but as much to herself as anyone.

"This has the stench of Zhindia Melarn all over it."

CHAPTER 2

The Spy's Spy

I t was still his home, and Braelin Janquay wasn't sure if he liked that or not. He walked the Braeryn of Menzoberranzan for the first time in many months, and had lived on the surface now for many years, but he felt like he had never left these haunts and also that he had never really been here, all at the same time. He took a deep breath, taking in the aroma, and laughed as he considered that this place was certainly living up to its nickname as the Stenchstreets.

But the smell did not repel him, as it would have for almost anyone who was not intimately familiar with it. For Braelin, this supposedly terrible place had been his sanctuary for much of his life—for all his days until Jarlaxle had hired him, trained him, and taken him on many grand adventures. Now he lived in Luskan, working for Jarlaxle and for Beniago, but Menzoberranzan, more particularly the Braeryn of Menzoberranzan, remained his home.

The Braeryn felt different this visit, however, for the place was eerily quiet and the people he saw on the street, even the ones he knew, seemed subdued and wary. One woman he had thought a friend gave him a hard look and rushed down an alleyway at his first move to engage her.

Braelin looked to the many scars on the streets and buildings, recent scorch marks from the demonic fires of Abyssal creatures, to explain the reception.

Some in the city and many who lived in the Braeryn knew that Braelin worked for Bregan D'aerthe, and Bregan D'aerthe's alliance in this civil war had not been formally announced. But it wouldn't be hard for these folk to think he sided with the Baenres, of course, and from what he had heard, the demons brought into Menzoberranzan by Matron Zhindia had been making survival very difficult for any who sided with the Baenres.

With that grim thought in mind, Braelin was aware that many here would betray him if it meant saving themselves from demonic retribution, or worse, from being dragged back to Zhindia and made into a drider—other rumors said that she was building a drider army to counter the Blaspheme.

Braelin Janquay had spent most of his life in the most chaotic and dangerous parts of Menzoberranzan, but he had never known it to be anything like this.

With the reception he was receiving driving home caution, he had taken his time, a roundabout route, learning all that he could before slipping along the shadows of this particular street in the Braeryn, one that held an establishment well known to be owned, or partially owned, by Jarlaxle and Bregan D'aerthe.

He eyed the building, the Oozing Myconid, now and warily looked for any signs that Zhindia had ruined it and killed the tavern keepers, or perhaps set a trap for Jarlaxle or any others loyal to Bregan D'aerthe who might venture inside.

He called upon a spell stored in a ring to show him any such traps near the front door, then a second spell to open the door with a magical knock from afar. He crept up and glanced about, making sure he was not seen, then scaled the wall beside the door and flipped over as he moved above it, head down, feet hooked on the eaves of the roof. Securing himself more firmly, he then produced a clever tube set with mirrors—a peekaround, it was called by members of his trade—to peer inside.

The place seemed normal, if quiet.

Given the recent demon attacks in the Stenchstreets, Braelin was surprised that anyone was inside at all.

He looked to the bar across the way, and smiled despite his wariness.

For Azleah tended that bar, and she looked as beautiful as when Braelin last saw her, before this new swarm of tumult had begun in the City of Spiders.

He tucked his peekaround away, hooked his strong fingers on the thin top jamb of the door, and rolled down gracefully as he swung into the establishment, letting go at the exact moment to let him hit the ground and right himself with such smoothness and fluidity that any who had not watched the entirety of his entrance would have thought he had simply strolled in through the doorway.

Azleah had seen the flourish, though, as her grin revealed to him. She pretended not to look at him as he made his way across the dimly lit room, but he knew that she had seen him, had recognized him, and was pleased to see him again.

Braelin made no such attempt to hide his stare. Azleah was the most beautiful woman he had ever seen. She was short by drow standards, but Braelin, too, barely topped five feet. Her hair was silvery white with hints of gold, her eyes shining amber, and her nose a mere button sandwiched by her dimpled cheeks.

She finally looked up at him openly when he slapped his hands on the bar.

"What is your desire?" she asked, and her choice of words wasn't lost on Braelin. He fancied her indeed, but the best part was that he knew that she fancied him as well, perhaps even more.

"Same as always," he answered cavalierly.

"Why, Braelin Janquay, I am working, and there are others in here," Azleah said.

"Oh, I see. I thought you meant for a drink."

"Of course, you did."

"The same as always," he repeated and looked to the shelves of fine liquors rising up on the wall behind her.

"Good timing, then," she said and pulled a bottle from under the bar, Braelin's favorite beverage, Myconid Elixir, a clear, potent alcohol made from the potatoes farmed in a nearby myconid garden—the very alcohol that had given this place its name centuries before.

Braelin's lips turned to a frown. "No, wait, I have changed my mind," he said, reaching over just as Azleah was preparing to pour.

She looked at him curiously, suspiciously.

He pointed to the top shelf. "Perhaps the limited elvish Feywine," he said.

Azleah pulled her hand away and poured the Myconid Elixir. "No, you don't, Braelin Janquay," she said. "You just want to watch me climb up the ladder."

Braelin shrugged as if he didn't care that he had been caught. "I am a man," he stated. "I have spent most of my life being ogled by the women of Menzoberranzan. Am I to be blamed for turning the coin?"

"So you leer at every woman you see?"

"Only one."

"Am I to be complimented by that?"

"Am I to be complimented by the way you leer at me?"

Azleah drew a wide grin. "Only you," she said.

"Atmosphere is more than half the pleasure of the drink," Braelin said.

She put his filled glass before him. "Then find some time," she said. "I've plenty of atmosphere to share."

Braelin lifted the glass in toast to her before taking a sip, and Azleah, not one to give him the last word, collected the bottle of Myconid Elixir, spun about, and hiked up her gown revealingly as she climbed the ladder to replace it on the top shelf.

"I am happy to learn that you are still here, that this establishment remains untouched," Braelin told her sincerely when she came back to stand across the bar from him.

"Oh, the Oozing Myconid has been touched," Azleah replied darkly. "Repeatedly."

"Demons?"

The woman shook her head. "Allies of the zealot Matron Zhindia Melarn."

"Not Melarni themselves?"

"None of her own, I believe, no. I have spoken with Mizzryms and members of House Vandree. They come in here and advise me to see the truth of Matron Zhindia and of House Baenre. I suspect that it is not a truth with which Jarlaxle would agree."

"Vandree is with Zhindia, then," Braelin mumbled.

"And House Mizzrym."

"We knew that Matron Miz'ri Mizzrym would side with her," said Braelin. "Vandree is a blow to the cause of those who would oppose the Lolthians."

"Then the whispers are true," said Azleah. "Bregan D'aerthe will throw in with the heretics. I had expected Jarlaxle to see how fares the battle before playing his hand."

"He would prefer to remain apart from it all, but I suspect he is as determined to see this to the end, whatever end that may be, as is Drizzt Do'Urden himself," Braelin told her. "Something has come over our friend, though he will not speak of it. He went to the north, and there . . . was changed."

"So say the rumors."

"So say I, who have seen him firsthand. Rumors no more."

"He will declare for House Baenre, then."

"He is Jarlaxle. He will declare nothing, and act as best serves him—only in this case, he has made the decision that what best serves him and what best serves Bregan D'aerthe is for Menzoberranzan to be rid of the yoke that is the infernal Spider Queen."

He studied Azleah carefully as he spoke, looking for some hint that she didn't agree. He did note a mote of disappointment, but that much, he had expected.

"Jarlaxle might well be killed here," Azleah said. "He will become a primary target for Matron Zhindia, do not doubt. As will the Oozing Myconid and all who work in this place as soon as she is convinced that Bregan D'aerthe is her enemy."

"Jarlaxle already led an assault on her house only a few short years ago," Braelin reminded. "One that I remember so painfully well." He gave a little laugh, but could not hide the accompanying shudder. "If Zhidnia has not attacked the Oozing Myconid yet, then she is harboring doubts as to our allegiance, as well she should be."

Azleah fixed him with a sympathetic stare. She was one of the few who knew that he had been the victim of the Curse of Abomination in that time, turned into a drider by the Melarni priestesses. The mere thought now racked him with phantom pains and he found himself rubbing his legs.

He shook it all away with a reminder that Yvonnel had saved him, that Jarlaxle and his friends had rescued him.

"Jarlaxle brought Artemis Entreri here, and Entreri killed her only daughter—irretrievably, I am told," Braelin added, bringing the conversation back on track. "She'll never forget that and she'll never forgive it, of course, but she cares about losing her daughter only because it weakened her house and her position. She is a true Lolthian, that one. All she cares about is power, so even her anger at what happened before will be put aside for now as she tries to figure out if Bregan D'aerthe will be to her advantage or her enemy's advantage."

"How can you know that?"

"Because the battle has been going on for some time now and here I am, inside the Oozing Myconid speaking with you. What protection other than fleeing through secret ways would you and this place have if Zhindia was still holding grudges?"

"Despite the past, Zhindia doubts that Jarlaxle will turn against Lolth openly. Or she hopes."

"Perhaps she believes that Jarlaxle's hold on his band will be lessened and we are primary agents to turn against him."

"It is no secret that Braelin Janquay wishes to lead Bregan D'aerthe," Azleah teased.

That brought a smile and a bit of snorting to Braelin. "The open secret is a falsehood, then," he said.

Azleah hopped up on her toes and leaned over the bar, resting her elbows on the burnished wood and dropping her face—a very round face for a drow—into the palms of her hands. "Do tell," she prompted. "I had thought you an ambitious man."

"My ambitions only have to do with you," he said, and enjoyed how her eyes widened at his sincerity and fervor. But as much as he liked just talking to her, it was important he be clear in correcting her assessment—for himself, if nothing else. "I remain loyal to Jarlaxle. *Always* loyal to Jarlaxle. He found me on the streets, broken and wondering the point of life itself, and gave to me a home, a path, and a purpose. I do not wish to ever replace him, but am bound to make him confident that if something ever happened to him, all that he has built will be well served by me, if I remain alive. Never would I think of being the source of his demise, in any way."

"But if something happened to Jarlaxle, Kimmuriel would take the band, yes? What then for Braelin?"

"I would not be stupid enough to even contemplate any action against that one, who could, and would, read my mind and know my plans and so do things to me to make the Spider Queen herself shudder in whatever approximation of sympathy she might muster. And yes, my dear Azleah, take that as a bit of advice for yourself, as well. I have come to know Kimmuriel very well. He is not vindictive—no longer, at least—and is not unpredictable in terms of temperament. But he is no enemy any of us would ever want. If he should take the reins, I would not jostle the rothé's yoke."

"So, Zhindia's hopes that Bregan D'aerthe is malleable are dashed."

"Unless, perhaps, she is thinking of tavern keeper Azleah," Braelin said, turning it all back around on her. "It is an open secret that Azleah would like a band of her own, one led by women, which she believes to be the natural order of things."

Azleah moved back from the bar at that, her expression becoming very serious. "I do have one, a gang, and no mercenary band," she admitted. "No rival to Bregan D'aerthe, which I still willingly serve, but merely a complement of my own associates within a city that Bregan D'aerthe has all but abandoned."

She glanced about as if making sure that her next actions would not be noticed, then moved to a small drawer at the base of the shelves and brought forth an unremarkable-looking little book, returning fast and sliding it to Braelin.

It was full of her recent observations and advice, Braelin knew, and tucked the report safely away.

"Jarlaxle and Kimmuriel both know of my expanding network," she told him. "And offer their blessing and support."

Braelin tapped the interior vest pocket where he had slipped the tome, and nodded.

"Mutual benefit," said Azleah. "They know."

"But perhaps Matron Zhindia Melarn does not know this," Braelin slyly added. "Her hopes, in her own sexist way, would be on her ability to turn you into an ally, or perhaps the priestess Dab'nay. But surely she wouldn't hope, or care, to turn me or any other man high in Jarlaxle's ranks."

Azleah nodded, clearly catching on. "Let us keep it that way, for all our sakes."

Braelin finished his drink in a great gulp, then slapped the glass down on the bar. "I have much to do this day," he told her. "Perhaps later we can share another drink."

"Perhaps we can share more than that," she said boldly. "You know where to find me, but only because I let you know where to find me. And in a place where the atmosphere is more than half the pleasure."

Despite the dire portents all about him, Braelin left the Oozing Myconid with a spring in his step.

"I TOLD YOU," CHELLITH VANDREE SAID TO THE HUNZRIN priestess standing beside him as they watched the drow man enter the tavern in a most careful and unusual way. "There is no doubt. That is Braelin Janquay of Bregan D'aerthe."

"I didn't doubt you," Barbar'eth Hunzrin replied. "Why would I? A minion of Jarlaxle comes to the Braeryn to check on his tavern? It proves nothing."

"Braelin Janquay is more than a minion," Chellith argued. "There are whispers that he is third to the leaders. Why would Jarlaxle send someone so important if he meant to remain neutral?"

"He sent his best scout to a place where information is critical," Barbar'eth reasoned.

Chellith blew a long sigh.

"Do not let your ambition blind you to doubt," the priestess advised. "Your greatest wish is to become the Vandree weapon master when this is all done."

"I do not deny it, and striking such a blow would put me in great favor."

"Or get you—get us—tortured," Barbar'eth argued. "Matron Zhindia hates Jarlaxle, it is true, but she hopes to bring Bregan D'aerthe into her fold."

"And what does House Hunzrin think? If there even is a House Hunzrin left, I mean."

Barbar'eth knew her face was tightening, giving away her true feelings. She was playing the role of contrarian here out of caution and to draw out any information this Vandree scout might have of Bregan D'aerthe's standing. Obviously, he had nothing other than his speculation. She had been hoping for more.

"House Hunzrin survives," she curtly replied. "Few were killed in the raid beyond the replaceable non-drow servants."

"Yes, I am sure that Matron Shakti and First Priestess Charri are quite content."

"Your tone . . ." Barbar'eth warned.

"Can you not see the opportunity here? For me, yes, but for yourself as well. If those Hunzrins not in Matron Mother Baenre's thrall do not act out boldly, then . . ."

Chellith found the words stuck in his throat, for the muscles in his mouth wouldn't heed his desire to speak. None of his muscles would move to his mind's command.

He stood there, perfectly still, perfectly helpless, as if his body was trapped in some wrap of unseen metal.

"You have forgotten your place," Barbar'eth warned. She stepped back and reached into her belt pouch, producing a small strip of metal. She held it up before Chellith's eyes.

He knew what was coming before the priestess even created a small flame between the thumb and index finger of her free hand. He tried to break out of her spell of holding, but this one was strong, so very strong.

Barbar'eth began whispering, teasing him with her chant.

"I cannot ever allow a man to speak to me in such a manner," she said, shaking her head and feigning—so clearly feigning—some remorse.

No, Chellith knew her well, and knew she enjoyed this play.

His armor began to grow warm, and how he wanted to shed the chain shirt!

But he could not.

The discomfort became pain became searing agony. He tried to break from her magical hold, and failed again. He wanted to apologize, but he could not.

And she was lecturing him, warning him, reminding him that though they were friends and lovers, their companionship had an order to it that could not be denied. This was the Spider Queen's way, she was saying, repeatedly.

Chellith wanted to scream. He knew that his skin was blistering. They had been through this before, several times, enough so that the man looked like he was wearing a mail shirt of scars whenever he removed his armor and clothes.

Barbar'eth liked those scars. She would run her hand gently over them and whisper into Chellith's ear reminders that she made the rules, and his duty was simply to unquestioningly follow them.

He could smell flesh burning, *his* flesh burning. How he wished her magical paralysis took that particular sense away.

The pain was exquisite now. If her spell hadn't been holding him in place, he was sure he would fall over.

"Do you understand?" he heard Barbar'eth sneer, moving closer to him, and he understood that in his attempt to put his thoughts elsewhere he hadn't heard her the first few times she had asked that. Not that it mattered, though, for what was he to do? He couldn't even blink his eyes!

The priestess gave a disgusted harrumph and waved her hands out, spinning around.

The paralysis ended and Chellith fell to one knee, gasping. The armor cooled almost immediately, but the pain remained.

Still with her back to him, Barbar'eth whispered, her voice hissing like a snake, "You so enjoy snide insults aimed at my family." She spun about, her face a mask of rage. "Is the fleeting pleasure of the jibes worth it to you?"

"I was only . . ."

"Are they worth it to you?" she repeated, biting off every word.

"No, priestess."

"Who do you serve?"

"Lolth, Lady Lol . . ."

"Of course Lolth, you idiot. We *all* serve Lolth. But who does *Chellith* serve?"

"I serve Priestess Barbar'eth," he said.

"Now, tell me all that you know of this Braelin Janquay fool."

"He . . . he holds great . . . power . . . in the city of Luskan," Chellith said, but it took a while, for he was trembling and still gasping.

Barbar'eth sighed and began casting once more. She placed her hand on the man's forehead and sent waves of magical healing into his tormented body.

"He is the prime scout of Bregan D'aerthe," Chellith said, calming as the pain diminished.

"Then I ask again: Why would Jarlaxle risk him here?"

Chellith shrugged. "Why is the Oozing Myconid still operating? Why are the workers not dead?"

"Do tell."

"Because Matron Zhindia has not moved against Bregan D'aerthe."

"And yet you want us to do so without her explicit permission? Did you even think this inane plan through? Matron Zhindia will make driders of us! I should simply melt you for your stupidity."

"She won't if we can get Braelin Janquay to reveal to us Jarlaxle's designs in the war," Chellith said, obstinate despite his recent torture.

"If he is so valuable to Jarlaxle, he will never betray that."

"Does it matter?" Chellith asked.

Barbar'eth stared at him, at first in anger for his impertinence, but then curiously.

"We murder him," he continued, "and tell Matron Zhindia that he admitted to us that Bregan D'aerthe will side with the Baenres before we were forced to kill him."

Barbar'eth's puzzled expression didn't change for a moment. Then her eyes began to narrow.

"That is likely to happen, of course," Chellith said, his tone growing frantic in the face of Barbar'eth's deepening scowl. "Matron Zhindia hates Jarlaxle. She will believe what we tell her because it is only confirming that which she knows in her heart, despite any hopes she might have of sidelining that band of mercenaries."

Barbar'eth's expression softened. "So, even if Jarlaxle was planning to keep Bregan D'aerthe out of it . . ."

"Our actions will make of Jarlaxle and his band enemies of Matron Zhindia," Chellith said. "Can you deny the gain to House Hunzrin? Ever has Bregan D'aerthe been your rivals—your house and Jarlaxle's band fight for every morsel of trade beyond the city, and of late—"

He bit it off there, realizing that if he said the truth, that Jarlaxle was growing stronger and controlled much of the northern Sword Coast area on the surface, while House Hunzrin had lost all favor up there—by bringing a catastrophe in the form of phylacteries filled with demons to a Waterdhavian noble family—the reminder might not go over very well with the vicious woman, particularly since so many of her house were now imprisoned in their own compound by the Baenre heretics.

"We are on Matron Zhindia's side, of course, for that is the demand of Lady Lolth," Chellith said, his voice growing stronger. "But do we really want Bregan D'aerthe to join us? When we win—and how can we not?—would it not be a more profound victory by far, particularly for House Hunzrin, if Jarlaxle and his mercenary rogues were all sent to the Abyss to be shown the error of their ways?"

Barbar'eth came forward suddenly, grabbed Chellith by the cheeks, and kissed him deeply.

"I will bring in our friend," she whispered. "Oh, my clever lover, you watch the door, and when Braelin Janquay comes back out of the tavern, engage him with words."

"I'll tell him that I wish to join Bregan D'aerthe," Chellith replied with a chuckle. "Those arrogant fools think everyone wants to be a part of their ridiculous adventure."

Barbar'eth left and Chellith watched Barbar'eth move back down the alleyway, almost hypnotized by the confidence in her stride, her swaying hips; he was undeniably attracted to her, desired her and hated her all at the same time. As soon as she moved out of sight at the end of the alleyway, the Vandree warrior turned his attention back to the Oozing Myconid, just in time to see Braelin Janquay come out through the door.

Chellith stayed in the shadows for a bit longer, trying to recall anything he had heard about this man—not the information Barbar'eth had asked for, but regarding Braelin's fighting style or training. He didn't know much, but was certain that Braelin had never been to Melee-Magthere. Braelin wasn't the son of a noble house. In fact, there was no House Janquay in Menzoberranzan, and never had been as far as Chellith knew.

"No academy training, no weapon master to learn from," the Vandree warrior whispered to himself, bolstering his resolve. He could not imagine that any such commoner could match blades with him. Chellith had been third in his class and had trained extensively under Weapon Master Zintarl. How could any homeless rogue from the Stenchstreets ever hope to match that?

Realizing that there were Bregan D'aerthe allies within, Chellith waited for Braelin to get some distance from the tavern before moving out to intercept him. Even then, he barely came out of the shadows, and instead gave a short, sharp hiss.

When Braelin turned his way, Chellith began flashing his fingers in the drow sign language, relaying his name and asking for an audience.

The rogue looked around, then moved carefully toward the warrior. "House Vandree, you claim?" Braelin asked. "You are a noble?"

"Nephew of Matron Asha," he answered honestly, though he noted that his declaration of his house had moved Braelin Janquay's hand a bit closer to his weapon belt.

"A skull drinker," Braelin said, showing little respect. It was whispered throughout Menzoberranzan that the Vandree table was set with goblets made of human skulls. While true, the goblets were used only on special occasions, but the disparaging moniker of "skull drinker" was common when referring to one of Chellith's clan.

Chellith tried to hide his anger at the insult and did what he could to not end this commoner's life right here and now. "And you are a dwarf humper, I suppose, since you are of Bregan D'aerthe."

"Am I?"

"You are Braelin Janquay of Bregan D'aerthe, yes. I know of you and heard that you were in the city, and so I have sought you out."

"Heard from whom?"

"Whispers on the Stenchstreets."

"You spend much time here, then?"

"It is my only reprieve from the nonsense of the current winds blowing in the city, and from the glares of the priestesses of Vandree, most especially from Matron Asha herself."

"Do tell."

He snorted in derision. "You are of Bregan D'aerthe so I need not explain to you what is going on. No doubt, you have heard of the tightening alliances as the battle lines are more clearly drawn," Chellith said. "Do not waste our time with such a pointless question."

Braelin didn't respond at all, not even a blink.

"Just as I won't waste our time pretending where my house's allegiance lies; yes, you know that my matron has chosen the side of Matron Zhindia Melarn. Does that bother you? For I have heard that Bregan D'aerthe has not stated any position."

Still, not a blink.

"I am not here as an envoy from House Vandree to you, or to Jarlaxle through you."

"Which is exactly why I am trying to figure out *why* you are here, and why you sought to bother *me*."

"Because none in the Oozing Myconid have a direct line to Jarlaxle, and the fewer who hear my request, the better. I have little desire to become a drider."

Braelin seemed to relax, just a bit, at that. He spent a moment looking Chellith up and down before asking, "How do you know that we will not side with Matron Zhindia?"

"I do not *care*."

That clearly caught Braelin by surprise, as Chellith was hoping.

"I do not care which side Bregan D'aerthe takes, if any," Chellith elaborated.

"Then, again I ask: Why do you bother me?"

"I want to join."

"Join? You are a noble nephew in a ruling house."

"And it is nothing I ever wanted." Chellith paused and looked around for effect. "If you mean to betray me, please just kill me, but I must speak truly here. I wish to be gone from this place."

"We of Bregan D'aerthe might soon be here, as you just implied."

"But at least then, if am with you, I will know that I am fighting for something beyond the latest argument between the matrons of the city. House Vandree, Matron Asha, sides with Matron Zhindia because she worships Lolth and fears the vengeance of the Spider Queen. It is hard to argue that logic, I admit, but to go against House Baenre? That is madness!"

"So, your desire here is simply pragmatic."

"No, no," Chellith said, shaking his head as emphatically as he modulated his tone. "Maybe I am simply more loyal to my gender than to the priestesses who raised me, who beat me, who tore my flesh with their snake-headed scourges. I want to join with you to find some semblance of freedom, some semblance of worth beyond my potential as a mate or fodder in whatever squabble the women bring to Menzoberranzan. If that means fighting in the city, even against my own family, then so be it. Because when it is done, all that I ask is that Bregan D'aerthe takes me far from this place. I have much to offer."

He kept his voice emphatic and even pleading as he began to honestly list his achievements in the Academy and in his work for House

Vandree. He recounted everything he could remember, with embellishments, and then made up some more—anything to keep Braelin engaged.

He took heart when the rogue began nodding and smiling, even leaning in as if eager to hear more from this potentially valuable recruit.

"YOU ARE A RECKLESS FOOL, CHELLITH," BARBAR'ETH HUNzrin whispered to herself when she peeked around the alley wall and saw him go out to speak with the Bregan D'aerthe scout, even though that was exactly what she ordered him to do. She couldn't deny her excitement. The plan was indeed dangerous, so very much so, but when they brought the fabricated information to Zhindia, the powerful matron would no doubt be grateful—as long as they were convincing enough.

And surely Matron Shakti would be positively thrilled when the day was done and Bregan D'aerthe greatly weakened, if not utterly destroyed. House Hunzrin would claim all trade outside of the city as their domain once more!

Still, Chellith had a streak of recklessness in him—as she had just reminded him when she melted his flesh with his own armor. It would not surprise her if he messed this up and made the murder much more difficult than it had to be. Then she'd have to take matters in her own hand.

With that in mind, she put her worries aside and began to read the scroll of summoning, knowing that her complete focus and energy would be needed to properly control this particular beast.

She had called upon this one, Ingrou, before, and preferred it to the other of its hezrou kind . . . mostly because she enjoyed the silly, squeaky noise the massive and hulking frog-faced demon giggled every time it inflicted pain on another. The two had been together often in the last few tendays, and when the portal opened and the hezrou emerged, Ingrou seemed pleased to see Barbar'eth once more.

"Come along, my beastly friend," she said. "Let us play with a foolish man."

AS GOOD AS THIS CHELLITH VANDREE FELLOW WAS AT wearing a mask of eagerness and hope, Braelin Janquay was better at pretending to care. His nods were hiding the movement of his eyes, darting every which way. His expression feigned interest, but he wasn't listening to a thing the idiot warrior was saying, for none of it would matter a whit if and when Braelin ever took him to speak with Jarlaxle and Kimmuriel to request admission into the band formally.

Instead, Braelin was keeping his senses turned outward, past Chellith, keeping his hands ready, his thoughts ready, expecting the worst.

That was Jarlaxle's training at play.

He noted movement in the shadows of the alleyway. He smelled something terrible, disgusting, and strong enough that he could taste the rankness.

A moment later, he felt a tightening of his muscles, a magical intrusion trying to hold him in place, perfectly still, perfectly helpless.

He recognized it from the extensive training he had done with Dab'nay.

He *couldn't* blink. That truth pervaded his thoughts.

He felt his armor growing warmer, uncomfortably so, just as that woman emerged, dressed in the robes of a priestess.

Beside her came a huge, seven-foot beast that looked like a giant spiked toad with muscular arms and walking upright on two legs. Braelin thought of Jarlaxle's adventure in the north and the tales of the slaadi, but the odor—for indeed, this was the source of that wretched smell—told him that this was no slaad.

It was a demon, and a big, strong, ugly one.

Braelin Janquay reminded himself that he couldn't blink.

His armor was burning him now, but he couldn't even twitch at the severe discomfort.

"Look, my dear Ingrou," he heard the priestess say, and he noted that she wore the insignia of House Hunzrin, one that Braelin, like all members of Bregan D'aerthe, knew well. "We have a spy of Bregan D'aerthe, come to Menzoberranzan to help defeat Lady Lolth, and so deny you creatures of the Abyss this wondrous playground."

Braelin's skin was beginning to blister, he realized, and he could feel a great scream of pain bubbling up in his throat.

"Let me cook him a bit longer before you eat—" Barbar'eth said, that last word, the last she would ever speak, bitten off as surely as she hoped this hulking demonic toad-beast would bite off Braelin's head.

Braelin had trained with Zaknafein of late, but most of his martial skills had come from years and years of training under the tutelage of Jarlaxle, who loathed long battles. "Too much could go wrong with every passing heartbeat," Jarlaxle had often explained to Braelin in their sparring.

The draw was everything, and if done right, quite often the whole of the conflict.

As with now, when Braelin dropped his failing act of paralysis, brought his left hand to his right hip, drew, inverted, and stabbed his tapered short sword upward in a single, fluid motion, catching the priestess right under the chin and driving the fine and heavily enchanted blade up with such power that the tip pushed through the top of her head.

Braelin tugged the tapered sword down and the instant it came free, he executed a pair of backflips to bring him away from the demon and Chellith Vandree, landing from the second one at the same moment as the crumbling priestess settled into a heap on the ground.

The toad-beast surprised him with a strange, squeaky sound, like a laugh from something that simply didn't know how to laugh, as it turned to face him and flexed the clawed hands of its massive long arms.

"What have you done?" Chellith babbled, and to the demon, "Kill him!"

The hezrou demon took a step Braelin's way.

"She summoned you and now she is dead," the scout said, almost nonchalant. "You are free, and there is an idiot standing right beside you that *doesn't* have his sword drawn."

The demon took another step, but painted a curious expression on its wide-mouthed face and glanced over at Chellith, who was only then drawing his own sword.

"Wait . . . what?" the Vandree warrior said, his eyes widening as he understood the sudden turn.

The hezrou leaped upon him, toothy maw clamping about the forearm Chellith brought up to fend off the demon.

Chellith's free hand finally drew a sword and stabbed it into the hezrou demon's gut.

The beast roared in rage, its left arm coming up, then down hard on the crook in Chellith's sword arm, slapping the arm away, taking his hand from the impaling blade.

The warrior reached for it again, but the demon shook its head, and so shook Chellith's whole body, wildly, then spit out the shattered arm, Ingrou's free right hand coming across to bash the man and send him flying, crashing to the ground, unarmed, bleeding, and badly dazed.

As much as he was enjoying the spectacle, Braelin realized that he wasn't going to get any information out of the split-brained priestess, who wasn't even twitching anymore, and that this idiot warrior might prove of some value to him.

And while he might want to flee, he didn't feel good about leaving a demon in the Stenchstreets.

He wondered if Drizzt—through Jarlaxle—was rubbing off on him.

The demon crouched and tamped down its legs, ready to pounce upon the helpless man, but before it started the leap, an arrow drove into the side of its toad head; then a second, a fine and magical one, stabbed through its left arm into the side of its chest.

Surprised and confused, the hezrou caught a third and a fourth before it even turned to face Braelin, some dozen steps away now and grinning as he lifted the bow yet again.

Ingrou's telepathic growl reverberated in Braelin's mind.

It shook him—a demon in your brain is never something you want to experience—but it didn't distract from the disciplined scout's aim as he put an arrow right into the demon's forward-facing nostril.

As soon as the missile flew away, Braelin rushed forward.

The demon leaped ahead as well, and the drow dove into a forward roll, going right under the toad and coming around and up, putting a sixth arrow into the beast before he was even back to his feet, then two more before he had to toss his bow aside, spit his bloody short sword from his mouth to his left hand, and draw his long sword—his new and fabulous long sword—from its scabbard on his right hip.

My patience runs thin, he heard in his mind, and knew it wasn't the demon. No, it was his sword, the new one Jarlaxle had given him upon his return from the north, its fine edge glowing a thin line of red light.

"Come on, then, let's play," Braelin taunted the hezrou—but also encouraged his sword—and he rolled the keen-edged weapon in his right hand.

The sword remained angry with him, he knew, telepathically cursing him for using the other blade to murder the priestess.

"A demon isn't enough for you?" Braelin verbally replied to the sentient weapon. He felt a sudden urge to rush over and finish Chellith then, but ignored it and charged the hezrou.

Braelin launched into a flourish to try to distract and slow the demon, but the wounded and outraged beast just plowed through it and almost bowled over Braelin, with the rogue getting just down low enough to avoid the sweep of the hezrou's heavy, powerful arm. He dove out to the side, turning and letting himself fall into a roll, and stabbing twice at the beast's hip, scoring with both—and how easily and beautifully this deadly sword slid through demon flesh and demon bone!

Braelin flipped himself over and back to his feet and darted ahead as the hezrou turned. He rushed right into the thing, getting in close so that the lunging swipe of its fiendish right claw went behind him.

He almost thought that he had missed, so easily did his sword slip right through the demon's chest, and that surprise almost cost him dearly, slowing his response when the demon bit at him. He fell backward and down, letting his tapered short sword fall away and gripping the hilt with both hands, and pulled his long sword out—not straight out as was the typical way, no, but with an upward motion, yanking the blade through demon innards, ribs, flesh, and finally right back out free. So quickly did the keen blade slice through the demon and emerge that Braelin just let himself fall backward, and without obstruction, for the demon wasn't wrapping him with its arms anymore.

Braelin stumbled, but kept his feet under him, backpedaling fast, watching his foe.

The hezrou showed no sign of charging, and didn't even seem to be looking at Braelin at all. It just stood there, arms out wide, its head and body full of arrows, oozing demonic pus from many wounds, especially right in front, where it was so cleanly and deeply sliced belly to chin.

Braelin watched the feathered end of the shaft of the arrow he had put up the demon's nose, now pointing skyward and quivering.

Attack! Braelin's sword telepathically ordered, and he meant to heed that call, but not as the weapon wanted. He began to drop the sword, looking to the bow that was lying off to the side.

No! the sword begged. *Please!*

There it was, as Jarlaxle had warned him. Khazid'hea, the infamous weapon known as Cutter, was no longer ordering him. No, it was begging him! That brought a smile to Braelin's face as he considered that he was fully matching wills with the dangerous sword now.

Very well, then, he silently answered. He didn't retrieve his bow. He didn't retrieve his short sword. He took up Cutter in both hands and went at the hezrou demon directly, charging at it, dropping to a slide and slashing its legs, coming up fast and driving the sword angled under the demon's toad-like gullet again and again.

He could feel the satisfaction of the blade in his mind, the elation as it drove home repeatedly and drank its enemy's blood.

The hezrou was destroyed, Braelin knew, already beginning to emit Abyssal smoke as it began its banishment back home, but Braelin noted something else, some movement to the side, and so he kept stabbing furiously, seemingly out of control.

He stopped short and spun about, Khazid'hea sweeping down and across, intercepting the sword of Chellith Vandree and driving it out wide. Braelin turned right about to face the man, rolled his blade up, over, and then back down and out again, and so off guard was Chellith, so surprised that his backstab had been foiled, that he lost his sword altogether, the weapon flying across the way and bouncing on the stone of the street.

The tip of Khazid'hea was at his throat.

And how the sword wanted to eat!

But this one might prove useful, Braelin remembered, and conveyed to the weapon that sentiment.

Khazid'hea would hear none of it, compelling Braelin to strike, and so forceful was the telepathic command that the skilled Bregan D'aerthe rogue almost did it.

Almost.

Instead, he just slipped the tip into Chellith's throat, just a bit, forcing the man up on his tiptoes.

Braelin's free hand came up, his index finger going over his pursed lips. "Not a word," he told the warrior. "And if you do not follow perfectly, I *will* take your head."

He retrieved his weapons, then, and turned toward the Oozing Myconid.

"Why?" he asked as he neared with his prisoner.

"It was the priestess," Chellith stammered. "She is my master and told me to do this. She is Hunzrin and hates Jarlaxle's band."

Chellith rambled on and on for a few moments, until Braelin finally stopped him with, "The band you told me you wished to join?"

"She made me. House Baenre has taken her family out of the fight."

"What of your family?"

The man swallowed hard, or started to, but the movement brought the lump in his throat against the tip of Khazid'hea. He gurgled in pain.

"Matron Asha . . ."

"Go on."

"Matron Asha has sided with Matron Zhindia. That was true."

"And?"

"There is nothing more," the man pleaded.

"Then I leave you with this advice, Chellith Vandree," Braelin said. "Never give an interrogator all your information before they have agreed to spare your life."

Chellith's eyes widened in horror.

"What more?" Braelin demanded.

The man stammered and stuttered and wanted desperately to come up with something, anything, but after a moment, Braelin understood that anything Chellith said at that point would be a lie.

So, Braelin removed his sword tip, but out the side of Chellith's neck, slashing the man's artery.

He walked away as the blood began to spurt, Chellith sinking to his knees. He felt the satisfaction from Khazid'hea, even a whisper deep in his mind from the sword that it was beginning to think that maybe he was worthy.

Braelin sent the same message back to the sword. It wasn't a bargain, though, a notion of mutual benefit. No, it was a challenge, one Braelin was growing confident he could win.

Following Jarlaxle's training to the letter, Braelin produced a small rod and cast a divination, one that would show him magical enchantments, particularly those upon items that might be quite valuable. He relieved the dead priestess of some baubles and an interesting broach, retrieved Chellith's sword, which seemed quite enchanted for a weapon of a man who was not a house weapon master, then went back to Chellith, who was still kneeling, gurgling and choking.

Braelin studied him closely, but found no magical emanations worthy of his time.

"It didn't have to be like this," he told Chellith, who was staring at him, grasping at the tear and trying pathetically to stem the blood. "If you had wanted to join Bregan D'aerthe truly, I could have granted that."

Chellith nodded repeatedly, his eyes plaintive and begging.

Braelin looked around at the few witnesses in the shadows on the street, the end of an alleyway, and a couple on a balcony seemingly enjoying the show. All of them seemed rather amused, and why not? For these Melarni allies had been rampaging the Braeryn with their demons of late.

One last glance and disappointed sigh at Chellith, who was sinking into the street, and Braelin Janquay went on his way.

CHAPTER 3

The Battle Behind the Battles

Matron Asha demands an audience," house wizard Iltztran Melarn informed his matron.

"She *demands?*"

"Apparently. She is quite angry, so said her emissary."

"Angry?" Zhindia gave a derisive snort. "I have always questioned House Vandree's true understanding of and allegiance to Lady Lolth. Who was killed?"

"Chellith Vandree."

"Who?"

"A nephew," Iltztran explained. "A fair fighter by all accounts, and one aspiring to the rank of weapon master."

"But they have a weapon master."

"Of course."

"Then this one was a worthy gift to Lady Lolth," Zhindia said. "And one that does not cost them as much as it helps us in the greater scheme of the war."

"Matron—"

"She wants answers," Zhindia interrupted. "That is understandable. And so we shall give her answers beyond the obvious: that her precious nephew died in service to Lolth, fighting in the Braeryn. A greater loss was the priestess of House Hunzrin, of course, and the greatest of all, the banishment of the hezrou for a hundred years! Is Matron Asha Vandree angry about those losses?"

"The emissary mentioned only Chellith."

"Because Asha is selfish and stupid and cannot understand that we will pay great prices only because the reward is greater still."

"She joined in our alliance, and did so against her fear of our greatest ally. House Vandree has a difficult history with House Barrison Del'Armgo, who will become untethered if . . ." Iltztran stopped and abruptly cleared his throat to hide his forthcoming correction. "When," he said, "House Baenre falls."

"Untethered? Whose tether matters most?"

"Lady Lolth's," Iltztran answered immediately, recognizing yet another slip. He looked to Yiccardaria and Eskavidne, and relaxed a bit, for neither seemed overly concerned.

"Come," Zhindia bade him and all her entourage. "Let us see if our investigators have returned."

She led the way out to the main balconies of House Melarn, a wide and long walkway protected by the many pillars of stalactites supporting it every few feet. The sentries, wizards and archers and mostly men, all snapped to tight attention at the arrival of the stern matron.

"How long?" Zhindia asked the lone priestess, a young Melarni woman named Zovallia.

"Matron," Zovallia answered, bowing appropriately—to Zhindia and to the two yochlols. "Not long." She motioned out to the northeast. "I expect them to come into view any moment."

Zhindia nodded and turned to watch.

"With . . . witnesses," Zovallia added with a rather wicked emphasis.

That news pleased Zhindia. Zovallia's apparent delight in it pleased her more.

They heard the horrible droning of chasme wings before the

demons came into view, flying in a group, but two by two, for each pair held one side of a harness that carried a drow prisoner. There were fourteen chasmes, bearing seven "witnesses," and the whole of the group was led by a trio of succubi, who no doubt had convinced the harnessed drow that it would be in their best interest to come along.

The droning noise grew to maddening levels, so much so that one of Zhindia's archers fell unconscious to the balcony.

"Punish him," she told Zovallia, and gave it no further thought, moving to greet the succubi trio as they alighted on her complex.

"A single drow killed all three: the Hunzrin priestess, the Vandree warrior, and Ingrou," said Kariva, a most beautiful succubus with red hair to perfectly match the red bat wings that she folded to invisibility behind her shoulders as she stepped upon solid stone.

"An impressive victory," agreed the black-haired succubus Uvillia.

"We should catch him and play with him," offered Riffithia, the third of the group, whose eyes constantly shifted color—but remained remarkable and intense whatever their hue.

"*Him?*" Zhindia asked. "What do you know?"

"It was a man, yes," Kariva replied. "Several have confirmed that." She had to raise her voice to be heard over the now-deafening droning of the fourteen chasme demons.

Zhindia scowled and looked to those approaching beasts, with their ugly blue-gray insectoid bodies and their hideous and bloated human faces.

"Desist!" Kariva shouted and almost instantly the droning became the more normal hum of their large beating wings. "They do like to show off their droning prowess," she explained to Zhindia.

"Several, you were saying?"

"Yes, all but one of them admitted to being on the street, though more than one claim to have seen little. It is likely they all saw the fight, at least from afar. What we have garnered is that the fighter who slayed the three was a man, slight of build, quick with blades, and clever, so very clever."

"Line them up in my throne room," Zhindia ordered as the chasmes began ushering the captured drow to the balcony. She stalked off, Iltz-tran and the two handmaidens in tow.

"The succubi will be valuable additions," the wizard remarked on the way. "I am surprised they answered our call."

"You doubt Lolth?" Zhindia snapped at him.

"I am sure he does not," Yiccardaria intervened.

"I only . . . it is not my recollection that succubi, who are neither true demon nor true devil, answer to the calls of the priestesses of the Spider Queen."

"Cleverly reasoned, wizard," Yiccardaria congratulated him. "Apparently, the succubi hold a grudge against some of our likely enemies, particularly Drizzt Do'Urden and his friends who did harm to their queen, Malcanthet. These three were eager to be a part of this glorious battle, in any case, and that is to our great advantage."

"A hezrou is worth two succubi," Zhindia said dryly.

"In battle, perhaps, but the subtler advantages offered by the alluring Kariva and her sisters cannot be overlooked. They are smart, their magic is deceptive, and their ability to enthrall is undeniable."

"The blessing of Lolth has attracted powerful allies, then, and that is good," Zhindia decided, needing to put it back in terms favorable to her beloved goddess.

"And Lolth's blessings have made more of current allies, yes?" Iltz-tran put in. "I have to ask. I have followed Zovallia's journey since her return from Arach-Tinilith and now I witness her performing dweo-mers I had thought forever beyond her limits. She had been but a minor priestess before the recent events, but now?"

"Many of the young priestesses siding with our cause and battling the heretics, Zovallia included, have been blessed by an intervention of these two handmaidens," Zhindia confirmed, entering the throne room and taking her place on the throne.

"Through our work, the clergy of our half of Menzoberranzan have become far more formidable," said Eskavidne. "Zovallia has excelled, and is casting dweomers that would have been decades away from her abilities, and perhaps forever beyond her reach, as you noted, wizard. Faith in the goddess is an advantage."

"More than half," Zhindia corrected. "And more will join us when their ingrained fears of House Baenre cannot hold against the power we bear or the proof we are in Lolth's favor."

They left the conversation there for the time being, as Zovallia and the three succubi paraded the seven witnesses into the room, lining them before the throne.

Zhindia let them stand there in silence for a long while, sizing them up and down, making them sweat and hoping that some might wet themselves. How she enjoyed this feeling of complete power!

Finally, she slipped off her seat and began pacing the line slowly, hands clasped behind her back. "You were there, all of you, on that street when the fight commenced," she said. She stopped walking and blurted, "I will spare the first person who tells the truth of the fate that befell the Vandree warrior and the Hunzrin priestess!" with sudden volume and energy, startling them all.

"I did not witness it!" one said, while a trio of others proclaimed that they had only seen the fight from afar, and another couple remained silent. The last of the group shouted out, "It was a rogue, of Bregan D'aerthe, I believe!"

The room was buzzing, but Zhindia silenced it all by lifting her hand.

"Take those who denied seeing it to a room and enact a zone of truth there," she told Zovallia. "We will give any who lied to the Curse of Abomination."

"No, I did see it," one of those four blurted. "I was just afraid to speak!"

Zhindia called for silence again, as that brought more murmurs, and at least one more of those who claimed ignorance of the fight appeared to be ready to confess the truth.

The matron walked up before the trembling speaker, a young woman who appeared malnourished and who, like so many in the Braeryn, probably spent most of her days wandering about stupidly under the poisonous delusions of certain mushrooms.

"See? You can be prompted to honesty," Zhindia softly said to the poor woman.

She nodded eagerly. "I saw it, but I know not who—"

"Shh, shh," Zhindia prompted. "You did well in telling the truth." She nodded to a pair of guards, who rushed over to grab the woman by the arms. "Perhaps I will let you lead my drider brigade."

The woman's sunken eyes widened in shock as that registered and she began pleading for mercy.

"Take her," Zhindia told the guards, who dragged her away. The matron moved up before the two who had remained silent. One man chewed his lips nervously. The other, a woman, kept her gaze cast to the floor, muttering, "I saw nothing."

Zhindia snorted and chuckled wickedly, then moved before the man who had blurted out the name of Jarlaxle's band.

"Take the others away and interrogate them," she told Zovallia. "They are of no interest to me. Those who did not lie might find a place in our ranks, or a merciful death if you find them untrustworthy. Those who dared to lie in this holy place of Lolth will become the first of our answer to the Blaspheme.

"And you," she said to the man before her. "Bregan D'aerthe? What do you know of Bregan D'aerthe?"

"Nothing," he said. "Or little, and nothing more than what everyone else knows."

"Then how can you make such a claim?"

"He came out of the Oozing Myconid right before the fight," the man nervously explained. "That's Jarlaxle's place, they say. I was in there when he came in. He spent the whole time talking to the tavern keeper, and the conversations seemed to be . . . friendly."

"Tell me more," Zhindia prompted.

"I am not certain of his name, but I have seen him before. Braelin, I think, or something like that."

Matron Zhindia elicited a little growling mewl at that. She remembered that one, one she had given to Lolth only to have the cursed Yvonnel Baenre steal him back.

"Take this witness, feed him, outfit him, and put him in the ranks of our army," Zhindia instructed other guards. She looked at the man, who seemed truly terrified.

"You have earned the place to serve in the army of Lolth," she told him. "And when this is over, you will be a houseless rogue no more, but instead, a full member of House Melarn, the First House of Menzoberranzan."

If that was supposed to calm the poor fellow, it certainly did not. Zhindia understood it, of course. This one, like so many other cowardly drow, was simply hoping to ride out the war hiding in holes.

One did not hide from the Spider Queen, though.

She dismissed him with the remaining guards, then turned to her priestesses, her house wizard, the three succubi, and the handmaidens. "Braelin?" she asked.

"Braelin Janquay," Iltztran replied, nodding. "I have heard the name, and yes, it is one associated with Bregan D'aerthe."

"Then we must capture this Braelin Janquay," Zhindia said, not bothering to inform Iltztran that House Melarn and Braelin Janquay were not strangers.

Zovallia started to offer her services for that task, but Zhindia cut her short with an upraised hand, drawing the priestess's gaze across the way to three far better suited for such a job.

"Can we play with him before we deliver him to you?" Kariva asked.

"As long as he is alive when you give him to me," Zhindia replied.

CHAPTER 4

The Pressure Campaign

H e is going to get himself killed," Kaitain Armgo dared to reply.

Matron Mez'Barris glared at the wizard.

"I do not wish this!" Kaitain was quick to add. "But Malagdorl is determined to get to this Blaspheme leader whatever the risk."

"Which is why I appointed you to stay with him and magically extract him if there is a need," Mez'Barris responded.

"As I did in the first fight against the Do'Urden compound," the wizard hesitantly answered, knowing that he was on delicate ground here with Mez'Barris, who considered Malagdorl the reincarnation of her lover, Uthegentel Del'Armgo, who had been her patron and the father of her five daughters. Malagdorl was huge like Uthegentel, full of fury and muscle. And now he looked very much like that slain warrior of old, for Mez'Barris had given him Uthegentel's black armor and adamantine trident, and had styled his white hair in a row of crown spikes and filled his face with pins and rings. There had been much whispering about the Barrison Del'Armgo compound when Mez'Barris had made her adoration for the young man so obvious and taken him in so close to her, but of course, all of it was flattering to Mez'Barris and to her new consort, or whatever it was that Malagdorl, her grandson, had become.

"You took him from his victory, so Malagdorl says," Mez'Barris teased. "He would have finished with the Blaspheme witch then and there."

Behind the matron, Taayrul Armgo, her daughter and First Priestess of the house, nodded and smiled.

But Kaitain wasn't being baited into such an argument. Matron Mez'Barris knew well that he had saved Malagdorl that day, for this leader of the Blaspheme force of former Abyssal driders had found assistance in that fight and was surely going to defeat Malagdorl. Malagdorl knew it, too, though the overly proud warrior would never admit it.

"Mal'a'voselle Amvas Tol is no easy opponent," Kaitain said instead. "I have no doubts that your grandson . . ." He hesitated there, just because he enjoyed seeing Mez'Barris's face tighten in simmering anger.

"He is the weapon master of House Barrison Del'Armgo," she said through gritted teeth, and Kaitain suddenly rethought his taunting game. "You will refer to him in no other manner of familiarity."

"My pardon, my matron," Kaitain said with a bow.

"Continue . . . carefully."

"She is formidable," Kaitain explained. "As strong as any drow in Menzoberranzan, other than Malagdorl. She fights with the skill of a weapon master."

"And she would have *killed* Malagdorl? The pride of our house?"

"Not alone, no. Of course not. But in the tide of that battle, she found allies, where he did not."

"Even though Kaitain was there with him," Taayrul said from behind Mez'Barris.

"I was opening the portal to take us home, as I had been instructed," Kaitain said without hesitation, and without surprise that Mez'Barris's nasty daughter would take that thread to its absurd and insulting end. "The force Matron Zhindia sent to battle the Do'Urdens that day was not meant to win, but to make our enemy show their hand. And they did, and that hand was the Blaspheme. How much we did learn of them!"

He noted Taayrul snorting and rolling her eyes.

"But your matron had been explicit to me in her instructions," Kaitain went on, now aiming his words at the First Priestess. "We were there to observe, not to engage, and to remain outside the fray for matters as political as practical. My duty was to return us safely home, Malagdorl most especially, and so I did. In his fight with Mal'a'voselle, another had joined against him, a skilled warrior whom I believe to have been none other than the prize now captured and kept by Matron Zhindia, Dinin Do'Urden. This ally came in un-expectedly and had Malagdorl at a sudden disadvantage. I could not allow the risk."

"You did the right thing that day," Mez'Barris finally admitted. "But if Dinin, or whoever it was, had not joined the battle?"

"Mal'a'voselle Amvas Tol would be another name in Malagdorl's long list of vanquished foes, of course."

It wasn't what Kaitain expected when Mez'Barris leaned in and asked sincerely and quietly, "He can beat her?"

"He can beat anyone," Kaitain replied.

Mez'Barris nodded. "Then get him out to the West Wall. Matron Zhindia will be putting more pressure on that foolish Matron Zeerith, who rules House Do'Urden, as we try to weaken her alliance with the Baenres. The fighting will be constant in that region, and no doubt, the Blaspheme will join. Find a way, I charge you. Get Malagdorl his battle with this ugly woman from another millennium, and let him get his victory.

"And you," she said, glancing over her shoulder to regard her daughter. "You will go with them and make sure that Malagdorl is not too seriously injured. But hear me, both of you: Our weapon master's win will be honorable. He will kill this Mal'a'voselle creature of his own accord. Just do not allow her friends to intervene this time."

Kaitain locked stares with Taayrul, who was as unhappy with

having to go along as he was in having her, but bowed deeply and said, "Of course, Matron. Your every word is my command."

"THEY'LL NOT RELENT," SARIBEL TOLD MATRON ZEERITH inside the House Do'Urden compound.

Her brother, Ravel, added with heavy sarcasm, "Matron Zhindia is trying to show us a better path."

Saribel snapped a glare over to the wizard. She didn't disagree with Ravel, but sometimes such things were better left unspoken.

"They have not breached the compound at all?" Matron Zeerith asked her two children.

"No," answered Saribel. "But on more than one occasion, I believe they could have."

"As I said . . ." Ravel began, but quieted when another scowl came at him from his sister.

"You are rested," said Zeerith. "Now go and rally our forces. The Baenres will come to sweep clear our porch as soon as they have finished the newest demon wave in the Braeryn."

"Should we not hold priority over the fighting in the Braeryn?" Ravel asked.

"Perhaps Matron Mother Quenthel holds more faith in us than you do," Zeerith said to him. The matron was perturbed and on edge, and Ravel read that clearly enough to finally shut his mouth and keep it shut.

"Your magic is needed—now go," Zeerith finished with a wave of her hand, and the two left the audience chamber.

"You do not disagree with me, yet you hush me like a child," Ravel complained to Saribel when they were out alone in the corridor. "Zhindia is clearly trying to persuade us to abandon our alliance with the Baenres. Do you not think our mother should understand this?"

"Matron Zeerith," Saribel corrected, for such a term of familiarity as Ravel had used should not be spoken aloud where anyone might overhear, "is more than seven centuries old and has witnessed many wars in this city. She knows the way of things and doesn't need us troubling her with such repetitive information."

"Zhindia—"

"Matron Zhindia," Saribel angrily corrected.

"If we are fighting with the Baenre heretics, then why?" a frustrated Ravel returned, holding his hands up in the air as if he wanted to claw at something, anything, in anger. "The incessant knee-bending is exactly the indoctrination of Lolth, is it not? The constant reminder of our place in a hierarchy that allows us to even exist only under their suffrage?"

"We do not know the disposition of anything as of now. Better for you and for me to continue our proper practices."

"Our proper Lolthian practices, you mean."

"Yes."

"Because you expect Matron Zhindia to make an offer to Matron Zeerith, and are not certain which way our mothe . . . Matron Zeerith will go."

"Her responsibility is to our house, first and foremost."

"That is the Lolthian way," Ravel said, dripping sarcasm on every syllable.

"It is the practical way," Saribel said with her jaws clenched. She glanced all around, then pulled her brother into a small room and shut the door. "However Matron Zeerith decides, she must know we're with her."

"Are we?"

"For now, yes. When the blood dries, then we will choose."

"I have already chosen."

"As have I. What I say to you here matters not, because Lolth surely knows that my heart has abandoned her."

"Yet you still find divine power to cast."

Saribel shrugged. "The priestesses of the Lolthian houses have seen their powers increase, but those of us battling the order of Menzoberranzan have seen little decrease. It is an enigma."

"It is Lolth toying with us, with all of us," Ravel remarked. "Using us for her ecstasy in chaos. Is it any different than the many suggestions that she prizes Drizzt Do'Urden, the greatest heretic of our age?"

"He was, perhaps, but now is not. What Yvonnel and Matron Mother Quenthel—"

"Matron Mother," Ravel echoed with a laugh.

Saribel sighed in surrender. "What those two did on the field above is truly the greatest heresy imaginable."

"For all we know, Lolth gave them that inspiration and power."

"Why?"

"For this very civil war we now wage!"

"Your cynicism is—"

"Entirely justified, given the experiences of my life. You ask me to be Lolthian, and this line of thinking is exactly that."

Saribel wanted to answer, obviously.

But just as obviously, she could not deny the claim.

THE FORMER DRIDER THEY CALLED VOSELLY, A HUGE AND powerful woman returned from the grave she had found in the earliest days of Menzoberranzan, rallied her forces around her and led the charge headlong into the ranks of House Melarn and their allies. Working a sword in her right hand, a short spear in her left, the powerful and violent warrior ducked low and covered and ran right through an enemy fireball, then leaped and crashed in boots-first to scatter the lesser enemy fighters trying to secure a shield wall before her.

Like people possessed, behind her came the soldiers. *Her* soldiers, for Matron Mother Quenthel, on advice from Yvonnel, had named Voselly as commander of the Blaspheme. And what a powerful force it was! Returned from the grave, these drow had felt the ultimate torture of Lolth, serving as abominable driders in the Abyss itself, and for almost every one, that experience had not engendered fear, but simply rage, a wall of pure anger that now fell over the Melarni forces and their allies.

A person fearing death had no chance in battle against one who had come through the worst that death could bring.

The Blaspheme drove the attackers back from the area before House Do'Urden, back past the Westrift and toward the Mistrift and

Narbondel, felling four enemies for every Blaspheme returned to the grave.

Out of House Do'Urden came Ravel and Saribel, leading wizards and priests to bolster the rear lines, to heal the wounded, and to create defenses if the attack was pushed back.

As they expected would happen, for they had seen this play before.

As the rage of the Blaspheme played out, the counterattack began, and this time, few drow were in the enemy ranks, and those who were served more as coordinators and witnesses to the events as the new force supporting Zhindia Melarn and the Lolthians—an army of demons—flew down from the cavern's ceiling or came forth from the Mistrift to meet the Blaspheme charge.

"The major demons," Ravel reminded the wizards coming forth from House Do'Urden. "Destroy those who can bring in allies from the Abyss. Banish them for a hundred years!"

The Blaspheme held the line for a while, but inevitably had to turn and flee—through the protective circles the wizards and priests had constructed to slow the demonic charge. The wizards and clerics were now focusing their magical energy skyward, hurling fire and lightning and storms of sleet to defeat the flying chasms.

Ravel and two others scoured the skies looking for greater fiends, and whenever one was located, they cast ribbons of energy to entrap it and force it down to the ground.

And there, Voselly and her forces fearlessly fell over the demon and destroyed it.

But more came forth, and with the Lolthian drow behind them in support, defeating even the protective magic circles and countering the spells of cover. Voselly's force, now with the defenders of House Do'Urden, were forced back to their compound.

Another bloody day of stalemate and attrition, leaving both sides to assess their losses and those of their enemies once more.

"We're killing more of them than they are of us," Ravel insisted to his dour mother, Matron Zeerith, when the West Wall region of Menzoberranzan was at last quiet once more.

"There are many more of them than there are of us," Zeerith replied.

"At least seven major demons will not return," Saribel added, to bolster her brother's optimism.

"Do you think we can drain the Abyss of demons, child?" Zeerith scolded.

"Then where are the Baenres?" Ravel angrily answered, causing many in the throne room to bristle at his tone.

He had only said what so many of them were thinking, of course. Being so near to House Melarn and to the Fane of the Goddess, House Do'Urden was under particular stress, after all, with these battles occurring almost daily now.

Zeerith glared at her son.

"The Braeryn has been quieted by all reports," Ravel pressed on. "The Baenres won a great fight there and now seem in control."

"That is hardly the case," Tsabrak Xorlarrin insisted.

That one's voice carried great weight. Tsabrak was the most powerful wizard in the family, so powerful and influential that he had refused to change his name to Do'Urden and Matron Zeerith had supported him in his decision. For he was the current archmage of Menzoberranzan and perhaps the most powerful wizard in the entire city. And notably, rarely was he seen outside House Do'Urden engaging the enemies.

Not so long ago, Tsabrak had been the tool of Lolth in enacting the great Darkening over the surface lands known as the Silver Marches, in what was perhaps one of the most powerful displays of magical power in recent memory.

His allegiance here was tentative and critical, both Ravel and Saribel understood. Even Zeerith didn't dare to go against him at this time. That Tsabrak was here at all in these crucial moments was encouraging, but, if the nobles of the house weren't careful, it might also prove temporary.

"First, it was not the Baenres fighting there," Tsabrak continued. "It was that rogue Jarlaxle and his mercenaries. Second, yes, the Braeryn is quiet for now, but that is because Matron Zhindia has shifted her forces west to battle this very house, among other reasons, and far to the east, trying to break the Baenre grasp over Donigarten and the food supplies."

"Among other reasons?" Saribel asked.

"To support High Priestess Sos'Umptu in the Fane of the Goddess," Zeerith answered for Tsabrak.

"It makes sense," Tsabrak added. "Sos'Umptu remains a Baenre, of course, but she has already openly defied her heretical sister and family by offering refuge to those loyal to Lolth. There are even whispers that it was she who performed the Curse of Abomination on doomed Byrtyn Fey."

"She would not do that," Saribel argued, holding on to the hope that the wicked action against one of the oldest houses in the city, second only to House Baenre itself, had caused many of Zhindia's allies to rethink their loyalties.

"Anything is possible," said Zeerith, at the same time as Tsabrak corrected Saribel by reminding her of Zhindia's title.

"Possible, and more likely than you clearly wish to believe," Tsabrak added.

Ravel and Saribel left the throne room soon after, ordered to go and check on the perimeter defenses.

"Tsabrak does not engender confidence," Saribel noted as the two made their way through an empty corridor.

"Perhaps that is the very reason he has come to us," Ravel replied. "He is serving as the Archmage of Menzoberranzan, a title he has coveted for most of his life."

"And one given him by Matron Mother Quenthel."

"For us, for the Baenres, to win, it is likely that Gromph will have to return. Tsabrak is a proud and accomplished wizard, and there is no doubt that he blusters more since the events of the Darkening, but he would not wish to compete against Gromph Baenre if Gromph agreed to return to his position at Sorcere—certainly not if that meant an open challenge."

"I'm just surprised by the timing of it all, and by Matron Zeerith's dour mood and Archmage Tsabrak's pessimism," Saribel said. "He corrected us about the Braeryn without even noting that it was likely a better thing that it wasn't House Baenre itself, but was Bregan D'aerthe, that won the fight on the streets against Zhindia's demons."

"I notice that Tsabrak still called her Matron Zhindia," Ravel said as if that held some importance.

"He moves along the walkway between two houses, Melarn and Baenre," Saribel explained. "Tsabrak is veteran enough to understand that this whole war might be nothing more than a test by Lolth for all of us, and that the situation in Menzoberranzan might quickly revert to what it was before the events on the surface. In which case, were he to move too far in either direction, he would likely lose his position as archmage."

Ravel shook his head, buying none of that. "Too much has happened since Yvonnel and the Matron Mother stole the driders from Zhindia and reverted them to their drow bodies. Had that not occurred, we would be in full control of Gauntlgrym by now, with King Bruenor defeated and Drizzt almost certainly served up as sacrifice to the Spider Queen. I agree that we must always assume that things are not what they seem in Menzoberranzan, but you cannot still be thinking that there is some greater deception at play here than we understand."

"Understand," Saribel quietly murmured. "Isn't that the point? What do we really understand about anything?"

"This is no test of loyalty," Ravel replied. "This is a fight, almost certainly a fight to the death."

"And to the damnation."

"Only if we lose. I do not intend to lose."

"You should tell that to our cousin Tsabrak, the Archmage of Menzoberranzan."

"Matron Zeerith should be telling that to Tsabrak right now," Ravel curtly answered.

"Unless she is beginning to agree with him," said Saribel, and there ended the conversation as the siblings neared the end of the corridor, where several guards, Xorlarrin and Blaspheme, had been stationed.

CHAPTER 5

They Promised Me!

Y ou let them lead. You steal my glory," Malagdorl Armgo said to the wizard at his side. Hordes of demons passed by the huge drow warrior, sweeping to the north to battle the Blaspheme and other defenders of House Do'Urden.

"I only act as Matron Mez'Barris instructs," Kaitain replied. "These are the foot soldiers of our enemies. You will find opportunities to get your kills—ones that truly matter—when the first lines are shattered."

"To kill the weaklings hiding from the demons!"

"They are all weaklings, weapon master. The nobles will not come forth in these early battles—certainly not the nobles of the Xorlarrin clan, who will throw their magic from the balconies of House Do'Urden and will not risk anything more with the Melarni so near. We are not even certain of how much Matron Zeerith's heart is in this fight, as with all of those following the foolish Baenres. They see the cost of their disloyalty to Lolth in the face of Byrtyn Fey!"

Malagdorl was hardly listening to the last parts of Kaitain's lecture, for he was watching the retreat of the initial drow attack force, the ones used to goad the defenders away from House Do'Urden. More than watching his allies, though, he was watching one area of the battle that seemed to be going very poorly for the Lolthians, and apparently because of one enemy in particular.

"All weaklings?" he shot back at the wizard, then turned his full attention to that faltering area of battle, rushing forward and yelling, "Malfoosh!"

"Oh, by Lolth's skittering limbs, not this again," the wizard muttered and gave a great heave of resignation.

"They promised me!" Malagdorl growled, and it was true enough that Matron Mez'Barris had indeed assured him that he would get a chance to prove himself against Mal'a'voselle Amvas Tol.

He knew there was no way Kaitain, who had been there when Mez'Barris had made the promise, would dare interfere with Malagdorl's charge. Not against this one, who had sent him stumbling and wounded down an alleyway in retreat.

He could only hope that this would at last be the end of it.

VOSELLY HOOKED A TETHER TO HER SHORT SPEAR AS SHE dove into a roll to avoid the rock the flying chasme had dropped at her. "Come down, you little bug," she said, coming back to her feet and hurling the spear in a fast and fluid movement.

The chasme staggered in its flight, dropping a dozen feet when the barbed missile stabbed its thorax, and Voselly was quick to take up the slack and begin tugging it lower.

Predictably, the flying demon resisted only for a short bit, only as a feint, before turning fast, hard proboscis down, diving like a spear of its own for the warrior woman who had impaled it.

Not caught by surprise and purposely not looking up, Voselly used the sound of the approaching demon and the slack of the rope as her guide, keeping two hands on the cord until the very last moment, when she exploded into motion with a spinning, sidelong leap, drawing her sword as she turned and swept in across to take that proboscis, one of the antennae, and most of the bloated human face right off the abominable demon's body.

It crashed to the stone beside her with a sickening splat.

Voselly was already engaged with another fiend, a short, rounded beast with spindly limbs and rubbery skin, and a face that looked like it was selected from the ugliest features of a pig, an ape, and a rotting human corpse. It came on, swinging its clawed hands at the end of its long arms, but Voselly, who had spent centuries in the Abyss, understood the tactics of this minor fiend known as a dretch, and that its attacks were more a desperate flail than any coordinated and intended plan. She casually fended and countered while at the same time tearing her short spear from the dead chasme.

That task proved more difficult than dispatching the dretch, her twentieth kill in this fight that was so full of demon fodder beasts, dretches, and manes. She had defeated a trio of drow early on in the advance from House Do'Urden, killing one, sending a second running with wicked wounds, and leaving the third writhing on the ground to be taken prisoner, but other than those and the chasme she had finally taken from the sky, none of her kills had been notable.

Frustrated, the great warrior felt like a rothé farmer butchering a helpless cow.

Another dretch fell to her, then a pair of manes.

"They're trying to exhaust us with these dregs, which are so easily replaceable!" she shouted to her fighting companion, Aleandra of House Amvas Tol, who had been beside her for most of her life, and even in the Abyss in their shared state of abomination.

"An endless supply," Aleandra agreed.

They could kill a thousand this battle, ten thousand, even, and the Lolthians would refill those ranks in a matter of days.

Voselly knew it. They had to find greater demons to remove, for those were the beasts bringing in these lesser fiends.

At least a chasme was not so easily replaced as the dretches and manes. And the three drow . . .

Voselly heard her name, the nickname she had been given when she had served as a drider, shouted from across the enemy lines. It only took her a moment to locate the speaker, so distinct from the other drow in size and appearance, with his white hair gelled and spiked in a line across the top of his head.

Malagdorl Armgo shook his black trident at her and yelled her demeaning nickname again.

"The beast returns," Voselly muttered.

"You know him?"

"He is the one I battled when our lost friend intervened. This one is the Weapon Master of the Second House, Barrison Del'Armgo."

"He hates you, it seems."

"Because he knew that I would have beaten him."

"Don't," Aleandra advised, rushing up beside her.

Voselly turned a curious look her friend's way, scrunching her face even more incredulously when Aleandra kept shaking her head and pleading with her to ignore the challenger.

"Matron Mez'Barris has fully thrown in with the Lolthians," Voselly answered those doubts. "The Second House has made its choice. There is no reason to let this warrior man leave this battlefield alive."

She turned to discern a path to take her near to the challenger, but Aleandra grabbed her by the arm.

"Voselly, no, I beg you," she said.

"He will be a great loss to our enemies."

"You will be a great loss to us!"

"Your faith is endearing," came the warrior's sarcastic response.

"Even if you kill him, his allies will ensure that you are also slain."

"Then lead our forces against them more fiercely, so the friends of Malagdorl Armgo do not get that chance!" Voselly countered, and she leaped away, hacking the head from a dretch and stabbing a second with her spear, then slinging it away to knock aside a pair of ugly and bloated manes.

She smiled, noting that Malagdorl wasn't hanging back and waiting for her. No coward, this one.

He wanted this rematch as much as she.

"ORDER THE DEMONS ASIDE!" MALAGDORL INSISTED TO Kaitain.

"At the first sign of you losing—" Kaitain bit the sentence off when Malagdorl turned a scowl over him.

"If there is dire need, I will not hesitate to teleport us both from this battle," the wizard pressed on. "Matron Mez'Barris has been explicit in her demands."

"Dire," Malagdorl echoed. "Anything short of that and the least of Kaitain's problems will come from Matron Mez'Barris. You cannot win a fight against me, wizard, and even if you somehow managed to survive one, what course do you think Matron Mez'Barris would then take toward you?"

The warrior found himself quite pleased at Kaitain's helpless sigh, and even more so when Kaitain began doing as he had asked in clearing the path between the challengers of interfering demons.

He focused on Malfoosh then, replaying their previous fight as he knew she would be doing. He considered the back-and-forth of their weapon play, the way the woman had used the angled side of a stalagmite to escape his first trap. She had thought herself stronger, then, and had learned the truth when he had taken her sword from her.

Her spearplay thereafter had been cunning and fine, surprising him—nearly defeating him, he admitted to himself and to no one else.

But still, he had her beaten—he had been the quicker after their clutch, trident moving before her spear for the kill. The fight was his, until the woman's companion had rushed through, deflecting his attack and throwing him off-balance long enough for her to score a decisive stab.

Not this time.

He continued his slow and balanced approach, looking around for any allies of the former drider who might now similarly rush to her aid. The Do'Urden who had intervened the first time was off the battlefield, of course, in the clawing hands of Zhindia Melarn, but there was a woman, another of the Blaspheme, tall and strong . . .

Malagdorl did well to hide his smile when he saw that second woman, confident that she would not help his opponent, for he recognized her as Aleandra, who had betrayed Dinin's identity to Zhindia.

He honed his sight onto his opponent, and in his mind stopped thinking of her as Malfoosh. No, she was Mal'a'voselle Amvas Tol, a proud and formidable weapon master of an age past. He noted her stride, low and defensive. He had taken her measure in that first fight, but she had taken his as well. She had thought herself the stronger.

Now she knew better. And if not, more the pity.

He wasn't overconfident, though, and was wise enough to be wary. She would adjust. She would avoid clenches. She would be more careful in keeping her short spear and her sword away from the swings of his net.

It wouldn't matter.

She stayed on the balls of her feet with every approaching step, ready to dart to either side, or to retreat.

Malagdorl understood. She would make this a battle of stamina, not strength, of quickness and technique, not brute force.

Good. Let her think she had any kind of advantage. He would prove her wrong on the points of his trident.

When they came together, the rest of the world simply ceased to exist for Malagdorl, his concentration perfect, his vision clear and measuring every twist and turn.

She led with the spear, as he expected—but no, it was a feint, he realized as her hips hedged in their turn just enough for her to suddenly reverse the move, striding forward suddenly with her right foot, her sword arm coming across to bat the presented trident.

Malagdorl took that hit on his weapon and absorbed it by moving to his right with the blow. Instead of whipping the net back the other way over the batted trident to hook the sword, he rolled the trident underneath the sword and stabbed it straight out.

His opponent, expecting the net, and already adjusting to thrust her short spear under the tangle, had to abandon her attack and furiously retreat from the adamantine tines.

Malagdorl suppressed his pride, his self-congratulation for anticipating and defeating the woman's feint within the feint.

Instead, he reminded himself again that this one was formidable, immensely so: a lesser opponent would already be lifted into the air at the end of that trident for all to see.

But he was formidable, too.

Voselly came on again suddenly, retracting the spear, batting with the sword, and lifting her right leg in a vicious kick to Malagdorl's knee as the two moved closer.

Malagdorl rolled to his right, forcing the kick behind the knee instead of into the side, and avoiding the spear thrusting under the sword-and-trident tangle in the same movement.

Out flashed his right elbow, cracking into the woman's forearm and driving on, forcing her backward.

She held the weapon, managing to extract it cleanly, and got it up before her defensively just in time as Malagdorl took the initiative, grabbing his trident in both hands and thrusting it forward. She caught it between the tines with her upraised blade and managed, just barely, to turn it enough to her left to miss.

Out she stabbed with her spear, but Malagdorl drove his right hand—the rear one on the shaft of his weapon—down and to the side, the trident's shaft deflecting the stab. Then up and forward went that right hand, disengaging the trident and coming up before his opponent could bring her sword back in line. The butt of the trident clipped her chin and the tip of her nose, and she fell back out of range, shaking her head, squinting her eyes repeatedly in an attempt to chase away the pain.

Or not, Malagdorl realized, determined not to underestimate this one.

She wanted him to think her stunned, to come forward in a rush that he thought she could not then avoid.

So he did, or pretended to, roaring and leaping ahead, and the woman beautifully sidestepped and lifted her spear.

And Malagdorl, too, sidestepped as he came out of his leap, realigning as he landed and forcing yet another adjustment from Mal'a'voselle as the two crashed together. He felt her sword stabbing at his side, and brought his net over and down, hooking it and her arm and forcing it away. Her short spear was better served in these tight quarters than his trident, obviously, so he pressed in even closer, the two hooking arms.

And as with their first fight, each headbutted, slamming their skulls together, blood and sweat flying.

This is what she had needed to avoid, though. The clench favored the stronger, he knew!

Or thought he knew, until the clever Mal'a'voselle did not retract her head the next time they crashed together, but instead followed his retraction, pressing against the side of his face and biting his ear.

A shot of fiery pain ripped through him. He had been cut and scourged and beaten, but this was something new. A warrior endured pain or died, however, and he resisted the urge to just push her away, instead wrapping her in his arms suddenly and throwing himself backward and to the ground in a roll, forcing his knee beneath her, letting go of his net and tucking his arm between them.

With strength beyond anything anyone could expect of a drow, Malagdorl thrust that arm forward, throwing the woman away and out.

She tucked beautifully as she landed, getting her shoulders around to continue the roll alone, and twisting to the side to come back to her feet, both weapons ready.

Malagdorl didn't come back to his feet to meet that, however. He shortened his roll and spun up to one knee, adjusting and lifting his right hand up beside his ear.

Mal'a'voselle Amvas Tol turned beautifully to meet a charge that did not come, but wide and balanced with arms and legs—too wide to get a deflecting arm across, too wide to turn her hips aside.

The hurled trident came in between, its tines finer than even the Baenre armor she wore, the weapon stabbing into her chest.

Rising and charging behind the throw, Malagdorl grabbed at the shaft to drive it through her heart, but he wasn't quite fast enough, and the Blaspheme warrior managed to crack her sword across to knock the trident free. An underhand throw with her left sent the spear flying with speed and power that surprised Malagdorl as it drove into his belly.

But he ignored that, stopped short the deflection of the trident, and snapped it back to the right, pressing forward just enough for the tips to rake the woman's face, drawing deep gashes and tearing her left eye.

They came crashing together again, butting and biting.

Malagdorl roared in pain when he felt the impaling spear being twisted by the clever warrior.

He, the great warrior of Barrison Del'Armgo, nearly swooned then, nearly crumbled.

Nearly.

Instead, he realized that her left hand was low, so he grabbed at her short hair with his right and yanked her head to the side.

He felt a sword ram and dig against his left shoulder, but didn't even try to respond, didn't even move his left arm to somehow push it away.

No, his one focus came clear for just an instant, and nothing else mattered.

Malagdorl took a trick from her own book and bit her, clamping his teeth down hard on her exposed neck and thrashed and chewed.

He tore out Voselly's throat.

He felt her recoil and threw her back several feet, taking her impaled spear and more of his flesh with her.

He grabbed at his wound as she tried to slap at hers, to stem the spouting blood, but he knew a fatal wound when he saw one.

So did she.

Still, she looked past him to his left, and he glanced that way to see her companion, staring on in shock and despair.

She called to Aleandra in a gurgling and choking voice, begging for help.

Malagdorl didn't have to look back again to know that Aleandra Amvas Tol simply turned away. He could see it on the face of the dying Mal'a'voselle.

She sank to her knees and Malagdorl moved directly before her.

He spent a moment admiring his handiwork, grinning as he noted her torn eye, the deep gashes, the blood dripping from the three holes in her chest, the blood spurting from her ripped neck.

His smile went away when he saw something fall from her mouth and recognized it to be part of him, not her.

Reflexively, his hand went up to that halved ear. He growled and snarled, moving his face very near to hers.

"Lolth is waiting for you, Malfoosh," he taunted and lifted his trident, aiming it right for her face.

But no, he turned it down, and instead just laughed as he lifted his foot and pushed her over to the ground, letting her die more slowly and painfully, letting her think about the doom that awaited her.

Then he walked away, knowing he'd been the only true weapon master in that fight.

CHAPTER 6

Too Much of a Good Thing

Braelin watched the fight from a perch on a stalactite hanging down from the cavern holding Menzoberranzan. The armies swarmed like insects hundreds of feet below him, the air crackling with lightning bolts and fireballs that erupted like blossoming flowers on a surface field.

He watched the Baenre forces gain ground, driving the demons and Lolthians before them to the south and east, around the tip of the Westrift, and thought that Jarlaxle would be pleased.

But then came the ferocious counterattack: He smelled the ozone and smoke filling the air, felt the tingle from black bolts of Abyssal energy. Heard the screams, so many screams, the agony of the dying and the terror of those soon to die.

He couldn't deny his own horror, his breath coming in gasps, the smells of burned flesh—demon and drow and the many unfortunate enslaved peoples of other lineages thrown into the fray—wafting up to fill his nostrils, but neither could he deny that he wanted to be down there, wanted to be in this fight.

Only his duty stopped him. His duty held his bow across his lap when the chasme flew just below him—how easy it would have been to pick off the trailing demon!

But that was not his mission.

So he watched.

In particular he saw the spectacle of one fight—even from this distance, Braelin thought that it must be Malagdorl Armgo.

Whoever it was the weapon master was fighting, the victory against that particular opponent brought a great cheer from the Lolthians.

But that, in turn, brought a fierce counterattack by the Blaspheme and their allies, pressing fast and far enough to retrieve some of their fallen and then retreat.

Braelin knew that the outcome, the victory, for whichever side, would be costly and muted with wounds, and he knew the clear implications of this battle. No more was this a game of fast fights and faster flights, a back-and-forth of feeling out their opponents, drawing lines, and coaxing allies from the enemy ranks.

No, now the war for Menzoberranzan was on in full, and if half the drow in the city were killed, that would not exceed Braelin Janquay's expectations.

They were fighting for their lives, and more than that, for their afterlives, all of them.

Giving quarter was not in that equation.

The rogue closed his eyes and composed himself. Where was Jarlaxle? If he did not get here, and soon, then he would have little role left to play, however he chose to roll his die.

Which meant Braelin needed to get to the Oozing Myconid, to share his information, and help Jarlaxle place his bet, and—if he knew the rogue—load the dice in his favor.

He scaled around to the far end of the stalactite cluster and peered carefully all about before he made himself vulnerable. He had no fear of chasms, not when he had solid ground beneath him, at least, but there were greater demons in the city than those—he had heard rumors of a balor joining the Lolthian side, a rumor he had no desire to see proven true.

The battle raged far below, but up here seemed calm and empty of enemies.

He had to hold faith.

One last look, and he took three running strides along a ledge and leaped out, plunging toward the ground.

Before he lost the momentum of his leap, still moving east, Braelin called upon an enchantment from a ring.

Instead of falling, then, he was gliding down, drifting ever eastward and down, toward the Stenchstreets of Menzoberranzan.

"YOU HAVE ALREADY LOST."

"I have," Azleah answered.

"And you are glad of that."

"Of course, it is . . . you are, wonderful."

A smile came to Kariva, who now looked exactly like Azleah, even down to the little mole just below the left edge of the woman's rather thick nose. She wore an identical blue outfit: a blue-and-white-patterned wraparound dress that swept down from the left shoulder, off the right shoulder, around low on the back, then back low over the left hip, revealing the woman's—and the succubus's—tightly muscled belly. The knee-length hem was frilled, enhancing every movement with sweeping grace, and was slitted up the front of the right leg. Or the appearance of this leg, at least, for all of this disguise, down to the mole, was an illusion.

"This is his favorite gown?"

"It is!" Azleah answered, giggling.

"Of course it is," Kariva said lightly to her new best friend. "You are so pretty! I am so thrilled to be as pretty as you."

Azleah smiled widely, but it melted a bit and she suddenly wore a look of concern, as if something wasn't quite right about that statement, or about any of this.

"It is just a game," the succubus assured her, and kissed her, strengthening the charm. This one was no easy mark, she reminded

herself. It had taken Kariva and her two friends a long while to finally get this Azleah creature under their willpower. "Just to make him
laugh, and then, of course, I will leave you two alone. And look at me!
I am Azleah to any unsuspecting patrons who might come in, and so I
can keep them engaged and happy while you and your lover take your
well-deserved rest!"

The woman's smile returned and Kariva breathed a little sigh of
relief. This was becoming quite tedious, and she didn't need the added
tension of danger.

Not against this next target, who had so easily obliterated a hezrou.

He is on the street, approaching through the shadows, Kariva heard in
her mind, the telepathy of Uvillia.

"Say not a word," she told Azleah. "Just a smile and a sweeping
turn to let this beautiful gown fly wide and spin about you like a cy-
clone. Remember: you are the eye of that storm your lover so desires."

"Are you sure?"

"My dear Azleah, I have long perfected this game of ours."

"But you don't know him."

"I know that he is like Jarlaxle, and I know that one all too well,"
Kariva lied.

Azleah frowned again, and Kariva wondered if she'd gone too far
with this comparison. "Braelin is different. Jarlaxle is the master of
games."

Another kiss, another assurance. "Not all games, my dear Azleah.
There are some things that even Jarlaxle, like your consort, simply
cannot control and simply cannot resist."

He approaches.

"Now go, and be quick," Kariva told the tavern keeper. "His favorite drink from his favorite person." As Azleah went for the door,
Kariva lifted a finger over pursed lips to remind her to say not a word
yet again.

THE STENCHSTREETS WERE QUIET, EERILY SO, BUT THAT
was understandable with the large battle raging over in the western

sections of the city. Still, Braelin took his time and kept to the shadows as he made his way toward the Oozing Myconid.

He knew that the Lolthians would be investigating the deaths of the Vandree nobleman and particularly of the Hunzrin priestess, to say nothing of the loss of a hezrou demon. That was a blow worth knowing more about.

As he turned down the last lane, the Oozing Myconid at its far end, he considered whether to sneak all the way or walk openly. If there was going to be trouble, perhaps it was better to get it over with, after all.

He thought better of that, though, for however it might make him feel, Braelin's responsibility was more than just to himself. He had learned quite a lot regarding the rapidly declining situation here in the city and of the battle lines, and of the rumors that an unexpected and important prisoner had been taken by the Lolthians from the ranks of the Blaspheme. Included in those whispers were hints that Matron Zhindia would make of this prisoner a drider publicly, as a warning to all those who would oppose the Spider Queen, particularly to those who had been relieved of the Curse of Abomination to become living drow once more.

So instead of the door, the scout went up onto the rooftops, picking his way carefully. He wasn't afraid of any fight—in fact, he wanted one!—but this wasn't about him. It was about Jarlaxle's vision and the many who depended upon it, most especially the woman tending to the tavern he was now approaching.

He went to the roof of that building, spider-crawling down the front behind the giant mushroom to the left of the main door, then dropped down, glanced around, and moved inside.

To Braelin's surprise, the place was empty of patrons. It was early in the day, but still . . . he wasn't sure he'd ever seen the tavern deserted.

No, not deserted, he noted, seeing Azleah over at the bar, giving one last wipe of a cloth before tossing it aside and pointedly lifting a glass onto the counter.

She wore his favorite outfit.

She gave him a coy smile, and moved toward the door to her private quarters.

Braelin wasn't sure what to think, but he surely knew what he felt.

Had Azleah emptied the place in anticipation of his arrival? He thrilled at the idea . . . but how could she know?

She didn't glance back at him until she reached the door, where she gave him a mischievous little grin and a wink of her pretty eye, pausing there on the threshold.

Braelin went to the bar and the drink she had placed on the bar. Indeed, his favorite.

"Where is—"

She put her fingers to her lips—those perfect lips—and shushed him. Then she walked away, not glancing back at him.

Grinning, Braelin went over the bar with a flourish, scooped up the glass, and moved to the door to Azleah's room, where he was met immediately with a great hug and a passionate kiss, the woman immediately fumbling with his weapon belt.

He returned the kiss wholeheartedly, but with some further surprise, for it was unlike any Azleah had ever offered. Forceful and even with a bit of biting—something seemed to have stirred his lover in ways he had not known before.

He wasn't opposed to the change at all, and kissed back with even more fervor.

She held the kiss, backpedaling and taking him with her toward the bed, and he took care not to trip over his fallen belt and sword.

He opened his eyes, still locked in a kiss and a hug that was growing tighter and tighter by the step, almost painfully so.

And there, sitting on the edge of the bed, peering at him from around the footboard canopy, he saw . . . Azleah.

Stunned, confused, Braelin reached up to grab the arms of the woman clenching him, but found her grip only tightening more. He tried to pull back, to pull his lips away, but she would not let him, and kissed him even more tightly.

The pain in his lips from the teeth was nothing compared to the weakness he was experiencing. It felt as if his very life force was somehow being sucked out of him. He twisted and pulled, and there, along the right-hand wall, he saw . . . another Azleah.

Panic hit him when he felt another set of hands grab him on the left side. Confusion tore at him when he saw a fourth Azleah!

All dressed exactly the same.

All looking exactly the same.

He thought of a mirror-image spell Gromph had often used, but no, this was no such thing, for the duplicates were not mirroring moves, but acting independently.

It made no sense.

And then he felt soul-wrenching pain, and he knew for sure it was indeed his life force being drawn into this woman . . . or whatever it was.

And he thought that a good thing.

But how could it be a good thing?

His legs went weak. The woman from the right-hand wall was up beside him, grabbing at him.

He felt a cord going about him, his arms being tugged down and tightly bound.

But it was okay. These were his friends. These were his lover . . .

All of them?

Braelin shook that notion away and fought back against the kiss, finally breaking free and gasping for air.

The kisser pulled back from him. Her hair lengthened and became red. Her skin tone changed before his eyes.

She was whispering to him, but he couldn't hear the words.

He just knew, somehow, that he liked those words more than anything he had ever heard.

It was a mistake, even trying to listen, but as the magical barrage of charming continued, and in his weakened state, Braelin could only resist it for so long.

He had to get free and flee. He had to embrace the woman—the not-Azleah—and give in to her sweet words.

Azleah stood up from the bed—*the true Azleah?* he wondered—telling him that it was all right, that these were their new friends.

He didn't know what to make of that.

Braelin shrugged and twisted, and found that he was surely stronger than the two holding him. But not stronger than the cord they had put around him, a magical cord that tightened with his every twist.

The woman before him, no longer Azleah, he was certain, sprouted red wings shaped like those of a bat . . . and came forward and caught him again with a kiss.

The last thing he saw was Azleah—was it really her?—looking at him with a strange grin on her face from the side of the bed.

Strange and unthinking, the grin of a simpleton.

His last thought as he felt his life force draining away his consciousness was that they had Azleah, too.

PART 2

INSPIRATION

In walking the streets of Callidae, in talking to the aevendrow, the contrast with Menzoberranzan could not be more stark. This was the answer, for me and for Jarlaxle, at least, and likely for the other companions from Menzoberranzan as well, although I do not know if Zaknafein, Kimmuriel, Dab'nay, or certainly Gromph had ever so directly pondered the question: Was there something within me, within all drow, a flaw in our nature, a predetermination, a damning fate, of all the evils of our culture for which the other peoples of Faerun cast blame and aspersions?

Certainly, I never felt such inner urges or demons or wishes to cause harm. Nor, I am sure, did my sisters—at least two—or my father. I never saw such natural malice in Jarlaxle, or even in Kimmuriel, though he often frightened me.

But still, even knowing that, it was ever hard for me to fully dismiss the opinions that the peoples of other lands and species and cultures placed upon the drow, upon me. Catti-brie once said to me that perhaps I was more constrained by the way I saw other people seeing me, and there is truth to that little semantic twist. But it went deeper, went to the core *of who Drizzt Do'Urden truly was—or, more importantly, of who I ever feared I might be or might become.*

The expectation of others is an often-crippling weight.

I lived under that weight. And as strong as I am, as much as I've trained my mind, body, and soul, I see now how it stooped my shoulders just enough to not be able to truly stand tall around my companions. To want to hide, if even in the secret part of my brain, all the things they might have perceived about me and other drow.

But now I have the answer. Now we all have the answer, even those companions who perhaps never directly asked the question, and it is a wondrous thing:

We drow are not flawed.

We are not lesser. We are not malignant by any measure of nature. I do not know how high the ladder of evil deeds such truth climbs, honestly. I have seen wicked dictators of every species and culture to match the vileness of the most zealous Lolthian priestess. I have witnessed truly evil people, from dwarfs to halflings to humans to elves to drow, and everything in between and every species or culture only a bit removed. So perhaps there are some individuals who have within them a natural evil.

Or perhaps even with them, even with the most wicked, like Matron Zhindia Melarn or the magistrates of Luskan's carnival, who torture accused criminals with such glee, there were steps in the earlier days of their personal journey which corrupted them and brought them to their present state. That is a question that I doubt will ever show an answer, nor is that answer truly the most important factor, for in the present, in the moment, in their own actions, these folk, as with us all, bear responsibility.

The more important question to me in all of this, then, is how can an entire city—and nearly all within the city—be so held in thrall, be twisted to the will of a demon queen so completely that they lose all sense of what is right and what is wrong? Because surely that basic understanding is something that any reasoning being should possess!

In Menzoberranzan, I am coming to understand, there were far more akin to me than those gladly embracing the tenets of Lolth and her vicious clergy. Even Dab'nay, who long ago realized how much she despised all that was Lolth (and yet, remained a priestess and was still being granted magical spells from that being she despised!).

The answer, I now know, is fear. Of all the inspirations, the motivations any leader can give, the easiest is fear, and it is perhaps the most difficult to push aside. Dab'nay could secretly hate Lolth, but to proclaim it openly would have meant her death, if she was lucky. More likely, she would have been turned into a drider, sentenced to an eternity of unrelenting anguish.

Even the bravest would fear that.

Fear is a powerful weapon, and the tragic result of a despot is a tale too often told, and even easier to see in the more transient societies of the shorter-living peoples. I have seen kingdoms of humans taken to bad end by a lord with evil designs—we saw this with Lord Neverember and the Waterdhavian houses corrupted for personal gain. These are among the most predictable and saddest tales in the annals of the human societies, where one state or another decides to wage war, to steal land or resources from a neighbor. And also, thankfully, along with being the most common, such states are often the most transient. Kingdoms that were once avowed enemies are now grand allies and friends, sharing markets, intermarrying, prospering together.

The difference in Menzoberranzan, most obviously, is that the power there, the wicked lord with evil designs, was, and remains, not transient. A human leader will die—perhaps their successor will be of a better and more generous heart; if not the immediate one, then only a few decades down the road. Nor is the simple physical geography of the surface kingdoms conducive to any lasting and debilitating autocracy, for many of the people will come to know folk of other lands, and so will learn of the shortcomings of their society when placed against the aspirations and hopeful visions of their neighbors.

Such is not the case in the cavern of my birth. Not only is Lolth eternal and ever present, a dictator who will not unclench her talons, but the city itself is secluded. I am not unique in my desire to flee, nor am I the only drow who did run from Menzoberranzan through the millennia of Lolthian control. Perhaps I am not the only one who made it out of there, who somehow, with good fortune, survived the wilds of the Underdark, and with better fortune, found a home, a true place within a family. But for every drow like me who somehow escaped, I take heart in knowing that there are thousands who would like to escape, who see the wrongs before them.

Lolth's method is lying.

Lolth's inspiration is fear.

Lolth's full damnation of the drow in Menzoberranzan is that she is eternal, clutching tighter at every generation.

Now, we have a chance to break that hold, to free the city, to turn the whispers of the drow into open shouts of denial.

That is why I could not stay in Callidae. That is why I could not stay in the comfort of my homes in Longsaddle or Gauntlgrym, my wife and daughter beside me.

Because now—and only now, armed with knowledge and light illuminating what has so long been hidden—we have a chance.

—Drizzt Do'Urden

CHAPTER 7

An Impossible Choice

Azzudonna wiped the sweat from her face, her gray skin showing hints of the lavender blush that was so clear in her purple-streaked white hair and those haunting purple eyes.

Eyes so much like those of his son, Zaknafein thought, and he felt as if he was being transported back in time to those many sparring matches he had fought with Drizzt before and after Drizzt had gone to Melee-Magthere.

Zak chased the notion away, or at least tried to. He didn't really want to be thinking of Drizzt right then, however, because he understood well the likely danger, the terrible danger, his son was facing.

He shook his head and set himself again, feet wide and balanced, hands up to defend.

"If your mind is elsewhere, I will defeat you easily," Azzudonna teased.

Zak didn't answer.

Azzudonna sighed and threw the towel aside, then surprisingly turned away. "We are wasting our time here," she announced.

"You only say that because you know I will put you to the floor!" Zak called after her.

The woman stopped short and spun about, her almost perpetual smile nowhere to be seen. "When he is here mind and body, Zaknafein can do that . . . occasionally," she said, with only the last word showing any hint of humor. But her expression became a scowl. "When he is here mind and body, Zaknafein shows himself worthy of a place on Biancorso. This distracted man before me now cannot compete in cazzcalci."

Zak winced.

"If you doubt me, perhaps you can move to another borough and join another team, so that if you fool them enough to let you on their team, when we compete in the next event, I will show you the truth of my words."

"Move to another borough?" he echoed, his tone revealing more anger than hurt.

When his family and friends had returned to the south, Zaknafein had stayed in Callidae, in the borough of Scellobel and the house of Azzudonna. She was his lover, mind and body, soon to be his wife. She was his partner in everything now, his forever companion, so he hoped. And more than anything, Azzudonna wanted Zak to join her in her life's passion as a player on the Whitebears of Scellobel, the cazzcalci team known as Biancorso.

Cazzcalci was more than a game for the people of Callidae. Each of the four boroughs fielded a team of twenty-five battlers, and for those hundred Callidaeans, cazzcalci was their life. They trained all year for that battle of Twilight Autumn, when the summer sun gave way to the winter night above Callidae.

Zaknafein understood her anger with him—he deserved it at that moment. Since she had first met him on the day of his arrival in Callidae, she had mentioned him as a potential battler on her beloved Biancorso. She had watched him, even coached him that day when he battled against another woman who wished to become a member of Biancorso, and Azzudonna had looked at him even then as she looked at him now, her purple eyes sparkling.

The attraction had been mutual and instant, and it had multiplied many times over in the tendays they had spent together and the adventure they had shared. She had spent hours and hours at his bedside, bolstering his spirits when a slaad had infected him and his end seemed near, and now shared his bed. It was deeper than even that, though.

In the battle of cazzcalci, after her heroics on the rink, Azzudonna had been the one to start the chant "*Perte miye*, Zaknafein!" which had been echoed by the tens of thousands in the arena; the call, the pleading, that had brought the magic of the Merry Dancers, the magical lights of the northern night sky, swirling down to him, strengthening him, intoxicating him in their pure magical beauty, steeling his resolve to hold on and survive that which seemed mortal.

She had done that. Her love for him, expressed through the chants of all of Callidae, had done that, those eyes sparkling the entire time. Until now, when they didn't shine, but rather glared.

And that was Zak's conundrum.

He hated seeing those eyes look at him like that. Which meant he couldn't leave her.

Yet it also meant he couldn't return to the south, and from there to Menzoberranzan to join in the war against the Spider Queen, a war in which he—by fathering Drizzt, by sacrificing himself for Drizzt those centuries before, and unwittingly by being resurrected—had become a pawn.

His son was going to fight. Jarlaxle, his dearest friend, was going to fight. Dab'nay, once his lover, always his friend, was going to fight.

And he wouldn't be beside them.

He heaved a heavy sigh, his shoulders slumping, and he noted Azzudonna's expression and posture change. Her features softening, her stance shifting away from a fighting pose.

"Not today, then," Azzudonna said, her voice full of sympathy.

It struck Zak deeply to see that she loved him enough to trust him, to recognize and understand that something was wrong with him, and trusting, obviously, that he would tell her when he was ready.

"Not today," he agreed and began stripping off his fist wrappings.

SOMEONE LOOKING UPON THE LANKY YOUNG MAN MIGHT think him no more than a tall child, and certainly not formidable. But those who watched Allefaero battling the polar worms beneath the ice-filled borough of Cattisola knew better. Even those around the young student who worked the library in the Siglig had thought him more of a sage than a spellcaster. Surely, he was intelligent—no one doubted that—and the value of his understanding of the remorhazes could not be denied.

Still, when Allefaero ventured into the crystal caves beneath the city's lost borough on that initial descent beside Holy Galathae, even his biggest supporters had no hint that he would prove so potent an evoker, destroying many of the invading beasts, driving them back, indeed, saving the life of Galathae the hero.

The underestimation was inevitable and understandable, Allefaero knew. He was called "lanky," but in truth, he was skinny, incredibly thin. His brain worked wonders and he could read and remember a large tome in a day. But he ate little, which certainly wasn't a prescription for thickness in this cold climate. While other aevendrow his age trained physically, many hoping to one day serve on their borough team in cazzcalci, Allefaero read, and read, and read some more.

Knowledge was his power, quite literally, channeling his brainpower into his magical dweomers.

Yet even he had been surprised at the might of that in his first encounters with the polar worms, which were, indeed, the first battle encounters of his half-century of life.

Perhaps Allefaero's greatest gift was that he knew that he didn't know what he didn't know, and so he guided his quests for knowledge based on outcomes of past events instead of on tradition. He read those less regarded tomes in the vast library of the Siglig. Instead of dismissing the spellcrafting work of perceived failures, he took the time to learn if he could discover *where* they went wrong, and more than that, to understand what had led them on this or that particular path to begin with.

Which is why he stood now before the door of an old human, an exotic-looking Ulutiun man who over the years had become the butt of many jokes between the other scholars and wizards working in the library.

The "crazy old windblown shelduck" named Nvisi had predicted the continuing encroachment of Cattisola's ice wall many years before the stranger named Jarlaxle had figured out the secret beneath the canyon that housed the borough. But Nvisi's explanations and prognostications were always written with such strange syntax and word choice as to seem to some as ambiguous, and his manner of speaking was very different than that even of the other Ulutiuns in Callidae.

And thus, he was dismissed and mocked.

By all but Allefaero.

He knocked quietly on the door and heard mumbling within, but nothing distinct.

Rather than disturb the man at his work, Allefaero spent a minute to cast a spell upon Nvisi's metal doorknob, a spell Nvisi had taught him.

The knob shuddered and sprouted tiny limbs as it animated to life.

If Nvisi is not reading or writing, turn and open the door, he silently imparted to his tiny servant, and he smiled when the doorknob's new legs began twisting and the latch pulled back.

Allefaero lightly pushed open the door and let it swing enough for him to take in the room, his gaze going immediately to the occupant.

Wearing ragged and ill-fitting clothing, and many layers of it, and with his sparse crop of still-black hair all disheveled and haphazardly cut into many different lengths and layers, Nvisi surely appeared more a houseless and penniless vagabond than a scholarly wizard. His head was bowed, left hand tap-tapping at his left eyebrow, while he rolled some items—his magical gemstones, Allefaero figured—before him in his clenched right hand.

If he had noticed the door opening, he didn't show it.

"Master Nvisi?" Allefaero asked.

No response.

"Master?" he asked more loudly.

Nvisi's left hand dropped to his side and he looked up, though in his pacing, he was then facing the wall opposite the door. He glanced around confusedly and Allefaero called to him again.

It still took the short Ulutiun some time to realize that the speaker was behind him, and Allefaero was reminded as to why so many of his peers considered the notion of "Nvisi the Great Clairvoyant" somewhat . . . wrongheaded.

Finally, Nvisi turned around, a smile appearing immediately on the wrinkled and ruddy skin of his round face.

Allefaero sucked in his breath, a slight gasp that always occurred when he first looked upon Nvisi after a time away from the man and saw again those eyes, one bright amber, the other crystal blue.

"Allefaero," Nvisi greeted. "Too long, oh clever. Clever Allefaero. You listen to me. Allefaero listens to Nvisi."

The young wizard had a hard time unwinding that greeting until he realized that Nvisi was looking past him, to the door, now with both knobs visible because of the angle of the partially opened portal, tiny legs kicking on the hallway knob, tiny arms flailing on the inner knob.

Nvisi cackled at the sight.

"You taught me well," Allefaero said.

"Nvisi does not teach, no, no, no. Inform. Nvisi informs. He sees, he tells. He does not teach. No, no."

"Of course," Allefaero said with a bow.

"Nvisi is cursed, not blessed," the Ulutiun said, waving his hands, one still clenched, to cut that bow of respect short. Nvisi wasn't holding his fist tight enough, though, and a small purple stone flew from it as he waggled, bouncing across the room.

Allefaero moved to find it, but stopped at Nvisi's scolding "Eh eh!"

Nvisi gave a soft but sharp burst of two whistles and a fuzzy white-furred rodent, hand-sized and with no eyes and a large pink nose, scampered out from under a chair, darting across the room. It disappeared under a pile of boxes and papers beneath a desk covered in parchments, then came back out a moment later with the purple stone in its mouth.

"Doodles," Nvisi said gratefully when the sightless glacial lemming ran up his leg, weaved in and out of one of the shirts and another of the vests he wore, and dropped the gem into his waiting hand.

Wizards conjured their familiars from spirits, Celestial, fey, or fiend, but Doodles was none of those. He, or she—how would one know?—was truly a lemming, a living lemming, or perhaps the spirit of a formerly living lemming that was alive once more through Nvisi's magic, for the man had kept it by his side for as long as anyone could remember.

Or maybe Doodles had been many different lemmings. Some others whispered that Nvisi kept a lemming brood somewhere in the piles of papers and boxes and clothes strewn about his room, or perhaps somewhere else in the giant Siglig building. It wouldn't surprise Allefaero.

Whatever the case, there was clearly a bond between this strange small bi-eyed man and that tiny rodent which did not seem to be simply a magical creation.

Nvisi put his right hand into the front right pocket of the outer pair of pants he was wearing, then removed it without the other gems. He reached across with his left hand to add the purple stone into his right pocket, but couldn't quite manage it, so instead of simply transferring the stone to his right hand, he called to Doodles for help, and the lemming ran down his sleeve and deposited the stone for him.

All of that without sight, any sight, without eyes, even. Nvisi had once explained the seemingly miraculous efforts of Doodles the blind lemming to Allefaero as a matter of magic detection. He had cast that particular dweomer upon Doodles, so he claimed, over and over again until it became a permanent "sight" for the little lemming. Then Nvisi had bestowed magical auras, lines of varying energies, upon himself and everything in his private quarters.

Apparently it worked, for the lemming showed no signs of its blindness.

"Good, yes, very good, haha," Nvisi said, looking up as Doodles scampered away. "What?" he asked Allefaero.

"What what?"

"You talk like that and they soon will call Allefaero crazy like Nvisi!"

That wouldn't be such a bad thing, the young wizard thought but didn't say. He understood the question then, and replied, "I need a foretelling."

Nvisi's nostrils flared and he straightened nervously.

"It is important," Allefaero told him.

"Always they are, and always they are not what you think they are to be or not to be. The future is a trickster!"

"Please, I beg."

"Not surprised. Uncertain times. Allefaero wants to know. Mona Valrissa wants to know. They ask, always they ask, and they harrumph and shake fists and heads at Nvisi when they cannot understand."

"I know that the explanation of the visions are not your doing, not your fault," Allefaero replied. "You tell what they tell you to tell." As he heard the rolling cadence of his repetitive phrase, Allefaero realized that he might be turning more into Nvisi than he had imagined.

"A foretelling. Not Cattisola," Nvisi said, closing his amber eye. It popped open and his blue eye snapped shut. "Not for Holy Galathae and our visitors."

"For me," said Allefaero. "And for all of us. There is a great war commencing in the Underdark city that gave to us Jarlaxle and Zaknafein and the other udadrow. The war will touch us."

Nvisi gasped and nodded.

"I want to—"

"Stop!"

The young wizard went silent.

"One. One, only one! One vision, hour, image, explanation. I will not look to know too much. Such truths break the mind."

Allefaero understood. Nvisi was often visited by Callidaeans who wanted to know when or how they would die, and those requests had always elicited nothing but horror from the clairvoyant magician. Allefaero had been told that the reason was that Nvisi had seen his own death, and that moment, above all others, had sent him into this strange and unraveled existence.

The Ulutiun looked to his mantel and whistled. A small bell sitting on the right end of the shelf sprouted sticklike arms and legs and tiny eyes. It hopped up on its feet, pulled up the front rim of the bell as if it were the hem of an impeding skirt, then quick-stepped to the other side of the long mantel and gave a little ring of its bell to the hourglass sitting there—which responded accordingly by sprouting a pair of legs underneath and rising up, then a second pair of legs from up top. It gave a great leap—for an hourglass, at least—and executed a perfect flip, landing on its second set of legs and immediately retracting its limbs, becoming in appearance a simple hourglass once more, only now the sand was in the upper half.

"Hour. Yes, one," said Nvisi, and a pair of tiny arms popped out the side of the hourglass and adjusted the small butterfly screw accordingly for the fine sand to begin flowing to measure the requested length of time.

Then it seemed just an hourglass, and the bell flattened and seemed just a bell—except that it was a bell with eyes, staring intently and unblinkingly at the hourglass, ready to sound off when the sand had fully drained.

Allefaero watched it all with delight and found himself hoping that one day the others at the library would think of *him* as a "crazy old windblown shelduck."

"Want?" Nvisi said to Allefaero. "You know not that what you think you want you do not want! Men who know such things . . ." The diviner began shaking his opened and empty hand at the side of his head, rolling his eyes, mimicking one who had gone mad.

"No particulars, then," Allefaero agreed. "If you see my death, or those of a friend, tell me not."

Nvisi huffed and shook his head, as if the wizard wasn't playing fair with such a request. "But *I* see it," he muttered.

Sympathy hit the young wizard hard when he heard those words. Still—he must know. "I wouldn't ask this if it wasn't importa—" Allefaero started, but held up when Nvisi lifted a hand and nodded.

"One. Hour," the diviner said. He closed his eyes and began to whisper to himself, a babbling line that Allefaero couldn't begin to decipher—he knew the words, but their order, or rather, the lack of structure, made it impossible.

Still whispering, sometimes guffawing, the diviner shook his hand with the stones as if they were dice. A long while passed with Nvisi dancing about, singing, chanting, whispering, and often stopping as if he had lost himself in whatever spellcasting he might be attempting. But finally, he tossed the seven gemstones, each a distinct color of the rainbow, into the air before them, where they floated and rolled about, sparkling in different patterns, darting about each other to form different shapes, as if they were dots to be connected. Allefaero found himself wholly outmatched in trying to decipher those shapes, however, for they each lasted but a moment.

With each one, Nvisi gave a grunt and a nod.

"Endless fiends," the diviner remarked. "Abominations!"

Allefaero sucked in his breath, but this was no surprise to him, of course, for he had heard of the expected combatants in Menzoberranzan.

The gemstone dance continued. More mumbling and singing from Nvisi accompanied them.

"The web cannot be broken."

Allefaero didn't like that one, but then remembered that a web began all of this, and it was one that was cast *against* Lolth, and one that had reversed the Curse of Abomination, freeing driders from their torment and making of them udadrow once more. "Which web?" he asked, but Nvisi didn't hear him. The wizard recalled the warnings of ambiguity in Nvisi's prognostications and grit his teeth to force himself to just listen.

"Blood . . . betrayal, so much betrayal. Teetering, teetering, uncertainty. Loyalty against betrayal. Fear against hope. Which is stronger?"

Allefaero chewed his lip.

"A battle of flesh, a battle of truth and heart and . . ."

Nvisi was gasping, and trembling.

The gems began to move all about once more, and Allefaero understood those last remarks to be a question Nvisi was asking of the divination spell.

He looked right at Allefaero and gasped again, eyes popping wide in horror.

The wizard nearly swooned—had Nvisi just seen his death? Or the death of another?

Or worse?

"The overview," he said to Nvisi, though he had no idea if the man, dancing and singing softly in his trance, could even hear him, or was even aware that there was someone else in the room. It went on for a long while, so long that Allefaero glanced at the hourglass repeatedly, watching the sand draining away. He tried to intervene more than once, asking questions. He resisted the urge, for this was truly maddening, to reach out and grasp one of the stones and pluck it away to force Nvisi to give him something, some bit of information, anything.

The sand drained, the tiny bell hopped up and dinged.

"Callidae," the diviner said as the gemstones fell to the floor. "A chin lifted high, droplets falling from it."

With a great heave, Nvisi opened his eyes.

"What does that mean?" Allefaero asked.

"What?"

"'A chin lifted high, droplets falling from it.'"

"Where did Allefaero hear that?"

"You just . . ." he started to answer, but stopped when Nvisi bent low to gather a stone or two and called out, "Doodles!"

"Nvisi?"

"You must go," the diviner said.

"What did you see?"

"I saw war."

"Yes, yes, of course, but what does that mean?"

"It means ugly." Nvisi shuddered and shook his head. "Ugly more than Allefaero knows."

"I've been fighting beneath Cattisola," Allefaero argued. "I've seen death."

"Have you seen . . . have you seen?" Nvisi asked. "Shake and scream, shake and scream, forevermore, shake and scream." He furiously tapped his finger, quite hard, against his forehead. "The wounds in here? Haunting!" He held his hands up before his face, one opened like a claw, the other fisted, holding a couple of the gemstones. "The blood that cannot wash! Brother's blood on the murderer!"

He came forward as he spoke, forcing Allefaero to backpedal.

"My death?" the wizard asked, though he had promised not to. "Did you see my death?"

"Go! Go!" Nvisi shouted at him, bulling forward, chasing him back toward the hallway. The animated doorknob turned the latch, then kicked off with its tiny feet to swing the door open as Nvisi forced him through it.

"Ugly!" he shouted, grasping the door to slam it closed. "A chin lifted high, droplets falling from it!"

Nvisi gasped at his own words, as if shocked by remembering them, or by whatever it was that had incited them initially. He swung the door shut, the doorknob securing it.

Allefaero stood there for a long while, committing every utterance the diviner had made during and after the spell to his memory.

Trying to sort them out.

Fearing that their apparent ambiguity would leave him knowing less than he had before he had come to see his friend, his crazy old windblown shelduck friend.

CHAPTER 8

The Needs and the Wants

Gromph is back in the Hosttower of the Arcane?" Drizzt asked the unexpected guest at the Ivy Mansion in the town of Longsaddle.

Jarlaxle nodded.

"I'm surprised that he came back from the north," Drizzt said.

"He knows," Jarlaxle said.

Drizzt looked to Catti-brie, who had escorted Jarlaxle to the room and was now sitting off to the side, pretending to work on some magical scroll. She wasn't in a good mood, and certainly wasn't missing a word of this conversation.

"Knows?" Drizzt asked, though he was fairly certain that he understood what Jarlaxle was talking about.

"He knows that this is the chance," Jarlaxle explained. "Right now, this one moment, and his house, his sisters, his lover, and his daughter are leading the fight. To break the tyranny is now or never for him, for all of us."

"You think Gromph is coming with us to Menzoberranzan to wage war on the Lolthian drow?"

"He is considering it, surely. Else, he would have stayed in Callidae with the aevendrow beside Zaknafein."

Drizzt's heart dropped at the reminder that his father had not come south with them back to the Sword Coast. Zaknafein had quite obviously fallen in love with Azzudonna, and so he had declared himself a Callidaean, with the blessing of the Temporal Convocation and the mona currently holding the office to oversee the drow city's governing council. Zaknafein had heard clearly Jarlaxle and Drizzt's designs to join the war in Menzoberranzan, and he had rejected them.

Drizzt had dearly hoped to have his father at his side, but alas, it seemed not to be.

"Gromph could have remained up there in the farthest north outside of Lolth's spidery grasp," Jarlaxle said. "He understands, as I do, that the moment will pass, and swiftly. House Baenre is powerful, and they are bolstered by an army of resurrected drow stolen from the cruel judgment of Lolth . . ."

"But you don't think that enough."

Jarlaxle held up his hands and shook his head. "What I know is that the ambitions of the other houses are rooted deeply in the past, and that the power of the matrons of most of those houses sits squarely in their loyalty, and the devotion of their underlings, to the Spider Queen. What are they without her, truly? What hold do they have on the men of Menzoberranzan other than the edict of the Spider Queen that those men, simply by a matter of chance to be born as men, have to accept being lesser? The religion of Lolth determines the order of Menzoberranzan, and those at the top of that order will be loath to surrender it. Gromph sees it, and so he has returned."

"Which, in turn, leaves Callidae without a powerful protector. What might become of Callidae if Lolth wins in Menzoberranzan now?"

"Who knows the way to the aevendrow lands to tell the Lolthian victors if that is the case? You? I? Kimmuriel or Gromph or Dab'nay? We all understand our duty if we fall into the hands of Matron Zhindia Melarn or any of the zealots, and that is to die silently . . ."

He paused as Catti-brie rather loudly shifted her chair on the wooden floor.

"Of course, it won't come to that," Jarlaxle insisted, trying to shift the conversation away from such a grim possibility.

"Bah, but ye're all a lot o' fools," Catti-brie mumbled, and her reversion to her dwarven brogue told Drizzt that he was surely in for a long night.

"Why fools, pray tell?" Jarlaxle asked.

"Cuz ye're thinking in terms o' mortal might. I'm well aware of the division in the city, and that it be favorin' House Baenre at this time," Catti-brie said, turning in her seat and tossing her quill to the desk. "As aware as I am that Jarlaxle can say one thing out of one side of his mouth, and not a minute later, say the opposite out th'other side of his mouth. Might be. But I'm knowin', too, that Baenre's side, yer own side, isn't led by any goddess, or demon queen, or whatever it is we should be calling the witch Lolth. Drow against drow, ye've a chance. So I ask ye:

"Do ye think it'll be *stayin'* that way?"

"I don't know," Jarlaxle admitted.

"Exactly," Catti-brie said. "Fools."

"If King Bruenor were to call in his allies and join us . . ." Jarlaxle started.

"But he won't and ye know he won't!" Catti-brie came back.

"Then he won't," Drizzt interjected strongly. "But we are bound to try to break free of Lolth. This is, was, my home."

"Never was, by yer own words," Catti-brie reminded.

"But it should have been," said Drizzt. "And it *should* be for all the drow there now, particularly the young and all who will come in the years ahead." He shrugged helplessly. He had struggled over this decision for a long while now. Was this really *his* fight? Was it his place to charge back into a city he had so long ago left behind, returning only on a couple of occasions when circumstance had forced his hand, and fleeing the place thereafter as soon as he possibly could?

Now there was a civil war beginning in full, Lolthian zealot against those drow desperate to throw off the shackles of her tyranny—as

Drizzt had done. He couldn't deny that he had been an inspiration for this war, certainly.

But did that make it *his* war, *his* responsibility?

"... Gromph made his choice when he reignited the magic of the Hosttower to power us here in Gauntlgrym," Jarlaxle was arguing to Catti-brie when Drizzt tuned back in to the conversation. "It was a heresy to Lolth, whose handmaidens and representatives had made it clear to him to shut down Gauntlgrym's access to the magic. He disobeyed, and so King Bruenor and his subjects survived. Gromph did that. Lolth doesn't forget or forgive those who disobey."

"So, he'll only be joinin' in the battle because if the Baenres lose, he knows that he's sure to be eternally doomed?" Catti-brie scoffed.

"Well . . ."

"If Gromph had remained in Callidae, outside of any influence in Menzoberranzan, then it is likely that he would have lived out his life in peace, removed from the politics of the City of Spiders and any vengeance Lolth or her priestesses might have thought to mete out," said Drizzt. "The drow of Menzoberranzan have cowered in fear of Lolth for centuries, and that is what got us to this crisis. No more."

"I know one who didn't cower in fear, and who left, expecting fully that his desertion of a city so far down in the Underdark would certainly mean the end of his life," said Jarlaxle. "Yet here he sits."

"Free, and ready to go back," Catti-brie added, staring hard at her husband.

I have to, Drizzt mouthed at her.

She didn't blink.

"What of Bregan D'aerthe?" Drizzt asked the mercenary leader. "You hold Luskan, you rule Luskan, and the people there depend upon your band for stability. Are you all leaving to go to war in Menzoberranzan?"

Jarlaxle didn't seem certain of his answer, but he eventually shook his head. "Bregan D'aerthe's value to the cause will be greater outside the city. King Bruenor will offer supplies—more, I hope, as the battle plays out—but Bregan D'aerthe must operate to bolster that, to find other sources to grant us magical weapons and mundane necessities.

Beniago has proven himself clever and competent. He will continue to lead in Luskan and all about the region, with much of my people working toward that end."

"What does that leave, then? You and Kimmuriel and how many others will go to the city?"

"A handful, at least, perhaps many more than that, not counting those agents I already have within the City of Spiders. And obviously our belief that Gromph will decide to join is proven true. I am expecting reports from Braelin Janquay within a tenday, who is in Menzoberranzan, and I will use that to convince the archmage if he still needs convincing." He looked to Catti-brie as he spoke that, then pointedly added, "Penelope Harpell herself will be in contact with Braelin. It is good that we have so much support among the surface communities."

Catti-brie chuckled, but didn't respond.

"I wish you well in your coming battles," Jarlaxle said to Drizzt, glancing slyly at the angry Catti-brie as he rose to leave. "I am back to Gauntlgrym, and we will be in the tunnels of the upper Underdark this very evening.

"I daresay it might be a safer venue this evening," he said, a smirk on his face.

Drizzt's eyes never left his wife as he replied, "I will be there."

Jarlaxle started for the door, but Catti-brie jumped up from the chair and intercepted him, wrapping him in a hug. "I feel like this is goodbye," she said quietly and soberly, her bombastic Dwarven brogue fading. "Forever goodbye."

Clearly touched by the moment, Jarlaxle seemed at a loss for words.

"It was a great and grand adventure we had up north," Catti-brie said. "And one that will shape the future for me and my daughter, for Zaknafein and for so many others for years to come. I thank you for it."

Pointedly, Drizzt and Jarlaxle both understood, she had left them off her list.

Jarlaxle's expression showed that he was looking for words with which to respond, but Catti-brie stopped him short by adding, "I understand."

The rogue tipped his hat to Drizzt, kissed Catti-brie on the cheek, and rushed out of the room, all jokes abandoned out of respect to his two friends.

Drizzt studied his wife, her back to him as she stared at the open door to the hallway, Jarlaxle fast receding.

He could see the conflict within her, and understood it all so well. She knew what had to be done.

She hated what had to be done.

And dreaded what seemed almost inevitable.

That this inevitability was something different this time.

Something much darker.

"WHO DO I THINK WILL WIN?" GROMPH ECHOED BACK TO the questioner. He shook his head and gave a helpless little laugh. "It is the lair of the Demon Queen of Spiders, her primary playground on the Material Plane. My dear Kimmuriel, who do *you* think will win?"

"I think we have no choice."

"First, that doesn't answer my question . . . although it also does, in your own roundabout way. Second, though, there is *always* a choice."

"Indeed there is. So I put a question to you: Why didn't you stay in Callidae?" the psionicist asked. "I have been in your thoughts, Archmage. We both know this, and as I understand you so very well, I find your question an exercise in confirming and confronting your fears and nothing more."

"My work is here, not Callidae," Gromph countered, but Kimmuriel's grin remained.

"It is more than that. What is happening in Menzoberranzan is of great concern to you."

"You think that an accusation?" Gromph scoffed.

"An observation."

"And one I do not deny. Why would I?"

"Yes, but I know your hopes for our homeland," Kimmuriel said. "You made them clear when you allowed the magic of the Hosttower to flow back through the channels to Gauntlgrym to keep the primordial in its pit. The handmaidens had told you to shut it down, and you did, but in the end . . ."

Gromph's eyes narrowed threateningly, but Kimmuriel was confident enough in his statements to have no fear.

"I know where your heart is, Gromph Baenre, father of Yvonnel."

"I don't even know the child."

"Hardly a child, but yes, perhaps you do not know her. But you hope to. And even without her, you prevented Zhindia Melarn from conquering King Bruenor's people."

"By undoing that which I had done in sealing off the Hosttower's magic to Gauntlgrym in the first place. By becoming truly neutral in the conflict."

"And yet you had to understand what your neutrality meant. Do you deny your hopes regarding which side proves victorious in Menzoberranzan?"

"The heart and the mind are often in conflict," Gromph said. "I have perhaps another two centuries of life—more if my studies prove fruitful. I wish to live those centuries and more. And when I am finally done with this existence, I know that Lolth will remain very much entrenched in the afterlife."

"Then escape her."

"How? By feigning worship of some other foolish god?"

"You know your god, as do I, and they are the same."

Gromph was sitting, but that statement set him back on his heels.

"So, that's your plan," the former archmage of Menzoberranzan said after digesting it. "When Kimmuriel is no more with this physical realm, he will blend into the hive mind."

"The multiverse is a matter of divine numbers," Kimmuriel said. "The particulars of the tyrant gods are merely noise—temporary noise in the ultimate eternity of it all. We are manifestations of pure and singular thought, grains of sand on an endless beach or drops of water in the endless ocean that splashes onto that beach. The hive mind is a conduit into that pure and singular thought. It is my destiny to directly merge, to become less speck and less droplet, and more a viewer of it all. You felt the power when we channeled it from the hive mind to obliterate Demogorgon those years ago. You felt it, the ecstasy."

Gromph didn't blink.

"Do you deny that?"

"That is your escape from Lolth?" he asked.

"In the end, yes, from her and from all the pretend gods," said Kimmuriel. "It is the same escape you seek here, hiding in a magical tower dedicated to learning and testing your limits and your whims. Only of a magnitude greater than any number I might now assign."

"You sound like Drizzt and his talk of transcendence."

"In the end, there is one Truth," Kimmuriel asserted. "Whether through fear or hope or perhaps even through some divine inspiration, we all seek that one Truth. Perhaps the monks have found their path to this same place but with a different name. We live in a world with a multitude of beliefs and religions and assertions of what will come next—what reasoning being wouldn't ponder such things? Perhaps the paths to Truth are many and winding. Who are we to know?"

"Perhaps Lolth is the way."

"That I reject," said Kimmuriel. "Lolth and those godbeings like her demand actions contrary to nature, to conscience, to any reasoning and decency of what might be an eternal soul. The one Truth is harmony, not chaos."

"Even if we now must partake of great chaos and destruction to find it," Gromph said and tried to hold his scowl.

But Kimmuriel's grin told Gromph that his sour expression was failing badly.

"That is your escape in the end," Kimmuriel offered, promised.

"YOU ARE ANGRY WITH ME FOR MY CHOICE TO GO?" DRIZZT asked when he and Catti-brie were alone.

The woman, tears running down her cheeks, closed the door and turned to face him. "I am angry," she said, "but not at you. I am terrified for you, sad at what I expect, and jealous of you."

Drizzt started to get up, but Catti-brie's look showed him that she didn't want a hug from him at that moment.

"Jealous?" he probed.

"Of course you have to go. This is your destiny. This is the circle you trod when first you left Menzoberranzan."

Drizzt could only nod, saddened, but truly appreciative that Catti-brie understood.

"And here I stand torn," Catti-brie explained. "Because when I chose to leave Iruladoon, to return to this life and your side after the century of turmoil for you, and of peace for me, I expected that this path would be *our* path, not yours alone."

"But for our child," Drizzt whispered.

"But for Brie," Catti-brie confirmed, and gave a crooked, broken smile, her deep blue eyes glistening with moisture.

"You understand that I walk my path more willingly because of her and because of you?" Drizzt asked. "Surely, I would prefer Catti-brie at my side, both for her support and because of her, of your, strength. You are an ally of spirit and one of formidable magic, even measured against the powers of Menzoberranzan."

"And against the powers of the Abyss that will no doubt bolster your drow enemies in Menzoberranzan?"

"A balor would quake at the sight of Catti-brie's bared power," Drizzt said heartily, and now he did stand and move toward his wife, who couldn't help but give a little laugh.

"Don't die," she whispered in his ear when he wrapped her in a hug.

"If I don't, it is because I am unafraid," he replied after a pause. "Because I know that my legacy, my little Breezy, has Catti-brie guiding her."

He felt Catti-brie's arms tighten around him. He feared, and understood it to be mutual, that this might be their last hug.

CHAPTER 9

Into Darkness

Avernil entered the small chapel in Scellobel as quietly as he could manage, not wanting to interrupt the prayers of the paladin kneeling before the statue of their goddess Eilistraee. The priest spent a moment considering the paladin, her pressed white clothing and the perfect trim of her short blue-gray hair reflecting the discipline that had so ordered her life. He took a seat on the backmost bench and began a prayer of his own, seeking guidance, as was Galathae in this confusing time.

"We knew it would come to this eventually," came the paladin's voice a short while later, stirring Avernil from his contemplations.

He glanced at the woman. Holy Galathae, she was called throughout the city of Callidae, and the moniker was quite apt. She was a hero to the aevendrow many times over and had recently led the raid that had returned to the city many they had thought lost to the slaadi and the frost giants that inhabited the far end of their glacier home.

"For our descendants, I presumed," Avernil replied. "Certainly, I did not expect the udadrow to arrive in Callidae, and most certainly, not the group we encountered, good of nature and enemies of the demons."

"When Doum'wielle Armgo came to us, the die was cast," Galathae replied.

"Even then, she was a cast-off from this city of the Underdark, so near to the Faerzress. She will not return to the south and certainly not ever to that City of Spiders, I expect."

"She'll not, no," Galathae confirmed. "Nor should she. Doum'wielle Armgo has suffered enough because of this place called Menzoberranzan."

"Would you say the same of Zaknafein?"

The paladin shrugged. "Azzudonna tells me that she often finds him staring off into nothingness, his thoughts far away."

Avernil nodded. It made sense.

"What does your communion tell you?" Avernil asked.

"We are reasoning beings of free will. The goddess would not command us to go, nor deny us the journey if that is our choice."

"Do you believe that Mona Valrissa will be as accommodating?"

Galathae chuckled at that. "She has more practical considerations than Eilistraee might hold."

"You think the mona would deny you?"

"It is not her choice alone," Galathae reminded.

"Then, the Temporal Convocation. Do you think they will deny you?" he pressed.

"Were it just me, then no, they would not. But it will not be only Galathae petitioning to leave Callidae, will it?"

"I would opine that you and I are the most hesitant of the congregation. Some are elated at the possibilities here, thinking the war in the Underdark the very moment of truth for them, the very event for which they were called to service in this temple."

"Mona Valrissa will not be pleased at that. Nearly a hundred aevendrow leaving Callidae to fight in a war that is not Callidae's concern."

"Is it not?" asked the priest.

"In the eyes of Eilistraee, it is the concern of all drow, and all duty to those who know the truth of Lolth. But we are a small church in a single borough. Seventy-three aevendrow in a city of more than forty thousand. And those seventy-three might well endanger the city itself."

"Doubtful."

"But not impossible," said Galathae. "And even the remotest chance of such disaster has ever been taken seriously by the Temporal Convocation, with the weight of it falling squarely on the shoulders of Mona Valrissa Zhamboule. She has already taken a chance in allowing Jarlaxle, Artemis Entreri, Catti-brie, Drizzt Do'Urden, Kimmuriel, Gromph, and the priestess Dab'nay—a priestess of Lolth in practice if not in heart—to leave the city with their memories intact."

"And the most unusual dwarf," Avernil added, and the mere thought of Pikel had him smiling, and Galathae, as well.

"It has been a most unusual year," the paladin replied with a head shake.

"*Perte miye,* Zaknafein," Avernil recited. "These heroes from the south drove Ygorl from the slaadi fortress and dealt a great blow to our enemies. Jarlaxle's cleverness showed us the source of the loss of Catti-sola borough, and likely saved the rest of Callidae as we drive back the remorhaz hordes which the slaadi and their giant allies have unleashed upon our home."

Galathae's troubled expression brightened almost immediately. "Unusual is not always a bad thing," she admitted.

"The Dark Maiden Eilistraee grants us our choices. They will be guided by the heart, with open eyes to the dangers before us. Is that not a good thing?"

"That is *everything,*" Galathae agreed. "The very reason that Eilistraee's words so called to me."

"I had thought it was because of the Dark Maiden's reverence for the world of sunlight. Did you not once call her a sister goddess to Mielikki? Or was that simply to engender yourself to the priestess Catti-brie?"

"A sister in ethics and cause. I stand by that comparison. Did Mielikki not return Catti-brie to this life for her to do battle with the avatar of Lolth?"

"True enough, but what of this cause? The choice is yours, is mine, is for each of our congregation to make on their own. But you know that Galathae's choice will sway many."

"It is not a responsibility I desire," Galathae replied. "For myself, I know the course, and it is one that pleases Eilistraee."

"An easy decision?" Avernil asked, surprised.

"No decision such as this is truly easy. But as much as I love Callidae, as much as I would remain here and enjoy the life we have built, yes, I see no other choice."

"If Mona Valrissa allows it."

"She'll not stop me."

"Yes, but will she allow you to leave with your memories of Callidae intact? Would you sacrifice even that, the very definition of your life, if that was the first cost, and with the last being, quite likely, the end of your life?"

Without hesitation and with no sign of the slightest doubt, Holy Galathae replied, "Yes."

"IT IS FOOLHARDY," THE SMALL MAN NAMED VESSI SAID TO Azzudonna as the two shared a drink in Ibilsitato, the main tavern in the Callidaean borough of Scellobel. "This is a decision driven by pride and guilt, not by any rational thought."

"It is not my decision."

"And I wasn't speaking of you. Of course Zaknafein will decide to go. You must have known that from the start. His son is walking into mortal danger, as is the man who has been his friend since long before either of us were born."

"He hasn't yet decided," Azzudonna argued.

"When he learns that Galathae is determined to go, and will almost certainly be allowed to do so, do you think he will remain behind?"

Azzudonna didn't verbally answer, but she realized that her sour expression would be enough. Vessi knew her as well as anyone alive. He could see right through any facade she tried to paint on her face. Vessi might well be the only person in the world from whom Azzudonna couldn't hide.

"Do you really believe that Mona Valrissa will allow it?" she asked.

"Who can stop Galathae? She takes her orders from a goddess, not the representatives of the Temporal Convocation."

"And just as many expected that one would bring trouble when Galathae pledged to her those many years ago," said another woman walking up to the table, "so she has."

Azzudonna grinned at the approach of their friend Ayeeda, who helped run Ibilsitato.

Ayeeda tossed her bar rag over the back of a chair and pulled up a seat. She didn't return Azzudonna's smile, and the woman understood her hesitance, given the subject.

Galathae, too, had once been of their band, a group of five young aevendrow preparing and practicing together endlessly in an effort to earn a place on Biancorso, the Scellobel Whitebears. But that was before Galathae had become "Holy Galathae," before the word of Eilistraee had come to her ears and into her heart. They were still friends, these four, but with Galathae far removed now.

Azzudonna and Vessi had achieved their common goal of joining Biancorso. An injury had slowed Ayeeda's progress to the point where she had simply stepped aside in the trials, while Ilina, the fifth of the companions, had also found a church and now served as a high priestess to Auril the Frostmaiden.

"Galathae turned her heart outward from Callidae," Vessi said.

Azzudonna put her hand on the man's forearm. He and Galathae had been paired in those early days and had even spoken of having children together. But they had drifted apart as Galathae had become more earnest in listening to the call of the Dark Maiden.

"Galathae's allegiance to Callidae cannot be questioned," Ayeeda insisted. "Many times has she shielded this city at her own mortal peril. Without hesitation . . ."

Azzudonna's subtle head shake stopped Ayeeda, reminding her that Vessi was talking about more than Galathae's feelings for the city.

Vessi clearly caught the signal, too, though, and he just laughed. "I will forever care for Galathae," he said with a sincere smile.

"As will we all," Ayeeda agreed. "And I think her goddess a fine being with a goodly purpose. How can we not cheer one who would rescue udadrow from the Underdark? But Eilistraee is not for Callidae—not solely, at least."

"I remain surprised that the Temporal Convocation ever sanctioned that particular church," Vessi admitted. "For all that we agree in the goodness of Eilistraee, her demands are often counter to that which remains our most important duty."

"But her demands were not ever expected as anything tangible," Azzudonna argued. "Not until now."

"And here we are," Vessi said with a great sigh.

"Yes, here we are. Is there not a part within either of you that looks at the possible adventure?" Ayeeda said, surprising Azzudonna.

"You just said that Eilistraee was not for Callidae," Vessi argued, obviously also surprised.

"Forget Eilistraee. I don't know her teachings, nor do I care at this time. I'm talking about the promise of being a part of something grand and great. Jarlaxle and his friends are off on a noble adventure!"

"One that will get them all killed," said Vessi.

Ayeeda shrugged as if that wasn't of much concern. "When you traveled to the frost giant fortress and did battle with the slaadi, even the slaadi godbeing, was that any less dangerous?" she asked Azzudonna. "Yet you went—twice!—and look at the adventure those journeys brought to you. The adventure and the love, even. We practice, we train, we do battle occasionally, and we put every essence of our hearts into the pretend war that is cazzcalci. Now a true war stares at us from afar, beckoning, and we close the curtains and act as if it is not out there."

The speech startled Azzudonna and left her and Vessi unable to respond for some time, until Azzudonna finally quipped, "Are you sure that you haven't joined Avernil's flock?"

"Maybe I am tired of wiping tables and filling mugs and watching you two have all the excitement of battling in cazzcalci," Ayeeda replied.

"There is an ongoing battle in Cattisola right now," Vessi reminded.

"It is one for wizards and priests," Ayeeda replied. "Warriors do not fare so well against the burning bellies of the remorhaz. They'll not even allow us to descend the ropes into the crystal caverns."

"So you wish to go across the world and do battle in the darkness of the Underdark?"

Ayeeda shrugged noncommittally. "I cannot deny the allure of such an adventure, not when I would know that I am fighting for the cause of justice, and to help our kin, who do not deserve their fate at the hands of the demon dictator. It is a passing urge, I expect."

Azzudonna looked to Vessi, who shrugged, not disagreeing.

Nor could she, Azzudonna had to admit to herself. She would continue to argue with Zaknafein to keep him in Callidae by her side.

But if he went . . .

CAMIOUS VERIDAL WAS THE OLDEST MEMBER OF THE TEMporal Convocation and had served in this legislature off and on for more than three centuries. His home was located in the borough of Mona Chess, which housed the Siglig, the chamber of Callidae's governing body.

He was also of the same generation as the priest Avernil of the temple of Eilistraee, both old men who had spent centuries in Callidae.

Galathae was surprised when Mona Valrissa Zhamboule had announced Camious as the Answerer of the Inquiry this day, but, judging from the way Avernil hung his head after the announcement, she guessed that the priest had expected it, or feared it, at least.

Avernil and Camious had known each other and had butted heads fiercely in the distant past.

Galathae caught Avernil's attention to lock stares, the priest slowly shaking his head.

Galathae tried to deny his dourness, but she understood that having Camious serve as the lead inquisitor was not a good beginning to their requested petition.

Camious walked down from his seat in the semicircular gallery—a far walk, since Mona Chess, as the hosting borough, always seated their representatives farthest from the podium and the witness floor.

He took his time, mumbling to himself and occasionally looking to scrutinize the petitioners, his gaze mostly falling over Avernil, his old friend, his old adversary.

When he got down to the floor, Mona Valrissa introduced him again, then took her seat. Camious paced back and forth before the ten guests of the Temporal Convocation this day, all but ignoring Galathae, mostly eyeing Avernil, and then studying the other eight clerics of the church of Eilistraee who had come with the high priest.

"On the issue regarding the petition to depart Callidae in support of the udadrow," he began slowly.

Galathae regarded Avernil, who offered a stern gaze and another head shake, begging her not to intervene.

"I object," she said anyway.

Camious was not caught by surprise, clearly, and he paused and turned his hawklike gaze over the paladin.

"Petitions, not petition," Galathae corrected. "There are two, not one, before the Temporal Convocation this day."

"They are the same request," Camious replied.

"But not the same petitioner. If two came here asking for a leave from their work, would they be answered as one?"

"Are you not a member of Avernil's church?"

"I am indeed, proudly so, but my petition is not his, nor one for, of, or included with his church. Mine would be before you—indeed, was before you—prior to High Priest Avernil's request. They are separate issues, I insist, and one should not influence the other." She could feel Avernil's gaze boring into her, and truly, she hadn't wanted to harm the man or the chances for his request. But neither would she risk her own journey for the sake of the church.

"You undertake this mission for your goddess, our goddess," Avernil interjected, drawing a fierce scowl from Camious.

"I do, and from that which is in my own heart," Galathae answered him, even as the inquisitor began to instruct her not to respond to one who was not asked to speak. "This is my charge, I believe," she continued, now addressing the whole of the convocation. "The calling of Galathae by Eilistraee was for this moment, for these unexpected friends I came to know and to care for. For the inspiration of Drizzt Do'Urden and for Zaknafein and Jarlaxle. Are we to doubt the graces our gods offered to them after the miracle we witnessed at cazzcalci?

"And that is why I must go to them now and help them with their fight. And that is why you must grant me this, for all of us. For if you do not, I doubt that I, or many of you, will sleep without the choice haunting your thoughts hereafter."

"You speak well, Holy Galathae," Camious admitted, and his tone was indeed softer, and he was nodding, as if silently assuring her that her petition would be handled separately, as she had asked.

Camious started to say something more, but again, Avernil interrupted.

"As it is her calling, can ours be any less urgent and compelling?" the high priest insisted.

Galathae thought that Camious seemed perturbed, but only for a moment, the man clearing his throat and turning to view the priest directly.

"My old friend, my old rival," Avernil began. "You, all of you here, should take Holy Galathae at her word. She has earned every bit of your, of our, trust so many times over. Her calling is sincere, and her goddess, my goddess, is thrilled at the possibilities that have come to our kin, the udadrow. It was not mere chance that brought the visitors from the south to our city. Nay, they came to find us, I have no doubt."

"Jarlaxle said that they came to find Doum'wielle Armgo," Camious corrected. "And I can assure you that Doum'wielle, who, like Zaknafein, has been granted permission to change her mind and leave Callidae to join in this war in the Underdark, wants no part of it. They came to find her, and they found her, and even she rejects their adventure."

"She is not of Menzoberranzan," Galathae felt the need to say, though she realized that her own case would have been stronger if she just left it where it had ended earlier. "She is more elf than udadrow, and was raised among the elves of the surface. And these visitors came to us accidentally in search of her, yes, but because Jarlaxle believed that Doum'wielle could be of great service to his cause at this critical moment in the city of Menzoberranzan."

"And she will not serve, and if she will not, then why should—" Camious began.

"She is not of Eilistraee!" Avernil insisted. "And she is only half udadrow, and only under the corruption of the sword you would not allow to remain here in Callidae did she seek out that part of her heritage, to devastating consequence. Her choice is not to go, but that has little bearing on that which Galathae, and I and my clergy and believers at the temple of the Dark Maiden, are compelled to do. By our goddess, by the beliefs that we hold dearly in our hearts."

"More dearly than your love of Callidae?" Camious asked bluntly.

Avernil started to answer, but stopped short, realizing the trap, as Galathae, too, saw it. If Avernil offered an affirmative answer, they both knew, it would end his petition on the spot, for if he and his fellows loved something more than Callidae, they would not be allowed to leave for fear that Callidae would subsequently be betrayed. And if he answered no, then why was he so insistent on going?

There was no correct answer to that leading question.

"Yes, an impossible choice," said Camious. "And thus, you see the difficulty for us here at Temporal Convocation."

He looked from Avernil back to Galathae, then to Mona Valrissa. "The petitions," he said, notably using the plural, "should be considered separately, I advise."

He then bowed to Galathae, to Avernil and the other priests, then to Mona Valrissa and the assembly, and slowly walked back toward his distant seat, high in the back row of the gallery.

Before he had even neared that seat, the petitioners were escorted from the room and placed in an antechamber to await the decisions.

They lived in a glacier, but Callidae was not a cold place. That particular room, however, held a palpable chill, and neither Avernil nor any of the others even glanced Galathae's way.

She understood and accepted it. She had hurt their chances greatly. Had she stood with them, a petition for all or none, the Temporal Convocation would have faced a much more difficult decision, both because allowing one to leave was far easier than the departure of several score, and because she was Holy Galathae, a hero of the city many times over, and if anyone in Callidae had earned this dispensation, it was surely her.

So be it, she decided, and she didn't try to explain herself to Avernil and the others.

She had done what she believed she had to do.

So be it.

"I'LL NOT EVER LEAVE THIS PLACE," DOUM'WIELLE TOLD Zaknafein and Azzudonna. She had gone to their house to see them, surprising both. "But I have heard that you are leaving."

"I am," Zak confirmed.

"And you are surprised to see me?"

"I am," Zak repeated.

"I wanted to say thank you one last time. You saved me from a fate likely worse than death itself."

"We all did. Of course we did, for you and the others, and the vision of Callidae, which is so different from the land we once called home."

"Well, I wanted to say goodbye, and thank you." She chewed her lip, and Zak recognized that there was clearly something more that had brought her here. He didn't ask, didn't say anything, just stood meeting her gaze.

"May I see it one last time?" she asked finally.

He knew what she meant. "Why?"

"I want to prove to myself that I have overcome that infernal blade, and fully so," Doum'wielle explained. "I would take Khazid'hea in hand and dominate it, and tell it that it will never again shape my course—"

"The sword is gone," Zak interrupted, and Doum'wielle fell back as if slapped.

"Gone? I was told you were wielding it now. You had it when we left the cavern of the slaadi."

"Jarlaxle intended it for me, but there was no place for such a weapon here in Callidae," Zak replied. "It is gone, south with Jarlaxle. Khazid'hea has gone to war, which no doubt pleases the insatiable blade immensely."

Doum'wielle fumbled about for a response, and finally just nodded with a bit of acceptance and resignation.

"You would have denied the blade," Azzudonna said from a seat at the side of the small room. "Such a weapon as that would have no hold over Little Doe of Callidae!"

That brought a smile to Doum'wielle.

"When you go, will you be fighting against my family? Against House Barrison Del'Armgo?"

"I know not," said Zak. "The lines are being drawn, surely, but where they will be cut, I can't be sure. What I do know is that I will be fighting against Lolth, and against those who would impose her will upon the people of Menzoberranzan who deny her. The battle is to free the city of the Spider Queen, and if the Armgos—"

"I do not care," Doum'wielle interjected. "They are my family in name alone—I should not have even called them that. My home is here, my family is here."

"And that is a good thing," said Zak.

"Perhaps there will be a day when you can return to Menzoberranzan in peace, to visit and to see the changes that have been brought about through this war," Azzudonna added.

But Doum'wielle was shaking her head through the whole of that sentiment. "I have no desire. Never. Not to Menzoberranzan, nor back to the Moonwood where I was raised. I am Doum'wielle of Callidae, and I am content. I am free of the sword and I am free of my past. I cannot change what I have done, and I'll not forget it. But I accept it now, and I look in the mirror with no shadows hovering about my shoulders, with no stains showing in my eyes."

Azzudonna rose and came across the room to wrap Little Doe in a great hug. "And here you are loved," she whispered into Doum'wielle's ear.

"I wish you had the sword," she admitted to Zak when Azzudonna stepped back. "I am not curious as to what would happen when I held it once more, because I know what would happen."

"You just wanted Khazid'hea to know it," Zak remarked, and Doum'wielle smiled all the wider.

"I wish you well on your travels," said Doum'wielle. "Although this is not, and cannot be, my war, I know which side should win. Lady Lolth be damned."

"Lady Lolth be damned indeed," Zak agreed.

Doum'wielle bowed to the two and left without another word.

Zak watched her move down the lane for some time before he closed the door. He was pleased for Doum'wielle, and believed that the demons within the young woman had indeed been fully excised. He turned with that thought brightening his expression, but found a wall of scowl coming back at him from Azzudonna.

"You decided, then," she said.

Zak swallowed hard, realizing that he hadn't even told her, hadn't told anyone, that he had finalized his decision to go to war before blurting it out to Doum'wielle.

He hadn't even admitted it to himself.

"He's my son."

"I know."

"And Jarlaxle has been my friend for most of my life. You cannot understand how trapped I was in the house of Matron Malice Do'Urden. I was her toy and her assassin. My every move—"

"I know," Azzudonna said and rushed over to hug her lover. "I know, and know that you must go and answer this call, for if you do not, it will haunt you forevermore. And I will go with you."

Zak pushed her back to arm's length, staring at her hard.

"Would you let me wander off to a war while you sat here in

peace?" she asked before he could object. "If you are going, then I will be by your side, and when it is time to put our weapons to work, you will be glad to have me there."

"I do not doubt that last part."

"Do you think you can stop me from going?"

Zak gave a helpless laugh and pulled Azzudonna back in for a great hug. "I can't, I know, but I would if I could. What will be left of Zaknafein if you come with me and are killed?"

"That is the price of war," she whispered back. "What would be left of Azzudonna if I let you go without me and you were slain?"

"Mona Valrissa has already told me that I will be allowed to leave the city. What of you?"

"I will petition this very day," Azzudonna replied. "The Temporal Convocation is assembled and hearing the petitions of Galathae and the church of Eilistraee right now."

"We should hurry."

"Not 'we,'" Azzudonna corrected. "You being there will hurt my petition. They will think I am coerced."

Zak started to respond, but Azzudonna put her finger over his lips. When he settled, she replaced the finger with her own lips, a long and lingering and promising kiss, then she rushed by him and out the door, fast on her way to the borough of Mona Chess and the assembly.

GALATHAE AND THE PRIESTS OF EILISTRAEE WERE CALLED back into the Siglig after more than two hours, during which the priests whispered and grumbled, sometimes prayed, and Galathae remained perfectly silent in her meditation and prayers. She let the priests lead the way back into the hall to take their seats before the gallery, all of them looking to the sitting representatives, trying to get a feel for what judgment might be coming.

All except for Galathae. She kept her gaze to the floor, her thoughts inward as she moved to and took her place on the left of the line of chairs. She told herself repeatedly that they could not deny her request. She had earned their deference here, and trusted that they would properly accede.

For all of her logic and surety, though, there remained a bit of nervousness, which became a gasp when Mona Valrissa settled the gathering, looked to the petitioners, and said simply, "Your petition is denied."

Galathae was almost yelling out in protest as she looked up—only to realize that Mona Valrissa was addressing Avernil directly.

"Our petition is a call from our goddess!" Avernil protested. "By what power does this body deny—"

"This body holds responsibility for the city of fifty thousand souls," Mona Valrissa quietly replied. "Ours is not a decision made lightly. The idea of scores of aevendrow marching to war in Menzoberranzan is unacceptable."

"The whole city should be marching!" one of the other priests yelled.

"Would you trust outsiders more than your own people?" another yelled.

Galathae sucked in her breath. That was the wrong thing to say, she knew. From both the obstinate priests. Any hope Avernil might have entertained of changing the verdict was flown, certainly.

As if to prove her true, behind Mona Valrissa, the representatives began grousing and pointing fingers, more than one calling for rebuke.

For her part, Mona Valrissa stood straight and solemn. She didn't blink, her expression didn't fluctuate at all, her stare boring into Avernil, who seemed to shrink under the weight of it.

"Do you think you are the only ones who wish to go?" she said at long last, after her immovability had silenced the outburst from petitioners and representatives alike. "Do you think that I would not wish to go and mete out justice to this demon queen who has held our kin, my kin, in her thrall for these centuries?"

"Our god . . ." Avernil began meekly.

"Is one of many in Callidae, sanctioned by this body to you many years ago. I know of the Dark Maiden and understand her call to you now—it is a call that was discussed when first you created this church in Callidae, and a call about which you were then warned. And in that warning, it was noted that we in the Temporal Convocation are not here to service the wishes of Eilistraee or any other godly being. We serve Callidae and Callidae alone, the common good, the general welfare of all who reside here. That service requires us to now say no to your petition. However deep your devotion, however determined your priorities, in this place, the city is above your church and above any of the gods worshipped here. And the city demands that you cannot go to this far-off place to do battle. The risks are too great, and the chances that your arrival in Menzoberranzan will change the outcome of their war are too small.

"Your petition *is* denied."

"The ritual!" one priest called. "Do not hold me here! Take my memories, as you would do to any visitor who came to us and decided to leave."

"Not to *any* visitor," another of the priests snidely added.

She ignored the latter remark, and simply said to the former, "It cannot be done to one whose memories of Callidae are all that gives identity. Your petition is denied."

Galathae admired Mona Valrissa's control in not lashing out at the priest who had so rudely questioned the decision to allow Jarlaxle and the others to depart with their memories intact.

"For you, Holy Galathae," Mona Valrissa began, and the paladin held her breath in anticipation. "We would prefer that you remain here with us, serving Callidae, as you have done for all these years."

The priests sitting to Galathae's right began to grumble, thinking that she, too, was being denied, but Galathae held her composure and let Mona Valrissa have her say.

"Our trials here have only just begun. The powers our visitors brought to bear on the slaadi and the giants have set them far back, we believe, at least for now, but the crystal caverns beneath our city teem with the threat of the remorhaz."

Galathae nodded. She was among the first to do battle down there, and had nearly lost her life to the power of the great polar worms.

"We are saddened, Holy Galathae, by your desire to leave," Valrissa said. "The whole of Callidae will mourn your departure. I implore you to change your course."

Galathae didn't answer—she knew that Mona Valrissa wasn't really expecting an answer.

"With that said, you have earned our trust in this," Valrissa said, and Galathae breathed with relief, though she knew it was coming. To hear the words, though . . .

"We'll not dull your memories of Callidae, but if you go, you go under Geas Diviet."

"Willingly," Galathae said.

"I doubt the ritual is needed for Holy Galathae."

"I doubt it, as well. Truly and humbly. But still, I would not go at all without the Geas Diviet upon me. Should I begin to betray Callidae in any way, under torture, then know I betray all that I am, and so let the geas take me from this world before the betrayal can be uttered."

"Could you not do the same to us, then?" Avernil asked. "We, too, would accept—"

"No." Valrissa cut him short. "Too many. Far too many. For one Callidaean to join the battle in Menzoberranzan, there is little risk. For your numbers? Unacceptable. It will not be. That is our decision. Your petition is denied, High Priest Avernil. Yours, Holy Galathae, is granted under the Ritual of Diviet."

Some of the priests began to object once again, but Avernil finally hushed them.

"You could have helped my cause," he whispered to Galathae.

"It would have defeated my own, and to no change in your outcome," she replied. He silently groused at this, but didn't refute her words.

"The Temporal Convocation has other business this day," Mona Valrissa announced and motioned to the guardians of the hall, who moved immediately to escort Galathae and the others out of the Siglig.

As she was leaving, Galathae saw Azzudonna coming fast the other way, up the white stairs and into the building.

She could figure out easily enough what had brought her friend to this place this day.

She also could guess the outcome, and it was not one Azzudonna would like.

"YOU ARE PLEDGED TO BIANCORSO," MONA VALRISSA SAID to Azzudonna, who sat alone on the floor before the legislative gallery some two hours later. "Heart and soul, until your body fails or your life ends. Have you forgotten?"

"Of course not, Mona Valrissa," the woman answered.

"But you'll not honor your sacred oath?"

"So much has happened. I have been to the south. I have been to the lair of the slaadi and faced the Lord Ygorl. I have—"

"You have fallen in love," Valrissa interrupted. "And it is a beautiful thing. But do you place this lover above your pledge to Biancorso and the borough of Scellobel?

"To Callidae?"

"I . . . I . . ."

"Zaknafein has been given permission to depart, though none here desires that," Valrissa said. "And yes, these last months have been surprising for us all. And enlightening. But no, Azzudonna of Scellobel, your petition is denied. You have taken a sacred oath to Biancorso, one not so easily rescinded."

"Yes, Mona," the devastated woman replied, her gaze to the floor.

"Convince Zaknafein to stay," Mona Valrissa offered.

Azzudonna did look up to meet her gaze.

She didn't respond.

She didn't need to.

CHAPTER 10

The Quality of Mercy

Jarlaxle moved his hand out toward Entreri, holding the unremarkable-looking but entirely remarkable mask.

"The choice is yours," the mercenary leader said to his long-time companion.

Entreri stared at the item long and hard, considering the many days he had worn that mask. He had used it to impersonate Regis, to no good end. He considered, too, the days he had spent in the City of Spiders, which was the whole point of the offer now. A big part of him wanted to never return to that wretched place, but another savored the thought of paying back so many of his tormentors and the sheer joy he would feel in watching the entire societal structure of the udadrow culture burn down.

He was torn, but there was something else mitigating his decision, something he had heard whispered in Jarlaxle's Luskan tavern, One-Eyed Jax. He held quiet on that, though.

"We're leaving in an hour," Jarlaxle said.

"Bruenor said the trails were secure for the first two days?" he said, bringing up a different concern.

"As far as we can tell, yes. Bruenor has forward scouts pressing ever downward. There is no sign of any drow in the upper tunnels anywhere near to Gauntlgrym, nor would I expect any, given the recent reports that the fighting in the city has become open and commonplace. Their eyes are on each other, not on us."

"The Lolthians will be watching the tunnels for signs of the dwarfs coming to reinforce the Baenres," Entreri pointed out.

"I don't fear a scout or ten," Jarlaxle replied, and he glanced at the man standing across the small room, who had a way of detecting spies before they could detect him.

Entreri regarded Kimmuriel for just a moment, then turned his attention back to the magical mask, a person and an item he hated as much as appreciated. "Leave it with Gromph," he said.

"And?"

"And if I find the opportunity to follow, I will find you. And if not, I wish you well."

Jarlaxle stepped back from the man and scrutinized him up and down. "What do you know?"

"Perhaps some things that you know, and that you do not know that I know," Entreri answered rather curtly.

"My friend, what troubles you?"

"I have some business to attend. Nothing more. Does it shock you to think that my entire life does not circle Jarlaxle like a fly buzzing a road-apple?"

"Artemis?" Jarlaxle asked quite seriously, almost pleadingly. The mercenary leader was truly off his balance here, Entreri saw, and although he was perturbed with the man, he didn't want to push it too far.

"We have had a grand adventure in the north," Entreri said. "I am weary."

"But it was worth the trip, yes?"

"Maybe, but it was one begun under false premises."

"Ah, you harbor ill will for me . . ."

"No. I simply have other business to attend. We've been gone for months."

"And how long will this other business of yours take?"

"If I knew that, I'd give you my answer now regarding your new adventure."

"It is much more than an adventure this time," said Kimmuriel, walking over.

"It is," Entreri agreed. "And I hold no illusions this time that those who go forth to Menzoberranzan will all return. Not this time."

"And it is not your fight," Kimmuriel said evenly, with no judgment in his tone.

"No, it isn't my fight. But yes," Entreri added, aiming it at Jarlaxle, "you are my friend and we have been through much together. I would wish to be by your side in this most important play of your life."

"But you have business."

"I believe I do."

"I could help . . ."

"No." There was no debate in his voice.

Jarlaxle bit off his words and stood staring at the man.

"Give the mask to Gromph," Entreri instructed again. "If I am able, I will catch up to you."

"And if not, then this is farewell, and perhaps forever," said Jarlaxle.

Entreri wasn't happy about that reality, but it was hung out there as an undeniable possibility. He held out his hand and Jarlaxle clasped it tightly.

"First Zaknafein and now you," Jarlaxle said. "And here I thought I inspired loyalty." Jarlaxle couldn't hold a straight face as he quipped, and Entreri joined him in a laugh—and one that both hoped would not be their last to share.

"What do you know?" Jarlaxle asked Kimmuriel after Entreri had left them.

"I know that the road awaits and I am anxious to be on our way."

"Need I clarify?"

"I was not in Artemis Entreri's thoughts during your conversation."

Jarlaxle held up his hands and wore a perfectly disappointed look. "Is that not why I keep you by my side?"

"One does not 'keep' Kimmuriel anything. Besides, I thought he was your friend."

"When has that ever stopped Kimmuriel from mind reading?"

"Of late," the humorless Kimmuriel replied, and Jarlaxle became even more off-balance. "Do you not wear your eye patch to prevent my intrusions into your thoughts? Why would others not feel the same?"

"That is different."

"Why?"

"Because I am . . . Jarlaxle."

"Our road awaits," Kimmuriel said and walked away.

Jarlaxle turned to the door through which Entreri had exited, fearing that he would never again see the man with whom he had shared so many grand adventures.

REGIS AND DONNOLA WALKED HAND IN HAND DOWN THE platform of the tram that had brought them up from Gauntlgrym, then along the main boulevard in the rebuilt town of Bleeding Vines. Snow covered the yards and fields to either side of the cobblestone street, and a few flakes continued to dance in the wintry breeze.

"You wish you could be with him," Donnola remarked to the somber Regis.

"I seem to be missing out on many adventures of late."

"You just returned from a grand rescue in the far north!"

"And there my adventure ended, while the journey for others has continued."

Donnola laughed at her husband, who turned a scowl her way. "I do understand," she apologized, and hopped over to kiss him on the cheek.

"This feels like the completion of a circle and I cannot help my friends to connect the last points."

Donnola nodded sympathetically. "The events in the deep Underdark may indeed prove momentous, but you must see why bringing you to Menzoberranzan might become more a burden than a help. Wulfgar isn't going, nor even Catti-brie, and witness King Bruenor's hesitance in even offering the barest support to those who would overthrow the rule of the tyrant Lolth."

"He should send more," Regis stated. "He should open the portal and bring in armies from Mithral Hall, Citadel Adbar, and Citadel Felbarr, then lead twenty thousand fierce dwarfs to the drow city himself and be rid of the Lolthians once and for all."

"Spoken from the luxury of irrelevance," said Donnola. "Bruenor, not Regis, is the one who will have to attend thousands of funerals for his fallen minions. Not to mention having to concern himself for those that still live under his banner and look to him for safety and succor. And, as you know, it is more than drow against drow. That much has already been made clear. The Abyss itself is coming against those who oppose Lolth."

"We drove the demons from Gauntlgrym, we can drive them from Menzoberranzan as well. All of them, even Lolth!"

"Again, husband, I do not even disagree with you on the possibilities or the best course of action, but know that if Bruenor did as you wish, the carnage would be remarkable."

Halfway to their home, then, Regis paused and turned back to the tram and the tunnel to Gauntlgrym. He had hugged Drizzt farewell and watched his friend, along with Jarlaxle, Kimmuriel, Dab'nay, and threescore other Bregan D'aerthe agents, move through the dwarven complex's lower gate into the lightless tunnels of the upper Underdark.

The Companions of the Hall had been off on their own adventures many times of late, but had always been at their strongest when they fought together, as in the ice cave in the northern glacier. Now, it was Drizzt. Just Drizzt, although he was accompanied by Jarlaxle and Kimmuriel, both worthy and powerful.

Yet they weren't the Companions. And so the fear and the pain were still there, manifesting as a tightness in the halfling's chest.

He turned back once more and walked the rest of the way to their home. Regis stood back while Donnola fumbled with the key to their front door, then nearly jumped out of his boots, as did his wife, when that door was opened from within by an unexpected visitor.

"How did you get in?" Donnola asked, and Regis nearly snickered, considering the target of the question. What lock in all the world could even slow this man?

"I would have a word," Artemis Entreri replied, offering a slight bow to the woman. "With your husband."

"Have a word with both of us, then," Donnola replied after glancing back at Regis and noting his nod. "Come and sit by the hearth with me, while Regis brews us some tea."

Entreri stepped back and let Donnola lead the way. He even started the fire while Regis moved to make the tea, and soon enough, the three of them were sitting on the comfortable chairs before the blaze.

"I didn't expect to see you now, though I did earlier," Regis admitted. "I thought you would surely travel with Jarlaxle to the fight. Or at least to the lower gate to say your goodbyes."

"We already shared our farewells back in Luskan. I delayed to give them a lead to Gauntlgrym through the portal before coming through."

"Why the mystery?" Donnola asked.

"Not a mystery, just to keep my head clear," Entreri replied.

"Ah, you, too, wish you could have gone with our friends," Regis surmised.

"Perhaps. But first I have business. *We* have business."

"We?"

"I need your help. I will pay."

"You'll get my help if I can, but you'll not pay. Haven't we been through enough already to—"

Entreri stopped him with an upraised hand.

"You know of my search?"

Regis shook his head and Donnola said, "No."

"Your husband incited it," said Entreri.

Donnola looked curiously at Regis.

"The staff," Regis said, catching on. "Kozah's Needle. You went searching for Dahlia, or at least for some news as to why her staff was on the *Narwhal* when it sank."

"When the *Narwhal* was blown to pieces, you mean."

Regis winced a bit at the reminder. He had helped Jarlaxle sabotage the pirate ship, then watched from the deck of *Deudermont's Revenge* as the crew of the buccaneer tried to fire their smokepowder cannons, only to reduce their own ship to flying bits of lit kindling.

Bloody bits of kindling and bits of sailors.

"No luck in your search?" Donnola asked.

"I did not know of the staff, then went off to the north. I have only just begun. To date, I have found nothing, nothing at all."

"Then what am I to do?" Regis asked. "I did not see Dahlia on the *Narwhal,* and the staff was stuck into a pile of booty, which it surely would not have been if she had been on the ship."

"Unless she was on the ship as a prisoner," Entreri grimly replied.

"I noted no prisoners and saw most of the hold," Regis assured him. "Had I thought her on the *Narwhal,* I would have stayed our plans until I had a chance to set her free and get her to the *Revenge,* of course. You have to believe that. I know that she was important to Drizzt—and to you. I would not—"

"I did not come here to accuse you," Entreri replied.

"Then why?" Donnola asked. "You knew all of this before."

"Jarlaxle has found the wreckage and marked it," Entreri explained. "Beniago led the salvage work, what little could be found. But they didn't find Kozah's Needle."

Regis shuddered as he vividly recalled the explosions rolling along *Narwhal's* decks, turning planks into slivers. "The force of those blows could have launched it a half mile away," he said.

"And thus, Beniago couldn't find it," said Entreri.

"Because he didn't have someone of genasi heritage to deep dive for it," Donnola remarked, figuring it all out.

"Beniago will lend me *Revenge* and her crew to go out there. I just need someone to scout the bottom of the sea."

"It's been the better part of a year," Regis reminded. "The bottom's mud is likely covering anything that's left of the treasures."

Entreri reached under his cloak and produced a wand. "Mud won't hide magic as potent as that of Kozah's Needle from the detection spells within this."

"Beniago and Jarlaxle used magical detection in their salvage, of course," said Regis.

"They weren't looking for the staff. It was not Jarlaxle's priority, and I believe he feared finding it for what that might mean to me—particularly since he was desperate for me to travel with him to the north.

"But I am looking for the staff now. I need it, and I need Regis to help me find it."

The notion didn't thrill Regis at all. He was of genasi heritage in this body of his rebirth, and he could dive deep, so very deep, and withstand the cold and the pressure. But the darkness of the depths terrified him, and particularly about that wreckage, where he might have to face the results of his sabotage in the form of skeletons and half-eaten corpses.

"You and Dahlia came for me when I was lost in the hell of Sharon's cocoon," Entreri coaxed. "I have not forgotten that and never will. Now I ask you to come with me to find Dahlia—or to find her staff, at least."

"As a friend?" Donnola asked.

"As I said, I'll pay handsomely if I must."

"And of course, as I said, you will not, and of course I will go with you out to the wreck." Regis looked over at his wife, hoping he hadn't overstepped his bounds by making such a declaration and decision without first privately discussing it with her.

Except she clearly wasn't thinking along those lines, saying instead, "I'm going, too. And I'll be standing on the deck of *Deudermont's Revenge* waiting for you to come up." She turned to Entreri. "And if he doesn't come up, I'll throw you overboard to go get him, don't you doubt!"

Entreri seemed quite amused by that.

"She will," Regis assured him.

The grim man nodded. "I'm sure she'd try." He looked at Donnola and nodded again, even offering a bit of a head-bob bow. "And perhaps she'd succeed."

"Believe it," Donnola quietly muttered.

Entreri's respect for Donnola wasn't feigned, Regis knew, for his beloved wife, Donnola Topolino, had lived a life as difficult and violent as Entreri's, serving in the highest ranks of one of the most feared assassin's guilds in Aglarond.

Entreri nodded at Donnola and Regis, and with that, the three got ready to depart.

WE ARE HERE TO SCOUT AND REPORT, INZRAH MIZZRYM'S hands signaled to the drow across the tunnel.

They are only five and we are twenty, that drow of House Hunzrin signaled back.

We know not their intent! Inzrah emphatically flashed.

We know they are not Hunzrin. Who out here who are not Hunzrin are allies of our cause?

When the Hunzrin scout had no response, Inzrah motioned for him to fade back to the main group, waiting in a more complicated area speckled with natural pillars and a side tunnel. A perfect place for their ambush.

"Get an eye out," Inzrah told Benova Faen Tlabbar, the wizard accompanying this group.

"Already out and watching the approach of the small group."

"Do you recognize any of them?"

"At least two are of Bregan D'aerthe."

Inzrah smiled widely at that, until the Hunzrin scout cautioned, "Perhaps fleeing Jarlaxle's cause. Or perhaps with information that the matrons would greatly desire."

"They have no detection spells out near to us," said Mallorae, a priestess of House Mizzrym. "I have cast many wards and alarms. We can fade back before them and keep our spells of clairvoyance and clairaudience upon them until we truly know their intent, and perhaps learn more of why they are marching into the Underdark."

"No spells of detection from them at all?"

"None," the priestess answered confidently.

She was wrong.

JUST A SCOUTING PARTY, BOTH DRIZZT AND JARLAXLE heard in their heads, a message sent by the third of their flanking group who stood between them facing a stone wall in a tunnel parallel to the force from Menzoberranzan. *Inconsequential.*

"You can get us through to them?" Drizzt asked.

Jarlaxle answered before Kimmuriel could. "He can, but you will not like it."

They claim twenty in their group, but I see only a dozen, Kimmuriel telepathically imparted. *Expect that eight more are hiding nearby.*

"Warn the advance," Jarlaxle instructed. "And have the rest throw off their magical non-detection spells and rush to join the fight."

"We are only two days out of Gauntlgrym," said Drizzt. "Prisoners would be valuable. Even if they know little, we may need them for exchanges later on."

"If we can," Jarlaxle agreed.

Kimmuriel seemed distant from them, his thoughts and gaze focused on what was beyond the stone wall before them. He had heard their exchange, though, Drizzt knew, for he gave a little snort.

LET THEM CLOSE A BIT MORE, THE HUNZRIN SCOUT SIGnaled to Inzrah, who had his longbow leveled and drawn. *You take the one on the left. I'll take out the right side and we'll let the Tlabbar wizard drop the three trailing with his lightning.*

Ahead in the corridor, the five Bregan D'aerthe drow moved along without any outward signs of concern.

Inzrah smiled, thinking this would be easy and quick, and with five fine trophies to show to his matron and to Zhindia Melarn. She would be the Matron Mother of the city, he believed, and so better to be in her good graces—

That thought ended abruptly, and Inzrah's expression changed to one of curiosity. He started to lower his bow, but found himself lifting it instead, then turning to the right and letting fly, the arrow snapping across the narrow tunnel to drive through the Hunzrin's knee, and with enough force to stab into the other knee as well.

"What?" the man squealed in shock and pain.

Inzrah continued to turn, noting the startled expression of Benova Faen Tlabbar, whose hands were up in the throes of his spellcasting.

Benova fought through the shocking interruption and continued—until Inzrah's next arrow flew into his mouth, stabbing through the back of his head and dropping him to the stone.

Inzrah felt his senses return, as if someone else had been within him, controlling him, just in time for the priestess Mallorae Mizzrym to finish a spell of her own, one that froze the poor, confused archer in place.

Down the hall came the five soldiers of Bregan D'aerthe, in full charge now, firing hand crossbows.

Inzrah felt one bolt strike the back of his neck, felt the sleeping poison seeping through his veins. He saw the Hunzrin he had shot trying to recover, bow in hand and alternating between setting an arrow and grabbing at his stabbed knees. From his angle, Inzrah couldn't tell if the man meant to shoot at him or the approaching enemies, but it didn't matter, for one hand crossbow bolt after another stabbed into the downed fellow, whose movements became sluggish almost immediately.

Inzrah felt himself sinking to the ground. The last thing he saw was the approach of the rest of his band, a charge suddenly interrupted when three newcomers to the fight—so he thought—simply walked out of the wall to his right, one wading straight into the battle, a second throwing what looked like a large feather to the floor before him, and the third staring intently at the Mizzrym priestess, who for some reason seemed not to be doing anything at all.

And then there was a large bird, a giant, flightless creature, scattering Inzrah's soldiers, launching them about, pecking at them with its giant beak.

"How strange," Inzrah said before the sleeping poison took him away from the battle.

ICINGDEATH DEFLECTED THE SWORD BEFORE IT EVER GOT near to striking Drizzt. Drizzt rolled the scimitar cleverly to bring that sword down, then out, his other arm coming up fast to keep the drow's second sword at bay.

Coming right out of the wall, he and his two companions had caught their opponents by surprise. Drizzt had already taken down the nearest enemy when he came through with a slash to the back of the legs and a hilt punch to the face as the man fell; this one, too, was barely ready to engage him.

He had her dead, then and there. A subtle twist of his right wrist would angle Icingdeath perfectly to take out her throat.

He heard the moans of pain from the man behind him.

He dropped Icingdeath to the ground and instead struck the woman under the chin with his open palm, a stunning blow that sent her staggering backward.

A rush and forward flip with a double kick straight out as he came around caught her in the chest and launched her into the next enemies in line.

Drizzt barely touched the ground before he was back to his feet and he waded into the group, Twinkle fending defensively, his free hand and his feet launching devastating counterstrikes.

At one point, facing a woman wielding sword and dagger, Drizzt tossed his weapon straight up into the air, then caught it, turned, and launched a javelin that had been coming his way, sending it right back to stab into the belly of the thrower.

He moved as if to catch Twinkle, but the woman saw it and cut her sword across to intercept.

Except, Drizzt's motion was but a feint, and her reaction gave him the opening to wade in closer and hit her inside the knee with a sweeping kick that sent her stumbling to the ground.

From the right came the stab from another sword, but Drizzt got under it and behind it, rotating his shoulders as he thrust his right hand against the newest attacker's sword arm, pushing it across his body. In the same movement, Drizzt shifted another step to the man's side, left arm cocked and back, hips turning, shoulders turning, and fist driving up into the bottom of the man's ribs with enough force to lift the fellow from the ground.

Again Drizzt struck, shoulders reversing, left hand coming back, right hand going across the man's chest to prevent an elbow or a backhand and to simply occupy his opponent, who was trying to square up.

Which meant that he was turning perfectly for Drizzt's next left hook, an open-palmed strike that hit the man square in the face, snapped his head back violently, and left him falling straight backward to the ground.

The overmatched warrior didn't even groan when he crashed down, his senses already long gone from this place.

Drizzt's attention was immediately back to the woman, who was trying to stand up on her broken leg.

"Do not," he said, but she kept moving.

He hit her with a downward blow, his hand snapping her head, likely breaking her jaw, and planting her motionless on the ground.

Up came Drizzt, surveying the scene. The battle was on in full, or at least, what was left of it. In the sheer shock of the three simply appearing through the stone wall, all the formations and plans of the would-be ambushers had been turned against them with brutal and effective suddenness.

Several were down and writhing, others down and dead or dying, and still others with weapons dropped and hands held up, begging for mercy.

One fight that caught Drizzt by surprise, though, was off to the side, where a drow not of Bregan D'aerthe was battling one of the Menzoberranzan ambushers in a furious and reckless manner, leaping and swinging wildly, taking severe hits in exchange for returning a blow. She had two fighters against her and got hit every eyeblink, it seemed.

Blood poured from her side and her neck. The side of her head was matted with it. Drizzt couldn't understand why or how she was still standing, let alone fighting, or why in the Nine Hells she was battling her own allies.

But then he did understand, and he looked to Kimmuriel, who was staring at the woman, his golem now, and controlling her movements.

Drizzt didn't know whether to charge at Kimmuriel or at the battlers, but the decision was made for him when a sword went right through the woman's throat, driving out the back, severing her spinal cord.

Even Kimmuriel's psionic control couldn't battle through that.

The two drow who had been fighting her, both wounded in several places, suddenly found themselves facing a dozen Bregan D'aerthe fighters, all with bows leveled and ready.

They dropped their weapons and fell to their knees.

"So everything you told me at the monastery was a lie," Drizzt said to Kimmuriel while Jarlaxle was ordering his forces about the vanquished enemies.

"No," Kimmuriel replied, and seemed genuinely hurt by the remark.

"I thought you wanted a world of mercy and community."

"I do, and I'll help make it. But be not a fool, Drizzt Do'Urden. Our enemies are vicious and I am no pacifist. These people had a choice and so they made one. And their choices will include torturing their enemies, turning their enemies into driders, feeding the souls of you and me and all of us to the damned Spider Queen. Mercy? When possible, I would agree. When battle is on, win it first and worry about mercy after." He pointed at the woman he had been controlling, now dead on the floor, drowned in her own blood. "She was an enemy. Better that she is dead than the loss of one of our allies."

Drizzt wanted to respond, but he knew better. Kimmuriel's tactic had horrified him, but if he had been the one battling the two drow in that last fight, and particularly before he had trained with Grandmaster Kane and learned so many less lethal techniques, it was very likely that both of them would now be dead.

And I am no pacifist, either.

"Eight dead, twelve captured, and with eight of those badly hurt," Dab'nay said, coming over to Drizzt and Kimmuriel.

Drizzt looked past her to see Jarlaxle's approach.

"Burn the dead," Kimmuriel said. "Burn them to nothingness."

"And execute the twelve quickly and mercifully?" Dab'nay asked.

"No," Drizzt said emphatically before Kimmuriel could respond.

Kimmuriel stared at him.

"No?" Jarlaxle asked, joining the group.

"The tunnels behind us are clear, while those ahead grow more dangerous," Drizzt explained. "Heal our wounded with your spells, Dab'nay, then heal theirs as much as you can this day, so that they can make the journey quickly back to Mithral Hall."

"It is a march of two days," Kimmuriel reminded.

"Send a fast guard with them and make it there and back here in three days. They'll know that the tunnels before them are secure. King Bruenor will see to the prisoners."

"You think to turn these prisoners to our cause?" asked Jarlaxle.

"These little acts of mercy," Drizzt said, then looked at Kimmuriel and emphatically clarified, "when and where we can offer such, will cost us little and possibly bring great rewards as the war continues. Let the priests and wizards of the houses of our prisoners scry for them and learn that we are not acting cruelly."

"They'll think it weakness," Kimmuriel warned.

"Some will, and perhaps some will not," said Drizzt. "And then that will be their weakness. But more importantly, we know the truth of it. We'll fight this war and win this war, but we must do so without losing our own souls, else what's the point?"

Jarlaxle appeared impressed and looked to Kimmuriel, who didn't argue.

"Dab'nay, form a guard and go with them," Jarlaxle ordered. "Take the prisoners to King Bruenor with all speed."

Dab'nay agreed and seemed pleased with the decision. "And burn the dead?" she asked, making sure the order still stood.

"Yes," Jarlaxle said, but at the same time, Drizzt said, "No."

"If we leave anything of them, Lolth will bring them back, and likely as undead drider beasts," Kimmuriel argued.

"Take them to Mithral Hall as well," Drizzt said. "Treat the bodies with respect in the knowledge that any of us could have been among their ranks at one time in our lives, that all of us here going to battle the Spider Queen once served her with our actions."

"All but one," Jarlaxle noted, staring at Drizzt.

"A matter of good fortune as much as anything else," Drizzt replied.

"Have the prisoners carry the dead?" Dab'nay asked skeptically. "They'll have enough in holding up the wounded as we move along. You'll turn your three days into a tenday."

Drizzt looked to Jarlaxle for an answer, any answer.

Jarlaxle held up a finger, as if an idea had just come to him. He pulled off his great hat, reached inside it, and produced the simple black cloth of his portable hole.

"Use this," he told Dab'nay and he spun the cloth out to form a large pit on the floor of the corridor. "Drop the dead in and pick it up by the edges to become an unremarkable piece of cloth once more. Open it again in the chamber of the primordial in Gauntlgrym, and there give the dead to Maegera in its chasm of fire, and do so with proper ceremony and respect."

He looked to Drizzt, who nodded his agreement.

"I'll say a prayer for them," Dab'nay promised, and added with a wink, "but not a prayer to Lolth."

She started away and Jarlaxle called after her, "Strip the bodies of all magic before you put them in. All magic and anything of value. Give all but the very best of it to King Bruenor as recompense for his help with the prisoners."

"And the very best?" Dab'nay asked, but all she got in reply, and quite clearly all that she expected for a reply, was Jarlaxle's laugh.

"Our enemies will show us no such mercy, nor such respect for our bodies if we fall," Kimmuriel remarked, and when Drizzt and Jarlaxle turned to him, he added, "And that is why we must fight this war, and why we must win."

Drizzt nodded.

"But not *during* the fights, Drizzt Do'Urden," Kimmuriel then scolded. "Go and fetch your weapons. We battle to win, however we may, and we can show mercy once we have achieved victory and not before. We cannot give our enemies the advantage of ruthlessness when battle is joined."

Drizzt thought to argue, to remind the psionicist that he had waded through a line of enemies and taken all who had come near to him out of the fight—and had shown mercy to them in the process. But he couldn't press that point, because he knew that he would probably kill many drow before this war was over.

CHAPTER 11

Blessing Bluccidere

Zaknafein wasn't really surprised at the chilly reception he found when he entered the open-air amphitheater that served as the temple to Eilistraee. He had been informed of the decisions of the Temporal Convocation, and had heard whispers that the priests of the Dark Maiden were not overly pleased.

He thought that perhaps they should be more generous with him, as he was going to fight a war they desperately wanted to join. They were, after all, allies in spirit if not in body in battling this common foe.

He did understand their surliness, though. There was a bitterness here, and the wound was fresh. Resentment was a predictable emotion and it likely wouldn't last.

"She is in the back meditation chamber, furthest from the altar," a young priestess told him matter-of-factly before he ever asked.

Zak started to ask the priestess her name, but she turned away almost immediately and went back to her work cleaning the beautiful floor, a mosaic of tiny stones presenting a magnificent image of Eilistraee the Dark Maiden.

He kept his head down as he went through the main chamber, where most of the congregation had gathered in prayer and meditation. Zaknafein heard their quiet grumbles as he walked through, the words "unfair" and "ungrateful" tossed about many times.

Again, he reminded himself that this was a time of mourning for these would-be warriors, who were so anxious to take up the call of their goddess to do battle with the influence and corruption of Lolth.

He wished he could take them all with him, but he understood and could not disagree with the decisions of Mona Valrissa and the representatives.

He moved through the rear meditation circles, approaching the eastern wall of Scellobel, and slowed his footsteps when he heard a familiar voice chanting solemnly. He edged around a pillar and noted Galathae, kneeling, her blue-white sword upright on the floor, tip-down before her, her hands about its hilt, her forehead resting against her crossed thumbs.

He could barely make out the words of her quiet prayer, but he heard "Bluccidere" more than once.

She was blessing her sword, he realized. Azzudonna had told him of Galathae's weapon, which was carved magnificently from the deep, compressed ice, the flat of the blue-white blade imbued with runes of power from hilt to tip, so startling in contrast with the silvery mithral hilt and crosspiece, both decorated with gold. And the wondrous weapon was imbued with something else as well: the grace of Galathae's goddess.

So she claimed.

Perhaps that was true, Zak thought, but he, who had no god, had similarly imbued his weapons, or at least blessed them and felt kindred to them, with the strength of his own spirit. Either way, Zaknafein knew that he would be taking a powerful ally with him to Menzoberranzan, and for that, he was glad.

Galathae finished by kissing the gemstone balance at the end of the mithral hilt, a large, deep blue stone Zak did not recognize.

"My good lady," he quietly said.

"Well met again, Zaknafein," the paladin replied, rising. She lifted

Bluccidere vertically before her in a salute to the man, then sheathed it on her left hip. "Our great trial awaits."

"I will tell you as much of Menzoberranzan as I can recall on our journey," he promised, and not for the first time.

"I heard that Azzudonna's petition was rejected."

Zak nodded.

"She is pledged to Biancorso," the paladin said. "Such vows are taken seriously in Callidae."

Zak nodded again, though he thought that disqualifying condition—a pledge to a team engaged in a sport—rather silly, given the scope of the event awaiting them. Callidae first and foremost, he understood in theory at least, but this was a chance for the aevendrow to free their udadrow kin from the grip of a tyrant. To perhaps actually secure Callidae even more by interacting with the outside world. He tried to keep the disappointment off his face, since the decisions of the Temporal Convocation were not Galathae's fault. She was his ally, and one he was glad to have. He must have showed something, though, for she just nodded in sympathy.

"Have they reached out to Gromph Baenre?" he asked.

"No. And they won't. Anticipating such demands, and unsure of how they would be met by the Siglig, Mona Valrissa and Jarlaxle had already prepared. The mona thinks it best that we avoid the city of Luskan and the Hosttower of the Arcane altogether, as well as the dwarven realm. None should know that any of Callidae are marching to the Underdark."

"It's just you," Zak reminded with a chuckle.

"That is enough, and I go under a strict and enforced prohibition. If I am weak under torture—or even not, if I am compelled by magic or deceived in any way—and I begin to reveal anything of Callidae, the Geas Diviet will take me from this life and consecrate my body and spirit."

"Why didn't they do the same to me? Or to Drizzt or Jarlaxle, then?"

"Why would our enemies even think to ask you of another city of drow? With you, it is simply a matter of trust, and that trust, you have earned. The Ritual of Diviet is no small matter, and one they are very hesitant to perform."

"I'm honored."

"The wizard Allefaero will join us shortly. He is now trying to discern a proper chamber where he can teleport us. From there, as soon as we bid him farewell, we are on our own through the tunnels to the Underdark and Menzoberranzan."

Zak's expression revealed his alarm, he knew.

"You know the way?"

"Perhaps we will catch up to Jarlaxle and his band."

"And if we do not?" she asked, probing. "Do you know how to get us into the city?"

"There are many ways to enter Menzoberranzan, and many ways that seem to be but are not," Zak explained. "The trail is not marked, but that is likely the least of our problems. You do not know the Underdark. It is no place for a small party to be wandering." He pointed to her sword.

"Bluccidere?" she said.

"It will likely be put to use often in the tendays it will take us to navigate to the city, and that will only grow even more dangerous if we go off course. And we will, I fear. I know the general direction from beneath Gauntlgrym, I believe, but there are mazes down there and many choices and side tunnels and great chambers with dozens of exits." He shook his head helplessly. "I haven't walked these paths."

"But you know the general direction, the earliest tunnels we must take?"

Zak nodded and Galathae considered her sword. "That is all we will need. I asked if you can get us into the city. If you know the general way, I can get us to the gates of Menzoberranzan."

Zak looked at her curiously.

"Through this sword, I speak to my goddess. She answers my auguries through Bluccidere, which will tell us which choice is the best for reaching our goal. Our path will be true. Every tunnel or exit chosen will be the right one. I can get us there, but can you get us into Menzoberranzan?"

"Through stealth or blood, we'll get in," he promised.

"Come," Galathae bade him after letting that thought hang in the air for a few heartbeats. "Pray with me."

"I serve no god."

"That doesn't matter," Galathae assured him. "You are a warrior, a true warrior, and that means that you look inside often in meditation, to find your strength, to strengthen your heart and will, to consider your movements."

Zak couldn't disagree with that, and when Galathae turned, knelt, and planted Bluccidere once more, Zak took a knee beside her. He drew out the hilt of his weapon, shaped as a beautiful red-and-gold phoenix, wings wide to form the crosspiece, the tiny rubies of its eyes glistening with inner fire, as was the larger ruby that looked like the balled-up tail feathers in the pommel. With a thought, he brought forth the magical blade of this mighty weapon, a sheath of the purest light.

He inverted it as Galathae had done with Bluccidere, set its tip on the stone, and fell into a mediation with his forehead against the phoenix.

"Have you named it?" Galathae asked, drawing him from his thoughts sometime later.

"It is the Blade of Light, that is all."

"But it is more than a blade," Galathae reminded. "It can be a whip as well, or an empty hilt."

"Indeed," said Zak. "And that whip can reach into the very plane of fire and tear a rift."

"Which do you prefer, sword or whip?"

"Two swords," Zak replied, turning to show the less remarkable but still powerful shorter sword sheathed at his other hip, one he had been given to replace Cutter when the Callidaeans had demanded it be taken from the city. "But the whip is often quite useful."

"And does that second sword have a name?"

"It hasn't earned one."

Galathae laughed, understanding.

"Your main weapon needs a proper name," Galathae told him. "Tell me about it?"

Zak understood that she was just trying to pass the time while they waited for the wizard to keep any doubts about their course away, but he was happy to oblige. He told her of how he had taken the weapon from a vile man named Arrongo, a pirate, and then described how Catti-brie had used the magic of a forge fired by the primordial named Maegera to join the sword with the powerful whip into a singular weapon.

"She did the same with one of Drizzt's scimitars," Zak explained. "Twinkle, by name. She joined the broken Twinkle with Vidrinath, a magical blade from Menzoberranzan, to create a new and more powerful weapon."

"Catti-brie is formidable and clever."

Zak nodded, wondering, and not for the first time, how he had ever thought that accomplished and competent human woman was not worthy of his son. What a fool he had been when first he returned from his long sleep of death, bringing with him to the lands his son had come to call home a level of ignorance and prejudice that had almost driven him apart from Catti-brie and Drizzt forever.

"Maegera, then?" Galathae offered. "Or Maegera's Torch?"

Zak rolled the names about in his thoughts, but shook his head.

"Lolth's Bane?"

"We hope, but no. The demon is not worthy of a namesake such as this, and the fewer times I speak her name, the better."

"It will bring light to Lolth's darkness," said Galathae. "Illuminator?"

"This type of weapon is called a sun blade," Zak explained. "That would offend Lolth, I think!"

"*Soliardis!*" Galathae replied suddenly, and with a smile. "The Callidae word for the watchful orb of summer."

"Soliardis is a good name," Zak agreed.

"Tell the sword," Galathae said and went back to her prayer position.

Zak did likewise, using the quiet to ready himself for the trials ahead.

They left the meditation chamber shortly, moving through the main chapel, where the congregation remained.

Galathae led the way and picked up the pace, thinking to go straight through, but she and Zak were intercepted by High Priest Avernil.

He locked stares with her for a long while, then said, "I still do not approve of what you did in the assembly. Had you but even tried to help bolster our petition, you would be traveling with a powerful and capable entourage."

"And you still know the answer Mona Valrissa would have given," Galathae said gently, "even if I had joined our petitions as one."

Her relief was palpable to Zak when Avernil, though wincing more than once, nodded his agreement.

"We are frustrated, that is all," he said.

"I am, too, my friend. I would have greatly desired you and yours to be by our sides on this task."

Avernil seemed to appreciate that. "Then know that our hearts and hopes walk with Galathae and Zaknafein. Do the will of the Dark Maiden well, my friend."

It seemed to Zak as if a great weight had just lifted from Galathae's strong shoulders. She came forward and wrapped Avernil in a tight hug, whispering, "I will," over and over again.

Zak noted, but said nothing of, the moisture in the eyes of the typically stoic Galathae when they left the temple, making their way to a small park by the main entrance outside Callidae and into the borough of Scellobel, very near to the slide that had taken Zak and his companions on a swift ride into the city on their initial visit, and not far from the vineyard where Zak had battled Ahdin Duine in the half-barrel combat ring.

The wizard Allefaero was there waiting, along with a round-faced Ulutiun man whose lips were moving constantly as he fretted about a handful of some small items—small colorful stones, perhaps.

He was still talking when Zak and Galathae arrived, though too quietly for them to make out any words. He kept looking up, but not looking at them or at anything else, it seemed, his eyes darting about nervously, frenetically.

"I believe you know Nvisi," Allefaero said to the paladin.

Galathae nodded, but didn't seem overly pleased. She looked at Zak and rolled her eyes, then said to Allefaero, "You were not able to find a proper location?"

"I believe I did," he replied, "but I'll take no chances with such dangerous magical transport."

Galathae didn't seem impressed as she looked to Allefaero's companion, and just as Zak followed that gaze to the small human, Nvisi threw his seven rainbow stones up into the air before him, where they danced and floated, and darted about, their movements leaving trails of residual color in the air behind them.

That levitational magic seemed to suddenly cease and Zak started to crouch, expecting the gemstones to crash down and bounce about the ground. But they did not, instead landing as if on an invisible platform before the bi-eyed Nvisi, where they bounced about weirdly for a few heartbeats before settling and then hovering once again.

Nvisi kept talking to himself, pointing to each and making what sounded like a conclusion or proclamation about its position in the group.

More than a minute passed before the unkempt man gave a great chortle and swept the seven pebbles into his hand, proclaiming to Allefaero, "Aya, aya, aya!"

"Yes," Galathae quietly translated to Zak.

"'Aya, my choice is correct,' or 'aya, you have found a better . . .'?" Allefaero asked.

"Found a better," Nvisi rambled. "Your selection to land . . . your death. Too short. Head in the ceiling or feet in the floor. Joined to stone and only to die."

"Did he just say that your teleport would have killed us?" Zak asked.

Allefaero nodded, but Galathae simply shrugged it off. "Nvisi is . . ." she started to say, but seemed unable to give a proper word for it, so she just held up her hands and sighed in surrender.

"A diviner," Allefaero finished for her. "And the best in Callidae. His predictions—"

"Are so convoluted that they could always be true and always be false at the same time," said Galathae.

"A powerful ally, then," Zak muttered, prompting a quick snort from the paladin.

"That is simply not correct," Allefaero replied, looking to Nvisi, who seemed unaware of the ongoing conversation of which he was the subject. "Some people just have to listen more carefully."

"You are going to let him tell you where we should magically appear?" asked Galathae.

"I am. You do not understand his mumbles, nor do I, but he does. He sees the world differently, but accurately. He knows that which I need and that which you seek, and will guide us through a magic that we cannot understand."

"I would have more faith if I understood it."

"Do you know how I create a lightning bolt with a bit of fur and a crystal rod?"

"No, but others do the same."

"Because that magic is . . . commonplace to us. Nvisi's is different, perhaps unique, because he does not perform his divinations in ways that our own aevendrow diviners can begin to understand."

"Perhaps he is the Pikel Bouldershoulder of Ulutiuns," Zak quipped. "I think we've all learned to trust Pikel."

"It is hardly the same," Galathae insisted.

"You have tasked me with getting you to a safe beginning point below the lowest doors of this dwarven kingdom I have never seen," Allefaero put in. "Or had not ever seen, until Nvisi showed it to me. Do you know this place called Gauntlgrym, Zaknafein?"

"Of course."

Allefaero began describing it, from the great entry hall off the natural cavern, one shaped by defensive fortification, catapults and ballistae mounted on the floor, on stalagmites and stalactites, on the ceiling, even. He spoke of the raised platform and the strange carriage— the tram.

And Allefaero verbally navigated his way through the place quite accurately, down to the lower corridors and chambers, to the forge room and the chamber that held Maegera.

If that description wasn't enough to convince Zak and Galathae,

Nvisi tossed his pebbles once more, and this time they swirled about each other, each trailing lines of its color, and those lines began to sketch an image, one that Zak knew well: the Great Forge of Gauntlgrym.

The red, yellow, and orange stones filled the mouth of the forge with painted fire.

"Trust Nvisi," an astonished Zak muttered to Galathae, and Allefaero smiled widely, and added, "He knows things."

"But how does he know things?" Galathae asked.

"Neither the aevendrow diviners nor the kurit shamans nor even his fellow Ulutiuns have figured that out yet," Allefaero admitted.

"But he knows things?" Galathae echoed.

"He knows Gauntlgrym," Zak confirmed.

"Can he answer for himself?" the paladin asked.

Allefaero shook his head. "If you plan to leave this day, I wouldn't ask that of him, no."

When Galathae seemed less than satisfied with that answer, Allefaero reminded her, "When I teleport us, I will be going with you."

"Take him, too," Zak said, nodding toward Nvisi.

"That will work," Galathae agreed.

"Tell me when you are prepared to—"

"Now," Galathae answered before he had even finished.

Allefaero looked to Nvisi, then tapped the short man on the shoulder, drawing him out of his personal dialogue. When the Ulutiun looked at the wizard, Allefaero nodded.

Nvisi cast his stones again, floating them before Allefaero's eyes. He walked up beside the wizard, stood on his tiptoes, and began whispering, then giggling, then grumbling, and back to whispering into Allefaero's ear. Whatever Nvisi was doing seemed to affect Allefaero greatly, for his eyes glazed over and he seemed very much to be looking at something that wasn't there in this park in Scellobel.

The stones sparkled, throwing little bursts of light to reflect in Allefaero's eyes.

As if in a trance, Allefaero held out his right arm toward Galathae and took Nvisi's hand with his left. Galathae took the wizard's right hand with her left, then held her free hand out to Zak, completing the line.

Allefaero began chanting rhythmically.

Nvisi cackled.

The gems fell out of the air and landed on the ground—but not the ground they had been standing upon! No, a hard stone floor, the magical sparkles of the gems providing the only bits of light in an otherwise lightless chamber.

Doodles ran out of Nvisi's pant leg and gathered up the stones, stuffing them into chubby rodent cheeks before scurrying back up under Nvisi's ill-fitting pants.

"How? Where?" Galathae asked.

"We are somewhere below the lowest corridors of Gauntlgrym," Allefaero assured her, conjuring a magical light cantrip to bathe the small chamber fully, revealing three passages leading out of it.

Galathae turned all about. "But which way is which?"

"This way is east," Zak replied without hesitation.

"How do you know?" Allefaero and Galathae asked together.

"I do not know how I know, but I know. This way is east. East is where we must go."

The other two looked to Nvisi, whose attention shifted away from them as Doodles appeared out of one pocket and began spitting the gemstones one by one into the man's hand. When the lemming disappeared once more, Nvisi looked up and nodded his agreement with Zak.

"In Callidae we say, 'May the Merry Dancers light your path,'" Allefaero remarked. "I don't know what to say here."

"Farewell," Zak told him. "Just that."

So he did, and so the two warriors left down the eastern tunnel, while Allefaero cast a second teleport dweomer to bring him and Nvisi back to the park in Callidae.

CHAPTER 12

A Warm Homecoming

The team that returned to Gauntlgrym had no trouble rejoining the main group less than three days later, even though Jarlaxle's primary band had made fine progress and had encountered almost no resistance or monsters. Now at full strength, Jarlaxle's group of skilled and veteran rogues moved with great speed into the deeper tunnels.

On three occasions over the next few days, they encountered drow scouts from Menzoberranzan—or at least, Kimmuriel did, sending his thoughts ahead and understanding the allegiance and strength of every group before those sentries even knew the Bregan D'aerthe force was approaching.

Even without that advantage the psionicist afforded, none of the small groups would have offered much of a challenge to Jarlaxle's band. Every skirmish played out the same: a sudden and overwhelming appearance of Bregan D'aerthe, Dab'nay and her cohorts casting their spells to silence the enemy wizards and priestesses, the warriors there to end things quickly.

Drizzt and Guenhwyvar led the way in each time, once from the side through a stone wall as with the first fight, once from behind their enemies, and in the last fight, one very near to Menzoberranzan, in a straightforward charge right down the hallway, with Drizzt dodging arrows, catching more than one before tossing it aside, and breaching the front rank with a mighty and high-flying leap and kick—one, he knew, that would have made Grandmaster Kane quite proud.

Guenhwyvar barreled through, scattering drow or running them over, and so fast and disciplined was the teamwork of the drow and his longtime panther companion that they got right through the small chamber that was housing the enemy force and into the lone tunnel leading out the other way.

None of these enemies were getting back to Menzoberranzan to warn Matron Zhindia and her allies of the new force that had joined the battle.

The way to the northeastern entrances of the city, the tunnels called the Masterways, were now before them, clear to the gates.

But now, too, they were among corridors that Jarlaxle and his band knew so well. Instead of going straight into Menzoberranzan—and using Jarlaxle's portable hole to get through thin walls into more secret, parallel tunnels—they made their way to the east and the south, circling outside of Menzoberranzan's huge cavern past the Braeryn, along the Wanderways and around the less populated eastern reaches that housed the lake of Donigarten and the Isle of Rothe. Then back to the west, they went, again through little-used, little-known tunnels, Jarlaxle leading the troupe into the city right upon the raised southern stretch, the Qu'ellarz'orl, which housed the major clans of Menzoberranzan, including, most prominently, House Baenre.

"Who knows of your arrival?" Matron Mother Quenthel asked Jarlaxle soon after, when he and Drizzt were announced to her in the main audience hall. She hardly looked at Jarlaxle as she spoke, for she couldn't take her gaze off Drizzt, or more pointedly, off the massive black panther that licked its paws as it sat comfortably at the famous heretic's side.

"The twenty-three prisoners I turned over to your house guards and those allies we left behind in your courtyard," Jarlaxle answered. "No others."

"In my courtyard? All of them?"

Jarlaxle gave a little grin. "Well, not *all*, for of course, we have begun our reconnoiter."

"Of course," Quenthel said dryly.

"I thought you would be glad to see us."

"Our enemies control the gates to the city—for now," Quenthel explained, not affording him the appreciation he had just requested. "We have heard that they have many groups out in the tunnels to make sure the armies of King Bruenor do not come here."

"Or to intercept and take any supplies and weapons that might be coming from our dwarf friends up above," said Yvonnel, standing beside the seated Quenthel. She, too, wasn't really looking at Jarlaxle, but neither at Guenhwyvar, her gaze blatantly locked squarely upon this man, Drizzt, who so intrigued her.

"We encountered a couple of such outposts," Jarlaxle replied. "They are deserted now, and the only ones left alive other than the prisoners I brought to you are the prisoners from the initial group, who are now under the care of King Bruenor."

"There were other patrols about, easily avoided," Drizzt added.

"Because you have that cursed Oblodran creature with you, no doubt," said Quenthel.

"You will understand the value of Kimmuriel soon enough," Jarlaxle assured her, but her sour expression remained—a leftover from the days known as the Time of Troubles, when the gods went silent. In their absence, the psionicists of House Oblodra had tried to take over Menzoberranzan and unseat the Baenres.

Quenthel's reaction didn't surprise Jarlaxle, but as he considered it more, it did unnerve him a bit. The Oblodran advantage in that distant time was the absence of Lolth, and now, wasn't Quenthel trying to be rid of the Spider Queen from Menzoberranzan once and for all? Shouldn't she now see the Oblodran usurpation attempt as a kindred cause to her own?

No matter, he figured.

And hoped.

"Do you need guidance in where best to deploy your forces?" Quenthel asked.

"I suspect that Jarlaxle will be offering guidance to *us* on the same very soon," Yvonnel remarked before Jarlaxle could answer.

"I have eyes in the city," he admitted. "And have for some tendays now. I would, however, like us to discuss my role in these events. Me and mine are suited for . . . different sorts of operations, of course."

"At this point, it is simply a matter of skirmishes, mostly in the Braeryn, and one near-continual battle before the gates of House Do'Urden. We expect Zhindia to make a greater move soon to gain some visible victory," the Matron Mother explained. "Her demons enter the city by the heartbeat now and openly walk the streets everywhere but the Qu'ellarz'orl. She has not been that bold as of yet."

"Have we any demon allies in the city?" Jarlaxle asked.

"We have no demon allies," Quenthel said flatly. "Never again."

That sounded as sweet music to Drizzt's ears.

"Then Bregan D'aerthe will use our wiles and find our places in the fight," Jarlaxle said.

"And thin the ranks of Zhindia's demon army faster than she can thicken them," Drizzt Do'Urden promised.

DRIZZT DISMISSED GUENHWYVAR BACK TO HER ASTRAL home as soon as he left the audience chamber, then followed Jarlaxle out of the main building of Menzoberranzan's great First House. He wanted to make sure Matron Quenthel saw the panther, but otherwise didn't want to waste her time until he needed her again.

"You go back to Kimmuriel and the others," Jarlaxle told him, pointing to the barracks they had been given. "I'm going to meet these Blaspheme warriors. Perhaps I'll gain some insights." He paused for just a moment, considering, then added, "Send Kimmuriel to me, to the barracks in the northwest corner of the compound."

Drizzt nodded and headed on his way. He had to go around the back of the nobles' compound to get to the appointed housing for Bregan D'aerthe, and there ran into an unexpected encounter.

"Well met again, Drizzt," Yvonnel said to him.

It was clear that she had left the audience chamber right after them, moving out a back door to intercept. She moved to him and wrapped him in a great hug, one he gladly returned.

"I hoped that Jarlaxle would wander off," she said, pulling away after a long while. "I wished a few moments alone with you."

"It is good to see you," Drizzt agreed. "I'm glad you're on our side."

"And the same to you. How fares King Bruenor? How fares Regis and Artemis Entreri and the giant Wulfgar—has he settled with Penelope Harpell yet, or does he remain a free wanderer?"

Her concern for his companions surprised Drizzt, but as he considered it, he understood. In the short time Yvonnel had been around Drizzt and his friends, she had fit in more easily than he ever would have expected. She was quite an extraordinary person, one who saw the world differently than anyone he had ever met.

"Wulfgar and Penelope take their joy where they find it," Drizzt replied. "And however they find it."

"They are wise."

"The others are well. They hope for the best down here and look forward to a future that is better than the present and far better than the past."

"And Catti-brie and your little girl?"

"We call her Brie."

"Her full name is quite a mouthful," Yvonnel said with a laugh.

Drizzt smiled and nodded. "Indeed."

"Catti-brie must be devastated that you are here and she is not."

Drizzt's expression was all the answer that was needed.

"She is a wonderful person," Yvonnel said with complete sincerity. "Formidable, dedicated, desiring to do well, loyal. You are a very lucky man, Drizzt Do'Urden."

"I am, indeed. I only hope that I am able to return to her soon."

"If ever you and Catti-brie entertain thoughts of adding a third in your marriage . . ." Yvonnel said, and Drizzt could tell that she was only partly joking.

He snorted. "That would be more an offer for Wulfgar and Penelope, I think."

Yvonnel smiled widely and winked at him, and there it was, so clearly offered. He didn't take offense and wasn't really even shocked by her suggestions, nor would Catti-brie be, he knew. There was an honesty and openness to Yvonnel that made her as trustworthy in Catti-brie's eyes as was Drizzt.

"What you and Quenthel did on the surface . . ." Drizzt began. "The defiance, the heresy, the complete rejection of Lolth and her ways . . ." He shook his head. "You are spoken of as a hero to all around me up there, and it is a title most deserved."

It was the first time he ever saw Yvonnel blush, something he never expected to witness!

"It was the only choice," she said.

"You could have sided with Zhindia and won the war with ease, and Gauntlgrym and most of the north would be yours."

"It was the only choice," she said again, more determinedly.

"Because you are possessed with decency."

"Because I have a memory of that which was before Lolth. What you did in walking out of Menzoberranzan those many decades ago, what Jarlaxle has done recently with Luskan and his actions on the surface with the humans and dwarfs and halflings and elves . . . this is the future, Drizzt Do'Urden. This is who we must be to join the wider world, to the benefit of all."

"We will win here," Drizzt said.

"We have to," Yvonnel replied. She glanced back. "I must go. The reports will be coming in from the Braeryn soon. The whispers claim that a great demon force is gathering in the streets this day and the fears are that they will go to challenge our hold on the region of Donigarten." She turned back and gave Drizzt another hug, then kissed him on the cheek and whispered in his ear, "We will win. Now that you and Jarlaxle have come, I know we will. The city will look to you, and thus, wicked Zhindia will lose support."

Drizzt watched her go, reminding himself of his earlier remark to her. Yes, he was very glad to have Yvonnel Baenre, the daughter of Gromph and Minolin Fey, the namesake of Yvonnel the Eternal and possessed of that Matron Mother's vast experiences and memories, on his side.

Woe to Zhindia Melarn if she came against Yvonnel in battle.

THE BREGAN D'AERTHE FORCE MOVED QUIETLY THROUGH the back alleys of the Stenchstreets. The main boulevards of this region of Menzoberranzan, the land of drow commoners and houseless rogues, showed the rubble and scorches of battles against demonic enemies.

Matron Zhindia's Abyssal forces kept coming here, continually, though in small numbers, as she tried to convince those she could to join the cause of Lolth, and to punish those who would not come to heel.

Jarlaxle saw the tension in Drizzt. The mercenary leader understood that it was taking every measure of discipline Drizzt could muster for him to stay out of the battles, as Jarlaxle had demanded. They had traveled to this tumultuous section of the city, initially at least, for information that would be critical to the longer cause of the war. Still, many times in their skulk, Jarlaxle noted Drizzt's hands on the hilts of Twinkle and Icingdeath. He wanted Jarlaxle to turn him loose on the demons, and in those battles, there would be no mercy.

But that would escalate too soon, and Jarlaxle was certain a bit more time—and a lot more information—would mean the biggest difference in the long run. To his relief, Drizzt, though virtually buzzing with a need for action, agreed.

When they came to the back wall of one building, Jarlaxle took out his portable hole and opened the way into the Oozing Myconid. He signaled for Drizzt and several others to go in, then waved the rest to take up strategic positions nearby, covering the streets and the rooftops, ready for a fight.

He brought Dab'nay to his side, his hand then signing to her, *When* the fighting starts, we should try to keep Drizzt on the demons alone, and not on any drow enemies.

She nodded her agreement and understanding, then went into the back hallway of the establishment right before Jarlaxle, who removed the magical portal, fitting the seemingly unremarkable black cloth into the chimney of his great hat. Seven were in there, including Drizzt, filling the small rear corridor. A set of stairs was to the right, leading up to the second floor and a door on the right-hand interior wall to the left, which, from the sound of many patrons beyond, seemed to lead directly into the common room.

There are three dozen and two in the place, beyond our four operatives, Drizzt and five others in the corridor heard in their minds as the seventh of their group, Kimmuriel, telepathically relayed his findings.

Probe each table. Find the commoners, find the nobles, Jarlaxle signed to the psionicist. *Find the allies, find the enemies.*

A short while later, Jarlaxle and Kimmuriel moved down by the stairs and quietly conferred.

THERE ARE ENEMIES WITHIN, LYING IN WAIT FOR OUR ARrival, Dab'nay's fingers told Drizzt.

How do you know? he signaled back, though rather poorly, he realized, for he was out of practice with the subtle and intricate drow sign language.

Our enemies know this place, know it is Jarlaxle's primary point of contact, and were certain that Bregan D'aerthe would make an appearance in the city eventually. Perhaps they have staked out the place for parlay, perhaps for ambush.

The sounds from the common room grew louder in the small corridor suddenly.

Jarlaxle waved for Drizzt and Dab'nay to join him and Kimmuriel. When they arrived, he showed them the alcove beneath the stairwell, led them to crouch down low so he could reveal the magical passage he had constructed with his portable hole, one that went into the common room, but was concealed from the main area because it was down low behind the bar.

If I call you in, Jarlaxle's fingers flashed to Drizzt, *enter prepared for a sudden and vicious fight.* He paused and looked Drizzt in the eye, his expression deadly serious to emphasize his final signals: *If you do not kill them, they will kill you.*

Drizzt nodded.

Jarlaxle disappeared through the hole, Kimmuriel following.

Time seemed to pass very slowly for Drizzt as he stood in that corridor beside the magical opening. He considered the circles of his life's journey, ones that kept bringing him back to this place of his birth, always, inevitably, to end in violence.

The first time he had returned to Menzoberranzan, he had come to surrender, foolishly thinking that his sacrifice would keep the drow from attacking the friends, the new family, he had made on the surface world.

Catti-brie had come after him and had saved him, along with Artemis Entreri, who was already here in this dark place, and was coincidentally seeking his own escape. That had been a long, long time ago, more than a century.

Much more recently, Drizzt had journeyed to Menzoberranzan beside Jarlaxle when the demons had gone out of control within the city, threatening all. Drizzt had been imprisoned by Matron Mother Quenthel Baenre, then had been freed and used as the living spear, the living bomb, of kinetic energy created by the combined power of a united Menzoberranzan. He had hurled himself from a ledge at the demon lord Demogorgon, the destructive magic flowing through him but not consuming him, saving Menzoberranzan from the monstrous beast. On that occasion, Drizzt had done battle here with these same Melarni forces. He had killed drow, as he knew he would again.

For the better, he had to tell himself over and over again.

He believed in this cause, believed that it might be the most important cause of his life. But he hated the prosecution of it.

It was the only way, though. Reason had failed. Violence alone could free the drow from Lolth and her loyal allies, her unreasonably zealous allies. Drizzt took out the onyx figurine and whispered a name.

Over the bar and to the left, came the telepathic instructions from Kimmuriel, accompanied by an image of a large round table with nearly a dozen drow sitting around it. *Come in swinging heavy, on my call.*

Heavy, Drizzt thought, and therefore replied. *Blades drawn and ready to kill.*

"We have to take them down, and fast, Guen," Drizzt whispered to the giant panther he had just brought in to his side.

The signal came to his thoughts and the drow ranger rushed through the portable hole, stepping behind the bar and leaping atop it, then from it to the floor to the left.

A single spring from Guen had her past him before he landed, the panther barreling into the targeted drow group, sending the chairs, the table, and the Lolthians flying all about.

Drizzt flashed by the closest two as they scrambled to get up.

Too slow!

The two fell side by side facedown on the floor as the ranger rushed on.

Next was a wizard, fingers moving, arcs of lightning growing fast, but not fast enough to deter the charging Drizzt, who sent the man falling backward, crying in pain and clutching his suddenly fingerless hands to his chest.

Off to the side, an enemy priestess stood near the wall, filling the air around her with flying guardians of pure demonic magic.

The sight of her distracted Drizzt enough to slow his movement to deflect and dodge a flying javelin coming in from the side wall of the tavern. He did get the block, partially, but the tip of the missile gashed him painfully in the back of his shoulder and along his shoulder blade.

No matter, he had to get to the priestess, who was into her spellcasting yet again.

But then came a conjured floating spiritual warhammer, swinging mightily at his head . . .

JARLAXLE STOOD SHOULDER TO SHOULDER WITH TAVERN keeper Azleah along the right-hand wall of the tavern, the mercenary leader using his enchanted bracer to summon one dagger after another into his hand with every fluid motion, forward to the throw and back to receive the next missile. The stream ran out at a dozen enemies who had come forth after posing as simple patrons in the establishment, as Azleah had fortunately noted and quietly passed along when Jarlaxle was still crouching behind the bar with Kimmuriel.

He knew he couldn't cut them all down, but he was doing a fine job of holding them back with the barrage while his operatives joined the fight.

The tavern door burst in, and Jarlaxle initially grinned, but no, it wasn't his reinforcements, but a demon, a large one, and with a lot of smaller fiends close behind.

"Time to empty some wands," said the woman standing beside him, who knew him all too well.

Jarlaxle sighed and reached under his cloak.

GUENHWYVAR OPENED THE PATH, LEAPING BETWEEN Drizzt and the weapon, taking the hit of the spiritual warhammer and issuing a grunting growl in response.

Into the cloud of demonic guardians Drizzt went, accepting their bites and stinging horns and slapping limbs, taking only minor damage as he drove through to get to the priestess.

She went first, however, throwing forth her hand and uttering a series of sharp incantations, and when that wave of magic hit Drizzt, he felt as if he had walked into a diabolical disease of the lower planes. Pain washed through him, slowing him, nearly buckling his knees.

His pride had cost him, he knew. He had underestimated this

priestess, who, he now realized, had to be a noble of some house, a high priestess of Lolth, for this spell was no minor dweomer!

By the time he reached her, he was coughing up phlegm and blood, and his flurry of attacks all seemed off, as if some divine, or in this case demonic, hand was slapping at his scimitars to lessen their precision.

He did score one minor hit, catching the priestess along her right side as she lifted a snake-headed scourge to respond.

Then he was backing up, trying to rebalance, as those four living serpents atop the scourge hissed and struck, two lashing out with hooked fangs, the other two spitting venom at Drizzt's face.

He dodged deftly if slowly, his forearm scraped by the viper, the venom immediately burning like acid. Worse, a wash of spittle caught him as he fast turned his face. It seeped into his right eye, blurring, burning, blinding. He stumbled back another step to regroup, noting the priestess's free hand waggling, the wound on her ribs healing almost fully.

Powerful was the only thought that crossed Drizzt's mind in that moment.

These were not goblinkin, he reminded himself, were not peasants or minor fighters. These were drow of Menzoberranzan, seasoned in battle, trained from birth, powerful in their devotion to the Demon Queen of Spiders, and more than ready for battle.

Behind him, he heard Guen roar out in pain and rage. A quick glance showed him that his companion was battling a trio of drow warriors, dancing about, each with a pair of gleaming longswords.

The summoned guardians continued to nip at him.

He could feel the disease of the priestess's mighty spell continuing to churn at his insides.

She raised her scourge and strode forward to strike again.

JARLAXLE HADN'T WANTED TO USE ONE OF HIS BEST TRICKS so early in his time here in the city, but this was no minor foe! The hulking glabrezu pointed the upper of its two sets of arms his way, menacingly clacking the giant claws at the ends of those limbs.

Those powerful and murderous limbs were still together before the huge fiend's chest when Jarlaxle fired off his wand, a glob of goo flying fast to strike the demon right in those claws, then rolling back and spreading out over the monster. The goo dried as it spread, the viscous material hardening to restrain the demon and lock it in place.

Jarlaxle tipped his cap at the caught beast and drew out a second wand.

Before he could aim it, though, a beam of brilliant light shot down from the ceiling over the glabrezu, brighter than a light spell, as if some caster had stolen a ray of sunshine and thrown it down.

The demon howled in pain at the radiance of the beam, but it only lasted a few eyeblinks before winking away—and taking Jarlaxle's entrapping magical goo with it.

And taking, too, any thoughts that the beam of daylight had come from a Bregan D'aerthe ally.

Jarlaxle was rarely surprised, but his jaw hung slack. They knew! How did they know?

"They expected—" he started to say as he turned toward Azleah, and bit off his sentence at his second surprise, at the woman's long and tapering dagger stabbing in at his throat.

DRIZZT FELL INTO THE LESSONS OF GRANDMASTER KANE and used his mind to overrule the cries of his body, to block them out entirely and focus only on the present, the exact present, and what he must do to best guide the way forward.

He straightened against the priestess, but then lurched as if in pain, bending to the right.

The priestess struck, her arm coming forward, her four vipers coiling.

And Drizzt came out suddenly, with shocking speed, his left hand rising before him, holding Icingdeath horizontally to come up under the serpents, his right arm swinging out wide to the right, then up and around.

The vipers retracted behind the rising Icingdeath, coiling and striking as the blade went harmlessly up and out to the left.

But again, with quickness neither the vipers nor the scourge-holder could anticipate, Twinkle came over and down atop those serpents before they could fully extend. Two remained behind that chop, but the heads of the two that had struck at Drizzt fell free to the floor.

Drizzt came on, or started to, but a magical force sent him skidding back a few steps.

He had never seen such a spell from a priestess and wondered if she was something more—and that notion was confirmed when he noted her whispering, the words coming magically to his ears, barely audible, frustratingly indecipherable, truly terrible.

He felt those whispers stabbing into his mind, inflicting pain, and he knew that he had to flee.

But the seasoned warrior also realized that she was the one telling him that he must flee. He understood the illogical command for what it was, and he saw, too, the smug look on the priestess's face.

Confident, so very assured, even though half of her living whip had been decapitated.

Now it was she who was underestimating her opponent, not Drizzt, and with that in mind, he turned and started to run away.

One step, two, then swinging back with a sudden pivot, he threw himself at her as she was again in the midst of spellcasting.

He stabbed left and right—and should have hit solidly twice, but did not, her protections coming up suddenly to deflect Icingdeath wholly, a second ward stealing most of the bite of Twinkle.

And meanwhile, those summoned demonic spirit guardians bit at him again, while the two remaining serpents coiled and struck out at him.

Enough of that, Drizzt demanded, with his foot and not his words. He leaned back out of reach of the vipers, tucking his right heel under his left foot and pulling his right foot right out of his low boot.

Continuing the movement, he kicked his right foot up high. One serpent managed to nip him in the shin, but he didn't care and drove through it before the priestess could enact further deflective shields.

He hit her squarely in the face, using the life energy of his ki to send a stunning wave through that foot. He knew that he had scored a crippling blow when the flapping and translucent guardian spirits all about him faded, the concentration of her spell thrown away.

On he came as the priestess fell back, stabbing Icingdeath hard into her belly, through her magical armor and any remaining wards, biting into her entrails.

Across came his right-hand blade to take her head from her neck.

But no, she uttered a word—a single curse—and was gone.

Drizzt stumbled forward. He balanced and leaped about, searching.

But no, she wasn't invisible, nor had she blinked anywhere nearby. She was simply gone.

He knew the spell of recall, for he had seen Catti-brie using it before, and had even gone along on the divine teleport with her on several occasions. Thus, he knew, too, that it was a dweomer only the most powerful of clerics could cast.

His opponent had been wearing the dress expected of a noble house, certainly, but she was not wearing the robes Drizzt would have thought to be of a high priestess of Lolth. How could anyone not of that rank perform the spells he had seen from this one?

The thought haunted him. He wanted to dismiss it as simply a matter of the woman not wearing the proper garb—perhaps she was trying to stay unnoticed.

But she was young, very young. Too young to have achieved such a rank?

JARLAXLE FOUGHT OFF HIS INSTINCTS TO DEFLECT AS THE tip of the dagger entered his flesh—he figured it would be more impressive if he just stared down at the traitorous Azleah.

Perhaps he had intimidated her, perhaps not, but either way, as

Jarlaxle had known, the woman's thrust stopped right there, before the blade could dig in and do any serious damage.

He saw the abject terror on Azleah's face, felt a bit of a sting from her shaking dagger hand, and shook his head in both sympathy and disgust as that shaking hand retracted just a bit, the blade slowly turning about.

Jarlaxle spun back and put another glob of goo into the face of the glabrezu, which was very near to him now. Then, growling in frustration at having to use so many of his tricks, he sent yet another charge from his wand, this one at the hulking demon's feet, locking it in place to the floor.

The mercenary leader winced when he heard the struggling yelp of pain from behind.

He knew that Kimmuriel was seeing through Azleah's eyes—and that Kimmuriel would bring that needlepoint dagger right into one of those eyes. She would see it coming—and by her own hand!—and could not dodge or turn or even blink.

Jarlaxle reached for the feather in his cap, thinking to bring in the giant diatryma bird, but stopped when Bregan D'aerthe associates dropped down from the room above to land lightly on either side of him.

"It took you long enough," Jarlaxle remarked.

"You gave all three of the potions of etherealness to D'fava," the woman on his right said as the man on his left leaped forward to stab at the trapped glabrezu. "He used one on himself first, then, as he had become gaseous, had no way to pass the other two to us!"

"We had to cut our way through the ceiling," the man said, dodging an awkwardly angled claw, then moving behind that lumbering swing from the off-balance demon and driving his fine sword into the side of the glabrezu's chest. "And there's a bigger fight outside."

Jarlaxle began a stream of daggers again, throwing them past his two minions and their diabolical foe to strike at the lesser demons the glabrezu had brought with it. He noted movement to his left and saw Drizzt dart past, somersaulting into the battle with a rage that surprised him.

Until Guenhwyvar came loping behind the ranger, her shiny black coat torn in many places by drow blades.

Jarlaxle held his shots for a moment to look far over to the left, where Drizzt and Guen had been fighting.

Three drow lay dead across the floor and tables.

He glanced back at Drizzt, then raging through the ranks of lesser demons. He thought of the earlier fight where Drizzt had insisted on mercy. Not now, though, not even with the three across the room.

Jarlaxle wasn't sure how he felt about that. His army was certainly bolstered by the deadly Drizzt. But, to his surprise, his sensibilities were stung.

The glabrezu went down in the green goo, hacked by Jarlaxle's associates, who moved fast to support Drizzt in clearing the tavern.

Outside the Oozing Myconid came the screams of fury and pain, a larger battle joined in full. But a more lopsided contest than in here, as Bregan D'aerthe swept down from the rooftops and rushed in from the alleyways in greater numbers than the enemy forces had anticipated, clearly.

It was over quickly, indeed almost ended before Jarlaxle even made his way out the tavern door.

"Guenhwyvar will be gone for a bit," Drizzt told him, dismissing the panther to her Astral home to recuperate.

"Take control out here and set a perimeter," Jarlaxle told him. "If any more enemies come to the Braeryn, we will meet them and turn them back."

Drizzt nodded and moved off.

With a signal of approval to Dab'nay, who was directing the priestesses tending the Bregan D'aerthe wounded, and triaging, too, the wounded enemies, Jarlaxle went back into the tavern.

To his surprise, he found that Azleah was still alive, though now with only one eye.

Kimmuriel crouched beside her.

"I expected to find that dagger sticking out the back of her head," Jarlaxle said.

"She didn't want to betray us," the psionicist told him. "I felt her regret when I possessed her."

"Whether she wanted to do it or not, she did it, or tried to," Jarlaxle replied and reached up to rub the blood on the collar of his fine shirt. "If you hadn't stopped her, I'd be dead, and would there be regrets then, I wonder?"

"Yes," Kimmuriel answered without hesitation.

That surprised Jarlaxle again, and he looked down to the woman to demand an explanation. She was just sitting there shaking and rocking and holding her hand over her torn eye.

"She did it for Braelin," Kimmuriel explained.

Jarlaxle snapped his stare up at his friend, trying to hide his confusion. Had Braelyn been in on a plot to kill him?

"They have him," Kimmuriel explained.

"Zhindia has him?"

Kimmuriel nodded. "They will make a drider of him, publicly, so they promised Azleah, unless she killed one of us, you or I."

"Pity for her that she went for the more difficult target, then," Jarlaxle quipped.

"Only because you have me watching out for you, and I have only you watching out for me," Kimmuriel replied.

"Now I've failed and Braelin is forever lost to me," the distraught and wounded Azleah said, her voice trembling with the pain—even though a priestess had obviously done some healing to her.

"No, you fool," Jarlaxle countered. He turned to stare at the tavern's side wall, the one eye showing outside his eye patch becoming so intense suddenly that it almost seemed as if he was staring across the city and into House Melarn. "Because you failed, Braelin has a chance."

CHAPTER 13

The Diabolical Trap

Zaknafein and Galathae moved down the corridor at a swift pace. Galathae wore a fine suit of silvery chains, but it made not a sound, backed and lined as it was by the silk of the white spiders and the mucus of the strange hagfish bred in Callidae. Every so often, the paladin would stop and hold forth her sword of blue-white ice, then reach into it, or into herself, or perhaps both, Zak thought, to bring forth a mist of some sort, bluish in color, that seemed a ghostly image of that sword.

"The way is clear," she said, inviting Zak to move along with her.

"The sword told you that?"

"My goddess told me that."

Zak gave a little chuckle, one that brought a frown to Galathae's face.

"Bluccidere helps me to focus my thoughts," she said, her tone showing Zak that she was clearly perturbed by his continuing and obvious doubts.

"Your thoughts?" he sarcastically asked anyway, because he simply could not help himself. Zaknafein had heard too much of goddesses in the many years of his life. "Perhaps that is the source then, yes? Your thoughts. Your senses. Your instincts."

"To focus my thoughts to connect with the answers of my goddess. You do not believe in Eilistraee."

"I know nothing of—"

"But you think you know enough to tell me that I am wrong in my faith," Galathae interrupted.

"No, it's not that."

"It is exactly that," said Galathae. "I understand, though, and fully so, for I was as lost as Zaknafein not so long ago."

"So, now I am lost because I do not see this Eilistraee creature the same way that you do? And here I was, fearing that my doubting would offend you, when, had I known your intent to condescend, I would have tried to offend you."

"Condescend?"

"I am hardly lost."

"I did not mean—"

"You did exactly mean."

The two stared hard at each other for a few heartbeats, both showing expressions caught somewhere between indignation and apology.

Zak broke the tension when he began to laugh, and a moment later, Galathae joined in with him.

"I meant no disrespect," he said.

"Nor did I," said Galathae.

"Yes, you did," they both said together, and they shared a heartier laugh still.

"As long as your divine senses of direction and danger work, be they from some goddess, your sword, or your inner power, who am I to judge?" Zak remarked.

"Fair enough. And if you fight well, perhaps I'll keep you around."

Down the corridor they went, laughing.

And then, so suddenly and unexpectedly, falling.

"WONDERFUL NEWS!" AZZUDONNA SAID EXCITEDLY. "AND it is the right thing—"

"This is not what we discussed," Vessi interrupted. Allefaero, Ayeeda, and Ahdin Duine all turned to the small man in surprise, while the last at the meeting, High Priest Avernil, simply offered a scowl.

"What do you mean?" Azzudonna asked. "This is exactly what we four talked about that day in Ibilsitato."

"We *four*," Vessi agreed. "Four of us, and a fifth if Nvisi decided to join."

"That was before we knew Holiness Avernil's intentions," said Ahdin Duine.

"We are walking into a city against enemies who number in the thousands," Ayeeda added.

"Tens of thousands," Avernil said.

"But so, too, do our allies count such numbers," said Vessi. "We were supposed to be going in support of Galathae and Zaknafein."

"That, and to free our kin from the grip of a demon," Ayeeda said.

"Which is the more important issue," High Priest Avernil put in, staring at Vessi and not backing down or even blinking at all. "Being loyal to your friends is important and honorable, and surely a positive attribute in the eyes of Dark Maiden Eilistraee, but—"

"I give not a thought to Dark Maiden Eilistraee," Vessi snapped back. "That is your calling, not mine."

"But the notion of breaking tens of thousands of our kin free of the grip of a tyrant demon is the higher calling," Avernil stubbornly finished.

"Kin?" Vessi replied. "We know nothing of these udadrow. Nvisi is morè kin to anyone of Callidae than they."

"Even Zaknafein and Jarlaxle?" Ahdin Duine asked, looking at Azzudonna as she did and drawing Vessi's gaze to his dearest friend as well.

"No, of course I'm not talking of Zaknafein or Jarlaxle, or any of the other three who came to Callidae. But this was not our plan. We four were to travel fast down the tunnels to catch up to Galathae and Zaknafein, going in support of them. We four! Not Avernil and his hundreds."

"Only fifty or sixty will go," the priest interjected.

"Only fifty or sixty. Well, that makes it very different," came Vessi's reply, dripping with sarcasm. "I'm sure that the Temporal Convocation won't mind, then, that only fifty-five, or sixty-six, or however many the final count turns out to be, disobeyed them and abandoned Callidae for some desperate mission in Menzoberranzan."

"Fifty-five, or sixty-six, or however high the number becomes, is a far stronger force than the handful," said Avernil.

"And a far more *noticeable* force," Vessi replied.

"We'll be long away before they know we are gone," Allefaero assured Vessi.

"For a wizard, you really miss the point far too often. They will know we are gone, but even that is beside the main issue here. The reason the Temporal Convocation said no to Avernil's church and to Azzudonna was because they fear the udadrow will realize with the infusion of such numbers that another place, another city, another entire clan of drow have come to join the fight against their demon Lolth. Galathae alone would not present that problem."

"With her unusual sword of pressed blue ice?" Azzudonna asked, and reminded.

"Is it any more unusual than Entreri's?" Vessi argued. "And Jarlaxle is known for collecting exotic items. No, with fifty and more of us entering Menzoberranzan, we put Callidae at risk. I cannot be a part of that."

"I have to go," Azzudonna pleaded with her dear friend.

"I know, and I'll tell no one."

"I need you with me. Vessi, we've been through so much."

"We have, and I respect your choice, though I fear that Biancorso's chances in the next cazzcalci will be greatly diminished without you. But I cannot go, my friend. I cannot. Callidae is my home and my heart and I'll not join in this plan that so puts it at risk."

"We will become just more members of Jarlaxle's mercenary band, then," said Ayeeda. "Strays he collected on the surface and brought into his fold."

"That would be a good front for you down there," conceded Vessi.

"For us," Ayeeda insisted, but Vessi just shook his head.

"Galathae went under Geas Diviet," Vessi reminded, and stared hard at Avernil. "Will you priests demand the same of yourselves and of your flock?"

The priest considered it for a few moments, then shook his head. "No."

Vessi scoffed.

"We will, if it will satisfy your . . ." Ayeeda began, but Vessi waved the whole notion away.

"I cannot go, in either case. I cannot do this to my beloved Callidae." He kissed Azzudonna on the cheek, then Ayeeda, then bowed to the others and left the small house where they had gathered.

Callidae had suddenly become quite lonely for Alvinessy of Biancorso.

SOME TWENTY FEET DOWN, THEY LANDED HARD. ZAK MANaged to turn his legs to send him into an immediate roll and slide, for the floor upon which he landed was sloped, descending before him. Galathae crashed down less gracefully, though, sliding to the side and slamming her hip and elbow, then her head with lesser force. She gurgled, then groaned, and grabbed at her hip and tucked her arm in tight against her side.

By the time Zak could recover enough to stand—and on a badly twisted ankle—the paladin was softly chanting. Zak ambled to her and slid down beside her, immediately wiping a bit of blood that was streaming down over her temple from under the brim of her silvery helmet. Worse, the front and side of her tan trousers were showing blood, as well, and lots of it.

Her eyes didn't seem to focus and her chant—a spell of healing, Zak presumed—fell away to nothingness.

"Stay with me," he whispered to her, and he grabbed at her belt, thinking to reveal the wound there and stem the flow.

But Galathae's hand went to that hip and she whispered the name of Eilistraee.

Zak watched the woman's hip shimmering like the water on a pond in a slight breeze, and he heard Galathae's breathing ease.

She brought the hand to her head, brushed off her helmet, and continued to send forth those waves of healing until that wound, too, had mended.

Then she relaxed and looked up at Zak. "Ouch," she said quietly.

He helped her to sit up.

"Your goddess granted you healing without casting a spell?" Zak whispered.

"What is a spell but a prayer? I am a paladin of Eilistraee. When I most need her, she will be there for me. And yet you doubt."

"Drizzt can mend his wounds similarly, and no god is involved," the stubborn warrior replied, still keeping his voice low.

"You have witnessed divine magic all your life and yet you doubt," the paladin said with a shake of her head.

"The most powerful magic I have witnessed is that of Gromph Baenre, and I have never met anyone with less use for the gods than he. Or perhaps that of Kimmuriel Oblodra, who despises all notions of meddling greater beings."

"I, for one, am glad for such a meddling being," she said, indicating her healed wounds.

Saying nothing to that, he helped Galathae to her feet, the two looking back up at the wall they had somehow come through. There was no door to be seen.

"A trap," Zak surmised.

But Galathae was shaking her head. "My augury would have shown it to me. When I last asked the goddess weal or woe regarding our path, the answer indicated no such dangers as this. However you believe I get my magic, that cannot be."

"Unless the trap was put there after you cast your spell," said Zak.

"Which means that there are enemies in the tunnels above. We must get back up and find them!"

"But how? And where are we now?" Zak asked, turning about. He nudged Galathae, who held forth her sword, which was now emanating not a blue mist, but red.

"Enemies," she said.

Zak nodded and tried to take a more complete look at the large chamber, one with a ceiling spiked by stalactites and a floor broken by thin, tapering stalagmite mounds. The smell of death hung in the air—not as if it were a fresh kill rotting, but rather, as if this place was simply too full of murder to ever be rid of the stink.

"Stay close," Galathae whispered, and Zak was impressed at how quickly and fully she had recovered from her fall. Perhaps she, or maybe Drizzt, was onto something here with these added disciplines, he thought, especially as he tested his ankle.

They moved into the chamber, past the stone pillars, standing silent sentry like the stripped skeletons of some long-dead behemoth. At one point, Zak came upon a mess of entrails against a base of a stalagmite.

Galathae nodded when he pointed it out.

This was a place of death.

Zak stopped and held up his hand. Something had moved in the darkness to the right. He pointed that way, he and Galathae taking cover behind two pillars, with Zak at the very edge of the light emanating from Bluccidere, and not yet calling upon his own light-emitting blade.

They came in fast at Galathae, a band of zombies and skeletons of all sorts: humans, elves, dwarves, even a pair of skeletal minotaurs, their massive horns seeming all the more impressive attached to a bare skull.

Galathae met the first attack with a sweeping two-handed strike, shattering a skeleton and cutting a zombie cleanly in half. She had to immediately go to a one-hand grip, though, lifting her shield to fend the charge of a skeletal minotaur. She took the hit and went flying backward, but held her balance as she skidded against a rocky mound, the minotaur close behind.

Zak leaped out from his cover, calling forth the whip and cracking it *one*, *two*, *three*, tearing and ripping at the nearest monsters, including the second minotaur.

He snapped the whip again, drawing a line of fire on the minotaur's skull as it turned.

A zombie rushed in from the right, clawing for Zak's extended arm, but he casually sent his smaller sword across and under that extended arm, angled up to stab the zombie right in its open mouth.

He twisted his arm and jerked suddenly to take the top half of the undead thing's head off as he rushed past it, moving behind a group of monsters that turned as he passed—and put them between him and the raging minotaur beast.

Its charge was barely lessened as it barreled through its supposed allies, sending broken bones and shattered zombies and skeletons every which way. Head lowered, it bore down on Zak—who called his blade of light back, turning Soliardis into a sword of radiance once more, as he fell flat to the floor, rolling and turning at exactly the right moment for that powerful weapon to cut across the giant skeleton's ankles—and he was surprised and amazed at how easily Soliardis bit at the undead monster, severing both its ankles with that single strike.

Zak still got run over, but the minotaur took the worst of it, flying down hard against the floor and the next stalagmite in line—and with Zak up and charging in right behind, smashing it a dozen times before it could turn around to fight back—and by that point, it was little more than a pile of broken bones.

Zak moved around it, away from the other monsters, this time, trying to keep everything in front of him, and also trying to keep a watch on Galathae. He gasped when he saw her, for the minotaur had crushed in against the pillar where the paladin has been standing. He breathed easier when he saw Bluccidere come up through the back of that monster's skull, a beautifully executed uppercut.

The weapon master went to work on the minotaur standing before him, leading with his ice sword and waiting for those moments of best opening to send Soliardis driving in, the powerful blade, its radiance hungry to consume the undead, taking great chunks of the flailing monster with every hit.

They were turning the fight perfectly, he thought.

Until he saw a giant eyeball hanging in the air at the far end of Bluccidere's glow.

"Galathae!" he called.

Two bolts of black energy shot out from the eye, one at Zak, one at Galathae, who was still pinned to the stalagmite and could not dodge.

Zak did dive aside, but still got nicked and felt as if his very life force was being sucked out of him, as if the cold jaws of death itself had entered his body and begun to chew.

He came up out of the dive to see the floating eyeball blink away, and with a roar, he threw himself at his foes, determined to get to his companion, who had apparently taken the necrotic ray at full force.

GALATHAE FELT THE COLD ENERGY BITING AT HER. SHE shoved aside the destroyed minotaur and swept her sword across to drive back the monsters, then cast a quick spell of healing upon herself.

And felt nothing. Something—likely that beam of dark energy—was preventing her from healing.

Confused, but with no time to sort it out, the paladin began wildly sweeping Bluccidere, then bashing anything that came too close to her with her shield. Realizing that Zak was okay, and even finishing the group that had turned for him, she fought defensively, scored few hits but gave up none.

She nodded, seeing Zak revert Soliardis again to a whip, snapping it back and forth horizontally before him and taking the face from a trio of zombies that fell over one by one, like chopped trees finally surrendering to the earth.

They would win, she believed.

And then the wall grabbed at her, tentacles sprouting from all about the stalagmite, hooking her arms, pulling her shield from in front of her, weakening her swing so that Bluccidere did little damage to the fiends coming at her!

A skeleton's bony finger raked across her face. A zombie bit the forearm of her shield hand, pinching her viciously beneath her mail.

"No!" Holy Galathae said in pure denial, and with a roar, she drove herself forward, tearing and tugging, pulling her sword arm free, then whipping her holy blade down atop the chewing zombie's shoulder, nearly decapitating it and dropping it destroyed to the floor.

Across went her backhand, taking a pair of skeletons, and then Zak was there, thinning the ranks with equal fury from behind.

"No!" Galathae yelled, and she ripped herself free of the grabbing tendrils, staggering forward, shield-bashing the next zombie with such force that she launched it into the air and to the ground.

She started to advance, then stopped, so suddenly understanding it all, the lair of this hellish beast, as a giant, strange skull appeared from behind a nearby pillar, its toothy maw of bone opened wide, its enormous singular eye staring at her with obvious malevolence.

Tiny lights floated about its head—lights, she understood, that used to be the eyes at the end of fleshy eyestalks, long rotted to nothingness.

"Stay close," she told Zaknafein. She ran to the zombie she had shield-rushed and chopped it down as it tried to stand.

One of the lights floating about that skeletal creature issued a pair of purplish rays, shooting out to strike its companions.

Zak felt his skin hardening, felt as if he were turning to stone!

But he felt the warmth of Galathae's presence and the mist of Bluccidere, shimmering about his skin, defeating the petrifying attack.

"Clear a path for me!" Galathae yelled, and Zak brought forth his whip and began tearing lines into the plane of fire as it slashed across the faces of zombies and the skulls of skeletons, ripping them apart with wild abandon.

Fearlessly, Galathae charged the floating undead eye monster, Bluccidere in both hands, calling to the sword, empowering the sword, with every stride.

Another ray came forth from a different one of the tiny orbs floating about the skull, this one streaking a yellow line.

Zak felt himself lifted and thrown back.

Galathae, too, took the hit, but she powered through it, growling, determinedly stepping forward.

"I . . ." she roared, "smite . . . thee!"

Her overhead chop met the floating monster's attempted bite, the blue-white blade humming furiously with power, and she brought it down with all her strength and with all the holy power she could manage.

The sword struck, the air about her and her target suddenly glowing blue. The floating skull was driven down, the blade putting a large crack from above that huge central eye all the way to the crown.

But the monster was far from finished, and bit hard at the paladin's midsection, sending her twisting away in pain.

In came Zak, blades in hand, in a whirling and ferocious assault, stabbing and slashing wildly to force the monster back; then, as it floated back from his reach, Zak made Soliardis a whip once more and cracked it in a stinging sweep above the skull, across the floating tiny lights.

Not one but three rays came forth in response, each splitting to strike at Zak and at Galathae.

The first made him feel heavy, as if his limbs were wrapped in thick metal.

The second made him realize that he couldn't win and should flee for his life.

The third showed him the truth of the world, that the real monster here was Galathae, and so he should strike at her!

But he looked at her, bathed in holy light, serene and yet focused in her efforts to resist the rays—the same rays that had hit him. Her beauty—not physical beauty, but ethical beauty—comforted him, showed him the truth of the attempted charm, showed him that he could not be afraid, and allowed him to release the magical weights that were now slowing his movements.

He was on the beast in a heartbeat, whip leading, then Soliardis reverting to its sword form. Zak stabbed it straight into that central eye—and while it was stuck there, Galathae slammed Bluccidere down again atop it, widening the crack.

And then again as the eyes sent forth three rays once more.

The first sent both Zak and Galathae flying backward, as if a great invisible hand had just plucked them from their feet and thrown them away.

The second hit them in mid-flight, the same withering energy as

Zak had felt initially, biting at his life force, calling him to the realm of death.

They landed and tumbled hard across the floor, some two dozen feet from the skull as the third ray flashed in, a yellowish bolt that hit Zak and Galathae, but also a zombie that was stubbornly rising from the floor between them and the eye.

Zak dove aside and felt a strange pulse go through his body, and his eyes widened in horror as the zombie's entire form suddenly flapped as if it were a bedroll hanging on a wash line in a strong wind.

It flapped again weirdly, and then was simply gone, disintegrated to nothingness.

Zak turned to Galathae, who was still there, also gawking at the display of terrible power.

And then all that he saw on her face was determination, and she tried to claw her way up from the floor and charge back at the monster.

But she could not, nor could Zak, for that first ray remained, holding them like magical chains.

Zak struggled against the pull, but braced himself for more rays that were surely coming his way.

But no.

He and Galathae had truly wounded this monster, and it was no stupid thing, clearly. It floated away from them and the binding ray was gone, but replaced by a suddenly living floor, with tentacles and eyestalks rising all about the area where Zak and Galathae lay, confusing them and making it hard to move.

Galathae put Bluccidere horizontally in front of her and looked back to the area of the wall where she and Zak had fallen into the cave. She whispered to the sword, then let it point like some divining rod.

"There," she told Zak. "The door, the magical gate. Go!"

Zak started for the wall, which seemed to be climbable, but he paused when he got to the base of it, noting that Galathae had stopped some three strides from the wall, had turned about and was now chanting repeatedly, "Grant me this, Dark Maiden. I have come to wage your battle beside you. Do not let me die so far from my destiny."

"Come on!" he called to her.

She ignored him and kept chanting.

Zak started for her, but stopped. She had earned his trust. He didn't know what she was up to, but she clearly couldn't stop now to explain it.

He started up the rocky and uneven wall, picking his path carefully. About three-quarters of the way to the indicated spot, some fifteen feet up from the floor, he glanced back and whispered for his companion, for he saw the massive floating skull returning, and it was not alone, herding another host of undead monsters before it.

Galathae backed slowly toward the wall, still chanting.

The leading zombies and skeletons fanned out side to side, flanking her and preventing any attempt to flee. A group with the floating undead skull, including a trio of those minotaur skeletons, hurried for the paladin.

Thirty feet away, an eye cast another ray, but a singular one for Galathae, as if it had not noticed Zak up on the wall.

The woman held perfectly still and stopped chanting, and Zak feared that she was magically held and helpless.

He slowly pulled the hilt of Soliardis from his belt. He would get one chance, he believed, one strike to end this, or watch his companion be horribly murdered.

The eye and its companions were twenty feet away.

"Come on," Zak whispered under his breath, ready for his spring.

The monsters from the side charged at her hungrily. The eye was closest, only ten feet from her now, its toothy maw opening wide.

Zak held one heartbeat longer.

Galathae didn't, stabbing her finger ahead and to the floor, creating a spot of light under the floating skull, which burst outward and upward immediately, creating a twenty-foot cylinder in both diameter and height of shimmering, glowing magic that looked to Zak very much like the Merry Dancers of her homeland's winter sky.

The floating skull and its immediate entourage were in it, but the undead from the sides and trailing the skull ran up and crashed against it as if it was not merely light, but a tangible barrier. They could not cross into the area of light!

Zak's jaw hung slack, and he almost forgot the fight altogether for a moment, only realizing the danger as the eye kept coming. He turned to leap, but again, it was Galathae who moved forth, shouting, "Eilistraee! Bluccidere!" and presenting her holy weapon before her.

And all the area was bathed in radiant light, the undead monsters staggering suddenly.

All but the floating skull, which continued shooting rays at her, stinging her, tearing at her life force, slamming her back against the wall.

Tendrils sprouted from the wall to grab at her.

The maw opened wide and swept in at her and, finally, Zak came down from on high, both hands tight against Soliardis's hilt, driving the blade straight down with all his strength and all his momentum through the floating skull.

He bounced away heavily to the floor, staggering and dazed, and shocked to see the eye still there, still floating, still alive, or undead—still animate, which is the main thing that concerned him. And now, badly hurt, he had to pull his second blade, for a minotaur charged at him and he had nowhere to run.

Galathae tore free of the tendrils, crying for her goddess, and stabbed at the eye with Bluccidere, divinely empowered and crackling with energy. The holy sword struck and flashed and the skull recoiled in obvious pain, flowing lights like glowing ichor pouring from its huge central eye.

Galathae pulled Bluccidere back and released the boundaries of her enchantment of light, creating a blast of radiant energy all about, brilliant and blinding.

Zak cried out and covered his eyes.

His sight had still not returned when he heard Galathae shout out, "I . . . banish thee!"

He did see the strike, did see the floating skull simply disappear beneath it, with Soliardis, which had remained stuck in the bone from the strike of Zak's leaping assault, now falling freely to the floor. As his eyes adjusted, he saw, too, the smoldering mounds of zombies and skeletons, the lesser ones destroyed, the three minotaurs still standing, but smoking as if their very beings were melting away.

The one coming at him had stopped in its tracks, and so Zak struck, again and again, driving it back with battering slashes against its skull. He dove past it and retrieved Soliardis, then went into a frenzy, ignoring the pain from the fall and the life-devouring rays. The remaining two skeletal monsters, badly wounded from the stunning burst of radiance, lasted only a couple of heartbeats under Zaknafein's barrage.

He finished the last and staggered back for Galathae, who stood gasping, as if she had given all that she could and more.

"What did you do?"

"Something I have never done before," she admitted, and she shook her head as if coming out of a trance. "Do you still disbelieve?"

"In the goddess? Yes!" he said. "But I believe in Galathae."

Smiling, she shook her head again at his obstinance.

"Where did the skull thing go?" he asked, looking all around. "An undead beholder?"

"Banished to its home plane of existence."

"Then we have a lair to explore," Zak said, mustering some enthusiasm. "What treasures—"

"Banished if this is not its home plane," Galathae interjected, stopping him short.

"And if this is its home?"

"It will return soon." She looked plaintively at Zak. "I have little left to offer this day."

In truth, Zak had little as well. He pulled a fine cord from his belt and gave her one end, then went up the wall with all speed. Galathae began to climb behind him, though much more slowly, finding a handhold or a foothold, then taking some time to hold her place, and very unsteadily, as Zak tightened the rope between them.

He poked around for a bit, seeking where stone ended and illusion began, and finally tapped at a spot which was not there.

He found the door and fell through the magical opening onto the floor of the corridor they had been walking. He poked his head back into the lair of the undead beholder, for that was what he believed the floating skull to be, and began pulling with all his strength to assist Galathae's climb.

She was almost to him when the skull reappeared, right where she had banished it.

Zak reached down and grabbed Galathae by the shoulder, hoisting her, tugging her, with all his strength.

The eye looked up at them with pure malice.

He pulled Galathae through and pushed her flat to the floor, then rolled aside, and just in time as a white ray flashed through the dimensional opening, angled up, and where it struck the corridor's ceiling, the stone simply disintegrated, leaving an angled ten-foot-deep shaft up into the stone.

"We have to kill it," Zak said, but Galathae shook her head.

Zak crawled for the unseen portal and poked his head through just for an eyeblink, to confirm that the monster was still there.

Still crawling, he backed up. "We cannot leave this here for those who come behind us, or for our friends returning."

Galathae's voice was growing weaker by the word, her eyes rolling up in their sockets as consciousness flitted away. "Zak, I cannot."

He wasn't asking her to.

"Zaknafein!" she called weakly as the weapon master got to his feet and charged, both hands again on Soliardis.

He leaped through the portal and back into the other-dimensional lair, blindly hoping the monster had not moved.

PART 3

A GATHERING
OF HEROES

Of all the traits I find important in those with whom I surround myself, the one that matters most to me is the value of that person's word. Without that, there is no trust. Without trust, there is no chance at any true relationship. People who know me and see that I am friends with Jarlaxle might wonder about this, but the truth of Jarlaxle is that he has honor, that he would not coerce or lie or cheat on any matter of importance. He is a game player, and will bend the rules to his advantage more often than not, but he is not a malicious person and wouldn't lie to his friends if he knew it would cause harm.

Take his effect on Artemis Entreri: It cannot be understated. Entreri was possessed of many of these same qualities, though they were buried beneath great pain and unrelenting anger, mostly self-loathing. He had honor, but only in that it allowed him to hurt others.

Jarlaxle coaxed him from that state.

So when these two—add Kimmuriel, as well—give me their word, I have learned that I can trust that word.

Many times I have heard someone labeled as a brilliant tactician in battle or in debate or in commerce, whether with armies or weapons or goods or words, only to see that person up close and then shake my head and sigh in resignation—a sigh that once would have been disgust, but now I know is in response to something so common that I cannot hold that deep disappointment. For as I see the workings of their words and tactics, what I see is not brilliance, but in fact nothing more than immorality. For too often with these very powerful individuals, their true gift is a curse: they are simply not bounded by decency, and their ruthlessness that so many praise is to the detriment of them and—most important—of those around them.

They are foul beyond the expectations of those they dupe.

Coercing a populace to get behind you by lying to them isn't brilliant. Great orators playing an audience based on their predisposed beliefs—or, worse, fears—by making promises they know they cannot keep isn't a sign of brilliance or intelligence. Nay, it's merely a clear indication of a lack of ethics and character.

Cheating in a physical competition, as I learned most painfully in my years at the academy, doesn't make you a better swordsman—in fact, the result might prove quite the opposite.

Selling someone a miracle cure or coaxing them into a transaction that is meant to simply take their gold doesn't make you a titan of business in any moral universe. Sadly, though, in simple, practical terms, it often will make exactly that, a person who profits by sacrificing their character and inflicting pain on others in exchange, almost always, for excess.

This, too, is the battle for Menzoberranzan, a war for the commonwealth and the soul of my people. Lloth is lies and Lloth is terror, nothing more. But those indecent traits have brought her to unquestioning power in the houses of Menzoberranzan, and stripping her of that power may well prove impossible.

It is a try, though, that most of us have come to see as worth the fight and, perhaps, the inevitable sacrifice. It is a battle for what is right, a war that will resonate to all who survive it and to their children and descendants who come after.

We need not win and eliminate Lloth to open more eyes to the truth. Because if we can do that, then they will see.

And so, we shall see.

—Drizzt Do'Urden

CHAPTER 14

Two Roads of Responsibility

Looking out through her balcony window, Catti-brie couldn't help but be charmed. After a fresh snow, Pikel and Ivan Bouldershoulder had come to visit the Ivy Mansion, and more specifically, to visit Brie. The three of them were outside on the hill, where Ivan was using his masonry tools to help Pikel calculate and fashion the appropriate banks in the long ice slide they were building.

Catti-brie grinned wider when Pikel waved his new arm, stark white and seemingly made of pressed ice, to create a wash of water over the course, then ran along beside it, Brie galloping behind and falling on her face in the snow every third step. Pikel kept that new arm, the gift of Qadeej, out over the course, freezing the water below with its frosty magic.

It was all so simple, so gloriously play, and just that: play. Whatever the current darkness presented, Catti-brie held faith that her little love would be surrounded by so many good people.

But the darkness *was* there, hovering about her. She had been visited by dreams the previous night, ominous and foreboding and so seemingly final in their terrible outcome. Drizzt would face Lolth again, she feared, and she would not be there beside him.

She had a role to play in that fight, she felt in her heart, and one she would not fulfill.

Drizzt wouldn't have a chance.

"It was just a dream," she whispered, trying to shake the fluttering black wings away.

She took a deep breath, focusing on the events outside and wondering then why she was just standing here and letting the dwarves have all the fun with her little Brie.

A quick spell to keep the cold away and she went through the balcony doors and over the rail, enacting another spell that let her drift down the side of the hill like a feather on an autumn breeze.

She landed just in time to see Pikel and Brie go careening down the ice slide.

"Not enough bank for the both of ye!" Ivan yelled in warning from across the way, and sure enough, the dwarf and the toddler went up high on the next curve—too high, and over the bank, to go sailing down into a snowbank.

Brie's shrieks of joy became cries of fear.

"Pikel!" Catti-brie called, running down.

"Hehehe," the dwarf giggled, looking at the child, who was covered in snow. "Snowgirl Bweezy." The dwarf snapped the fingers of his magical white hand and a burst of warm wind rushed over Brie, blowing away the snow and turning her terrified wails into a gasp, and one that calmed her down enough, clearly, to realize that she wasn't hurt at all.

"Hehehe," Pikel laughed.

"Hehehe," Brie echoed, and her entire face was smiling once more.

"Ye gotta put another two feet and an overhanging curve to it if ye're to be sliding down together, ye dolt," Ivan bellowed, coming over.

"A little too daring there, Pikel?" Catti-brie asked, moving beside them. "Perhaps less of a slope?"

"Hehehe," both the dwarf and the toddler said together, and Brie added, looking straight at Catti-brie defiantly, "No!"

"Brie," Catti-brie said in her best mother voice.

The toddler looked away.

"Brie," Catti-brie repeated to no response. "Brie. Brie!"

"No!" the toddler said.

"Bweezy," Pikel called and the little girl swung about, her smile wide.

"Bweezy?" Catti-brie asked.

"Bweezy!" insisted Brie.

"Brie?"

"No, Bweezy! Not Brie!"

Catti-brie started to respond, but stopped mid-correction, mid-explanation. What was the point? Some battles weren't worth fighting.

"Breezy," she said instead and the little girl beamed and Pikel issued another "hehehe."

"Ye gonna stand there missin' all the fun, or ye gonna take a run?" Ivan asked Catti-brie.

Catti-brie only considered it for a heartbeat, before announcing, "I'm going to take a run."

So she did. And then again. And again with Breezy. And one with Ivan leading all four of them in a chain that had Catti-brie at the back of the line whipping around the corners and almost—almost—going over the banks on the curve.

These were the moments, Catti-brie realized then, and it was a reminder, not an epiphany.

This simple little play was what made life worth it. Not Bruenor's gold or Jarlaxle's network, and not some adventure or war—those were fortunate luxuries and painful necessities—but this, this simple, childish, joyful play, was what truly made it all worth it to Catti-brie. Because this was love, this was friendship, this was family.

It wasn't perfect because Drizzt wasn't here, but moments like this were the perfection they hoped to secure.

That Drizzt was literally fighting to obtain for them—the culmination of the journey that had followed him out of Menzoberranzan nearly two centuries before—and Catti-brie wasn't with him.

She was surrounded by laughter and love and light.

But the darkness still lingered.

"IT WILL BE A GLORIOUS JOURNEY," GRANDMASTER SAVAHN told the two women she had come to see at the Ivy Mansion in Longsaddle. "Ilnezhara will arrive in the morning and your darling Brie will enjoy the world opened wide before her, flying in a season that she has not seen from so far above."

"Breezy," Catti-brie said.

"Yes, quite. The dragon sisters do love to fly up high, where the winds are strong. Fear not, for we have saddles with tethers . . ."

She stopped when she noted that Catti-brie was smiling.

"What is it?" Savahn asked. "There are great winds up there."

"I think she means the name," Penelope remarked, though she seemed no less lost about what Catti-brie had found so humorous.

"The name?"

"My daughter," Catti-brie said. "She has decided not to answer to Brie any longer. We are to call her Breezy. In familial situations, at least, though I suspect it won't be worth your—either of your—trouble to refuse."

"She is headstrong," Penelope agreed.

"Breezy?" Savahn paused and considered that for a bit, then nodded her approval.

"Uncle Pikel's doing, only with him and with her, it is *Bweezy*."

All three shared a laugh at that.

"So fitting," Savahn agreed. "Very well, then, Breezy it is, and your little Breezy will know a glorious ride with me back to the Monastery of the Yellow Rose, if you agree."

"I'm not sure that I do," Catti-brie said, drawing looks of surprise from both Grandmaster Savahn and Penelope.

"She will be perfectly safe, I assure—"

"Of course, she will," Catti-brie immediately answered, her tone and expression making it clear that she had nothing but trust in the monk. "It is just that—"

"That you're missing Drizzt, and feeling guilty about letting him walk into darkness without you," Penelope interjected.

Catti-brie shot her a scowl, confirming that the Harpell wizard had been correct.

"Because you should be there with him," Penelope pressed, and Catti-brie's expression turned to one of surprise.

"It is my understanding that your reason for returning to this life those few years ago was to wage exactly this battle beside Drizzt Do'Urden," Savahn added.

"I returned to do battle with the avatar of Lolth in the service of my goddess Mielikki," Catti-brie replied. "And so I did."

"This is not part of that same battle?" Penelope asked.

"I know not, but things have changed."

"Because of your child," Savahn said.

"Of course, and because my relationship with Mielikki, and more than that, Drizzt's relationship with Mielikki, has changed."

"It is the child," Penelope stated.

"Breezy," Savahn said with a disarming smile, lowering the tension in the room.

"Of course it is," Catti-brie admitted.

"But not for her safety," Savahn stated.

"Nor her training," Penelope added.

"You fear that she will not remember you," said Savahn. "Every parent has those moments of fear, and every grandparent, surely. The notion that you will become just a distant whisper to a child you so dearly love is not a comforting one. I am sure it is with heavy heart that Drizzt went to meet his destiny, for certainly he feels the same as you do now."

"And I am here to make sure that Breezy will know him should he not return," Catti-brie said.

"As if King Bruenor would let that happen!" Penelope said. "Or Regis and Donnola, or Wulfgar. Or either of us here."

"Are you telling me to go to Menzoberranzan?"

"Hardly that," said Savahn. "But we are showing you that the possibility is there, should you choose to go. Fear not for Breezy, no more than Drizzt does. She has many who love her, many who see her promise, many who love her parents. Were it not for Breezy, where would Catti-brie now be?"

"Banishing and destroying demons in Menzoberranzan."

"And with all we've just discussed?"

Catti-brie shrugged her shoulders and shook her head. Her heart was telling her to go and not to go at the same time.

"Should you decide to go, Gromph has the item known as Agatha's Mask," Penelope said. "It was offered to Artemis Entreri, but the man would not travel to the Underdark with Jarlaxle."

"I appreciate all you both have to say, but I have a lot to think about. Do not leave with my daughter, not yet. I'm not sure of my course, and even less sure of the farewell I should offer to her if I decide to go."

"Do not be distressed, my friend," Savahn said, but the words were nothing more than puffs of air to Catti-brie, who was truly torn. She found Breezy and retired to her room with her child.

Thinking.

GROMPH SLOWLY CLOSED THE LID ON THE MAGNIFICENT coffin in the secret side room of the mansion he had constructed in a dimensional pocket accessed from his chambers in the Hosttower of the Arcane. The mansion was now a permanent fixture, solidified by daily renewals that Gromph had cast for a year. The entrance, protected with many wards and non-detection spells, was cleverly hidden behind a secret bookcase in his appointed rooms.

Tens of thousands of gold pieces had gone into constructing this sarcophagus, to say nothing of the physical and emotional pain Gromph had endured in creating that which lay within it.

The chimes rang again, a melody pure, a cadence mournful.

With a sigh, Gromph left the chamber and moved along that dark corridor, then up the stairs to pass through a wall that only appeared to be a wall, stepping out through a glass case filled with illusionary trinkets and into the dining hall of his fantastic home. A dozen nearly translucent, ghostly figures moved about, setting the table for the guests he anticipated would arrive this very night.

One ghostly servant moved up to him slowly. While others were dressed in the attire one might expect of serving waiters or cooks, this one wore the image of a formal suit seen at the courts of noblemen in Waterdeep.

"It is Lord Parise Ulfbinder?" Gromph asked.

The servant nodded and Gromph breathed a sigh of relief. He needed to speak with the man, a Shadovar lord and a trusted resident of the reconstructed Hosttower, privately, and he feared that the ever-curious and perceptive Lady Avelyere might arrive at the mansion before Parise.

Avelyere knew that something was going on, Gromph had come to believe. He felt bad for deceiving her, which surprised him, for though he had come to think of Avelyere as a friend, Gromph Baenre had never been bothered by lying.

In Menzoberranzan, lying was surviving.

That thought left a grin on his face as he followed the ghostly servant through the chamber and down the hall past the sitting room to the foyer.

Two guards stood by the doorway of shimmering purple light. Unlike the magical creations that served him in this place—preparing his food, making his bed, bringing him whatever clothing, items, or books he desired—these two were something different, something far more tangible. Twelve feet tall and carrying huge spike shields and serrated blades, the formidable constructs had taken Gromph four months each to complete, but what wizard worth the status of archmage shouldn't have a couple of iron golems guarding the mansion that took him a full year of diligent and persistent spellcasting to make permanent?

When the chimes rang again, Gromph nodded to his butler, who pulled down on the golden-stranded rope hanging to the side of the purple entryway.

Something unseen behind the swirling violet hue shifted, two walls of iron sliding back, allowing a man to come through the thick fog.

He came in glancing left and right nervously, as he always did, as almost everyone who was not Jarlaxle or Kimmuriel always did when passing between the metal sentries.

"Archmage, it is good to see you," Lord Parise Ulfbinder said with a bow.

Always the polite one, Gromph thought, seeing the flattery for what it was, but appreciating the respect nonetheless.

"I am glad that you managed to return early," Gromph replied.

"I rode back to Luskan on a cloud," Lord Parise replied with a chuckle. "Good fortune alone put Caecilia on the same road as I—well, above the road, if you will, as she, too, hurried back for the council you have called for this evening."

"And you found the Twisted One?"

"Indeed, Archmage. He was in Baldur's Gate, as you predicted."

"With?"

"Again, as you predicted," Lord Parise replied.

Gromph nodded. "How did you explain them to Caecilia? I assume you did as I bade and brought them beside you."

"As I was instructed. And the giantess asked no questions about it. She knows Jarlaxle's associate, of course, and has heard the whispers as to why he would not venture to the deep Underdark beside Drizzt and Jarlaxle, and so understood or at least suspected why the two might be together, and together with me returning to Luskan."

"Jarlaxle's friend knows nothing of this other matter with the Twisted One?"

"Of course not. Nor would he care."

"And Avelyere?"

"She is intrigued by the tasks I have put to her, as you asked of me," Lord Parise admitted. "But she is no fool and knows that the business of the Archmage of the Hosttower is yours alone to share."

"Do you understand your role in my designs?"

"The role of caretaker, nothing more, and I am humbled that you have chosen me for this most trusted duty."

"You are protecting more than my possessions."

"Eagerly, my friend. Eagerly."

Gromph nodded to Parise's left arm, and the man pulled up the loose sleeve of his voluminous robe nearly all the way to his shoulder, revealing a wound more than two inches square that had been cut out of his flesh, just behind his bicep.

"I am growing old, Archmage, and feeble, and I do not much like it."

"What is that common saying among you humans?"

"Growing old is better than not growing old," Parise said with a laugh, but he cut it short and in a serious tone added, "But now I know better. And now you have shown me a possibility I cannot resist."

"Thank the Twisted One. This school of the arcane arts is his specialty. He taunts death and intends to cheat it."

"I already have thanked him. I will bring him when the last of your guests this evening have departed, as you instructed."

Gromph nodded.

"May I see it?"

Gromph considered the request for a moment, particularly given the impatience and eagerness in the tone behind the words. Not for the first time, the powerful drow wondered if he should have trusted this duty to one less . . . ambitious and accomplished.

A few heartbeats later, he shook the notion away, reminding himself that this place he had created from no more than magical strands, and more especially for the golems and treasures he kept within the pocket dimension, needed to be maintained and protected. His caretakers had to be powerful of their own accord, and influential within the hierarchy of the Hosttower of the Arcane. The possibilities for him to fill the needed posts formed a very short list, and given the dark nature of the plan to be concealed and protected, even shorter.

Kimmuriel would have been his first choice, but Kimmuriel was gone to Menzoberranzan, along with his second choice, Jarlaxle.

Catti-brie would have been his third, except that her heart was still tied to Mielikki, though the bonds were strained. And that goddess, called the Forest Queen, for all her own recent meddling with the realm of death, would probably not approve of Gromph's little game here.

That left Lord Parise Ulfbinder, a Shadovar man Gromph had come to think of as exceedingly honorable and good to his word.

Also, Parise was a man rich enough in coin and yet not quite powerful enough in spellcasting—though powerful enough to understand the concept—to be tempted by the promise Gromph was able to make.

Because of course, the other factors weighing on Lord Parise Ulf-binder were also of consequence, particularly his approaching mortality.

Having lived under a true and vicious tyranny, having thrived there by convincing his nemeses that they would be better off using other tactics in dealing with him, Gromph understood that the best way to assure allegiance and the fulfillment of duties was the concept of mutual benefit. Lord Parise had the means to do that which Gromph was doing, but he did not have the ability.

Gromph had the ability, and had promised to help him as soon as this current messy business was attended, however it played out. Parise wouldn't let that one chance go to waste, Gromph knew, and thus, his home, his treasures, and his meticulous and expensive preparations would be capably protected.

"You will not know everything about the most important chamber, of course," Gromph threw out there anyway. "From Kimmuriel and the Hive Mind, I have learned ways to hide certain . . . dweomers from any sort of detection, sense, or spell a thief might utilize."

Parise stiffened a bit at that. Gromph had used a tone to make it sound like a warning, not a threat, but the dire consequences implied made it both.

"Will you remain or return for the feast and council?" Gromph gently asked the man.

"May I remain for a bit?" Parise asked, clearly overwhelmed by the apparent invitation. Lord Parise was an important man at the Hosttower of the Arcane, but he was not among the elite wizards who comprised the Seven Scholars.

"Of course. You should become familiar with the home and to the staff, particularly to the door guards, who are not so forgiving."

Parise chuckled at that, but only a bit, and with more than a little nervousness behind it.

Gromph was glad of that reaction. He was welcoming the man,

promising the man a great gift, offering his trust in the man. But it was a good thing, he knew, for Parise to be a little bit afraid of straying from his directed course.

Even the clarity of mutual benefit could only take a bargain so far.

"YOU THINK HER DEAD," THE HALF-ELF TIEFLING ASKED IN a raspy voice that seemed deprived of air.

Artemis Entreri looked to the younger man's staff, which was made of bone and set with a tiny humanoid head atop it, to remind himself that the feebleness of that voice could be so very deceptive. He had seen this one's destructive power in action in the forest of Neverwinter Wood a long time ago. Very little unnerved Artemis Entreri, but the manner of death facilitated by the necromantic spells of Effron Sin'dalay was not anything he ever wanted to experience.

Effron shifted his uneven shoulders to unravel himself from the fold of his dark robes, then managed to pull himself up from the seat of the too low, too cushiony chair. He grasped his staff in his right hand for support, his left arm hanging limply behind him.

"You love her," Effron said.

Entreri shrugged. "Once," he admitted. "But now, it seems more a duty that I owe to her."

"A duty you think I should share."

"We are all broken. She is not an exception."

"So?"

"So without us, what does she have?" He wanted to add, forcefully, that she was Effron's mother, but he understood that the truth of the relationship was likely why Effron was having a hard time in seeing any of this from his point of view, and was resisting any notion that he should aid Entreri in his search for Dahlia.

"She is dead," Effron stated.

Entreri had only recently met up with the man, and had had to this point only a single and short conversation with him regarding Dahlia and the discovery of her signature weapon out in the wreck off the Sword Coast.

"You *know* this? You did as I asked and used your magic to search the nether realms?"

"I know only what you told me. The conclusion seems rather obvious."

"But you could not even bring yourself to make the attempt, as I asked."

"It is not so easy a task," Effron snapped back, clearly not enjoying Entreri's presumptuous tone, "and one that could take many tendays. Those realms of the dead are vast, and populated by the often bitter and uncooperative souls of many millennia."

Entreri started to respond, but the door to the small room pushed open and Lord Parise entered.

"Come, Effron, you and I have much to discuss before I return you," he said.

"I will be back in Baldur's Gate this very night," the tiefling insisted.

"Before then, of course," said Lord Parise. "I have an engagement with the other masters of this tower this evening, and we will long be finished before I prepare for that event."

"You will try as I asked?" Entreri said to Effron as the twisted man shambled for the door.

"I am in such demand," he replied with a snort. "Everyone has a request."

"Some of us pay very well," said Lord Parise.

Entreri rolled his fingertips against his palms. Not too long ago, he might have cut down the pompous ass on the spot, taken his wealth, and thus paid Effron very well for the trouble of searching the nether realms.

Now, though, he just offered a withering glare.

"After the gathering this evening—" Parise began.

"Am I invited?" Entreri asked.

"Of course not."

"Good."

"After, when we are done, Archmage Gromph would speak with you."

Lord Parise ushered Effron through the door, then closed it behind him, leaving Entreri alone in the room. He had come along willingly back to Luskan with Effron and Lord Parise, thinking that this was all about his search.

Now, he was beginning to realize that it was mere coincidence that had put him with the Twisted One, or perhaps that Gromph and Parise had used his street knowledge and ability to find Effron to lead them to the necromancer. Or perhaps just the opposite, and Effron had led them to him.

Whatever might be going on, Entreri wasn't happy about it at that moment. The room was comfortable, the hearth warm, the food delicious and ample.

But Dahlia was out there, perhaps alone and trapped.

Or more likely, she was dead.

And instead of enjoying the comforts of an archmage's hospitality, he had to *know*.

CHAPTER 15

Friendly Fire

A zzudonna and Ayeeda led the procession down the tunnel—or at least, they were the leading members of the band from Callidae. Floating in the air before them, some twenty feet ahead, was a conjured spectral hand carrying a flaming torch, the work of Allefaero, who remained a few ranks back with Nvisi and Avernil.

The journey had been uneventful since Allefaero, with Nvisi's guidance, had put them in a tunnel below the dwarven stronghold of Gauntlgrym, with no signs at all of either enemies or allies anywhere about.

The two wizards chatted easily, watching their steps, but no longer fully on their guard, and so they were taken by surprise when the torch ahead simply vanished, along with Allefaero's magical floating hand.

"Hold!" Azzudonna, Ayeeda, and Allefaero said together, the wizard pushing his way up front to look down the now darkened corridor.

"Where is your mage hand?" Avernil asked, coming up behind Allefaero.

"The spell is dismissed. I know not why."

"Would that take the torch with it?" asked a concerned Azzudonna, for the torch was no magical construct, although Allefaero had used a cantrip to light it.

"No."

Allefaero called forth a second mage hand, then motioned to Ayeeda, who presented a second torch for the hand to grasp.

The wizard lit it with a spell, then instructed the hand to move down the corridor. He stopped it some ten feet ahead, noting a rope lying among the stones and mounds of the uneven floor, one coming from the left-hand wall and angled toward the middle of the corridor.

Allefaero sent the mage hand to the left-hand wall, the group noting where the rope had been secured. Then back to the middle of the tunnel went the torch, and slowly ahead. A dozen feet, fifteen feet . . .

They noted that the rope stopped. Allefaero moved the torch toward the end point and left it there, hovering above the rope for a few moments, all of them peering intently, trying to figure out the riddle.

Azzudonna and Ayeeda drew their weapons and started ahead, the wizard and the priest right behind.

As they neared, Allefaero moved the mage hand away, just a bit, but enough so that it blinked away as the first had done.

Not too surprised, the wizard cast a light spell, filling the area.

"There is tension on that rope," Azzudonna noted. "That's not the end of it."

"A portal," Allefaero said.

"Do not," came a voice from the side, weak, but recognizable to the group.

Azzudonna sprinted to a jag in the wall, finding it to be concealing a small side alcove. And there, she found Galathae, struggling to sit up.

HE WASN'T SURE IF HE HAD PASSED OUT OR NOT, WASN'T sure if he had struck the floating skull creature or not, wasn't even sure where Soliardis might be, or his other blade.

All that Zak knew was pain. His ribs ached and one leg was bent horribly to the side, in a manner that it should not be. He could only open one eye for some reason.

He figured it was caked blood holding the other one closed, but he couldn't be sure.

I'm not dead, he thought, but didn't have the strength to say aloud. *Yet.*

He tried to roll but could not, for the movement sent fires of pain shooting up from his obviously broken leg. He couldn't even turn his head without pain, but he did manage to look up at the wall from which he had leaped, the wall that held the secret portal, and beyond it, Galathae. It was beyond his feet—or at least the one foot of the leg that wasn't bent out to the side—looming above him. Teasing him.

He had to get back to her, but wasn't sure it was possible.

Perhaps she would regain her sensibilities and use her healing powers to bolster herself and come for him. He thought back to her last words and wondered if she even knew he was in here.

He thought himself very foolish as he considered that—and did his best to ignore that he was practically praying to Galathae's goddess himself—and began wondering about his next move when a torch appeared up high on the wall, likely coming in through the portal. For a moment, Zak's heart leaped, thinking it Galathae. But no, it was held by a spectral hand, which blinked away.

The torch tumbled down, bouncing off jags in the stone, landing right beside Zak's leg and immediately beginning to light his pants on fire.

He couldn't reach it with his hand, so he drove the unbroken leg out to the side, ignoring the pain of the violent movement and the sting of the torch, pushing the flaming brand away.

He had to reach down and pat at his leg, so he did, again lighting internal fires of pain as he tried to make sure he didn't begin to actually burn.

It took him some time to pat out the sparks, and longer still to settle back and catch his breath, forcing down the agony the many movements had brought.

Another torch held by another spectral hand appeared high above him.

"What madness is this?" he whispered helplessly.

The hand winked away and the torch bounced and flipped along the uneven wall, careening outward off one jag and falling free right for the prostrated man once more . . .

THE HEALING SPELLS OF A DOZEN CLERICS WASHED OVER Galathae, strengthening her and sealing her wounds. She stood up with no trembling and stretched and shook her head to clear the last of her sleep. She came out of it with a short-lived smile before asking seriously, "Where is Zaknafein?"

"Yes, where?" Azzudonna volleyed back to the paladin.

Galathae wore a confused look, as if it had only then struck her that these other Callidaeans should not be in this place. "The mona allowed you to leave?"

"A tale for another time," Azzudonna insisted, growing impatient. "Where is Zak?"

"I . . . we came out."

"The portal," Allefaero interjected.

"Do not go in there!" Galathae said as some of the others moved back toward the rope lying in the corridor.

Many gazes turned her way.

"It is the lair of a strange and powerful monster," she explained. "An undead . . . a floating skull with a singular, huge eye. Magical powers, rays of energy . . ."

"A death tyrant," said Allefaero, Callidae's resident sage of all enemies monstrous. "An undead beholder. Formidable indeed from all that I have read."

"Do not go in there," Galathae repeated.

"Is Zak in there?" Azzudonna demanded.

Galathae stuttered for an answer, her head turning this way and that as if she was trying to remember all that had happened. In the end, she could only shrug

Azzudonna rushed for the rope and took it up.

"Nvisi!" Allefaero called. "Weal or woe?"

The diviner began muttering and tossed his rainbow gemstones.

Before they could finish their dance in the air before him, Azzudonna half disappeared, leaning out of the corridor and into the extra-dimensional space beyond.

Nvisi's cry of "Weal!" was barely heard, for Azzudonna's head came back into view, the woman yelling for Avernil. "Hurry, priest!"

Then she was gone, turning about as she went into the extra-dimensional chamber, rappelling down the wall with the same agility and skills she had perfected in her years of patrolling the glacial walls housing the canyons that formed her homeland.

She felt the rope jostle a bit as someone took it up behind her, then heard a gasp and looked up to see the upper half of High Priest Avernil, the man on his belly, half in the hallway above, and half within this magical chamber.

Several light sources showed in the chamber, far below: that of Soliardis, muted as it was, stabbed through the solid bone of a giant skull; a few tiny beads of red glow, floating about the monstrosity; and the two torches below, one to the side of Zak, the other between his splayed legs, burning him, as he tried to maneuver his clearly broken form to be rid of it.

Azzudonna dropped the rest of the way to the floor and rushed for her lover.

Before she arrived, a heavy rain pelted down, a sudden, magical rush of water that quickly dimmed and extinguished the fires, leaving her in only the light of the magical sword and those curious floating beads. She dropped to her knees and crawled for Zak, quickly crouching beside him. "We're here," she whispered, her hands about his face, her eyes growing wet with tears. "We're here, my love."

A magical light filled the area, revealing the extent of the carnage: the destroyed skeletons and zombies, the destroyed death tyrant.

Avernil came down and nudged her away, beginning his healing spells.

Galathae was next. She fell over this man who had saved her life in the previous fight and lay her hand upon him, calling forth the greatest gift of her goddess, her most powerful blessing of healing.

Others fanned out about them, Allefaero going straight to the death tyrant and pulling forth his quill and book to begin making sketches and taking notes. He even managed to snatch a couple of the floating red orbs, and placed them away in a small and secure coffer that magically sealed.

More magical lights appeared about the chamber, the Callidaeans fanning out to defensive positions behind the stalagmites, weapons drawn, spells ready.

"What is this place?" someone asked.

"A lair," Allefaero answered. "The lair of a death tyrant. Someone, I would presume our enemies from Menzoberranzan, placed an entry portal in the hallway to trap any coming from above to do battle against Lolth."

"Might Jarlaxle and Drizzt be in here?" a very concerned Ayeeda asked.

"Unlikely," Zaknafein said, sitting up, his voice strong once more. He shifted his leg back in from the side with only a minor grimace of pain, then stood, accepting help from Azzudonna. "If Jarlaxle and his band had fallen into this place, that monster would have been long destroyed, and the trap more clearly marked."

"We tumbled in before we even realized it was here," Galathae said.

"Then let us be away," offered Avernil.

"No, not yet," Zak said. "It's a lair. You know what lairs have?"

"What?"

"Treasure."

"We have a duty before us," Avernil protested.

"And there might well be items in here that will aid in that duty, even if it is only coin that will bribe the unaffiliated drow of Menzoberranzan's Stenchstreets to fight on our side. This is a practical matter, high priest, and not a matter of greed. The lair will unlikely be very large."

"But there may be more monsters," Galathae cautioned.

"Not for long," said Zak, and he stepped over and tugged Soliardis from the skull and led the way toward the rear of the main chamber. "Set guards in the corridor above, and drop more ropes and a litter, if you can construct one. Let us clear this place quickly and be back on our way."

CHAPTER 16

The Double-Crosser

W as it worth it to you, Braelin Janquay of Bregan D'aerthe?" Matron Zhindia whispered to the prisoner as they stood in the highest levels of House Melarn. Above them were the doors and stairway that ascended to the cells, the dungeons of this house that was built among the stalactites of Menzoberranzan's cavern roof.

"Was what worth it?" the battered man replied.

"Your embrace of the heretics. Did it bring you joy?"

Braelin shrugged. "I have sided with no one. I am merely a scout informing my superiors, who, to my knowledge, have professed no side-taking in this conflict."

Zhindia's voice grew shrill. "You murdered a Hunzrin priestess and a Vandree nobleman!"

"I defended myself—would not any drow in the service of Lolth do the same? Does Lolth encourage submission to those who attack—"

His sentence was cut short by a stinging slap from Matron Zhindia, one that had Braelin seeing spots before his eyes.

"I have witnesses who say you began the fight," she told him.

Braelin shrugged and shook his head. "If I had started the fight, do you think I would have been stupid enough to allow the Hunzrin priestess to summon a glabrezu to her side? Or if she already had the demon beside her, do you think I would have been stupid enough to—"

Another slap.

"Yes," she said, "I think you are that stupid. Perhaps you will realize this when your legs are being quartered and your drider body bloats with rot and stench."

"You are choosing sides for Jarlaxle," Braelin warned.

Zhindia laughed at him and nodded to the guards.

"Jarlaxle will not forgive you twice," Braelin quipped, drawing another slap.

A crank was turned to the side of the room and the heavy trapdoor above Braelin pulled up and into the chamber built into the ceiling. A pair of guards grabbed the bound man roughly by the arms and enacted the magic of their house emblems, levitating up and taking the prisoner with them.

They were beating Braelin before the trapdoor even swung closed once more.

STRIPPED TO NOTHING BUT A LOINCLOTH, LYING IN MUD and his own feces, his many open wounds festering, and with little more than the roaches he could catch to eat, Dinin Do'Urden wanted nothing more than to end his life and to deprive his merciless captors of their pleasure in torturing him.

They wouldn't allow that.

He tightened up as he heard the outer doors of this miserable place open, then relaxed when the guards came into view, dragging another poor prisoner by the ankles, stopping every couple of steps to kick him.

Good, Dinin thought as he considered the newcomer. There were only a dozen miserable captives remaining in this prison—in this wing, at least (though it wouldn't have surprised the captured Dinin to learn that Matron Zhindia, who took such delight in doling out torture, had many more prison wings). Three of the cells in this prison were smaller and double secure, most notably the one holding Dinin at the end of the row and facing the doors. Similar cells flanked his on either side, their barred doors facing each other just outside his own. The small cell to his right held a pair of women, the one on his left contained a single woman warrior, rumored to be of the Blaspheme and taken in the same raid that had cost him his liberty. He had tried to call out to her once, but that had earned him a beating that both swelled his mouth and drove home that such interactions would not be allowed.

Beyond that cell, down the hall to the left of his door, was the play area, where the guards and some occasional visitors took the prisoners for the most exquisite games of agony and mutilation.

One of Dinin's fingers and three of his toes were there.

Across from that area was the largest cell, a communal cage full of rogues from the Stenchstreets, even a couple of *iblith,* or non-drow. There had been at least twenty in there at one point, but simple attrition from the eagerness of the torturers had whittled that number, and no fewer than four drow had been taken for the Curse of Abomination as Matron Zhindia continued to build a drider army.

Thus, Dinin was glad to see an addition, and happier still when he realized that it was another drow. His odds of being next to suffer the ultimate curse had lessened, if, as he feared, Zhindia's bargain with him was simply a taunt to make him even more miserable when she gave him to Lolth as a drider. How could he not fear that, after all, given the torture and mutilation he was now receiving? Whatever sympathy he might feel for the new prisoner couldn't matter.

Anything to delay that most terrible fate.

"This one's important," said the man on the left who was dragging in the newcomer. "Gets his own cell, says Matron Zhindia."

"All three small ones are full," the other replied.

"Fix that," said the first, and his partner dropped the prisoner's leg and started for the rear of the prison.

Dinin held his breath again, for being relocated would certainly mean another round of torture, if not a visit to the priestesses making driders.

But no, the guard went for the woman to Dinin's left. He unlocked the cell door and walked in.

Her cries of pain began almost immediately.

The guard dragged her out by the hair, and every time she reached up to try to grab his arm and alleviate the pain, he paused, turned, and slugged her in the face. He moved as if to put her in the next cell down the line, which was now holding only another single Blaspheme warrior, but changed his mind and took her to the play area instead—practically shrugging as if to say *Why not?* Dinin could hear the chains and shackles, and could picture her hanging from the ceiling or attached to one of their nefarious devices, and chained by her wrists and ankles.

The newcomer was thrown into the now empty cell and spared, temporarily at least, from a beating, as the two guards went to the chained prisoner in the play area.

Dinin tried to block out her screams.

He failed miserably.

BRAELIN TRIED TO CALL UPON HIS MANY YEARS OF TRAIN-ing, looking for some way to strike back there and then. He knew that his situation would not likely improve and that any chance he might have of escape would have to be now, before they got one of his wrists chained.

He had practiced a clever move that might steal the sword of the man chaining him, and a quick trip would leave that man stumbling, giving him a free lane to the second guard, who was still over at the play area torturing a prisoner.

A clever move, but one not possible in his current state. His tormentors had handled him perfectly, those snake-headed scourges filling him with poison that made his arms seem as if wrapped in a weighty metal. He couldn't move fast enough.

He thought to try anyway—perhaps a quick death would be the best he could hope for.

But no, he couldn't bring himself to do it, couldn't bring himself to abandon all hope, however logical that course seemed. He needed to live, to help Azleah, who was in dire trouble.

Or perhaps she wasn't, and that made him angry and fearful in an entirely different way.

He didn't want to die not knowing the truth, as much as he feared it.

"I will stay alive for her," he heard himself whisper as the bracelet clicked shut about his wrist.

"For who?" the guard asked him, then slapped him when he didn't immediately answer.

"For Lolth," Braelin lied. "She knows the truth and will not be pleased—"

He ended with a grunt as the guard kneed him in the gut. "Matron Zhindia is Lolth's voice in Menzoberranzan, heretic," he said. "You would do well to remember that."

"For the short time you have left to live," said the man out beyond the cell door.

"Don't worry about the hardness of the floor," the first added, slugging him across the face and stepping back. "You will fill it thick with your fresh, soft offal soon enough."

Braelin slumped to the floor, his arm stretching up above him. He watched the guard close the door and paid attention as the key went into the lock. He listened carefully, trying to determine how many tumblers the lock had.

He could not begin to decipher it, and even if he had, he could only hope to reach the door with one hand, and that just barely. He'd never be able to pick any but the most basic of locks in that position.

And he doubted that House Melarn, so practiced with prisoners, would use a basic lock. The one on the door, at least, was a keyhole. The one holding his wrist was magical, attuned to a metal bar the guard had used to secure it—and one needed to open it, likely. There was nothing on this smooth bracelet to pick.

He was caught and he was doomed, he knew, unless Jarlaxle or someone else—perhaps Azleah, he dared to hope, for it was too much for him to bear in that dark moment to think that this woman he loved had betrayed him—found some way to free him. She had been overwhelmed, surely, given that there were three succubi. Three! Likely she was also charmed—he had almost fallen for their supernatural allure, himself.

Azleah was as cunning as any drow he knew, even including Jarlaxle. She would understand the concept of temporary sacrifice for ultimate victory. Braelin had to hope that any victory she had in mind would include him!

Around the corner, he heard a jail cell open, then close, and a moment later, the second guard joined the first outside his cell door. Braelin noticed then that this one's gear was not as fine as the first's. He had no idea whether that might matter down the line, but he had been taught by the best in the business that no detail was too small to note.

"Are we betting or not?" the second guard asked.

"With no odds?"

"Of course with odds! It would be a fool's bet to wager that this newcomer would be sent to the Curse of Abomination after that one. Matron Zhindia will take her time and make a spectacle of turning the brother of Drizzt Do'Urden into a drider."

Braelin's ears perked up at that.

"Aye, but this one is Bregan D'aerthe," said the guard who had chained Braelin. "Quite a message it will send when he is made into a drider, but possibly not one Matron Zhindia is yet ready to send."

"Has Jarlaxle declared a side?" asked the second guard.

"This one did it for him by murdering a couple of allied nobles, including a priestess. So what odds are you offering?"

"Three chances to one that Dinin Do'Urden is the first of the two to be given to Lolth."

"Four."

"Three, and if that is not enough for you, Preego, then you wager on this Bregan D'aerthe heretic," said the second guard.

"Good enough, then. Fifty silver and drinks for a month on . . ." The first man paused and looked at Braelin. "What is your name again?"

Braelin hesitated.

"Speak now or I will come in there and make you tell me." He rattled his key chain—two distinct keys, Braelin noted, along with the empowered magical rod that had sealed the bracelet restraint.

Braelin thought to lie, but to what end? Zhindia knew his name and had spoken it in her court. It was no secret. "Braelin," he said. "Braelin Janquay of Bregan D'aerthe."

"Did you see that, friend?" the guard named Preego asked the other. "He speaks it with pride, as if it means something important."

"Does that change the odds of the bet?"

"No."

"Then my coins are on Braelin."

"Braelin Janquay of Bregan D'aerthe," Preego tauntingly corrected, staring straight at the prisoner as he spoke.

"Such fancy words for a man chained and lying in someone else's filth," the other guard said.

"We should teach him that we're not impressed . . ."

The guard took out the key again and put it in the lock, and Braelin realized he had made a mistake, a point that was driven home to him repeatedly and quite emphatically in the play area of the dungeon.

He didn't remember being put back in his cell.

"YOU MUST BE IMPORTANT," BRAELIN HEARD DISTANTLY, the voice coaxing him back to consciousness.

"You have Preego Melarn as your jailer," the voice—the one they had named as Dinin Do'Urden, he thought—went on. "Preego is the best of the torturers, you see. He will inflict exquisite pain, as you've already felt, but he'll not accidentally kill you. Only those Matron Zhindia wishes for her own purposes are afforded the courtesy of Preego Melarn's attention."

"Like the brother of Drizzt?" Braelin asked before he could reconsider. He hadn't quite sorted through that information as of yet. What did it really mean for Zhindia and the Lolthians, and more important, for Jarlaxle and Bregan D'aerthe, to have the brother of Drizzt in her clutches?"

"So it would seem."

"Then you are who they say? Dinin Do'Urden, brother of Drizzt Do'Urden?"

"I am. Returned from serving the Spider Queen in the Abyss for a century and more as a drider."

"Sounds like a fine life."

"I am too beaten to laugh, my friend."

"I have heard of you," Braelin said. "Jarlaxle has spoken of you."

"He rescued me when my house fell from grace. A temporary reprieve, but one I'll not ever forget. How fares Jarlaxle and Bregan D'aerthe?"

"Some of the Bregan D'aerthe aren't doing so well," he noted, the irony heavy from his prison cell. The joke was a delaying tactic as much as anything, as Dinin's question had the ever-cautious Braelin on alert. "As well as any, I expect. This war has brought great tumult to the drow."

"And great promise."

"We shall see. I know that Jarlaxle would wish to remain neutral, of course, as is his, and Bregan D'aerthe's, way."

"That appears to not be working so well," Dinin replied. "With you in Matron Zhindia's prison."

"A misunderstanding."

"Is that not always the case?"

They both laughed at that, and both groaned a bit in pain from the effort.

"Tell me of this Preego."

"He is everything one might expect from an ambitious relative of Zhindia Melarn. He enjoys his work, but is very careful."

"As I just learned."

"Count your fingers and your toes," Dinin said. "Ten of each? How about your ears? If all of those remain, then no, my unfortunate friend, you have learned nothing of Preego Melarn as of yet."

Braelin just sighed and slumped back against the wall, his right hand, like Dinin's, high up above as he settled onto the floor. He had always feared that it would end like this for him—as was true with most drow, particularly male drow, and even more particularly for those houseless males who had no Lolth-loving matron to protect them.

"If you discover a way in which you might kill yourself with these clever bindings we have, please do tell before you attempt it," said Dinin, and Braelin's mood grew even darker.

He managed to fall into a deep reverie, escaping the tumult and desperation for just a bit before a harsh voice growled, "You stay back!"

He opened his eyes to find a spear tip right in front of his face, and reflexively crushed back against the wall.

"And stay down!" the guard Preego yelled at him. "Whenever I am coming with your food, you stay back and stay down. The first time you do not, your meal will be dumped upon the floor, where you can lick it out of your own waste. Do you understand?"

Braelin stared at him blankly—he hadn't moved an inch.

That did not seem to matter. The long spear prodded forward, tearing his cheek.

"I understand," he said with all the strength he could manage, which wasn't much.

Preego retracted the spear, then lifted his keychain from his belt, selecting the one for Braelin's cell and unlocking the barred entry. Eyeing Braelin slyly, the Melarni torturer then laid his spear in the corridor beyond the cell and placed the key ring atop it, before pushing in the door and stepping into the cell, where he dropped a bowl of some rotten-looking stew onto the floor, where it bounced and spilled all about.

Braelin reached for it, but Preego slammed his foot down on the prisoner's hand. "Did I give you permission to eat?"

"No," Braelin gasped, wondering how many bones had been shattered, and knowing the number to be greater than one.

The man kicked Braelin in the face for good measure, then spat in his food bowl and went back outside, closing and locking the gate.

"Now, eat," he ordered. "And sleep. I want you wide awake when I've time to play."

Braelin learned a couple of hours later that it was not an idle threat.

Braelin nine-toes.

HE LOST ALL SENSE OF TIME, FOR THERE WERE NO PERIODS of reverie and alertness, just hours, days, of darkness, and foulness, and torture. He and Dinin rarely spoke, though both took comfort in the conversations, even if neither had the strength to keep a discussion going for any length of time.

What proved even worse for Braelin was that he did not become numb to any of it, not the wretched, rotten food, the vomiting, nor the smells, the sores, the festering wounds. And certainly not the beatings, for Preego Melarn was indeed an expert in inflicting pain.

He grew weaker hour by hour, and kept hoping he would just die, always aware that they would never let that happen.

He began trembling every time he heard the click of the outer dungeon door—or maybe it was the clang of the trapdoor out beyond the dungeon and leading up to the main complex being shut. Did it even matter? He almost wondered if his captors had a wizard eye in the room, for they seemed to arrive at the exact moment when he had found some small bit of respite in his reverie.

Most of the time when the main door to the complex banged open, it wasn't Preego, but some lesser guard torturing some lesser prisoner, or, on two occasions, taking a prisoner away.

To be made into a drider.

When it was Preego, and not simply delivering food, Braelin understood that he had less than an equal chance of avoiding torture, for Preego would take Dinin half the time, yes, but more than once, he then took Braelin to the play area when he was finished with the Do'Urden captive.

This time he was startled from his sleep by the clank, and heard the footsteps approaching.

It was Preego.

"Please take him," Braelin whispered under his breath, and he felt bad for wishing such ill on Dinin.

No such luck this time, though. Preego Melarn stopped at his cell door, and he was not holding a bowl.

"To the wall!" he ordered, sounding angrier than usual.

Braelin was already huddling back, pressing himself so tightly against the wall that it seemed as if he were trying to meld with the stone. There was nowhere else to go, and he worried that Preego would find his lack of retreat as an indication of defiance. He watched every movement of the guard in terror, like a dream where he could not run fast enough from the monster.

Preego removed his key ring from the hook on his belt and placed the key in the lock, then turned it.

The click rang out painfully in Braelin's ears, as did the squeak of the metal hinges as the door opened, just a bit.

Just a bit.

And still, heartbeats later, just a bit.

Braelin peeked out from under the arm he had used to shield himself, looking skeptically, incredulously, at Preego Melarn, who just stood there at the slightly open door, staring back at him.

No, not staring at him, Braelin realized after some time, but rather, just staring.

Blankly.

Unblinkingly.

The rogue uncurled himself and edged closer to the door. He called to Preego softly, heard the person across the hall and Dinin over in the cell to his right both make sounds of surprise.

"Huh?"

"Hmm?"

Braelin uncurled further and stood up—aware that with these actions he was risking brutal retribution if his instincts were off—then slowly edged out from the back wall of the cell, inch by inch, until he reached the limit of the shackle holding his wrist. Still slowly, so very slowly and cautiously, he lifted his free arm out and turned his shoulders, leaning as hard as he could against the pull, stretching as far as he could for the cell door and the immobile Melarn guard.

Who still didn't blink.

Braelin heard a soft whisper down to the left, near the play area, and he curled back, anticipating the worst.

Instead, he felt waves of warmth—wonderful, healing warmth!—flowing through him.

He didn't know what to think. Jarlaxle? Or was this, perhaps, some twist to the Melarni torture techniques, offering hope and pain relief before snatching it all away once more?

Still, Preego Melarn didn't move, and Braelin realized that it was no act by the man, for no one could not blink for this length of time.

He uncurled again, stretching, stretching, but the door, though a bit open into his cell, was still beyond his reach.

"What is happening?" he heard Dinin whisper, but he ignored it. Mostly because he wasn't quite sure.

He turned himself about and stretched away from the wall again as far as he possibly could, then planted his foot firmly on the ground and bent to the side back toward the wall, lifting his other leg straight out toward the door and inching his way even further.

Another wave of healing magic came flowing through him.

He heard Dinin gasp. "What do you want?" the Do'Urden said, and he wasn't talking to Braelin.

Thinking the whole thing a trap and a tease didn't deter Braelin, though. Quite the opposite, it spurred him on. He thrust his leg to its limit and managed to hook his toes around the frontmost bar of the gated door, and pulled it back as hard as he could, though his foot slipped off the door in the process.

But he had the door further opened, and thus its edge closer, with Preego's arm now fully extended, and more, with the guard leaning forward, and magically paralyzed still, with no way to counterbalance the sudden tilt.

The torturer fell against the door, swinging it in, and leaving him to tumble to the floor of Braelin's cell, facedown and hard. He was close enough for Braelin to grab his shoulder and roll him aside to get the key ring, yanking it from the man's hand.

He fumbled only a moment before reaching up with the enchanted bar to unlock the clasp about his wrist.

A voice stopped him.

"You tell Jarlaxle," a woman said.

Braelin froze and glanced back, then sucked in his breath when he saw the speaker, wearing the robes of a high priestess of Lolth, standing outside his cell and looking right at him.

"You tell Jarlaxle," she said again, and when Braelin just continued to stare at her in confusion, added, "Do you know who I am?"

"You look familiar . . ." he started, but shook his head.

"I am Kyrnill."

"First Priestess Kyrnill Melarn," Braelin blurted.

"No," she said. "I am Kyrnill *Kenafin*. You tell Jarlaxle and you tell High Priestess Yvonnel Baenre and the Matron Mother that I did not intend to double-cross them. That I, too, was deceived."

"What?"

"They will understand."

"Let me out," said a woman in the cell across the hall. "I will tell them."

Kyrnill ignored her.

"Let me out, or I will tell the guards that you—" the woman reiterated desperately, but Kyrnill swung about and silenced her with a glare.

"Will you, now?" the First Priestess of House Melarn said.

"I . . . I . . ."

Kyrnill held her hand out before her, palm up, and cast a spell, magically summoning a red-and-black spider into her hand. She blew at it, and it already had a web strand up, for it floated off her palm and across the way, gently down to the floor before the opposite cell door.

When it landed, one spider became two, then four, then eight, then double that and double again, and all the spiders began skittering for the bars, now with Kyrnill casting new spells upon them all, so that they continued to enlarge, and by the time they reached the cell, they barely fit through those bars.

The screaming began immediately.

"You tell them," Kyrnill said one last time to Braelin, and she waved her hand in a circle before her face, spoke a word of recall, and was gone.

Braelin tapped the clasp, which fell open.

He went to Preego, pulling his dagger from its sheath on his belt, then stumbled over the man, who offered not a movement or a groan in response, and out into the hall.

"Kill him!" Dinin said, rushing as far as his own chain would allow toward the front of his own cell. "Let me out!" Each command was equally as frantic.

Braelin glanced across the way, to see the two poor women prisoners slapping at the spiders, which were now as big as a drow's head.

Braelin's thoughts spun as he considered his options. He played through the sequence that best served him. His strength was mostly back from the unexpected spells of healing, so he leaped back into his cell and dragged Preego Melarn in after him, hauling the man to the back wall, where he meant to strip him and chain him in his stead.

All the while, Dinin was calling to be let out and for Braelin to kill the Melarni.

But Braelin ignored him and ignored the sounds, the sobbing and shrieking from across the hall where the spiders feasted on the two women, the tumult from the other prisoners farther down toward the main door begging to be released. He blocked it all out and methodically went about his task. He had Preego sitting propped against the wall when the man gave a little groan and began to come out of the spell.

Preego opened his eyes just in time to see Braelin's open palm coming in fast to strike him in the face, driving his head hard against the stone.

Then a second time, and a third, and then a knee came in with great force, bringing the sharp sound of a cracking skull, and Preego's head lolled to the side.

Braelin pulled off the man's armored vest and shirt, stripping him to the waist before clamping his wrist in the wall shackle. He stripped him fully and quickly donned the outfit, then looked down at the one weapon, the knife, that Preego had been carrying.

Preego wasn't dead. The escape could be justified as a matter of simple survival, and if he left Preego Melarn alive, perhaps that would keep some measure of politesse alive between Jarlaxle and Matron Zhindia.

But how he wanted to kill this man!

He stumbled out into the hall, pulling the door closed and locking it.

Across the way, the magically summoned spiders seemed to be gone, leaving one of the women lying limp on the floor, the other curled up against the wall and crying softly.

Braelin didn't have that key—there was nothing he could do for them.

He did have the key to Dinin's cell, however, and that brought an entirely different set of conundrums swirling in his mind. Freeing this one, the brother of Drizzt, would be an act beyond Matron Zhindia's forgiveness, surely, and would almost certainly declare Bregan D'aerthe as siding with the heretics.

But how could he leave him? How could he go to Jarlaxle—to Drizzt!—and tell them that he had left Dinin here to suffer?

He went into Dinin's cell and released the man, who was still weak from hunger and from the beatings. Braelin began to reconsider his choice as he helped Dinin out of the cell—how could he hope to escape with one so battered beside him?

Dinin pulled away suddenly, stumbling, falling against the again-locked door of Braelin's cell.

"Go to the play area," Dinin bade him. "They have salves there, and perhaps other items to aid us."

Braelin nodded and rushed down, coming to an abrupt halt when he heard a cell door open back behind him. Reflexively he reached for his belt, for Preego's belt, only to find that the key ring was gone. He spun to look back into the dungeon to see that Dinin was not in the corridor. The door of Braelin's cell slammed shut.

He rushed back to it. "No, do not!" he called to Dinin, who was slapping Preego across the face, ordering him to wake up.

The Melarni guard coughed and shook his head, looking up at Dinin just as Dinin grabbed him by the hair at the sides of his head, yanked his head forward, then rammed it back into the wall, again, and again, and again.

Preego's unchained hand came up to grab and slap at his attacker, but Dinin would not be stopped or even slowed.

The back of Preego's head hit the stone a dozen times and more, until a soft crunching sound came with every impact.

Finally, Dinin let go and fell back.

"No, too easy!" Dinin said. He fumbled about for the key ring, which was on the ground beside him, then sorted one key and grasped it tightly in his fist, the end pointing out.

He drove it through Preego's left eye, twisting and turning, then tugging it back to pop the eye out with it.

Braelin looked away. Preego had offered no resistance, but he wasn't sure if the man was dead, or just far, far from consciousness.

He hoped the man was already dead.

Bloodied, Dinin came to the door and unlocked it, joining his rescuer.

"Now we can leave," he informed Braelin, tossing him the key ring.

Braelin locked the cell door. He glanced across the way at the two women, offering a sympathetic but helpless glance to the one still upright, and went down the hall to join Dinin at the torture area, where the Do'Urden had indeed found some salves and was rubbing them over his many wounds.

He hoped he hadn't made a mistake helping this one.

CHAPTER 17

To Forgive Is Not to Forget

I will speak with you after the gathering, Gromph heard whispered into his thoughts after expressing his pleasant surprise to see Catti-brie attending the meeting beside Penelope Harpell.

They called it the Seven Scholars, but there were only five permanent members, including Gromph, Caecilia, Penelope Harpell, Lady Avelyere, and Kimmuriel, who, though not a wizard in the conventional sense, could provide answers to questions far beyond the capability of the others because of his familiarity with the illithid hive mind. The other two seats were reserved for Catti-brie and Yvonnel Baenre, infrequent attendees both.

He looked at Catti-brie, catching her stare, and gave a slight wink and nod in response to her telepathic message.

Gromph then lifted a small bell and rang it, signaling the ghostly waiters to deliver the feast.

"Shall we wait until after the meal to begin our discussion this evening?" asked Lady Avelyere, who was always a stickler for etiquette.

"Have we much to discuss?" Caecilia the cloud giantess asked.

"That would depend on how much progress we each have made in our respective quests," Gromph answered. "And yes, I think we should begin at once, for I expect a long and exquisite meal this night." He looked to Catti-brie. "Penelope has explained to you the subject of this discourse?"

"I did not know she was coming until I found her waiting for me at the fiery teleport here in the basement of this very tower," Penelope answered. "A pleasant surprise."

"Nor did I expect to be here until shortly before that point," Catti-brie added. "I was with King Bruenor after seeing my daughter away to the monastery with Ilnezhara and Grandmaster Savahn. As it was an easy path here to Luskan, I decided to accept the invitation and partake of good food and better discussion."

"I think you will find the discussion very interesting and quite relevant," Gromph replied. "We five—now four with Kimmuriel off to Menzoberranzan—have been trying to craft a new spell of great utility and power, one involving the schools of divination and conjuration, and even a bit of chronurgy."

Catti-brie tried to appear appropriately interested. She took a glass of wine from one of the waiters and started to thank the server before remembering that this waiter was no more than a conjured magical specter.

"You have heard of the vortex warp?" Gromph asked.

Catti-brie shook her head.

"A short-distance teleport," said Caecilia.

"A dimensional door, then," Catti-brie said.

"Well, no—not quite. It is for other targets and not simply the caster. Allies or enemies, even monsters, can be thrown, and they need not be willing. Quite a handy dweomer—I will share it with you when next we meet."

Catti-brie lifted her glass in toast to the giantess.

"Think of all the creatures we can summon," Gromph said, then paused as the plates were brought in by a line of waiters, who set them down.

"Do begin," he told his guests.

"We can summon demons and shadowspawn, devils, animals for our nature-minded fellow casters. All sorts of beasts and elementals . . ."

"To say nothing of the nonliving possibilities," Caecilia added. "Bonfires, servants, a radiance to light a room . . ."

"What is missing from that list?" Gromph asked Catti-brie.

She replied with a shrug, not quite sure where all of this was going.

"People," Gromph answered. "We can teleport others beside us. Right now we can recall our companions along with us to our home. But we cannot—as yet—summon others *to* us."

"Is that not a matter of expressed free will?"

"We bend the will of demons and devils to make them do our bidding," Caecilia pointed out.

"But yes," Penelope said to Catti-brie, "it is a matter of ethics and free will. This is why such a dweomer is more complicated. If we intend it as a tool for gathering friends, or even as a manner of rescuing companions, it would involve more than mere conjuration."

Catti-brie offered a little wry grin aimed at Gromph, to not so subtly remind him of how much his life away from Menzoberranzan had changed him. That he was even allowing the ethical implications of fashioning a new spell at his table was something the Gromph Baenre she had first met would never begin to consider.

He returned a scowl, of course.

"So," she continued, "it requires divination magic to let the intended target know of the coming spell and gain their willingness?"

"Yes," answered Avelyere. "As with most spells, we must first look at all the potential problems . . ."

"What could go wrong with a fireball, after all?" Gromph said dryly, and when Catti-brie looked at him, she saw that he was staring her way.

He was trying to show her that he was still that hard-hearted and merciless grand wizard from Menzoberranzan, she recognized, and she thought it rather . . .

Cute? Or pathetic?

No matter, she realized. Gromph's ego bristled at any thoughts of emotional softness.

She turned back to the matter at hand, this notion of a conjuration *and* divination spell that would bring forth specific individuals. How she wished such a dweomer had existed when Drizzt had departed for Menzoberranzan!

Or even now, even when all of this was settled, how much easier would it be to bring Breezy back and forth between the Monastery of the Yellow Rose and the Ivy Mansion in Longsaddle!

Why hadn't this spell been created before? she wondered.

But as she considered it, she began to understand the potential danger here. An infiltrating wizard could bring in an army! Would any walls protect cities, or places like Gauntlgrym?

She looked around at the gathering and listened to their continued points and discussions, and for all the potential benefits, she wasn't sure she wanted their efforts to prove fruitful. She did appreciate their thoughtfulness and care, however.

Catti-brie thought that perhaps she should attend more of these meetings, if only to understand the lengths these wizards were willing to go—and the moral questions that came up.

If at all.

Then she remembered why she had come to this place, and it had little to do with magical research. She was here to see Gromph Baenre, and wondered if this present meeting would be her only chance to sit in on any.

She turned her thoughts away from the conversation, then, and on the grim task before her, and on her daughter—of course, on her daughter. She had sent Breezy away with Savahn earlier that day, perhaps for the last time.

The words of the others could not land on the distracted woman, then, even such alarming warnings that included terms like "trap the soul" and "magic jar," and other sorts of comments regarding phylacteries where they might store a piece of the intended target's spirit.

Yes, Catti-brie was glad that they were thinking all of this through, but at that moment, it seemed more a theoretical exercise, and nothing nearly as pressing as the very real choices and dilemmas now sitting before her.

As good as the food and drink were, she hardly touched them through the remainder of the meal and the discussion, and was only partially aware when the ghostly servants began clearing the plates—she waved away the one that came for her food, though again she didn't know why she had bothered with that—and when Gromph began saying his goodbyes to his fellow scholars.

"The food seems to have interested you less even than our discussion," Gromph said, and he was very near to her, which surprised her and took her from her contemplation.

"I have enough in my belly and a lot on my mind—too much, I fear, for such weighty conversations regarding the ethics of a dweomer that may never even become a reality."

"You did not come for my good food and better company?" Gromph asked, and Catti-brie started to respond, almost took him seriously, before realizing his sarcasm.

She was off her usual perceptiveness, and that, she knew, could not hold.

"I came because—"

She stopped when Gromph tossed something beside her plate on the table.

It looked like a plain white stage mask used by performers in the traveling troupes that crisscrossed the Realms.

But Catti-brie knew this item, and knew that it was anything but plain.

Agatha's Mask, it was called, and donning it could make someone appear exactly as any different person, even a member of a different humanoid species.

Undetectably.

It was the perfect disguise, and it was, as far as she knew, unique.

"I cannot replicate it as Jarlaxle asked," Gromph said, as if reading her thoughts. She remembered his work with the psionicist Kimmuriel and glared at him, suspecting that very thing.

"What?" he asked innocently—and he *was* innocent of reading her mind, Catti-brie realized as she considered it more closely, and his comment just a coincidence.

"He asked me many months ago, perhaps foreseeing the very events that now surround us," Gromph explained. "But no, it cannot be replicated by any magic of which I am aware."

"Perhaps such an endeavor would be a better use of the time of the Seven Scholars."

Gromph shook his head. "Oh no," he said. "For all the potential troubles of the spell we are now discussing, this mask holds promises more nefarious by far."

"You say as you toss it to me."

"I know why you are here and I know that you need it. You are traveling to Menzoberranzan to fight beside your husband."

"And you approve of my choice?"

"It is not my place to approve or disapprove. I know that you are going, and since you are going, this mask is your best chance to survive. I could polymorph you into a drow, I suppose, and place a dweomer of permanency upon it, but I fear that Drizzt prefers the look of a human for his pleasures."

Catti-brie replied with a scowl, "Every word you speak points to differences, and not in celebration of those differences."

"I just said that he . . ."

The woman's scowl deepened and Gromph said no more.

"Well, there you are, as you wish," he said. "Do you intend to walk the tunnels to Menzoberranzan alone?"

"I have done so before, and that was before I found my calling as a priestess of Mielikki and as a wizard."

"A very powerful wizard," Gromph said, the seemingly sincere compliment catching her off guard.

"But no, good lady, you will not be walking alone," he added. "And will not be walking nearly as far as you might think."

Whatever remnants of the scowl Catti-brie might have had on her face were wiped away as she considered that statement. "You're coming to Menzoberranzan?"

"That is my place. For all I hate of this war, I have come, at long last, to understand that I cannot avoid it. This is my fight, too."

Catti-brie nodded, thinking that they two would be a formidable pair indeed. She doubted there were many wizards across Faerun, and surely no one in Menzoberranzan, who could come close to matching his terrible powers. And, as he pointed out, she was no slouch herself.

"And I hope that one more will join us," Gromph said. "And you, dear Catti-brie, might be just the person to persuade him."

At his prompting, she followed Gromph through a series of corridors and rooms, coming to a door,

"I will join you presently," Gromph told her. "I have promised to show an associate about this mansion I have created. I am sure you will understand."

Catti-brie nodded and gave it not another thought. She turned to the door and pushed through, coming into a lavish sitting area with big, comfortable-looking divans and couches, overstuffed chairs, a bar covered in fancy bottles full of liquids, with crystal glasses nearby and a ghostly bartender waiting for commands.

She spotted the bare feet of a man hanging over an arm of a couch, and recognized the sword belt, or more particularly, the skeletal hilt of the sword sticking up from it as it leaned against the couch.

She found herself unsurprised.

"You seem quite comfortable," she told Entreri, walking over.

He opened a sleepy eye. "Weary from the road."

"I should be surprised to see you here, as I heard you were traveling to Waterdeep and then south, but I am not."

"I am not here by choice, or not for any choice you might understand. Why are you here?"

She held up Agatha's Mask.

"I already told Jarlaxle I didn't want it," Entreri said with a snort.

"It is not for you."

"Then who—ah, you? You are going to Menzoberranzan?"

"I am, with the archmage. This fight matters."

"Not to me."

"I know you better than that," Catti-brie said.

"You think too much of me."

"I think very little of you," she flatly stated. That got his attention and he pulled himself up to a sitting position, reaching for his boots, but never blinking as he stared with obvious surprise at Catti-brie.

He didn't put the boots on, just had them ready nearby, and continued to stare, his puzzlement clearly undiminishing.

"For all the time circumstance has put us together, does it occur to you how little we have spoken?" Catti-brie asked.

"We have fought together, and well, and for common cause."

"And we have fought against each other, for opposing cause."

"That was a long time ago."

"I remember still when we first met. Do you?" Catti-brie asked.

"Like it was an hour ago."

"I have forgiven you, but I have not forgotten."

"I struggle still to forgive myself, but nor have I forgotten."

"The dwarves . . ."

"Fender Mallot and Grollo," Entreri said and when Catti-brie's eyes widened with surprise, he added, "I told you. I have not forgotten."

"But have you forgiven yourself?"

Entreri shrugged.

"I understand," Catti-brie said quietly.

"We have all killed, aye?"

"Sydney," Catti-brie said, lowering her gaze. "Her name was Sydney."

"The wizard?"

"Dendybar the Mottled's assistant. I still feel the warmth of her blood on my arm. I still hear her final gasp, the last air leaving her lungs. I was barely a woman then."

"I was still very much a boy when I made my first kill," Entreri replied and he shrugged when Catti-brie looked at him.

"I had to," the woman said.

"So did I, over and over again. It became easier—too easy. It became more than a matter of survival, and more a way of life."

"Do you remember them all?"

"Of course not," he said.

"But you remember the two dwarves—or was this recently mentioned to you?"

"I remember that day vividly and always have, as you remember Dendybar's assistant."

"That was my first, and I hated it. And I still do."

Entreri shrugged and nodded.

"So why do you remember them, Fender and Grollo? Because it was murder?"

"I only said that I remember the day. I only learned their names much later. A century later."

"Why?"

"I thought it important."

"For them or for you?"

He shrugged again. "Did you come here to berate me?"

"I'm not berating you."

"To speak of old times, then? And if that, then why focus on such grim moments? I thought that we were all past that—forgiven, yes, if not forgotten."

"We are," Catti-brie admitted. "Perhaps it is just your unwillingness to continue on your journey that has irritated me. Your friends need you and you have abandoned them."

"An old friend needs me more." That caught her short, wondering who he meant. He continued, "And what of you? You let your beloved walk into darkness without you."

Catti-brie closed her eyes and realized that her tactics in trying to shame Artemis Entreri into going might have been a mistake. Seeing him lounging in such comfort, that undeniably formidable and even less deniably vile sword leaning on the couch, had been such a discordant image that she had gone down this path before thinking it through.

"Which is why I go now!"

"And where are Wulfgar and Regis? Where are the famed Companions of the Hall when Drizzt needs them? Or King Bruenor, who could summon several dwarven armies and march to Menzoberranzan—"

"Enough!" she interrupted. "Please?" She patted her hands in the air and took some time before opening her eyes. Entreri sat there on the couch, looking up at her, but there was no judgment in his eyes, just empathy.

"It's a complicated world," Entreri offered. "Which is why Gromph asked you to convince me to go."

"He did, but I know not why."

"Because I know House Melarn. I was with Jarlaxle and Drizzt when we overwhelmed the place. I know it well, and"—he reached down and produced his jeweled dagger—"this dagger terrifies Zhindia Melarn."

"You think he means to use that against her? To terrify her into surrender?"

"Perhaps. I expect that he has little desire for a prolonged fight and intends to decapitate the Lolthians quickly. Perhaps this is the executioner's tool he believes will accomplish the task."

Catti-brie considered it for a few moments. "I wonder, though, why he would ask both of us along. If I mean to use the mask . . ."

"I don't need it," Entreri assured her.

"Then you are coming?"

"I haven't decided. I find myself needed in two different places."

"Menzoberranzan and elsewhere?"

"Yes—as well as in my heart and in my head. I know you are no friend of Dahlia Sin'dalay—or Dahlia Sin'felle, as you probably knew her. But she needs me, needs someone, and though we parted ways not as friends, I cannot let that call go unanswered."

"If she is indeed still alive."

Entreri nodded.

"Have you learned anything?

"Only that her twisted son is still a foul creature."

Catti-brie raised her eyebrows at that.

"He doesn't care," Entreri explained. "But no, I have little information regarding Dahlia's path. She was in Waterdeep more than a year ago, and one woman told me that she went to Baldur's Gate, though I doubt the truth of that rumor."

"Baldur's Gate would make sense if she wound up with pirates."

"So would Luskan. Or half the cities on the Sword Coast. Or on a ship out to sea, for that matter."

Catti-brie couldn't disagree, though if Dahlia had gone through Luskan, she doubted that Jarlaxle would have been oblivious to it.

"I offer a deal," Entreri said. "I will go with you and Gromph, and let us cut the head off this Lolthian beast, and if you and I return alive, or even if you alone return alive, the hunt for Dahlia resumes. You will help me, on your word. Further, you will seek to find and aid her, if she needs it, on your own if I am . . . unavailable."

"You know my history with Dahlia," Catti-brie protested. "You know Dahlia's history with Drizzt."

"So do not ever forget it. But forgive it. That is what we do, is it not?"

Catti-brie really didn't have an answer for that. But it didn't matter. "You have a deal," she told Entreri.

"Marvelous," said Gromph Baenre, materializing beside the two of them.

"I knew you were there," Entreri remarked, and Catti-brie didn't doubt him.

"Rest up, make your preparations," Gromph instructed. "Our road will be shorter than that of others as soon as I can determine where to begin it."

"Can't you put us right into House Baenre?" Catti-brie asked.

"I could, but in that case, our road from there might be determined by the designs of others. My plan is more . . . direct. And our arrival might be noted by those who secretly work against our cause."

He looked at Entreri as he said it, Catti-brie noted, and given what the man had just told her, it made sense.

"You don't trust the Matron Mother?" Catti-brie asked.

"I am drow, and a male, so of course I don't. More, I have several sisters and a bevy of nieces, all who once and perhaps still pledge themselves to the Spider Queen. We would all be fools to expect that everyone in House Baenre, or everyone who claims to side with House Baenre, truly is an ally."

CHAPTER 18

The Optimism of Ignorance

With the help of Nvisi's clairvoyance, the Callidaeans searched the lair of the death tyrant in short order, navigating every twisting corridor and the many levels of several chambers, locating every nook and cubbyhole, and finding anything and everything that hinted at magical properties.

To Zaknafein's sensibilities, the haul was minor at best. They had found no useful items other than a single arcane focus in the form of a magical candle that could light and extinguish with a mere thought from its holder. Not insignificant in the Underdark, but not exactly exciting to someone with darksight. Any other treasure came mostly in the remnants of those many poor souls who became undead servants of the lich-like beholder: tattered clothing and rusted armor and weapons; a few small sacks of coins, mostly copper and silver; a backpack holding some exploring gear and another with a few potion bottles, though only one remained intact and seemingly usable, which Nvisi determined to be a potion of healing of the very least kind.

Still, the Callidaeans seemed perfectly giddy as they climbed the rope back out into the corridor above. They chatted excitedly among themselves about this great and interesting side adventure, and the things they had seen that none of their city had likely ever before witnessed.

Back out in the corridor, Allefaero dispelled the magical doorway to the death tyrant's lair, sealing it off forever.

They shared a large meal right there in the corridor, the priests summoning fine food and drink appropriate for the great victory that they'd had nothing to do with. Zak sat with Azzudonna and Galathae throughout, with Ayeeda and Ahdin Duine occasionally joining them.

Not far from them, a group of Avernil's priests sat in a circle, penning what seemed to be heroic poems about "vanquishing the tyrant eye."

"You must understand, this has already been quite an adventure for them," Galathae said to Zak.

"Is my surprise that obvious?"

Azzudonna laughed.

"You must admit that was a powerful creature in there," said Galathae.

"Quite deadly, Allefaero informs me," Azzudonna added.

"And quite dead by the time you all arrived here," said Zak. "Yes, a terrific fight for me and for Galathae, one that tested us to our very limits, and almost, had it not been for a bit of luck, beyond those limits. But this is the Underdark, and so you should all get used to such dangers."

"We of Callidae are not all utter novices to battle, Zaknafein," said Azzudonna.

"Of course not. But neither were you participants in *this* battle."

"But many here are young and eager," Galatahae interjected. "They have not known many battles—some have fought none at all—and even in those occasions, they were mostly fights well directed by their superiors, and with designed roles, as in the chamber of Cattisola of late, when some descended to battle the polar worms, with the priests, some of these same ones now here, waiting in the chamber above to perform their healing talents."

"True. And for many, the trip into the skull's lair was likely the first time they have ever been in the fortress of an enemy, any enemy," Azzudonna added. "It can be a thrilling thing, you agree."

Zak blew a sigh. "Look at them." He did just that as he spoke, noting the wide smiles, the sheer elation that they had gone into the lair of a monster. Even though that monster was vanquished before they arrived, its minions destroyed as well, it was indeed a new and exciting moment for these Callidaeans.

Now, Zak sat with these two trusted companions, one he admired greatly, the other he loved dearly. Galathae and Azzudonna were surely worthy of his trust, whatever an enemy might throw at them. He knew that Allefaero, too, was formidable, as well as some of the others, like Avernil and the two warriors, Ahdin Duine and Ayeeda. But still, watching the celebration around him, and regarding a creature they had not even seen animated, had doubts flitting about the thoughts of Zaknafein, undeniably so.

"I understand their excitement, but I do question their mettle. Do they really understand what they are walking into here?" Zak asked the two women.

"Do I?" asked Galathae. "Do you?"

"I do, yes," Zak assured her. "You?" He looked from Galathae to Azzudonna. "And you?" He could only shrug.

"Need I remind you that we of Callidae are not secure in warm beds, our bellies filled, our hearths warm and safe?" Galathae said.

"My journey to the cavern to rescue you and the others was not my first fight," said Azzudonna, and Zak realized that the women had taken his questioning quite personally.

"I know," he reassured them. "What you do not know, however, is Lolth, and the power and devotion of her zealous priestesses. You've faced monsters, even thinking warriors, but I can't harp enough that you've never seen this kind of cruelty. This fight now awaiting us will be one without quarter, without mercy."

"We know that," said Galathae. She nodded her chin toward the others, leading Zak's gaze there. "So do they. I promise you—they are ready. Let them enjoy their adventure before every celebration is tempered with the sense of loss from those among us who will fall."

"Don't be fooled by their joviality," Azzudonna told Zak, and she put her hand on his forearm. "They understand that the price might be high."

"The price might well be everything," he corrected.

"And they are willing to pay it in service to their goddess."

"Then maybe we're all a bit foolish," Zak muttered under his breath.

"Do you have a plan for when we arrive?" Azzudonna asked the both of them, ignoring Zak's pessimism.

"No," Zak answered. "No. Other than finding Jarlaxle and joining with him, I had no real idea of how I and Galathae would find our place in this fight."

"It's different now," Azzudonna said. "Avernil leads this group."

"Then he can find their place, while you and I and Galathae find ours."

"Galathae's path is with Avernil," Azzudonna declared.

Zak cocked an eyebrow at that and turned a sidelong glance at the paladin, who nodded her agreement with the statement.

"It has changed now, Zaknafein," Galathae said. "This is a formidable force you see before you, and mostly because of their trust in and love for each other and the divine powers given by the Dark Maiden. We should remain to the side of those forces allied with us in Menzoberranzan, aside even your friends now with these new additions."

"To the side?"

"Yes. We of Callidae know how to fight, do not doubt. To the side, we will provide an unexpected boon to our allies and ensure that our ways do not interfere with their own battle measures. With you guiding us through the maze of Menzoberranzan, we will strike hard and fast and leave our enemies reeling."

"You underestimate—"

"I do not."

"I only wish to fight beside my son."

"Of course you do," Azzudonna said. She moved closer to Zak and kissed him on the cheek.

"And perhaps that will happen," Galathae said. "But Allefaero brought Nvisi for a reason, I am sure. He is an eccentric one, his ways unknown, but his powers of seeing the future roads clearly are not in doubt to any who know him. We will find a path to best serve Eilistraee, and Azzudonna will almost certainly remain with us. Will Zak?"

Zak sighed and thought it over. He motioned his chin back toward the crowd of celebrating Callidaeans, examining every object and every coin as if they had taken the treasure hoard of Tiamat herself.

"They look like children, and ones I am leading to a slaughter," he lamented.

"You are not leading them," Galathae reminded.

"They are celebrating the victory as if the Spider Queen herself fell in that lair. And they weren't even involved in the fight."

"But I was right down there beside you. Did I disappoint?"

He gave a little chuckle as he considered the powerful paladin. "Hardly."

"They won't either. You will see."

"Allow them their little celebration," added Azzudonna. "And do so with the knowledge that they know well what might be coming, and if it be their deaths, they will willingly sacrifice all in service to Eilistraee, fighting for their beliefs."

Zak surrendered with a head bob. "I do not intend to die down here, and I certainly do not intend for you to die down here. Not after what we have found, my love." He reached up and gently stroked her white-and-purple hair. "It is something I never knew existed, something I did not witness in my centuries in my homeland. Something I never saw until I stepped back from my own mistaken judgments about my son's human wife and realized their bond honestly."

"You had lovers," Azzudonna replied with a wry grin. "Dab'nay, yes?"

"That was comfort. That was an escape from the realities around us. She is a wonderful woman, and I will always care for her. But it wasn't this. It feels as if we have only just met, and at the same time, as if we've been together forever. I cannot imagine my life without

Azzudonna. I am glad to see you, always, and yet, I am terribly afraid because you are here."

"I'm not going to let you die," she whispered, moving close for a kiss, and then whispered in Zak's ear, "And I know you will not let them kill me."

THE TROUPE WAS ON THE MOVE AGAIN SOON AFTER, MAK-ing good progress, their steps light, as they journeyed deeper into the Underdark. With every break, the clerics provided food and drink, and healing spells for sore feet, while Allefaero set magical alarms and Nvisi threw his colored gemstones, reading their dance, discerning their way, and checking, too, for any dangers that might be lurking nearby.

And there were many, but all were natural predators, be they animal or monster, and not Lolthian drow. Down one hallway, a mated pair of displacer beasts, large six-legged felines with a pair of whiplike tentacles sprouting from their shoulders, had built their den, one that Nvisi warned was filled with a quintet of cubs.

Zaknafein knew the danger of displacer beasts, but he didn't need to warn the Callidaeans, for they, too, were familiar with the strange monsters, which they called dirlagraun.

Skilled in conjuring more than plain bread, the priests magically created thick slabs of meat, while the wizard Allefaero conjured a floating magical disc. They loaded the magical cart and sent it down the side passage, piled with steaks that would keep the dirlagraun well fed for many tendays.

It occurred to Zak that the true terror of the Underdark was ever the element of surprise. One could never let down their guard in these tunnels and caverns, for to do so would invite an ambush.

In the Underdark, there was always some creature, something truly monstrous, preparing an ambush.

But with the continuing clairvoyance of Nvisi, that edge of disaster was dulled, and the troupe navigated day after day with little trouble, taking many short rests, and with Allefaero conjuring small, hemispheric domes of protection for the longer rests.

It proved to be the easiest journey Zaknafein had ever taken through the winding ways of the Underdark, and though he didn't know how that might translate when true trouble found them, as it eventually would, his confidence in his companions only increased. He put aside his fears at watching their seemingly overbalanced joy at raiding the lair of the monster he and Galathae had slain, and began to understand that any childlike or wide-eyed openness he might witness among them was not the whole story of these brave aevendrow.

He thought of their play in Callidae, where they danced and sang and giggled foolishly over tall tales and bawdy games, and then he thought of their more serious play, of his fight with Ahdin Duine in the half-barrel of frozen grapes, and of cazzcalci, the blood sport.

Yes, these aevendrow were easy to underestimate.

And any who did were foolish indeed.

They were near to Menzoberranzan, then, Zak knew, with some of the tunnels and multitiered chambers very familiar to him. They passed a fungus garden, the land of giant myconids, the mushroom people. Zak had been in this place in ages past—the ever-enterprising Jarlaxle had dealings with the myconids on more than one occasion, and traded with them for the mushrooms that formed the primary ingredient of some of the most popular drinks at his tavern in the Braeryn. Little seemed to have changed, for this entire Underdark world was quite literally set in stone.

Zak thought of his homeland, Menzoberranzan, the city and the cavern that had stood for millennia. Every drow family tried to put their mark on it, be it with circling stairways flowing from stalactite to stalactite, highlighted with faerie fire of varying hues, but those were such little details, he thought. He was sure that the city looked very much as it had soon after its founding.

Set in stone, like the ways of the Lolthian priestesses. And here they were, trying to change all of that.

He tried not to dwell on that seemingly impossible task as he sat alone on a flat stone taking a meal during a break in the march.

"How near are we to the city?" he was asked, and he turned to see

Galathae coming over to join him, with Azzudonna and Ayeeda close behind.

"By the measure of winding tunnels, or a straight line through stone walls?"

"Straight line," said Galathae.

"Likely no more than a mile. But we've another full day of marching, at least, through the winding tunnels. Why?"

"Nvisi has found something," Galathae explained. "Come."

They moved past many resting aevendrow, some eating, some taking a bit of reverie, and passed several side chambers in the uneven tunnel, which was barely five feet wide at some points, and as much as five or six times that at others.

Zak heard excited whispering—Allefaero and Avernil, he thought—as they came up on one side chamber, a multicolored glow spilling out into the corridor before them. Turning the corner, they found those two, along with Nvisi, who crawled about the floor, his seven gemstones floating in the air before him, forming various shapes, while the Ulutiun wizard created a sculpture across the floor of the chamber, an illusionary image of another chamber.

"What am I looking at?" Zak asked.

"A cave," said Allefaero. "Nvisi has used his distance sight to view a cave, not far from here."

Zak moved closer to the small man, even got down on his hands and knees next to Nvisi, who seemed not to notice him, but just kept drawing, or sculpting, or whatever it was, to bring his vision to form.

Yes, a cave, a large chamber.

"Where is this?" Zak asked.

"Do you recognize it?" High Priest Avernil asked.

"Maybe." Zak peered closer, truly impressed by Nvisi's work. He looked over at the small, round-faced man and was surprised to realize that Nvisi's eyes weren't even open. He was creating the image through his mind's eye alone.

"That is not Menzoberranzan," Zak said.

"No, of course not," Avernil agreed. "It is a cavern nearby, so Nvisi believes, and one in which our enemies are creating great mischief."

"How so?"

Nvisi said something unintelligible, then rolled his hand over the far end of the chamber he was creating, leaving a small illusionary fire burning there—although perhaps not so small, Zak realized, if it was to scale and the chamber was as big as it seemed.

He peered closer at the fire, noting that it was contained within a brazier.

"They have opened a gate to the lower planes in this outer cave," Avernil explained. "Nvisi says the barrier between the planes—"

"The Faerzress," Zak interjected.

"We call it the Mezzonel, the winding fabric of Piu."

"Piu?"

"Piu . . ." Avernil lifted his gaze and his arm, looking all around, sweeping his arm as he did. "The Everything. All that is and all that will ever be. Piu."

Zak nodded. "The multiverse."

"However we might name it," Allefaero interjected, getting them back on topic, "in this chamber, Nvisi says, the Mezzonel, the Faerzress, is weak and thin. The Lolthians have found it, or more likely have been guided to it by their demon queen, and are using it to efficiently bring in hordes of demon allies. It would seem that we have stumbled upon a sort of barracks for our enemies."

"How do we know these are our enemies?" Zak asked.

"They are summoning creatures of the lower planes," Galathae answered. "Demons."

That didn't prove anything to Zak, but he thought it best to keep that notion private. Certainly, Matron Zeerith Xorlarrin or one of the Baenres would not think twice of bringing in demons to do battle with Matron Zhindia's forces. Only a few years previous, Matron Mother Quenthel had filled Menzoberranzan's streets with demonic monsters.

The aevendrow didn't need to know that.

"We should go to House Baenre immediately with this information," Zak said. "Send a couple of us, perhaps. Myself and Allefaero. I can show him the way and his magic can get us there more quickly."

He noted the confused look Avernil was giving him throughout the reply, and the grin on Galathae's face as she looked at him, then at the priest.

"If we ever do go to this House Baenre, it will be to tell them that we have shut down this gate," Avernil explained.

"We are barely more than threescore in number," Zak reminded.

"Threescore with the blessing of Eilistraee," Avernil replied.

Zak grimaced. That sounded too much like the common refrain of Menzoberranzan, except replacing Eilistraee for Lolth.

"We have foresight of them, but they do not have such an advantage with us," Galathae explained.

"How many demons?"

"A horde, yes, but mostly minor fiends," the paladin replied. "They will be destroyed quickly."

"If Matron Zhindia's forces are summoning them, then know that there are udadrow there, powerful priests and wizards."

"Which is why surprise is our critical advantage here," said Avernil.

"They are not far from Menzoberranzan," Zak countered. "Do you think they would ease their guard with known enemies so near?"

"I am certain that they have many eyes watching the movements of any sizable drow force from within the city. But we are not coming at them from within the city."

Zak wasn't convinced, but neither was he expecting to change any minds. He just shook his head in resignation.

"We will go soon," Avernil promised.

"Make sure these are Lolthians," Zak did warn without going into details.

When Avernil started to question him, Zaknafein held up his hand and shook his head, offering no further elaboration. He blew a long sigh as the priest walked away.

"He is not so bad," Galathae said and Zak glanced over to see her grinning widely.

"I learned long ago not to trust clerics," Zak replied lightheartedly.

"Paladins are worse."

"So I've noticed."

"I want you with me when the fighting starts," Galathae said more seriously. "Our styles complement each other well. Azzudonna will be there with us as well."

Zak nodded.

"We will be on the outside rank of the square, likely the front."

"It's where I prefer to be," Zak assured her.

"Most on the perimeter carry a shield. Would you like one?"

"No. I have trained with two weapons since I was a child. No shield."

"I will protect you," Galathae promised. "As I did in the lair of the death tyrant."

"The lair of the monster I defeated while you lay wounded in the corridor above?"

"Protecting lessers can sometimes be painful," she said without missing a heartbeat.

Zak was finding that he quite liked this one.

But not in the same way he liked the woman now approaching, who plopped down beside him and gave him a fine kiss.

"My heart pounds for battle, and for what we will do in celebration after," Azzudonna whispered in Zak's ear.

He pulled her closer. "Think about staying alive first," he cautioned. "Then we can think about *being* alive."

"Take care to remember your places and your loyalties to all of those around you when the fighting starts," Galathae said to them both.

"Your concern is noted," said Zak, his voice even and serious, as was appropriate.

"I know," Galathae replied. "But it is always a necessary reminder when loving couples enter battle side by side."

"I'll not let a Callidaean fall because I am overcautious with Zaknafein," Azzudonna also answered.

"I will leave you, then," the paladin said, and she rose to go.

"I prefer that you stay," Zak said, and with a look to him, Galathae sat back down on the stone. "I would hear of our battle formations and plans while we wait for the diviner, should a fight find us. I have never seen a group so thick with priests and so thin with warriors and wizards."

"You will find it a pleasant surprise, then," Galathae said, and she took out a small knife to scratch some battle plans on the floor for Zak to see.

"NVISI IS LOOKING MORE CLOSELY," ALLEFAERO INFORMED Galathae, Zak, Azzudonna, and a few others who had come over to join them in their impromptu strategy session a short time later.

Zak looked back past the approaching wizard, noting Nvisi crawling about the floor, again creating magical illusions of some sort. He rose and brushed his hands against his pants, then followed Allefaero and Galathae back to the diviner, where his eyes became locked upon the magical image Nvisi had formulated. It wasn't a picture, but more a sculpture—a semiopaque replica of the chamber, it seemed, detailed now with stalagmites and stalactites, an altar at the end of an intricate summoning circle, and all of the entrances—complete with magical notes written into the sand explaining where those tunnels led, and which would be their entry into the enemy room.

Zak had seen great planning by priestesses in his days as a weapon master, with scrying pools and even miniature models of an enemy house, but nothing remotely as complete as that which Nvisi was creating.

If it was even real, Zak thought but did not say. Allefaero obviously thought this strange human a great asset, but what if he was actually more delusionist than diviner?

As Allefaero continued his explanation, it became clear that they were going to build their attack plan, in detail, according to Nvisi's premonitions and visions.

Zak had been in many battles. Rarely had they played out as planned.

"Zaknafein?"

As the sound of his name registered, he realized that he had tuned out the talk around him and that this was not Galathae's first call to him.

"Do you think it would be wise for you to go and offer insight to Nvisi as he dives ever deeper?" she asked, obviously not for the first time.

"I don't know, as I don't know this chamber."

"But you know the udadrow," Allefaero pointed out.

Zak shrugged. "Perhaps, but it is more that I once knew them than I know them now."

"You have seen such demon summoning, yes?" Galathae asked.

"Every drow in Menzoberranzan has witnessed such joyful moments," came the reply, and it was one that Zak could not help but tinge with sarcasm.

"Then any insights would help," said Allefaero. "The summoning circle? The altar? Even the strengths and weaknesses of demons?"

"You don't know about demons?" Zak asked with surprise.

"Our experience with creatures of the lower planes is quite limited," Galathae answered. "We know of the slaadi."

"Slaadi aren't demons," Zak said, only to muse a little before adding, "Or maybe they are. Their lord is, or was, I am told."

"Galathae's powers and those of the priests were more impressive against the slaadi than those of wizards," Allefaero said, then quickly added, "Of *some* wizards. We find that the creatures of these other planes of existence are often less affected by the typical elemental evocations of fire and cold and lightning."

"I think that true of demons as well."

Allefaero nodded and smiled widely, looking to Galathae, which Zak thought curious in that moment.

"Come, Zaknafein," the wizard bade him, and he followed to Nvisi, then offered his insights regarding the altars of Lolthian priestesses and the particulars, the few he knew, of summoning circles.

It was a short session, though, for things began to move fast then, as Nvisi had a sudden insight that attacking quickly would favor them. High Priest Avernil called his flock to gather.

"We use an eight-square, shield walls all about," he said. "Second rank, second flank protects the warrior wall. All others send forth weapons and bring summoned guardians about us. Nvisi will direct Galathae to lead us across the battlefield."

"What of Zaknafein?" Allefaero asked.

"He is beside me, right, with Azzudonna beside me on the left," Galathae answered.

"Perhaps Zaknafein, who does not know our ways, should stand to the rear guard and observe more than fight," Avernil said.

"You only say that because you have not seen Zaknafein fight," Galathae replied, looking to Zak with an admiring grin. "I have. He is beside me. We will want him first and foremost when we encounter the greatest of our enemies."

Avernil bowed to her, then to Zak. "I defer to your judgment on this, Holy Galathae."

Zak locked gazes with the paladin. He felt good with her beside him, and with Azzudonna close by.

"Allefaero will escort Nvisi and amplify his directions," Avernil added. "Mid-group, of course. I trust you will find the proper place for your powers, wizard, and I do not pretend to tell you how and where to throw your devastating spells."

"Most will be in support of the efforts of the priests," Allefaero answered. "To counter the efforts of those spellcasting against us, udadrow and demon. But yes, I do believe I have some helpful tricks to play."

With practiced efficiency that brought Zak a bit of hope, at least, the aevendrow formed into tight, even ranks. Those in the front rank carried two weapons, but the warriors on the outside flanks all carried a short spear and a large shield made of magnificent pressed ice. Those shields had hooks on the forward edge, depressions on the back, and the aevendrow secured them together, building a true wall of defense.

Again, Zak noted the precision. Clearly, this formation had been practiced and predetermined, since those warriors on the left flank carried shields on their left arm, opposite of those on the right—thus, even the shields had to be reversed in hook and depression.

He had never fought this way, and found himself intrigued by being a part of these tactics.

"On your time, Holy Galathae!" Avernil called from the central area of the square.

The more than two dozen priests in the formation began chanting softly.

"Nvisi!" Galathae called. "Guide me."

She began to move immediately and at a brisk pace, the square distorting only for a moment before the aevendrow resumed a near-perfect formation.

Down a corridor they marched, quickly but quietly. They came to a fork and Galathae didn't hesitate, veering right and moving along a straight corridor that ended at a stone wall.

"Nvisi says they will come in behind us," Allefaero said.

"Scrolls," Avernil ordered, and the priests broke ranks, each producing a scroll tube as they went, then unrolling the contents within, which were of summoned sealskin, and so lay flat. They checkered the corridor behind the square with them.

"If we have to retreat, speak the name Callidae repeatedly as you flee this corridor," Galathae warned Zaknafein.

The warrior nearly laughed aloud, realizing then that the priests were laying premade glyphs and wards. Avernil put down the last one, a line of sparkling dust, nearest to the square.

That would be the trigger if the enemy did come in from the rear.

"Hold, then charge!" Avernil told them when the corridor was prepared.

Zak heard Allefaero casting and guessed what was coming, and so he was not surprised when the wall before him simply vanished, revealing the chamber Nvisi had so meticulously—and astoundingly accurately, Zak realized immediately—replicated.

Even as the wall disappeared, two dozen and more glowing weapons appeared floating in the air before them, leading the way, and by the time the fighting square had rushed into the Lolthian summoning chamber, so, too, had come the spiritual guardians, the air all about them swirling with small celestial figures, flying about like an angry swarm of stirges. Translucent, the angelic guardians took the colors of the Merry Dancers—indeed, Zak could not help but think of that wintertime Callidaean sky in viewing them. He was nearly overwhelmed by the intensity of the sight, but those around him were not, clearly. He had seen the spiritual guardians of a priest before, but not like this, not with more than a dozen priests casting their spells all together and overlapping.

The square was met almost immediately by a group of minor demons, humanoid wretches that Zak knew to be manes. He had Soliardis and his ice blade up and ready to meet the charge, but nearly gasped when those demons met the leading edge of the guardians and began chipping away into pieces as the summoned spirits magically struck at them with divine radiance.

The manes seemed to be smoking, so many bits were flying away.

Not a mane, not a piece of mane, got close enough to Zak for him to strike at it.

Hardly even considering the move, he willed his magical blade into its whip form.

They had come in along the side of the roughly rectangular chamber not far from the altar and summoning circle. Nearly a score of drow were there, including several priestesses, with a handful of major demons, and so many, many more of the minor fiends, dretches and manes.

Allefaero struck next, filling the air above the altar with a sleet storm—but one like Zak had never witnessed. The raining cloud, too, looked like the Merry Dancers of the northern sky, and the falling sleet pellets glowed with radiance.

Zak managed a quick glance back at the wizard, to see him wearing what looked like a crown of floating stars.

He didn't know what that might mean and didn't have the time to sort it out.

For the demons came on, and came down, several chasmes knocked from the sky by the wizard's sudden storm.

Glabrezu, nalfeshnee, and vrocks—so many vrocks—charged in, pushing forward the manes and the dretches, which were reduced to nothingness by the swirling magical guardians. The major demons, too, were attacked by the swarm of conjured radiant beings assailing them, but they would not be so easily destroyed.

"Weapons to the udadrow!" Avernil commanded, his voice amplified by magic above the din of the sudden battle. In response, those floating maces and swords and spears flew forward past the demons to attack the enemy drow.

And so, too, came a pea of flame, green flame, flying over Zak's head and forward past the demon rank to explode into a giant fireball, but one unlike Zak had ever seen, for its flames were green and purple and not the normal colors one would expect. And they sparkled, seeming more like Merry Dancer radiance than fire.

Whatever it was that Allefaero had delivered, the demons certainly didn't like it. Several more chasmes fell burning from the sky, screeching horribly and melting as they thudded down.

So, too, screamed the udadrow caught within the blast.

The nearest major demons came on, but to a one, they were staggering, their forms diminishing, with bits flying off and smoke wafting all about. Dozens of spiritual guardians attacked each one incessantly—the demons had come into a killing zone, and every moment they remained within the diameter of the priests' collective dweomers, they were assailed and diminished.

And then finished off with great efficiency by Zak, Galathae, Azzudonna, and the others of the front rank, with most destroyed before they had even scored a single hit against the Callidaean group square.

The plan was working, undeniably so. With Nvisi's clairvoyance and divination, the aevendrow had caught the enemy wholly by surprise.

Somewhere behind came a series of explosions, which at first alarmed Zak. He realized, however, that in the corridor just beyond the passwall created by Allefaero, enemy support had come in from behind.

Exactly as Nvisi had foreseen.

And exactly where the priests had placed the many glyphs they had prepared in advance.

Zak trusted in those spells, focusing on the fight before him. A vulture-like vrock demon, green radiant flames from Allefaero's fireball coating it like a cloak, charged his way, and he prepared himself to take it on . . .

. . . only for the spiritual guardians to down it even as Zak lifted his whip to strike.

"Now, with me!" Galathae cried and rushed ahead, Zak and Azzudonna at her flanks.

The paladin bulled her way right through the failing demon ranks, out of the press and confusion, the smoke and the flying guardian spirits. That instant of clarity showed them the remaining enemies, the drow at the altar, and several large demons lying in wait—although everyone there, mortal and fiend, had also felt the vicious bite of Allefaero's green fireball.

But these were priestesses of Lolth, and Zak understood that they were far from finished here. He had to get to them quickly, before they could recover from the initial assault.

Easier said than done, however, as a huge and hulking four-armed beast leaped in his path. Zak knew this fiend, a glabrezu, with its crab-clawed upper limbs and giant humanoid form, like a great horned gnoll. Unlike many demons, this one's power lay not in its spells, but in its sheer physical toughness and ferocity.

He could defeat it, he was confident, for he had done so before, but it would take time.

Time he wasn't sure they had. Over the demon's shoulders he could see the priestesses casting spells: dispatching the magical weapons, healing each other and their demonic allies, and at least two of them dropping columns of fire onto the aevendrow behind him.

He had to get to them.

He had to get through this glabrezu—and fast

He leaped and stopped, using his momentum to sweep his whip forward and crack it across the face of the glabrezu, which snarled and bore in on him, those massive claws clicking eagerly.

And a brilliant light appeared, blue white, and Galathae appeared, rushing past him, leaping high with Bluccidere held higher for the massive demon, shouting a word Zak had heard in the last fight.

"Banish!"

Her sword came down across the armored forearm of one of the glabrezu's claw arms, a blow that should not have been serious, as the creature perfectly parried, and a single blow would not get through the heavy carapace-like shielding on that thick arm.

But the magic of it, divine magic gifted from Eilistraee, *did* get through, flowing from the sword and into the monster, stabbing at its very existence on this Material Plane.

A blinding flash, a smell of sulfur, and the glabrezu was, quite simply, gone.

Galathae landed awkwardly and overbalanced, stumbling forward, and Zak turned to follow and protect her, but changed his mind as Azzudonna came flashing past in pursuit of the paladin.

His companion thus covered by his lover, Zak went instead at the altar and the trio of priestesses standing there.

One snarled at him and lifted a four-headed scourge of living, hissing snakes his way. A second crossed the hands of her outstretched arms before her in the spider symbol, thumbs as pedipalps, eight fingers as legs—a typical casting pose for a Lolthian priestess—while the third dropped a globe of darkness over the group.

Zak almost laughed, having seen this play a dozen times before.

His mind had already clarified his course. The snakes of the scourge needed no visual help to find their target.

The coming spell from the priestess was one that would strike the area before her, so she needed no clear target.

With another enemy approaching, that globe of darkness would have immediately changed the battlefield in the favor of the Lolthians, but with Zak, it only obscured the true power of the priestesses' attacker. For the reputation of Zaknafein Do'Urden had been written with the blood of such opponents, so his response was equally as ingrained.

His right arm went out across his chest, a sweeping crack of the whip, followed by three short and sudden snaps. Down he dove into a roll, still moving forward, but angling left.

He felt the waves of heat, a fan of flames, just above him, a yelp of pain to his left.

He turned Soliardis into a light blade once more as he came around and up, reversed his grip and kept charging, but stabbed a backhand as he passed the second priestess, taking grim satisfaction in her groan of profound pain as the sheath of stabbing light drove in through her side.

That left one, who had been standing just to the left and slightly behind the altar: the priestess who had summoned the darkness.

Back to the right he went, sliding down to the base of the altar. As he came against it, using its solidity to brace him as he stood, he reached out left with his ice blade and tapped it hard against the stone, immediately retracting and diving forward, rolling over the rectangular stone.

The priestess dropped her enchantment of darkness and reached forward with the scourge, her other hand glowing in sickly green ooze that would inflict a terrible disease or curse.

Except Zak didn't care about either of those things, because he was behind her, while she was attacking the spot where he had tapped the stone.

Guided by fury, a growl escaping him, he slashed across with his light blade, Soliardis easily defeating the meager magical armor worn by the priestess, cracking through her skull and sliding through the soft tissue of her brain.

The top half of her head flew away and she dropped straight down, the snakes of her living scourge writhing and spitting furiously.

Zak slid a step farther from them, knowing that some of these vipers could spit their poison with great accuracy. He took a moment to reorient himself and measure the attack.

The priestess before him was obviously dead. The one he had stabbed coming up out of his roll lay similarly still, but the one he had whipped still stood and still held her scourge, now with only two serpent heads on its tentacles. Blood poured from the priestess's hand and wrist, just as outrage poured forth at Zak from her grimacing expression. He smiled at her, and the priestess's eyes widened.

She should have been looking the other way.

Azzudonna hit her with a flying body block from behind, launching her forward and to the ground. The aevendrow warrior barely seemed to touch the floor as she landed, so fast was her rebound to her feet and her quick-step to stomp one of the remaining scourge vipers, her sword stabbing down to take the other.

She flipped her spear in her hand as she went forward, driving the butt of it down hard on the back of the Lolthian priestess's head.

That threat under control, Zak considered where to go next, but only for the moment it took him to see that the battle was all but over. The Callidaean square had dispersed into fighting groups, most going back to the corridor to hold the line there, or more accurately, to pursue the few remaining udadrow of the group that had tried to come up behind the attacker and crossed into the glyphed field of exploding runes.

An enemy priestess and a pair of guards, both men, remained very much alive in the chamber, but had dropped to their knees, hands held high in surrender. Others lay on the ground, dead or wounded, and it did Zak's heart well to see the Callidaean clerics going to the fallen—their own and their enemies' (the drow, at least)—and calling upon their powers to bring healing and relief.

Another group of Lolthians were pulled in from the corridor right before Allefaero's passwall dweomer ended, resealing that temporary entrance. They were all wounded, burned and blasted from the varying glyphs that had been tripped out there. They, too, offered no further resistance.

Which brought another issue, Zak realized.

He moved off to one of the exits and sat down to recuperate and to guard while his companions went about their business. Azzudonna joined him soon after, and directed his attention to Holy Galathae.

"She is consecrating the altar, the brazier, and the magic circle," Azzudonna explained. "The Lolthians will not use this chamber again for their vile purposes."

He nodded at that. "How many have we lost?"

"Many were wounded, but only a few seriously," Azzudonna replied. "One is gone, I fear, and another two fight for their lives. Still, it was a great victory."

"And what of them?" Zak asked, motioning to the prisoners, who were being herded in a small group against the wall behind the altar.

"High Priest Avernil and Galathae will interrogate them—you know from your first journey to Callidae that we are very practiced at this."

"And then? We haven't the forces to guard them as we continue."

"Nvisi is already at work on that, deciding the best course. If there is a place where we can transport them, we will do so, of course."

"And if not?"

Azzudonna shrugged. "That is up to them. We will know if they are speaking truthfully. If they cannot be trusted to be out of the fight, at the very least, then that is their choice."

"You will execute them."

"Would you?"

Zak thought on that long and hard, surprised that it was a difficult question at all. Two of the Lolthians had died by his own hand, including one lying with half her head severed. And those were certainly not the first priestesses of the Spider Queen who had felt the rage of Zaknafein, and likely would not be the last.

"Yes," he answered. "I would. When this is ended, however it ends—or even if it ever ends—we who are not of Lolth will not continue to strike against her flock. But they will come after us through eternity. Any mercy we show now to those who will not honestly desert the ways of Lolth will only lead to more misery later."

"War is ugly," Azzudonna said.

"So is servitude," Zak replied. "And so is Lolth."

He was glad when Azzudonna leaned into him and kissed him on the cheek at that moment.

CHAPTER 19

An Offer She Can't Refuse

M atron Zhindia will see this one now, Braelin's fingers
flashed in drow hand code to the guard coming the
other way up the natural corridor that led from the
house proper to the dungeon cells.

The guard, armed with true swords and not merely a knife like Preego had carried, nodded and continued toward them.

The ploy seemed to work as the guard walked right past them,
with Braelin keeping his head down and maneuvering Dinin roughly
to keep the prisoner between him and the sentry. He breathed easier
when the sentry didn't notice that he wasn't Preego Melarn or any of
his other house companions, and thought it grand that it was so easy
to impersonate the "voice" of another in the hand language.

The way was clear all the way to the trapdoor, which, however,
was locked, and would be opened by no key Preego had carried.

"The other guard has the main key," Dinin said, turning back for
the hall.

Braelin shook his head and fell to the floor beside the trapdoor,
breaking the seal on the key ring. He bent the ring to further separate

the ends, then slid one end into the lock, putting his ear against the plate to listen.

"We haven't the time," Dinin warned. "It would be easier just to kill the man and be on our way."

Braelin didn't want to do that if he didn't have to. He still wasn't sure which side Jarlaxle would choose, if any. He could only hope that he hadn't already made the choice for his friend and mentor.

He wriggled the metal about until he found a bit of a catch, then listened carefully as he worked his improvised pick about to manipulate the tumblers.

"He returns," Dinin warned.

Braelin hopped up and pushed Dinin in front of him as the guard entered the small foyer.

"Excuse my foolishness," the guard said, producing a ring with many keys. "You cannot get out without this. I should have thought . . ."

He paused there and cocked his head, apparently only then realizing that Preego Melarn, or any of the other guards, would have known this, too.

Before it could fully register, Dinin leaped upon him and bore him down to the ground, wrestling for his life.

The guard went for one of his swords, but so did Braelin, who had all the leverage, and then had the weapon.

He put the tip to the man's throat, ending the struggle. Flat on his back, the guard let go of Dinin and lifted his empty hands up by the sides of his head. Dinin took his second sword as he climbed off the man.

"We should put him in a cell," Braelin said.

Dinin put him to the sword instead, driving the blade into the man's throat, then angling it to reach up into his brain as he pushed deeper.

Braelin grabbed him and shoved him aside. "What are you doing?"

"Giving them what they deserve," the son of House Do'Urden replied through his clenched teeth. "Only a bit of what they deserve."

"Jarlaxle won't like it."

"Jarlaxle isn't here. Jarlaxle did not feel the bite of Zhindia's snakes, nor the torture given by this guard and all the others, nor the looks of enjoyment upon their faces as they did so."

Braelin stepped back and let it go . . . because he *had* felt those things. "Take his clothes and be quick." He shook his head and sighed. "And wipe that blade."

They went through the trapdoor into the main house soon after and made their way along the corridor. Fortunately, both of the guards had house emblems, which would allow them to levitate down from the balcony and into the main cavern of Menzoberranzan, if only they could get there.

"We split up when we get out of this house," Braelin instructed. "You know the Braeryn?"

"Of course."

"Then get to the Oozing Myconid." It had almost been said as a reflex for Braelin. The Oozing Myconid was, of course, the standard meeting place for any involved with Bregan D'aerthe here in Menzoberranzan. But that had been before Braelin had been trapped in there—trapped, perhaps, by Azleah herself with the help of those wretched succubi.

Could she still be trusted?

"No," he thought and said, shaking his head, his heart sinking. He simply couldn't be certain.

"I know it."

"Forget that path," Braelin corrected. "Get to House Do'Urden—it is nearby. Speak with Matron—"

"Zeerith, yes," said Dinin. "I know the place."

"But do they know you?"

"They know me as Dininae of the Blaspheme. Priestess Saribel knows me."

"Then find her and remain with her until I come to you and figure out a better course."

"I once served Bregan D'aerthe and would like to again," Dinin said.

"That is a matter for Jarlaxle and Kimmuriel, and I know not where to find them. Get to House Do'Urden, and then worry about such things if we're all still alive."

"YOU SEE HOW SIMPLE THIS IS?" MATRON ZHINDIA SAID TO Kyrnill, the two standing in Zhindia's private chamber, staring into a small pool of water that was showing them the exchange between Dinin and Braelin. "Just dangle before them what they most want and they will take the hook. Like stupid fish."

Kyrnill Kenafin nodded and even offered a little laugh in reply, although any mirth she was showing was fully faked. She hated this play, for it was inevitably tying her up even more deeply into the many webs strewn about her. Now she was double-crossing both the merciless Zhindia, who had shown such joy in inflicting the most horrible agony, and Yvonnel, who was probably the most powerful person in Menzoberranzan, with arcane magic to rival that of the Archmage of Menzoberranzan, or worse, that of the previous archmage! And with divine magic that seemed above even the Matron Mother of Menzoberranzan.

Double-crossing either Zhindia or Yvonnel was straining and difficult, particularly given the dire consequences of getting caught—by either! And now she would likely find herself enmeshed with Jarlaxle and worse, with Kimmuriel Oblodra, that strangeest and most dangerous psionicist. Yes, cheating Zhindia and Yvonnel was surely dangerous, but double-crossing Bregan D'aerthe, or more particularly, double-crossing Kimmuriel Oblodra, was simply impossible.

So many webs, so many threads she needed to keep track of, so many knots tied by strings easily cut but much harder to keep straight . . .

The two men wearing the black-and-red uniforms of Melarni dungeon guards crossed through the southernmost rooms of the house's uppermost levels, approaching the balcony.

"Soon, now," Matron Zhindia remarked.

"How can you be sure that Braelin is wearing the correct emblem?"

"The fool Preego fell to Braelin," Zhindia replied.

Kyrnill nodded and let it go. The truly awful Zhindia had sent her nephew to be taken down, likely wounded, possibly killed, simply in order to deliver this cursed house emblem to Braelin Janquay.

And the Bregan D'aerthe operative had behaved exactly as she had predicted. The plan was simple, and Kyrnill had to admit, simply elegant, even if her part in it was not quite so simple.

"Kariva and her sisters are in position?" Zhindia asked the hand-maiden Eskavidne, who stood across the scrying pool, watching it all with obvious amusement.

BRAELIN THOUGHT IT STRANGE THAT THEY MET NO RE-sistance all the way to the balcony, but he wasn't about to curse his seemingly good fortune.

"Straight to House Do'Urden," he reminded Dinin when they cautiously exited to the terrace. Out by the railing, they noted that the area below them seemed clear enough—House Melarn was built fully among the hanging stalactite mounds, with no structures or large guard posts on the ground of the cavern. "You take the direct route. I'll head south and meet up with you there in a short while."

Dinin nodded and clambered over the rail. He leaped away, tapping the house emblem, then slowly drifting toward the floor.

Braelin followed almost immediately, tapping the emblem as he stepped off the ledge. He, too, began to float down, but much slower than Dinin had.

Dinin touched down and glanced back up, pausing for just a moment before sprinting away toward the boulevard called Lolth's Promenade, ducking for the shadows and soon out of sight.

Braelin was still floating, barely halfway to the ground.

Something was wrong, something more than the slowness of his descent. The armor of Preego Melarn was the typical chain shirt worn by most warriors in Menzoberranzan, but suddenly it was growing uncomfortably warm. And uncomfortably tight, becoming quite restrictive.

Braelin made to remove the leather vest above it, but that, too, was tight, so tight that the buttons would not easily unfasten. Worse, the tightening sleeves of the shirt continued to hinder his every move, and indeed, began forcing his arms down by his sides, stiffening as if he were more in a prison than a shirt.

He tried to thrash, for the heat was growing more than uncomfortable, burning him now.

The ground was close.

But so, too, were three familiar forms flying down from out of the shadows under the balcony from which he had leaped.

Three succubi, laughing at him as they approached.

"Where is the other?" the one with startling red hair asked as they neared.

"He ran off," said a black-haired fiend.

"Well, go and get him, both of you!" the first shrieked. "I can play with this one all by myself."

Braelin's thoughts spun, trying to make sense of it. Had the balcony been clear of guards because Matron Zhindia had set three powerful fiends waiting beneath it? It seemed ridiculous. Why would she do that?

Just for me?

The notion was lost in a burst of intense pain from the heating armor.

He touched down and began running, arms still stiff at his sides, but got only a few strides before the red-haired succubus caught him from behind.

"Oo, you are so warm," she purred, holding him tight with a powerful grip.

Braelin turned fast within that grip and tried to headbutt the fiend, but she moved too quickly and he stumbled past, then was tripped hard to the ground as she kicked out his trailing ankle. He couldn't break his fall and landed hard and awkwardly.

She grabbed him again as he lay facedown, and he heard her huge feathered wings come out wide, then begin to flap.

He rose up into the air, back to the same balcony, then was dragged back into House Melarn, where several guards surrounded him and hoisted him to his feet.

The burning armor had cooled again, at least, and his clothing was loosening once more. Before he could move them well enough to resist, his hands were pulled tightly behind his back and there shackled.

Suddenly, Braelin wished the armor was still burning him, that it would just kill him and be done with it. For he was once again Matron Zhindia's prisoner, and he had no doubt he would not remain in such a blessed state for much longer.

"SHE WAS MAL'A'VOSELLE AMVAS TOL OF HOUSE AMVAS Tol, from the earliest days of Menzoberranzan," handmaiden Yiccardaria told Matron Mez'Barris Armgo and the gathering in the city's Second House. "They would not heed the word of our Lady Lolth, among the first and greatest heresies of the early age. This one, their weapon master, was perhaps the greatest warrior in Menzoberranzan, and she only heightened her skills in her centuries serving us as a drider."

"Yet Malagdorl defeated her," Mez'Barris replied, turning her admiring gaze on the mighty warrior.

"He did, and his feat did not go unnoticed."

"He is the greatest warrior in the city," the matron boasted.

"Perhaps," said Yiccardaria, and Matron Mez'Barris bristled, yet knew better than to challenge Lolth's handmaiden. "But more great warriors are coming, no doubt. But yes, there is no weapon master, no master at Melee-Magthere, who can match weapons with your Malagdorl."

"Tell that to Lady Lolth, if you will," Mez'Barris said, still with an edge of offense in her voice.

"She knows. That's why I am here, at her bidding, to congratulate you and this great warrior."

Mez'Barris smiled.

"And to grant to Malagdorl Armgo a title beyond Weapon Master of House Barrison Del'Armgo," the yochlol went on. "He is beyond your house now, Matron Mez'Barris."

A flash of alarm crossed Mez'Barris's face, and if any had doubts of her amorous trysts with this great man, her grandson, those were surely diminished in her reaction.

"Malagdorl is now Weapon Master of Menzoberranzan," Yiccardaria announced.

"He serves House Barrison Del'Armgo!" Mez'Barris insisted.

"He does, Matron, he does," the yochlol assured her.

The matron's confusion was evident on her face. "I have never heard of such a title as this."

"The city has an archmage in Tsabrak, a first priestess of the Fane of the Goddess, a matron mother," Yiccardaria reminded.

"And all three side with the heretics!"

"To their folly. For now Malagdorl Armgo is the city's weapon master, the true epitome of the fighting spirit of Menzoberranzan." She walked past Mez'Barris's throne and up to the large man. "More than that, Malagdorl Armgo is now to be recognized as Lolth's Warrior."

Malagdorl smiled and nodded, seeming quite pleased with the title, and more so with himself.

"How many have you killed in this war?" Yiccardaria asked him.

"Twenty-three." He shot a scowl at the wizard Kaitain when he spoke, as if challenging the man to argue with the number.

"Impressive," purred Yiccardaria. "Even without the kill of Mal'a'voselle Amvas Tol."

"Were I allowed the freedom I desire on the battlefield, it would be ten times that number."

"No doubt. But should our enemies find some way to defeat Malagdorl, their joy would be even greater than ours in the fall of Mal'a'voselle. We cannot ever give them that. Do you agree, Matron Mez'Barris?"

The matron sat on her throne, seeming dumbfounded by the whole conversation, and simply nodded.

Malagdorl, though, issued an almost feral growl.

Yiccardaria giggled at that, hopped up on her toes, kissed him, and whispered, "Lolth will make of you a god."

"We will formalize this in House Melarn," Yiccardaria told Mez'Barris. "Within a tenday. Great gifts will come with it, to enhance your armor, to strengthen your body, to grant you magical protections and insight. You have only begun your journey, Lolth's Warrior.

"Only just," she finished, and kissed him again.

He wrapped her in one arm and hoisted her from the floor.

Across the way, Mez'Barris sat with a grin stamped upon her face. The honor to her house could not be underestimated.

But watching Yiccardaria passionately kissing Malagdorl brought a murderous rage bubbling up within her, jealousy coursing through her.

A helpless one, though. This was Yiccardaria, one of Lolth's favored handmaidens. Whatever she wanted, Matron Mez'Barris had to give.

THEY HAD HIM LYING ON THE FLOOR, HIS CURSED OUTFIT locking his arms in place. He could turn his head and move his legs, but he took great care not to, as a priestess stood to either side, a third at his feet, a fourth at his head, all holding scourges and watching him intently, and obviously eager to inflict some pain.

"My sisters return," the red-haired succubus told Matron Zhindia. "The other has escaped."

"To where?" Zhindia returned.

"Perhaps he jumped into the Westrift," said the fiend.

Zhindia stormed over and shoved aside the priestess at Braelin's left. "Do you understand what you have cost me?" she raged at Braelin. "Do you understand that you have declared Bregan D'aerthe's intentions now? Take heart, fool, for you will remain alive long enough to see them all—Jarlaxle, Kimmuriel, Drizzt, and Dinin—put to abomination. And you will already be there in that state as Lolth's servant."

Her smile was perfectly wicked, and Braelin tried hard to hide his revulsion and horror, not wanting to give her the satisfaction.

He suspected that he was failing.

"But you have been there before, Braelin Janquay, and in this very house, haven't you? Oh, I remember. Do you? Do you truly? The way you cried and screamed when your legs quartered? The gurgling noises that came from you as your belly bloated?"

Braelin swallowed hard.

"This time, we will do it publicly, for all to see your weakness, for all to see you become a true symbol of the devils that have treated the Spider Queen with such contempt."

He tightened his jaw, fighting the fear. He thought of Azleah—had she really done this to him? No, he couldn't believe that.

"Are you ready for your performance?" Zhindia teased. "I brim with the power of Lolth, so eager to begin!"

"We must let it be another, Matron Zhindia," came a voice from over at the throne.

The ambiguous statement had Braelin's mind spinning. He craned his neck and managed to view the speaker, and even allowed a bit of hope when he saw it to be the handmaiden Zhindia had called Eskavidne.

"You have a play here for great power," Eskavidne explained.

"It *will* be a play of great power," Zhindia snapped back.

"I bid you to consider the longer play offered to you if you give this agent of Bregan D'aerthe to Matron Mez'Barris to publicly perform the Curse of Abomination," Eskavidne said.

Braelin slumped. He had dared to hope that she meant another victim, not another torturer.

"Weapon Master Malagdorl has been named as Lolth's Warrior—he is now the weapon master of all of Menzoberranzan, champion to the Spider Queen herself."

"Then Mez . . . Matron Mez'Barris has already been given more glory than she deserves," Zhindia spat. "*I* am the principle of this war. *I* am the one who stepped forward to protect the honor of the Spider Queen when the heretics—"

"The longer play, Matron Zhindia," Eskavidne interrupted. "The only value of this man, who is not Dinin Do'Urden . . ."

Braelin expected Zhindia to spit at him, or kick him, or growl, at least, at the reminder of the lost prisoner, but she surprised him with her calmness, just nodding as Eskavidne continued.

"He is a friend of Jarlaxle and a high agent in Bregan D'aerthe, who are dangerous enemies, particularly given their ties to Drizzt Do'Urden and his friend the dwarf king."

"They are against us and we don't want them," said Zhindia.

"They are and we do not, indeed," Eskavidne agreed. "Consider, though: If Matron Mez'Barris bestows the curse, then her alliance is fully sealed. We both understand how important House Barrison Del'Armgo is to our alliance for Lolth. Let her curse him and parade him about, then let Lolth's Warrior cut him down in a duel, *then* you can bring him back from death as an undead drider before the cheering crowds. Those in the Blaspheme remember their moment of transformation into a drider, but they remember more the years, the decades, the centuries they served in the Abyss as undead playthings for Lolth. And the masses will remember the final act, not the initial one."

Zhindia made a little sound, and it wasn't a happy one. "I am to clean up Matron Mez'Barris's mess?"

"Think longer. This display I have described will bond your houses together very closely."

"And Mez'Barris will want to be the Matron Mother."

"As all matrons do, surely. Rest easy knowing that Lolth will not allow that," Eskavidne assured her. "But Matron Mez'Barris—*Matron* Mez'Barris, I remind you—will be satisfied in another way, as you will be. In several other ways, perhaps."

"What are you speaking of?" Zhindia demanded, her tone showing both annoyance and intrigue.

"Do you truly believe Narl'dorltyrr suitable as a weapon master of the First House of Menzoberranzan?"

Braelin saw the man shift angrily and uncomfortably across the throne from the handmaiden. The man beside him, whom Braelin knew as Patron Sornafein, smiled, but only briefly as Eskavidne bluntly added, "Or Sornafein as your patron?"

Braelin looked to Zhindia for a reaction. One thing he knew of this house was that Zhindia actually loved Sornafein, by all accounts and observations. He was the only thing anyone had ever known her to love, other than power and Lolth.

"Take care your words," she said, and then to minimize any threat to a handmaiden of Lolth, added, "I beg. You were there when Sornafein's mortal wounds were healed by the power of Lolth. He is worthy and undeserving of death or abomination."

"So, if I told you to make of him a drider, would you?"

Zhindia chews her lip, hesitated, looked plaintively at her lover, and said obediently, "Of course."

"Well, fear not," Eskavidne assured her. "Sornafein is worthy enough, and you may play with him whenever you choose. You can even continue to have him formally as house patron. But you should consider the possibilities, Matron Zhindia."

Zhindia shook her head, clearly confused.

"And the tightening of your alliance with Matron Mez'Barris, who will accept your ascension to Matron Mother," Eskavidne explained, and plainly added, "What glory to you and to House Melarn when you birth the child of Malagdorl Armgo, Weapon Master of First House Melarn?"

PART 4

IMMORTALITY

How many hours have I spent penning these essays, clearing my thoughts in lines of words, winding and weaving until I know what I know?

And knowing, too, that what I now know is not what I might believe as the story continues later, as my journey teaches me new truths—and I pray that I will never close my heart off to such insights.

For that is what this is: a story. I think of my life as a story I am writing. It is in my control. I am the author, for only I can be the author of this story.

As it is for all of us. Just as I am the author of my story, so you are the author of your own story. And while I know it's presumptuous to think anyone would care to read what I write, I can hope, at least, my daughter might one day find these words. So, for the first time, I write to you, my imaginary reader—and what an absurd notion this is to me!—but I feel it helps frame what I've always tried to tell myself. Namely, whatever twist, whatever station, whatever circumstance, the story remains yours to write, yours to feel, yours to make. There are, of course, so many things that cannot be controlled, but regardless of those, the outlook, the emotions, the handling of the offered journey is the lifebook that is written.

The journey. For me, from my earliest days, my earliest memories, the journey has always been more important than the goal. Learning to fight and to navigate the drow academy was more important than becoming a great warrior, as the former would lead to the latter, to whatever level I might elevate.

I cannot determine if the sunrise will be brilliant or one dulled by clouds too heavy, but I can always control my own reaction to it. I can always find the hope in those early rays or misty glow. I can always smile in response and remind myself that I am blessed to witness whatever the dawn has shown to me. That, I know, is better than lamenting the clouds, after all.

Too, I cannot control the clouds. As I cannot control so much regarding the circumstances around me.

But my reactions to them, and my choices because of them . . . those are my own, and mine alone. That is my journey and no one else's.

I rarely, very rarely, go back and read these essays I have penned. Or perhaps I should call them "sorts," for that is what they are: a sorting, an unwinding of the complicated and tangled threads that block my path through my journey. One might think—I might think—that perhaps I would refer to them often. But no. Such a read is rare, and never for more than one sort at a time. On those infrequent visits to the epiphanies of my past, it is simple curiosity, I know, which takes me there. Curiosity and not some re-realization of an insight as I seek answers to any knots in the life-threads currently before me. Perhaps I might measure some growth with any new perspectives that I bring to the read, as my experiences have thickened.

But always on those occasions, I read with great care and decided detachment, for I do not wish this chapter of my lifebook to be determined consciously—or worse, completely—by any former insight. Not in that way. The experiences are there, settling in my heart and soul, but my guidepost must be that which is now before me, the present. To do otherwise would be to catch myself up in those very fears of change that I have recently noted as one of the driving inspirations of our enemies in Menzoberranzan.

Now, though, with the dramatic changes that have swirled about me—

the discovery of Callidae, the raging war in Menzoberranzan, the birth of my daughter and seeing her grow—I have changed the play. I have given myself permission to go back and read these essays, all.

Perhaps it is because of my training with Grandmaster Kane.

Perhaps because of once transcending this mortal body.

Perhaps it is because of Callidae and the aevendrow, for in learning of them, the world has changed for me so suddenly and in so many ways.

Perhaps it is because of Brie—aye, that possibility rings most true. I will want her to read these, and hope that we will speak of them, both so that she can know me—can know her father more completely—and because any help these might give her in finding ways to unwind her own threads would bring to me great joy.

To teach what we have learned, to share what we have come to believe, to pass on the stories that taught us . . .

That is immortality.

That is a good and comforting thought when war rages all around me, when I place my hopes against a seemingly impossible army of demons and powerful zealots.

Whatever the case, this is my life, my story, my journey . . . and mine alone. And perhaps it is nearing the end—the fighting is all around me, ferocious and formidable.

But no, I cannot think that way, else I stop writing this tale!

So much has changed, and yet, so much has remained the same. I stayed true to that which was in my heart. Yea, I have clarified my feelings repeatedly, but the core of it all, the hopes, the desires, the truths, have remained solidly and inextricably a part of the heart of Drizzt Do'Urden.

This is my story. This is my journey.

Is that story fully told?

I think not!

There remains too much possibility, too much joy—joy that I alone can create within this life I am living, within this personal book, this life-book, my story and mine alone that I am writing.

I will see the next sunrise until . . .

—Drizzt Do'Urden

CHAPTER 20

Reversal of Fates

T his is unexpected," Eskavidne remarked, she and Yiccardaria standing amid the carnage in the summoning chamber just outside Menzoberranzan.

"Lolth guided us here," Yiccardaria reminded her. "Unexpected indeed. An unexpected intrusion into the affairs of the City of Spiders! An unwanted shove to the stone we set rolling down the mountainside."

"The Lady did not care which side in our little game proved worthy of victory, but now, it would seem, she is not about to let the disciples of that one play with our rolling stone."

"She will push back, sister, and it will be glorious!"

"But our bet . . ."

"We still don't know who will win, the Baenres or the Melarns," Yiccardaria said.

"We know who *won't*, but the Dark Maiden and her foolish followers are perhaps of no consequence to our bet, though again, they likely are. And we know which side will be most wounded by the Spider Queen's countering shove."

"The playing field has been unbalanced against Zhindia," Yiccardaria agreed. "And so we must at the very least alter our odds."

"We both know the odds will tilt in favor of the Baenres, my side in the wager," Eskavidne replied. "Eilistraee, curse her name, has seen fit to interfere, but now the great Queen of Spiders will push back harder. The Baenres' gain here in this chamber is indeed their loss."

Yiccardaria sighed. "If Zhindia wins, I will do most of the training of Byrtyn Fey," she agreed. "I will give you some fun with that one."

"And if the Baenres still prove powerful enough to win, I will give you no pleasure while you watch me do all the training of Byrtyn Fey," Eskavidne said.

"Agreed." Both smiled and nodded.

"It will still be so much fun," Yiccardaria said. "Whatever the outcome."

"As long as the Dark Maiden loses, then of course!"

"Shall we go and bring the new player to the game?"

"Indeed. To the Fane!"

Dinin sensed the pursuit, heard the flapping of succubus wings.

"They don't want to catch me," Dinin told himself over and over again, trying to stay calm. He was suddenly rethinking his treatment of the Melarni nobleman. Had they found Preego and decided to annul the deal? Was he about to be carried in by these fiends back to Matron Zhindia for torture and then the ultimate punishment?

He lowered his head and ran on, nearly crying out in terror, only at the last moment reminding himself that there were likely other combatants in the area, and from both sides. He was wearing the outfit of a Melarni guard and so certainly did not want to be surprised by any of the Blaspheme or other Baenre allies before he could properly explain!

The sound of the wings receded. Dinin dared to stop and glance back and up, breathing a sigh of relief. As he had hoped, the pursuit of the succubi was a show for Braelin Janquay and for any others who might be spying about the area. His escape had to look perfectly authentic.

He set his sights ahead once more, running northwest along the Westrift toward the house built into it that had once been his home, trying to pick a path through the shadows that would get him close enough to surrender without being slaughtered by a Xorlarrin lightning bolt, or chopped in half by a Blaspheme warrior who might mistake him for a Melarni.

He skidded to a stop and dove into an alcove in the piled rocks lining the Westrift. A group of drow were moving quickly, away from House Do'Urden. To join a fight, Dinin believed, for one was raging not far away, over to the northeast near the Fane of the Goddess.

His heart calmed a touch when he recognized them as Blaspheme, including at least two he had fought beside.

He came out slowly, hands held high, calling, "Dininae! Dininae of the Blaspheme! Help me!"

Spears and swords went up to the ready. Whispers among the group lasted only a moment before he was called over to the Blaspheme war party. Questions came at him from every side, but he just shook his head and kept repeating, "Get me into the house."

They did, quickly, and Dinin found himself standing before Aleandra, introduced to him as the new leader of the Blaspheme forces supporting House Do'Urden.

She vouched for him to Saribel and Ravel, who in turn took him to Matron Zeerith, where he recounted his story in full.

His cover story, given to him by the Melarni.

"I would be soon, if not already, returned to the Curse of Abomination were it not for Braelin Janquay of Bregan D'aerthe," he finished, after recounting many true details of his torture at the hands of Preego Melarn and the subsequent payback he had given to his tormentor. "Alas that one of Matron Zhindia's succubus fiends recaptured Braelin as we made our break from House Melarn."

Zeerith stared at him for a long while, making him shift uncomfortably.

"Is it true?" she finally asked.

"What?" Dinin replied, looking up nervously.

"Is it true that you were a special prisoner for Matron Zhindia?"

The man was at a loss, trying to gauge many things here. Was she doubting some or all of his cover story? Or something else, perhaps—he still wasn't sure if he wanted to reveal his identity so early on.

Perhaps it would be better to remain Dininae until the battles were more resolved.

"There are whispers that you once lived in this house," Zeerith said more pointedly. "There are whispers that your significance in this battle might be much more than that of a mere drider returned from the Abyss." Dinin realized then that if he remained Dininae, he would likely be sent right out and back into the fight. If he got killed, or even recaptured, Zhindia and Lolth would be sorely angry with him—and death on the battlefield would not keep him from Lolth's retribution, he feared.

"They are true," he admitted. "I am, or was, Dinin Do'Urden, son of Matron Malice and the elderboy of House Do'Urden."

"You knew your way around in the corridors below!" Aleandra unexpectedly put in, poking her finger his way in her epiphany—one that everyone there, Dinin included, thought genuine.

Matron Zeerith raised her hand and glared at the woman, who shrank back, for daring to speak out of turn. Zeerith focused on Dinin, her stare making him feel very small indeed.

"Well, this is . . . interesting."

"I DID NOT EXPECT SUCH AN ENTOURAGE THIS DAY," MA-tron Mez'Barris said to the group entering the space that served as her private audience hall and family chapel, a medium-sized chamber with a domed ceiling whose eight long and two short rafters, and bulbous central area, looked very much like the silhouette of a spider. Statues lined the walls from beside the entry door all the way around to the wall behind the slightly raised dais and throne. Unlike any other house in the city, many of these depicted the men of House Barrison Del'Armgo, including perhaps the most impressive of the bunch, against the wall to Mez'Barris's right.

Braelin Janquay kept his head down mostly, but couldn't help but notice how much that statue of Uthegentel resembled the hulking man standing just behind Mez'Barris's throne. She had made Malagdorl Uthegentel's visual twin, that was for sure.

"Greetings from Lolth's Web," Matron Zhindia said.

Braelin understood that she was using the name of the region that housed her house as a not subtle reminder to Mez'Barris of her suddenly elevated stature.

"We have come bearing gifts," Zhindia continued.

"Have you come with answers?"

Beside Braelin, Zhindia shifted uneasily at that, and on the other side of him, Yiccardaria and Eskavidne each gave a little gurgling laugh.

"Is there anything in particular that troubles you?" Zhindia answered. "We are preparing the grounds for a great battle even now, and expect the entire western reaches of Menzoberranzan to be bathed in Abyssal smoke within a few hours."

"What of House Hunzrin?" Mez'Barris returned immediately.

She snapped her fingers when Zhindia didn't immediately reply, and the startled Braelin looked up to see the wizard Kaitain rush up to his matron's side, holding a large mirror, struggling to keep it steady.

Malagdorl took the heavy thing with one hand and held it out at the end of his outstretched arm with ease.

Kaitain rubbed his hands together and cast a spell and the glass became cloudy almost instantly, only then gradually clearing to reveal the image of Matron Shakti Hunzrin, a woman Braelin knew well.

"Matron Mez'Barris," Shakti greeted through the scrying device, and she bowed. "The clairaudience was already engaged and heard your response, and I am honored that you continue to consider the unlawful fate visited upon me and my family.

"This is the Bregan D'aerthe traitor who slew priestess Barbar'eth?" Shakti asked.

"And Chellith Vandree, yes," answered Zhindia.

"I thought you were to make of him a drider," said Mez'Barris.

"It seems fitting that such an honor should go to Matron Mez'Barris, given the glory brought to you through the heroic exploits of Lolth's Warrior," Zhindia answered, and Mez'Barris's expression showed that to be the perfect statement in this place at this time, despite how badly the Matron of House Barrison Del'Armgo was trying to hide it.

"You make of the traitor a drider, Matron Mez'Barris," said Zhindia, "and then let Lolth's Warrior serve him to the Abyss for the Spider Queen's pleasure. And let him do it with this."

She drew out a sword, its fine edge glowing with a line of barely perceptible red light. Its hilt and crosspiece were plain now, but Braelin knew the blade intimately and understood that its wielder could change the hilt, willing the sword into whatever design they desired.

Matron Zhindia presented the sword horizontally across her open palms and moved toward Malagdorl.

"This is Khazid'hea, the Cutter," she told the great warrior. "Its edge is as keen and strong as any, and it is possessed of willpower and ego. Khazid'hea demands to be carried by the greatest warrior. By Lolth's words, that is you, Malagdorl Armgo."

"That sword was once wielded by the great Dantrag Baenre, and by Berg'inyon," Yiccardaria said. "Drizzt Do'Urden has wielded it also."

"And Zaknafein Do'Urden," said Eskavidne. "And the human, Artemis Entreri."

Braelin saw Zhindia stop and fight hard from shaking with anger at their recounting. Oh, how she hated Entreri!

On the throne, Mez'Barris harrumphed and shifted, her body language going cold.

"And Tos'un Armgo," Yiccardaria said, which seemed to calm Mez'Barris down somewhat.

What game were they playing, Braelin wondered, naming all these warriors?

"None of them were worthy of it," Zhindia then declared, and seemed to have shaken off her distress at the mention of Artemis Entreri. "None, not even Tos'un—with all apologies, Matron Mez'Barris. They are fine warriors all, but Khazid'hea demands the *best*, the truly exceptional. And that is Malagdorl Armgo. Only Uthegentel Armgo before him would have been worthy of this blade. And now, it is Weapon Master Malagdorl's to pair with that magnificent trident."

"To cut apart the Bregan D'aerthe assassin who killed my priestess," Shakti Hunzrin demanded.

Braelin understood that he was truly doomed, and from all sides.

Matron Shakti likely didn't even care about that minor priestess, but she knew, as everyone here knew, that turning him into a drider, then cutting him apart so that he could serve Lolth, was designed simply to end any possibility of Bregan D'aerthe surviving a Lolthian victory in Menzoberranzan. Shakti Hunzrin wasn't just looking to be freed of her capture by the Baenres guarding her compound, no. She was looking to rule all the trade after the Lolthians won here in Menzoberranzan.

And he had given them the excuse to do it.

He tried to shake that thought away. He couldn't have simply escaped that fight on the street outside the Oozing Myconid. He had done what he had to do.

Well, maybe not with Chellith Vandree, but that was irrelevant to this particular conversation.

Much was seeming irrelevant as he watched Malagdorl take the sword, staring hungrily at Braelin.

"When the time comes, you can go and free House Hunzrin, Matron Mez'Barris," Zhindia said.

Mez'Barris looked to the handmaidens to ask, "Are we to openly declare against Bregan D'aerthe, then?"

"Braelin murdered two nobles of our allies," Zhindia said, getting only a glare from Mez'Barris in response.

"Well?" Mez'Barris demanded of Yiccardaria and Eskavidne.

"Bregan D'aerthe has already joined the fight against us in their battle in the Braeryn," Yiccardaria said. "Drizzt Do'Urden himself was among their ranks."

Mez'Barris nodded, yet still did not commit.

"The final battle looms, and when it comes, my army will engage the bulk of the Baenres, their Blaspheme abominations, and allies— if they have any remaining—leaving your path to House Hunzrin open," Zhindia explained. "If you are quick and clever, perhaps you will be able to join the larger fight and cut off the inevitable retreat of the few survivors as they scramble back to the Qu'ellarz'orl and their doomed house."

Matron Mez'Barris didn't much appreciate being talked to like that, Braelin noted, as her eyes narrowed in a hard glare at the upstart

Zhindia Melarn. He took no comfort in noting that Matron Zhindia didn't so much as flinch at the scrutiny.

"First, I will publicly deal with this . . . creature Braelin," Mez'Barris replied. She looked right at Braelin, a wicked smile creasing her face. "Within the hour."

Zhindia started to respond, but Mez'Barris interrupted with, "Take your leave now, Matron Zhindia. See to your part in this grand play for Lady Lolth."

"As you see to yours?" Zhindia asked, though it wasn't quite a question.

"Indeed."

Zhindia, the handmaidens, and the rest of the Melarni delegation departed, leaving Braelin kneeling before the throne of Matron Mez'Barris.

"May I do it, Matron?" said a younger woman, whom Braelin recognized as First Priestess Taayrul, the eldest daughter of Mez'Barris. "I would so like to make this one my first victim of the Curse of Abomination. Lolth will give me the power! I feel it!"

"Silence, fool child," Mez'Barris snapped at her. "And get back away from that houseless filth. And you as well!" she scolded Malagdorl, who was merely leaning just a touch in Braelin's direction. He was holding the vicious sword, though, and called a pair of guards over to take the scrying mirror. All in the room who knew of Khazid'hea could well imagine what the bloodthirsty sword was suggesting to the ferocious warrior.

"Both of you consider our role, here and now," Mez'Barris demanded. "Are we to be pawns of Matron Zhindia Melarn? Consider this: Who will take the role of Matron Mother when Quenthel Baenre is permanently deposed?"

The two looked at each other.

"Zhindia will!" Mez'Barris told them. "Or thinks she will. But no, we will strike a decisive blow, and not just with this . . ." She sputtered and waved her hand dismissively at Braelin. "Organize the assault on the Baenre guard at House Hunzrin and have them ready to go immediately upon my command," she told Taayrul and Malagdorl.

"You'll not wait for word of the larger fight?" First Priestess Taayrul dared question.

"I need no words from another matron to act. We have our own agency," Mez'Barris replied. "Let the whispers seep out regarding our new prisoner and our intent to curse and slaughter this Bregan D'aerthe assassin this afternoon.

"And you, wizard," she said to Kaitain. "Find a source, use a source—I don't care who!—to let Jarlaxle believe that I am not so convinced that Bregan D'aerthe would be foolish enough to side with the heretics."

"You're coaxing Jarlaxle in," Taayrul said.

Shakti Hunzrin gasped and began to protest.

"Jarlaxle might well survive this," Mez'Barris said over those grumblings. "But Drizzt Do'Urden will be the cost. They are in the city together, as we just confirmed. Jarlaxle is a scoundrel and a heretic, but he is loyal to his followers. He will come for Braelin Janquay, and we will be ready."

"His allies are formidable," Kaitain reminded.

"But we know them," Mez'Barris replied. "We have studied them and we know how to beat them, don't we?"

"Even the one with the strange magic?" Taayrul asked.

"Especially that one," said Kaitain confidently.

"HOW IS IT POSSIBLE?" MATRON ZEERITH ASKED. "NO ONE escapes the prisons of House Melarn."

"We were helped. Or Braelin was, at least. He was in the cell beside my own and managed to save me," Dinin explained to Zeerith and the other nobles of House Do'Urden, as well as Aleandra and one other, Yvonnel of House Baenre.

No response came forth from any of those assembled, other than incredulous stares.

"It was a woman, a priestess, a high priestess, the first priestess of the House, I believe."

"Kyrnill," Yvonnel remarked.

"Yes, Kyrnill!" Dinin said with great excitement.

"Kyrnill *Melarn* aided in your escape?" the obviously skeptical Zeerith asked.

"Yes, well, no . . . in Braelin's escape. And she corrected him when he called her that."

"Kyrnill Kenafin," said Yvonnel.

Dinin nodded with great enthusiasm, Yvonnel noted.

"I heard them talking after she had paralyzed the guard. She said she was Kyrnill Kenafin." He paused, his expression indicating that something else had just come into his mind. "And she wanted Braelin to speak with you!" he said, pointing at Yvonnel. "She said—"

"Not here," Yvonnel interrupted. "You and I will discuss this later."

She felt Zeerith's cold stare, but didn't really care. She wasn't about to expose the dealings between House Baenre and the double-dealing Kyrnill to the entirety of Zeerith's clan, particularly not to Archmage Tsabrak, who had a lot to lose were he to side with the heretics.

"Are we to believe there is a war building within House Melarn at this crucial time?" Zeerith asked Dinin, but she was still looking at Yvonnel.

"Perhaps a small power struggle, but if there is, it will be crushed in short order," Yvonnel replied. "More likely, this is posturing by Kyrnill." She was thinking that it was more likely posturing by Zhindia than by Kyrnill, but she couldn't quite decipher the game here, the webs within the webs. There were many sticky web strands to explore, particularly since it was Braelin that Kyrnill had freed.

Or so this Dinin claimed.

Regardless, the first priestess had certainly been involved. Was Kyrnill making a play for the support of Bregan D'aerthe? Was Zhindia?

She looked to Matron Zeerith, the concern quite visible on the old woman's face.

"We have to hope it is true and that crushing it will be no easy task for Matron Zhindia," Zeerith said. "We need help inside our enemy's camp if we are to begin negotiations with any reasonable expectation of some concessions."

Zeerith was desperately looking for an out, Yvonnel thought, and a glance at the others in the room showed that the matron was not alone in that—although both of her children, Saribel and Ravel, didn't seem to share the sentiment.

The fight, it seemed, was more likely in their own camp than in that of the Lolthians.

"Release Dinin to me now that he can relay the message of Kyrnill," Yvonnel said abruptly, thinking it better to end the parlay before it could openly deteriorate, and until she could get a better understanding of what might really be going on within House Melarn.

Zeerith gasped at that and hesitated, but Yvonnel didn't back down in posture or expression, her stern stance a reminder that she wasn't really asking here.

Without waiting for word, she left with Dinin, going to the room with the gate to the tunnels that would lead back to House Baenre—a path that this member of the Blaspheme knew well. She wasn't surprised in the least when he recounted the full story of Kyrnill's rescue of Braelin and the woman's words to be relayed to her, but she still wasn't sure what that might mean, or how many layers there might be.

One thing she did know, however, was that this man Dinin Do'Urden, the brother of Drizzt, was out of the fight.

IN ANOTHER SMALL ROOM IN HOUSE DO'URDEN, SARIBEL and Ravel fumed.

"We should join Bregan D'aerthe and be away from Menzoberranzan, if that is even a possibility," Ravel said.

"The battle has even yet been truly joined," Saribel argued.

"And Matron Zeerith is already wavering. She doesn't think we can win. You heard her—she was talking about negotiations!"

Saribel considered that for a moment, then admitted aloud something that had been echoing in her thoughts for a while. "No, it is not just that. She fears the possibility that we might win. She is seeing the truth of the implications to herself and to the order that has given so much to her over the centuries."

"She has always thought many of the rules of that order were wrong," Ravel countered. "Look at how well the men of this house are treated. How many times have we heard her grumbling about the more vicious aspects of Menzoberranzan and the waste of the infighting? She was against the war begun on the surface by the Hunzrins, then escalated by Matron Zhindia, thinking it the loss of a grand opportunity! Even after King Bruenor chased us out of Q'Xorlarrin and took it as his own kingdom, Matron Zeerith thought Bregan D'aerthe's gains on the surface could bring new levels of prosperity, even if much of that flowed through King Bruenor."

Saribel was shaking her head through it all. She wasn't about to disagree that Zeerith was an opportunist and so would put practicality over pride—of all the matrons in Menzoberranzan, none was more concerned with outcome than Zeerith.

But this was something more.

"She has grown darker since Tsabrak has returned to the house," Ravel remarked.

"Tsabrak Xorlarrin, who refused from the outset to accept the name of Do'Urden," Saribel reminded. "And who seems less than excited by the conflict in the city. He has fulfilled his dream of becoming the Archmage of Menzoberranzan, and now that is at risk, whatever the outcome."

"Yet he is still a mere man," Ravel replied. "His dream, for all of his talent and power, could never place him higher. *You* could command him and he would have to obey."

Saribel gave him a sour look.

"I am not trying to diminish you, sister, and do not mean to—"

"Stop," she interrupted. "Please. You do not need to apologize to me, or grovel, or whatever it is you have been conditioned to believe. Isn't that one of the central points of this revolt again the Spider Queen and her demanded order of things?"

"I only meant—"

"I know what you meant and do not disagree, but you do not understand how brave you have been for most of your life in daring to question, in daring to sometimes disobey, in daring to sometimes stand up. You do not understand Tsabrak because you are not like him."

"I do not understand, I agree. The idea of subservience because of what? Because I was born a man?" He shook his head. "Why would I support that?"

"In part, because you were fortunate enough to be of noble birth, and more fortunate than that, even, to be born in the house of Matron Zeerith Xorlarrin."

"So was Tsabrak."

"Yes, and so were the many, many men of Menzoberranzan who will not side with our cause, and not only because they fear the consequences of a defeat. That is what you are missing here, brother. Many of Menzoberranzan's men, whatever might be in their hearts, will side with the current structure because they gain power and luxury through their attachment to the matriarchy. They have found their way to levels they find acceptable."

"At the cost of those men who are not so fortunate, or attractive, or useful to the status powers," Ravel spat.

Saribel shrugged even as she nodded.

"It is pathetic," Ravel said.

"Yes. Yes, it is."

YVONNEL FOUND BREGAN D'AERTHE IN THE BRAERYN, AS she had expected. The Stenchstreets were quiet—Jarlaxle and his band had tamed the area, so it seemed.

Jarlaxle was in the Oozing Myconid, sitting around a table with some others, apparently plotting some action, given the map spread on the table and held down at each corner by a drink.

"I'm glad you're here," he greeted Yvonnel. "We could use your help."

"For Braelin? You know?"

Jarlaxle nodded, his expression full of what seemed like disappointment.

Disappointment that she would doubt him, Yvonnel realized.

"Zhindia has him," Jarlaxle said.

"Where is Drizzt?"

"Drizzt?" Jarlaxle seemed surprised by the question. "He's doing what Drizzt does. He's out on the streets, scouting. And fighting whenever the need arises. Demons keep wandering into the Braeryn. Minor fiends, mostly, but also the occasional buzz of chasmes, or even some stronger demons. They are quickly dispatched, and usually by one of his scimitars. Why?"

Yvonnel looked around at the group. "I will explain later," she said, and she was glad that she had moved Dinin out of the way into the bowels of House Do'Urden and had not brought him with her to the Braeryn. "Kimmuriel?"

Jarlaxle nodded toward the stairs to the second floor.

With a nod in return, Yvonnel took her leave, bounding up the stairs to the only closed door. She found Kimmuriel within.

With his help, her consciousness was soon back in a selected room in House Melarn.

I cannot talk now, Kyrnill Kenafin immediately telepathically informed her.

Where is Braelin Janquay of Bregan D'aerthe?

He isn't here. He was given as a gift.

To Lolth?

No. I cannot talk.

The suddenness and sheer power of her rejection of Yvonnel's psychic intrusion hinted of desperation, and so she let herself come back to her mortal coil in the room with Kimmuriel.

"I heard," Kimmuriel told her as soon as she blinked her eyes open.

"Where would Zhindia send him?" Yvonnel asked, though she had her suspicions already. If he hadn't been given to Lolth, then who was the next most important person to Zhindia Melarn? Two possibilities came to mind.

"What are we hiding from Drizzt Do'Urden?" came Jarlaxle's voice from the door, and the rogue entered and closed it behind him.

Yvonnel took a deep breath. "Braelin tried to escape House Melarn, and almost made it. He took with him one of the Blaspheme who had been captured by Zhindia."

Jarlaxle shrugged.

"One you know. One Drizzt would surely know."

"We have no time for riddles."

"He called himself Dininae."

"And . . ." Jarlaxle started to ask, but he stopped, his jaw hanging open—a sight not often seen. "No."

"Yes."

"Dinin Do'Urden?"

"Yes."

"We shouldn't tell this to Drizzt," Kimmuriel offered. "Not now. Not until we know more."

"Dinin is in House Do'Urden, near to the entry to the tunnels to House Baenre," Yvonnel explained. "We should keep him far from the fight or risk returning a great prize to Zhindia."

Jarlaxle was nodding through it all, clearly digesting and concocting, as was his way. "We should speak with him at once to get the lay of the prison in House Melarn."

"Braelin isn't there," Yvonnel told him, again clearly catching him off his guard.

Jarlaxle looked to Kimmuriel, who nodded his agreement with Yvonnel.

"Then where?" Jarlaxle asked.

"Get your scouts out on the streets," Yvonnel told him.

"There are many streets in Menzoberranzan."

Yvonnel held up two fingers. "There are two places to focus upon."

Less than an hour later, Jarlaxle returned, bearing news from Aleandra Amvas Tol that a certain prominent weapon master of a powerful house was now carrying a very notable sword to complement his adamantine trident.

"We can't hope to attack Barrison Del'Armgo," Kimmuriel said.

"Then we'll find a different way," Jarlaxle replied. "I've done many favors for Matron Mez'Barris. Perhaps she will bargain."

"Perhaps she will kill you," said Kimmuriel.

Jarlaxle shook his head. "If she tries, then know that she underestimates me," he said with a grin. "And we both know how that turns out."

CHAPTER 21

Strike Team

Catti-brie was surprised by Gromph when he met her in his study in the Hosttower. He wasn't wearing the robes of his station at the Hosttower, but the old ones that he had gained as Archmage of Menzoberranzan, emblazoned with spider images. He carried a staff she had not seen, one of iron, inscribed with sigils and runes along its entire length. Magnificent runes, to be sure, but from afar, it seemed rather a plain stave, slender and straight, the shaft splitting near the top and weaving out, then in to join again, once and twice before the third break, which ended in a simple flair.

It was an intriguing artifact, yet her eyes went back to the robes of the Archmage of Menzoberranzan. She stared at him, slowly shaking her head in confusion.

"You have said your farewells to King Bruenor and the others?"

She nodded, still staring.

"The robes?" Gromph asked.

"Your new ones were truly mighty, were they not? I was told that the robe of the Archmage of the Hosttower was an item almost unique and the stuff of legends."

"You were told correctly," Gromph said. "But this garment is very similar, created from a recipe given to me as Archmage of Menzoberranzan. It took me years to fashion these raiments, and their power is no less, though a bit different in focus."

"Better suited to the battles in the City of Spiders," Catti-brie reasoned.

"Probably not," Gromph casually answered.

"Just more fitting for the task at hand, then?"

The great wizard shrugged.

"Then why wear them?" There was a bit of suspicion in her voice, as much as she tried to hide it.

"Fear not, my friend. I am not wearing these in any allegiance to the Lolthians. They will be destroyed, I promise."

"Then why? To show them your ultimate defiance of Lolth?"

"I have my reasons. Let us leave it at that." He paused for a moment, then added, "I would allow you to wear my other robes, but alas, their magic and your heart would never correspond."

The offer shocked Catti-brie more than the curious comment puzzled her.

He explained—again, surprising Catti-brie, as she hadn't often gotten such discourse from Gromph: "My robes of the Hosttower are gray, reflecting my state of mind and my way of looking at the world. Such items as these are not simple implements. They are extensions of the being wearing them, an amplification of the wizard's heart and soul. You are more . . . generous than I. Your robes would be of white cloth, not gray. My garment would be of little use to you."

Catti-brie had heard of such things, so she accepted the explanation without question—until she realized the color of the robes now worn by Gromph.

"Were I a being intent on evil, what color would be appropriate, then? Gray?"

"Black," said Gromph.

"Like the robe you're now wearing. The robe you assure me reflects no ill intent."

Gromph shrugged as if it did not matter. "This robe will no longer attune to me. It is, to me, just a robe."

"Then why would you wear it into this terrible fight? Why wouldn't you don the robe you claim reflects your heart?"

"I told you. I have my reasons."

Catti-brie stared at him hard.

"Do you think I need it?" Gromph asked and scoffed. He pulled aside the collar of his black robe, revealing a necklace full of rubies.

"This is the least of my toys," Gromph assured her. "I have lived for centuries. I have been an archmage for centuries. I have been an associate of Jarlaxle for centuries. He collects so many interesting little baubles, while I have garnered, or created, many of the mightiest magic items known to Faerun. Like this."

He held his hand in the air and spoke a command word, and in his grasp appeared a brilliant helm of shining silver, lined with gems, so many gems! Perhaps a hundred of them: opals, blue and orange, glittering diamonds, and red rubies. The helm was open faced, but with a strip to cover his nose, and one to either side to hold it firmly against his cheeks. Two small wings angled up from the front plate, and all of these garment appendages, too, were gem lined.

"I have heard of this item," Catti-brie said, barely able to get her voice above a whisper.

"I assure you that it is greater than you would imagine. And it is not even my prized possession." He chuckled and tossed her his staff.

As soon as she caught it, Catti-brie could feel the power of the staff. It pulsed with the magic of all the wizard schools. Her own ring, the one with which she could speak to the fire primordial within the chasm of Gauntlgrym, called out to her to summon a mighty fire elemental, and with the staff, she knew that she could!

"You are one of the few who have ever held a staff of this power," Gromph told her. "With it alone, I have an arsenal of spells. Fire and lightning, detection, invisibility, protection and enchantment, conjuration . . . its powers are vast and varied."

"I feel them," Catti-brie said. "You can throw many spells with this every day, it would seem. All without the typical study or memorization."

"*Many* many, true. But I don't anticipate that I will need it for that." Gromph poked his finger against his temple. "I have enough power within to deal with anyone or any demon that I expect will come against us, I assure you, and a dozen other lesser items—wands, both of these rings—to offer the diversity of spellcasting that I might require."

"Then why bring it?"

"Security, even though I trust that I've enough power without it."

"Your confidence is bolstering, I admit. But let us not underestimate our enemies here."

Gromph scoffed at that. "Hence the staff. And yet you wish to lecture me on the powers of Menzoberranzan? On the might of demons?"

Catti-brie felt a bit embarrassed.

"I am going to Menzoberranzan to do battle," Gromph told her as she handed back the magnificent stave. "I am going to Menzoberranzan to destroy not just the servants of Lolth, but the very concept of Lolth. There is no compromise here, Catti-brie. There is no doubt or hedging in my heart or mind. I have chosen to go to war, and when Gromph Baenre goes to war, woe to those who try to stand against him."

She didn't doubt that. Even without the legendary items of power he now displayed, she knew that there were few—so very few, if any—who could stand against Gromph Baenre.

She was surprised again, and so was Gromph, when the door opened and the third of the group entered the room.

It was Entreri, of course. She understood that immediately, but recognizing him was an entirely different matter, for he appeared very much like a drow.

"It's not magical," he said to her and Gromph. "It is the greasepaint of a stage performer and the wig of a prostitute. I told you that I didn't need the mask."

"We leave soon?"

Gromph tossed her Agatha's Mask and said, "We leave now."

"THE PRIESTESSES AND THEIR GUARDS ARE ALL DEAD OR captured," the courier from House Vandree informed the nobles of House Melarn and the visiting handmaidens. "The demons obliterated."

Zhindia wanted to reach out and throttle the woman for bringing her such terrible news. She had expected that the altar her allies had constructed in the cavern outside of Menzoberranzan would allow her to bring in a continual stream of monsters to keep pressure on the heretics, lesser fiends to continually taunt and terrorize the Braeryn, and forces enough to keep large swaths of her enemies occupied far from her main objectives. But now the summoning chamber was gone.

"What of the altar and the magic circle?" she asked sharply.

The courier swallowed hard.

"You are a priestess of Lolth," Yiccardaria said to the trembling visitor. "You need fear nothing here."

The yochlol had said it more as a warning to her than to the bearer of the grim news, Zhindia realized.

"They are consecrated holy ground," the courier said.

"Of course . . ." Zhindia started to reply, but the expression of the visiting Vandree priestess told her that such was not good news.

"Not to Lolth," she confirmed. "No longer."

"Desecrated, then?" she asked.

"Yes, and consecrated."

Zhindia didn't quite understand. Her enemies had rejected Lolth, but they hadn't begun prayers to any of the other gods that she had heard of. Could it be dwarven clerics, then, come from Gauntlgrym and praying to Moradin? Or Catti-brie, the wife of Drizzt, known to be chosen of Mielikki?

"To whom, child?" asked Yiccardaria.

Another hard swallow. "To the Dark Maiden Eilistraee."

Zhindia's face grew as set as stone. Flanking her, the handmaidens gasped.

"You are sure of this?" Zhindia asked after a long and uncomfortable silence.

The priestess lowered her gaze. "Yes, Matron Zhindia. The power of the consecration is undeniable and it sings with the Dark Maiden's voice."

Zhindia looked to the handmaidens. "Have they found allies?"

"Likely some of the heretic priestesses have heard her voice," Eskavidne said. "We knew of course that Eilistraee would try to help those who oppose us."

"They scored a great victory over a powerful force, and not one of our priestesses or demons escaped to warn us," Zhindia reminded. "This seems like more than just 'help.'"

"And what do you intend to do about that, Matron Zhindia?" Yiccardaria asked.

Zhindia hardly heard her, deep in thought, her mind spinning. "It was probably Bregan D'aerthe," she decided. "They have priestesses from our city and they have allies who would no doubt welcome the voice of Eilistraee in this fight."

"And what do you intend to do about it?" the yochlol asked again.

"Have we a hint of who did this beyond the consecration?" Zhindia asked the courier.

"No."

"Armies in the tunnels about us?"

"No, Matron Zhindia. King Bruenor has not come. No force of any size that we can detect has come."

"But a powerful enough force to defeat several priestesses, a dozen guards, a handful of major demons, and a horde of dretches and manes," Zhindia mused, then declared again, "It was Bregan D'aerthe, and likely with some help from the Baenres."

"Again, for the last time I ask, Matron Zhindia, what do you intend to do about it?"

"I intend to not wait." She looked to the first priestess, Kyrnill shrinking from her stare.

"You have done as ordered?" Zhindia snapped at her.

"Yes."

"Convincingly?"

"I believe—"

"You *believe?*"

"Yes," Kyrnill answered without hesitation. "Yes, convincingly."

"Then it is in motion already," Zhindia said. "All of you, go now and have every capable priestess in every allied house call to the Abyss with summons. Instruct every demon capable of bringing in demonic soldiers to do so, and that includes every demon they bring in which is capable of opening new gates behind them upon their arrival. Now. House Barrison Del'Armgo's alliance is sealed. The fight is on in full, and we will have victory soon enough."

"Where?" Kyrnill asked.

"House Do'Urden to start. House Do'Urden becomes again House Xorlarrin and joins our cause, or Matron Zeerith is the second matron cursed to Abomination. Make it clear to her."

"What word to House Barrison Del'Armgo?" Yiccardaria asked.

"Let Mez'Barris's force liberate House Hunzrin—she wants that alliance and we give it to her. And let them deal with Bregan D'aerthe. They know their role. To work, all of you! Gather the storm! This very night marks the end of this war. House Baenre will lose their allies and we will finally be rid of that traitorous family."

THE THREE LANDED IN A DEEP CAVE, SMALL BUT LIT BY glowing lichen around its edges and a multitude of glowworms crawling about its ceiling and walls. Also, a circle had been etched upon the floor, set with designs and runes that Catti-brie understood.

"Do all wizards of the Underdark have such sanctuaries for their teleports?" she asked.

"You have met many priestesses of Lolth and battled my family. Would you secure an escape were you me?"

"I would have one only, and it would be on the surface, and I would never return," Entreri answered as Catti-brie nodded to Gromph. "Now what?" Entreri said, for there seemed to be no exit from the room.

"We are far below Menzoberranzan," Gromph explained. He

moved up to a wall, searched about for a particular place, then held his stave before him and whispered a command, enacting a spell that temporarily vanished a section of the stone, opening a path to a tunnel. "We have a trek ahead of us, and a flight," he said, and started out.

"It is strange that a cave like this would exist," Catti-brie noted, following the archmage out. "No force of nature—"

"Gromph is a force of nature," Entreri cut her short, and the archmage laughed.

Catti-brie let it go with a sigh and a shrug. She had no idea how Gromph or anyone else might have carved out a cave like that within the solid stone, but she didn't doubt for a moment that Gromph had been the one to do it, and then build within it his secretive landing place.

Out in the corridor, they moved through winding ways on foot. It was a quiet place, save the occasional dripping of some distant water or the flutter of a bat or some other Underdark aerial creature, and dark, although there was enough lichen and glowworms to give a bit of light, and all three, through item, magic, or innate ability, could see well enough in the low light.

They took many turns, crossing past forks and side tunnels and chambers with a myriad of exits, but Gromph never slowed or hesitated.

The air became lighter, Catti-brie sensed, though the tunnel remained low and narrow. She understood when some sounds began to echo—not natural sounds as before, but calls, screeches, even the crackling boom of magical thunder. She understood when they exited the tunnel into a gully, a deep gully, the sounds and flashes far, far above.

"The Clawrift," Gromph explained. "We are on the bottom."

Entreri pointed up to a distant point, a shelf that seemed less jagged than the darkness of the other rocks high above. "Bregan D'aerthe was once based in that area," he said.

"Very good," Gromph replied. "I would not have expected a human to have such a fine sense of direction in the deep Underdark."

"And there, too?" Catti-brie asked, indicating a lower point, a shelf not much higher than the floor of the rift, where a cluster of giant stalagmites lay at a strange angle, some broken, some still showing their full tips, and one even hinting at the glow of faerie fire.

"That is what remains of House Oblodra," Gromph told her. "Thrown in here by Matron Mother Baenre in the Time of Troubles nearly two centuries ago. They sought to use the silence of Lolth to their advantage with their psionic powers. Lolth didn't like it. Take a good look as we pass nearer to it, and let it be a reminder of the power we are up against."

The archmage summoned a magical steed, then, a nightmare horse with fiery hooves and a mane of flames. Entreri, possessing a similar magical item, did likewise.

"Need I make you a spectral steed to keep up, or will you ride with one of us?" Gromph asked Catti-brie.

She returned a sour look, then lifted the unicorn pendant on the chain she wore and blew into it. A moment later, she was astride Andahar.

Gromph laughed at the sight of such a creature in so dark a place. "We have miles to go," he told them. "There is a secret tunnel, straight and uncluttered, that will take us to the Westrift, near to our target, and a chamber we can rest in and properly prepare our spells. Keep your word of recall fresh in your thoughts, Catti-brie, I beg."

"Your concern for me is touching," she quipped.

Gromph shook his head. "I do not need to spend the rest of my years listening to Jarlaxle, Drizzt, or any of your annoying friends whining at me for allowing you to come along."

"*Allowing?*"

"Put the mask on and let us be gone from this place," Gromph stated. "I do not like being so near to House Oblodra and its residual haunting energies, and I wish to be done and back in the Hosttower within a day."

And without waiting to know what the other two wished, he spun his steed about and trotted off across the base of the Clawrift, picking his path carefully about the many broken stones, and many more broken bones.

CHAPTER 22

Donjon

She had a spell of invisibility on her, and another to allow her to fly, but many times, Yvonnel wanted to drop both and assail the covens of Lolthian priestesses who were filling the streets near the West Wall of Menzoberranzan with demons.

The fight was imminent. Not a skirmish or a testing play of back-and-forth assaults, no.

She reminded herself repeatedly of her limited options and power here. She was a powerful force, true, beyond perhaps any other drow in Menzoberranzan, but she was, after all, a single person against thousands. While she might take out one of these summoning areas with an open fight, her efforts in such an assault would make little difference in the war compared to the potential of the desperate plan she now followed.

Still, she flew past her destination, just to get a look at the fighting in the street before House Do'Urden.

It had gone from a skirmish to a larger battle now, with allies pouring in on both sides. Lightning and fireballs, sleet storms and ribbons of energy to take chasmes and other flying fiends from the sky, flew from the Do'Urden balconies.

Yvonnel took heart that the house was well defended. Zhindia's losses in getting into that easily defended place would be considerable, if she managed it at all.

No, Zhindia and her allies would manage it eventually, Yvonnel knew. Yvonnel's side was full of mortal drow, while the ranks of their enemies were thick with demons drawn from a near-inexhaustible supply in the smoke of the Abyss.

Attrition would wear Yvonnel's allies thin.

Which made her mission all the more urgent. She soared past House Do'Urden, crossed the Westrift, then flew over House Duskryn, landing before the long pavilion leading into the Fane of the Goddess and coming visible as soon as she touched down. Then she walked, calmly and deliberately, for the chapel ruled by her aunt, almost daring the guards, drow and jade spider alike, to try to stop her as she moved ahead.

She heard the whispers, those of surprise and those calling for someone to act, but none moved against her.

The great and ornate doors swung open as Yvonnel ascended the stairs to them, though no drow sentries pulled them—it was Sos'Umptu letting her know that she had already been recognized and announced, no doubt.

She steeled herself and strode right through the entryway, only briefly glancing at the larger constructs, the towering jade spiders standing guard to either side. They swayed when she entered, undulating up and down, as if eager to spring and tear her apart.

Through the relatively narrow entry corridor, she entered the main chapel, a beautiful large chamber in the shape of a spider's body, and with eight legs leading out to a ring of smaller chapels. Several jade spider constructs stood about the place, randomly, it seemed, and motionless, though Yvonnel knew they could be called to animation and action quite easily.

Many eyes turned her way as she entered—not spider eyes, but those of priestesses. She tried to read their expressions, but saw too many emotions there, from awe to seething hatred, to get any sense of intent.

"Where is the First Priestess of the Fane?" she asked the nearest, who just continued to stare at her.

Her answer came in the scuffling noises from the rear of the chamber, and she looked up to see Sos'Umptu entering from a hallway, flanked by large driders. Something more, something like a cloud of shadow, was behind them, but it was shrouded in darkness and she could not make it out. It stayed just out of the room as Sos'Umptu led the driders to stand before the visitor.

"The courage of a heretic to enter this sacred place," Sos'Umptu said, shaking her head. "Or is it simply stupidity?"

"Or am I truly a heretic?" Yvonnel answered.

Sos'Umptu stared at her incredulously. "Perhaps you have forgotten what you did on the surface. I have not."

"I have forgotten nothing."

"Your theft of the driders was sacrilege," Sos'Umptu said. "Your irreverence to the goddess in that web you wove, and beyond that, the ridiculous tale you spun, was equally heretical and blasphemous."

"The power to weave that web came from where? And the notion to do so was based in the tale you decry as heresy, one that was given to me by Lolth herself in the memories of Matron Mother Yvonnel the Eternal. As were given to Quenthel."

"The false history of Menzoberranzan!"

"The memories of your mother, who ruled this city for millennia and was there at the founding," Yvonnel countered. "Memories given to us by the order of Lolth."

"It was Gromph and that El Viddenvelp illithid creature who gave Matron Mother Quenthel the memories in the hope of making her more formidable, a more acceptable Matron Mother, after the demise of Matron Mother Triel. Gromph, not Lolth, was behind this infusion, so who can speak to the veracity?"

As she tried to concoct her response, Yvonnel took some hope in the fact that Sos'Umptu had used the formal title of Quenthel, with no disrespect evident in her tone.

"I can," Yvonnel replied. "It was Lolth's doing that I was blessed with the memories. The very avatar of Lolth went to the Festival of the Founding and made sure that I would garner the same attention, did she not?"

"Irrelevant. We are reasoning beings of free will. Our choices are not predicated or predicted by any of the gods."

"Are we?" asked Yvonnel. "Then why is the action on the surface so . . ."

"Blasphemous?" Sos'Umptu cut in. "You were given a great gift, yet you used it to undermine the very being that demanded your divine ascension. You, Yvonnel Baenre, should have taken the seat of Matron Mother, and done so to the glory of Lolth. You, from the moment you learned to manipulate your physical being to become a woman, a full woman, a high priestess of more than noble birth—of *divine* birth. The throne of Menzoberranzan was yours! And then again through circumstance, it was yours to take, Yvonnel the foolish. When you led the way to destroying Demogorgon in this very city, doing such great service to our beloved Lady Lolth, none, not even Matron Mother Quenthel, would have stood against your ascent to the title of Matron Mother and the first seat on the Ruling Council."

"I led the destruction of Demogorgon to save the lives of drow, not in any service to Lolth."

"And that was your error, and that was your disaster!"

Yvonnel had never seen Sos'Umptu so animated, so excited and clearly enraged. Even in the memories of Yvonnel the Eternal, such outward emotion and venom were not to be found regarding this particular Baenre daughter.

"Why have you come to this place?" Sos'Umptu demanded.

"To find a better way. If we cannot deflect this war, the streets of Menzoberranzan will run with the blood of drow."

"As the streets of Gauntlgrym might have run thick with the blood of our enemies, but for you."

"We can find a better course."

"What better course?"

"Parlay. Compromise. Perhaps those who reject Lolth could leave . . ."

"You speak nonsense because you know you are doomed."

The driders flanking Sos'Umptu produced long spears. All about the chamber, the priestesses took cover and began chanting, while the jade spiders began to encircle Yvonnel, Sos'Umptu, and the driders—even those two giant constructs from the entry hall.

"Do you think I fear you, priestess?" Yvonnel asked.

All of the doors of the chapel chamber slammed closed, except for the one through which Sos'Umptu and her entourage had entered.

"They are magically sealed as well, Yvonnel the Heretic," Sos'Umptu told her. "You cannot use your spells to be gone from this place, and you cannot open the doors. I did not dare hope that you would be so stupid as to walk into my lair, yet here you are."

"I do not intend to leave," Yvonnel returned. "I ask again, is there not another way?"

That ball of smoky darkness behind the First Priestess of the Fane flowed forward to either side of Sos'Umptu, like shadowy hands seeking to embrace her. She didn't move her feet, but she receded as those shadows closed in around her, gliding back from Yvonnel as if the shadowy ball was drawing her into that hug.

And then Sos'Umptu was gone, lost within the roiling and shadowy gray fog.

The driders leveled their spears. The priestesses cast their spells. The jade spiders charged.

Shaking her head in sadness and disappointment, for she had expected much more from the intelligent and level-headed Sos'Umptu, Yvonnel held forth a small glass bead, enacting her spell and creating a globe of protective magic about her.

Several balls of flame appeared in the air above her head and sent down lines of fire, but the magic couldn't penetrate the globe, the flames flaring and spreading about it, but coming nowhere close to Yvonnel.

One Yvonnel became four, with three mirror images of herself dancing about her, acting as she acted to confuse her enemies. The powerful woman, versed in the arts arcane and divine, knew that she had to strike and strike hard, for her globe of invulnerability would not last long, nor would it stop those monsters moving to physically attack her.

Lightning flew from her fingers, blasting at the spider constructs, then at the driders. She threw a fireball back by the entrance, engulfing the huge jade spiders and more than a few of the priestesses, who screamed out in agony.

Yvonnel became a whirlwind, spraying missiles of magical energy. The enemies were upon her, and with a puff of smoke, she was gone, stepping through a dimensional door to the far side of the room.

And there she threw her most destructive spell of all, filling almost the entire chapel with a swarm of falling, flaming meteors, crashing down, smashing jade spiders, pummeling the driders and the drow.

"Where are you, Sos'Umptu?" she cried.

The meteors stopped.

The chanting of the priestesses stopped.

The spiders seemed no longer animated.

The wounded driders put up their weapons and shambled to the sides of the hall.

The fires extinguished.

The whole room was suddenly calm and quiet.

Yvonnel looked all about, confused. What had happened to her spell? How could anyone steal that powerful storm of magma from her?

The shadowy cloud drifted down from the ceiling to the center of the chapel, and there dissipated to reveal Sos'Umptu once more.

"Do you even begin to understand the power of this enemy you have made?" she taunted, and her voice sounded different, unworldly, multitoned and echoing.

"Do you intend to fight me, Sos'Umptu?" Yvonnel returned. "Or to send more of these minions in your place."

"I?" Sos'Umptu asked innocently, and threw her head back and laughed, though it seemed more than a single woman laughing, seemed as if the other priestesses and the driders, the jade spiders and even the chapel itself were laughing at her and mocking her.

The cloud of shadows formed about Sos'Umptu once more, and the woman began to float upward.

No, Yvonnel realized. She wasn't floating.

She was growing.

And the shadows went away, revealing Sos'Umptu as a drider!

But she kept growing, and no, she was not a drider, for she was beautiful, not bloated in abomination. Too beautiful to look upon. Beautiful and terrible all at once, and huge, dwarfing the driders about her, bigger even than the jade spider constructs that had come in from the entry.

And Yvonnel understood and knew she was doomed.

"Behold!" the creature that had been Sos'Umptu demanded. "I am the avatar of Lolth. Kneel to me. Beg for my mercy."

Yvonnel couldn't catch her breath. She didn't doubt the claim. Sos'Umptu, the First Priestess of the Fane of the Quarvelsharess, had brought in the Spider Queen, had given herself, her mortal body, to Lolth.

"Kneel!" she demanded again, and when Yvonnel did not, Sos'Umptu thrust forth her hands and spewed lines of webbing that enwrapped Yvonnel's feet and legs, cocooning her all the way up to her waist and holding her fast to the floor where she stood.

She tried to counter with a spell, but her words came out as nothing but gibberish and her head throbbed with stunning pain and noise.

Eight legs clacking on the hard floor, the giant godlike being approached.

"What am I to do with you, Yvonnel the Twice Blessed?" she teased. "All of the gifts that I gave to you. Such a waste. All of the glory I gave to you in your fight with Demogorgon. You would be Yvonnel the Eternal once more, reborn, to lead again. But no, you threw it away. And for what?"

Yvonnel found that she could speak once more. "You gave me much, but nothing quite as valuable as the truth," she defiantly roared. "And in that truth, you gave to me compassion, and hope. Was that my mistake, or yours?"

"I do not make mistakes."

"Your minions will die by the thousands here in this war."

The giant being shrugged. "Mortals die. It is what they do. And how they die is my pleasure and my power. How will you die, Yvonnel?"

The woman squared her shoulders and said, "I will not go to Lolth in death."

"Who can say?"

"I just did."

The giant laughed. "Killing you now would be so easy. Taking you in my arms and going back to the Abyss would be so easy. Perhaps too easy. You know the many names that I am given, of course. Speak them."

"Lolth," said Yvonnel.

"Continue."

"Lolth," said the stubborn woman, and the giant laughed again.

"Lady Lolth," the avatar corrected. "The Demon Queen of Spiders. Queen of the Demonweb Pits, the Mother of Lusts. You have heard all of these?"

Yvonnel didn't respond.

"And the truest," the avatar continued, "the Weaver of Chaos. I do so enjoy the unpredictability of the world. To roll the stones down the uneven mountain and watch their bounces and deflections. What would Yvonnel do with the knowledge I gave to her? With the opportunities that were placed before her? The excitement of watching you choose! The joy!"

Yvonnel shook her head, not sure if this creature before her was diabolical or rational at that moment.

"It did not matter," the avatar said to her. "Do you not understand? Your actions? The 'truths' you learned? They did not matter."

"Then what does matter?"

"My pleasure. My chaos. My power. Me. Just me."

"Then what future?"

"Who cares?" The avatar laughed at her, and it was sincere, she knew.

"You care enough to bless the matrons," she said.

"Do I?"

"You care enough to start wars—in the Silver Marches, in Gauntlgrym, in your own City of Spiders!"

"The ultimate chaos. War."

"Then why are you angry with me? With my actions on the surface and the theft of the Blaspheme? What could cause more chaos in the world than what I've done?"

She laughed even louder and that answer told Yvonnel the truth. Lolth wasn't angry with her. Anger would imply that Lolth cared.

"What am I to do with you?" the avatar said.

"You will never have me, foul beast."

"I already have you."

"You will never have my heart."

"But I will have fun nonetheless." She held forth her hand and an item appeared upon it. At first, Yvonnel thought it a spell book, a large and decorated one like her own, or even greater, like the one Gromph carried. But no, the avatar reached over with her other hand and removed from it a lid, for it was a box, not a book.

Lolth's avatar dropped the cover to the floor and began to flick her hand back and forth over the box, and with each pass, a white plate of some unknown material flew forth at Yvonnel and began spinning, like some type of throwing star.

These were no missiles sent to strike her, however, but rectangular plates that came near to her and began flying about her, rotating as they went.

Again and again, they flew forth, a dozen and more. Perhaps two dozen, Yvonnel thought, for they were flying circles about her too fast for her to properly count.

"Twenty-two," the avatar said, as if reading her mind. "And each with a fate. Some good. Some damning. Some that will bring you greater power—perhaps enough to turn the tide of this war."

"You lie!"

"I do not lie. You know that I do not. You may find wealth in one of these cards. You might find items of great magic. You might find allies of great power, or enemies beyond you. You might find curses or blessings, your greatest wishes, your greatest fears."

"What games do you play?"

"I'm not playing this game—you are."

"What is the game, though?"

"One that entertains me."

"Fiend."

"Your lack of gratitude disappoints me, Yvonnel Baenre. I could simply kill you. You know this. I could take you to the Abyss and imprison you forever, make of you a drider and let my handmaidens torture you for eternity. You know this. And yet, I offer you this chance, and it is real, on my word."

"Your word," came the sarcastic reply.

"Twenty-two cards flying about you in chaotic swirl. For a being of your power, half—perhaps more than half—will prove beneficial to you, perhaps greatly beneficial. And even of those that are cursed, if you survive, you will be set free. You see, you must pick one—until you do, those strands of my web will hold you right there where you stand, and within them, you know that you have no ability to cast your magic. So there you will stand. Forever, if I choose, or until I decide to simply take you to my home and play with you. All you have to do is pick."

"Why am I to believe you?"

"Do tell me, dear, what other options do you see? One ivory card, just one. One chance to escape a dilemma you cannot otherwise overcome. One."

Yvonnel tried to sort it all out, searched her memories for this magic before her—had Yvonnel the Eternal ever encountered such an item as this deck of cards?

"Now or never!" the avatar demanded.

Yvonnel reached forth, trying to pick as the cards swirled about her, trying to find some pattern, some clue.

But there was none.

She plucked one of the ivory plates, and an image appeared upon it while she held it in her hands.

She saw a door, a barred door, like a jail cell. And a symbol, like one from a card of a Talis deck, a single black, upside-down-heart shape.

The avatar laughed and the webs unraveled and fell to the floor.

And Yvonnel's every bit of clothing, every bit of jewelry, everything in her pockets, everything upon her that was not her, fell to the floor.

For Yvonnel was gone, gone from this plane of existence.

Simply gone.

CHAPTER 23

The Soft Defense

Should we join with our allies there?" Dab'nay asked Jarlaxle. She was with him on the rooftop of a building not far from the Qu'ellarz'orl, along with Drizzt, Kimmuriel, and a few other Bregan D'aerthe soldiers. Streaming down from the plateau of the noble houses came lizard riders, wizards on spectral steeds, and kobolds, orcs, hobgoblins, even a few giants and ogres. "That is the army of Barrison Del'Armgo, surely, and they are going after House Hunzrin, to free it from the Baenre grasp."

Jarlaxle shook his head, to Dab'nay's dismay.

Drizzt wasn't surprised by Jarlaxle's refusal. Perhaps the threescore of Bregan D'aerthe could make a difference in the coming fight in the area about House Hunzrin, perhaps not. But there were hundreds of Barrison Del'Armgo soldiers and enslaved peoples heading that way, and Jarlaxle wasn't about to commit to anything until his scouts returned.

Or at least, until his most informative scout of all, Kimmuriel, finished his spying within House Barrison Del'Armgo.

It didn't take long.

"The Armgos are indeed intent on attacking those imprisoning House Hunzrin," Kimmuriel informed them. "The liberation of Matron Shakti Hunzrin is foremost in the mind of Mez'Barris, so believes her palace sentry who could not resist my intrusion into her thoughts. House Barrison Del'Armgo will throw in with the Hunzrins fully, and discard Bregan D'aerthe without concern by performing the Curse of Abomination on Braelin Janquay."

"If I can get to her, perhaps I can show her a better course," Jarlaxle said.

"Matron Mez'Barris is clever enough to realize that so damning Braelin would forever turn Bregan D'aerthe from her," Dab'nay argued.

"The sentry was still excitedly mulling the visit by Matron Zhindia Melarn and a pair of handmaidens," Kimmuriel said. "It was Zhindia who made a gift of Braelin and of . . ." Kimmuriel paused and blew out a little chuckle. "And a gift of Khazid'hea for Mez'Barris's favored grandson, Malagdorl."

Jarlaxle knew then that parlay was out of the question. Malagdorl was the world for Mez'Barris. She would do anything for him, and such a gift! If she was playing the blade's edge in this war before, if there had been any hope of bringing her over to the side of the Baenres, that notion now was lost.

"Send associates to the four corners of the compound of Barrison Del'Armgo," he instructed Kimmuriel, who could spread his orders faster than any, of course. "Instruct them to cause distraction, but nothing too alarming. They are not to engage, not here. They are to keep the eyes of the remaining sentries outward only. Then they can go off to House Hunzrin and see what mischief they might make on the Armgo force that has gone there."

"And what of Braelin?" Dab'nay asked.

"That's our job," Jarlaxle replied. "We two with Kimmuriel and Drizzt."

"Braelin and the matron and others were apparently within the Barrison Del'Armgo family chapel, just beyond where I left the sentry," Kimmuriel warned. "I did not dare enter, for fear of being detected—the place is heavily warded and Mez'Barris's wizard, Kaitain, is clever, and is not fully ignorant of psionic power. Also, there are demons roaming within the house, and not merely dretches and manes."

"If Braelin is in that chapel, then perhaps the ceremony to curse him has already begun," Drizzt offered.

"Send them," Jarlaxle repeated to Kimmuriel. "Now, and be quick. Then you are getting us into Mez'Barris's private chamber. If she will listen, we will talk. If she will not, then we will destroy the nobles of the Second House and take Braelin back, whether or not she has performed the ceremony. Braelin has been a drider before, and Yvonnel returned him. She will do so again if it is necessary."

Kimmuriel closed his eyes and mentally departed to inform the group leaders.

Jarlaxle turned to Drizzt. "Mez'Barris is a formidable foe. By all accounts, Kaitain would be as deserving of the title of archmage as Tsabrak, and I need not tell you of the strength of Malagdorl. When we go in there, there can be no hesitation, no attempt at mercy."

"Which one would you ask me to kill first?" Drizzt replied, and there was no waver in his tone.

SOS'UMPTU BAENRE FELT THE POWER COURSING THROUGH her, glorious and beautiful. She felt as if she could reach across the city and grab her idiot sister and tear her apart.

But no, she had felt the connection, the strength of Lolth herself, keenly when the Spider Queen had returned control of her now giant and drider-like body to her soon after dispatching Yvonnel to some unknown and distant dimensional prison, but the epitome of that power had come right then, and had begun diminishing almost immediately.

She had felt Lolth still with her, still inside her.

She never wanted Lolth to leave. The goddess's presence within overwhelmed Sos'Umptu, had her shaking with ecstasy, had tears streaming down her face.

She felt her legs coming together, reshaping as she physically shrank, and there was movement inside of her that was not her own, a strange and disconcerting sensation that made her think of pregnancy—which of course brought its own tangential lines of thought, particularly since she had just dispatched a woman who had been blessed in the womb only a few years before!

A great sensation, a rush of blood within and of air through her lungs, and the first priestess was once more in her own body, the body of Sos'Umptu Baenre, a mortal drow. And the internal disturbance settled, too, for in that final transformation, a second being appeared as if materializing from the tumult within Sos'Umptu, a second drow woman now standing right beside her.

A beautiful drow woman. Too beautiful. Painfully beautiful.

It was not an emissary of Lolth, she knew. No, no.

It was the image of Lolth herself, reaching out to her from the Abyss.

Sos'Umptu fell to her knees, as did every other drow in the Fane of the Goddess.

"Many of my handmaidens have come to Menzoberranzan, my city," Lolth said.

Sos'Umptu wanted to look upon her, but dared not lift her gaze.

"They brought me here, to you, in full confidence that you would be an acceptable and accepting host."

"I pray you found me acceptable."

"Indeed, Sos'Umptu Baenre. Indeed. Rise now, I command. Look upon me. Let me see the love in your eyes."

Sos'Umptu slowly stood and even more slowly lifted her gaze.

The image reached out and put her hand on Sos'Umptu's forehead, and it felt tangible and warm. The priestess closed her eyes and heard whispers within her mind, two words, repeated.

A name, she realized, and her eyes popped open wide.

"Summon," Lolth instructed. "Bring forth the great fiends. Let them lead the way into the compounds of my enemies. Trample them!"

"My lady," Sos'Umptu breathed.

"My handmaidens await me in the chapel of House Melarn."

Sos'Umptu didn't reply, but she did wince. Lolth had chosen *her* to serve as vessel. Matron Zhindia Melarn was not worthy.

"The chaos will swirl to calm," Lolth assured her, as if reading her mind—which of course she was, Sos'Umptu understood. "When it does, all will be answered."

"Of course, my lady Lolth, my queen, my goddess," Sos'Umptu said.

"There are none worthier than you, child," Lolth said. "Now to your work and finish this foolishness."

The beautiful woman twirled about, one hand lifting over her head. She spun as if on ice, faster and faster, her arms lifting and rolling about each other, making of her a blur.

And she was gone.

Below her, on the floor, centered by her spin, a magical circle remained etched into and glowing upon the chapel floor. A circle of power, and one Sos'Umptu understood to be fitting for bringing in the great demons whose names echoed in her mind.

"IT IS BEAUTIFUL," AZZUDONNA WHISPERED TO ZAK-nafein when they at last entered the cavern of Menzoberranzan. Zak could hear the others of the group similarly gasping and whispering.

They had come in through a side tunnel, barely a crack in the wall wide enough to admit them single file. The area in the cavern before the entrance was littered with boulders, providing them ample cover—for now.

They were very near the Westrift—looking across it to his left, Zak could see the multicolored faerie fires outlining the Fane of the Goddess, which was quiet now. But the other way, southwest along the wall and just past the Westways, the more conventional entryways to this section of Menzoberranzan, the flashes of lightning and fireballs were clear to see.

Right in front of House Do'Urden, he knew.

"You wanted a fight," he told the nearby Avernil, and indicated the region. "You'll get your fight."

"I want no fight, Zaknafein, but we are called to battle," the high priest replied. "It is no choice. It is the demand of Eilistraee, and do not doubt that she will be there with us."

"We will probably need at least that," Zak said.

"I find your lack of faith disturbing," said Avernil.

"Do you? Why?"

"I know why I am here. I know why Holy Galathae is here. I know why so many of my congregation insisted on joining, but your reasons for being in this place and in this fight are personal."

"And no less visceral than your own, I assure you."

"Perhaps too much so."

"Not everyone who accompanied us from Callidae is of your church, Avernil."

The high priest shrugged as if it did not matter. "We have already shown the power of Eilistraee revealed, and still you doubt."

Zak studied the man hard, considering the implications of his boast, and realizing that if Avernil was feeling truly undefeatable because of his goddess that they were all in trouble. "That was on a favorable battlefield," he reminded. "We caught our enemies by surprise because of Nvisi and Allefaero, not because of your goddess or your faith. What you see now before you is a battle of great powers joined."

"We will go in as before, in our impregnable square," Avernil said. "I expect that surprise will again be our ally, as those enemies will have no idea of the arrival of our group."

As Zak began to argue, Avernil called out, "Form!" and the Callidaeans once more gathered in their square, moving out from the rocks. Zak found himself next to Galathae in the front once more, with Azzudonna across from him.

"This will not be as easy," he warned.

"We have the goddess," Galathae tried to assure him.

"They have one as well. And this is *her* home. Remember?"

Behind them, Nvisi began to make some undecipherable noise, and Zak turned to see the man with his gemstones floating before him. "Woe," he mouthed to Allefaero, who in turn called out for Avernil.

But Avernil wouldn't heed the call. "To war for Eilistraee!" the high priest yelled. "Go! Go!"

Galathae would not disobey, and so she started ahead, the square moving in unison behind and beside her, walking, then trotting. They drew nearer to House Do'Urden, where wizards, priests, archers, and spearmen hurled death down at the swarm of demons and drow forces assaulting the house. Fire and lightning flew all about, to the balconies, to the ground, and into the air, where a pair of scorched flying fiends came falling down, trailing smoke before splattering on the ground.

The Callidaeans drew nearer.

"On your order, Holy Galathae!" Avernil called ahead.

The priests were chanting now, spiritual weapons floating in the air beside the moving square, nearly translucent spiritual guardians swirling all about.

Not far ahead, a drow priestess turned their way, calling to her companions and pointing, clearly confused.

"Charge!" Galathae yelled, and the square roared ahead.

The front ranks of the spiritual guardians began slapping and biting at the priestess and her allies before the group of Callidaeans even physically joined the battle. Manes and dretches fell apart under the assault. The priestess threw her hands up defensively, calling out and stumbling to retreat. Beside her a pair of men fired their hand-crossbows wildly and similarly turned to run.

Allefaero's lightning bolt laid all three low, and continued past them to blast into a group of demons beyond them as well. Those fiends, those that were not obliterated, turned and charged at the square, and more came in from the sides, then, the moment of surprise at its end.

But the spiritual guardians remained in their thick dance, assailing the charging enemies before they reached the lines. And the spiritual weapons rushed out to meet the charge, floating maces and morningstars and swords glowing bright with magical power, stabbing and battering the fiends, who struck back ineffectively—and in that pause when the demons attacked the weapons made of pure divine magic, the guardians continued to batter them.

Finally, some reached the square, the interlocked shields along the sides holding fast, spears stabbing out, and in the front rank, where no shield wall was set, the demons met instead Bluccidere and Soliardis, the spinning sword and spear of Azzudonna.

The square kept moving, leaving a trail of smoking, dissipating demons.

From the balconies of House Do'Urden came cheers, the defenders obviously recognizing that reinforcement had come, if not who those reinforcements were—and now aimed their strikes before the moving block of divine destruction, or above them to take the aerial threats from the sky.

Zak couldn't deny the elation he felt, the comradery, the surging power—

Was this Eilistraee?

Dare he hope in belief?

"Forward, ever forward!" Galathae ordered, and she needn't have, for behind her, the Callidaeans were singing, the priests maintaining their spells, Allefaero lashing out with mighty magic—lightning bolts of radiant energy!—at those most powerful demons coming near.

Zak dared to hope.

But then horns began to blow from the balcony of his old house, and he glanced that way to see drow pointing out beyond the fight, back toward the Westrift.

"Rothé piles," Zak muttered when he looked that way, when he saw doom approaching.

"What is that?" he heard Azzudonna gasp. "What are those behemoths?"

"Goristro," he mouthed, his voice barely a whisper.

Around the edge of the Westrift, turning fast for the battlefield before House Do'Urden they came, three gigantic demons, appearing like massive orange-furred minotaurs, twenty feet tall and more, and nearly as wide at their great shoulders.

They carried palanquins, a wide litter for each beast, and upon those were drow, calling down, ordering their army forward. Scrambling all about the hulking goristro came more demons, and not merely the little dretches and manes, no, but true demons: vrock and glabrezu, hezrou and nalfeshnee. Serpent-bodied marilith slithered at the sides, six arms of each waving swords glowing with Abyssal power.

And a balor, perhaps the greatest of the major demons serving the demon lords, Zak noted.

A balor.

No . . .

Two.

"A PATH AS FREE OF DROW AS YOU CAN FIND," JARLAXLE instructed Kimmuriel.

"There are corridors thick with demons," the psionicist replied. "Mostly minor fiends, but some fierce, notably glabrezu. It seems that Matron Mez'Barris favors glabrezu."

"They probably remind her of her grandson," Jarlaxle remarked.

"There is one narrow path that will take us near to the doors, a zigzagging affair no doubt used by the Armgos as an escape route, should it ever be necessary," said Kimmuriel, ignoring—as he usually did—Jarlaxle's jape.

"Full of demons?"

"Full of demons, and likely heavily trapped."

"The fewer Armgos we kill, the more willing Mez'Barris will be to hear my words," Jarlaxle said. "That is our course."

"And I will lead," Kimmuriel said. "But do keep your giant bird at the ready and not engaged in battle. I might need it."

That brought curious stares from Drizzt and Dab'nay.

"Recall your fight with Demogorgon," Jarlaxle reminded Drizzt.

Drizzt nodded, catching on. In that battle, which was really nothing more than a single strike, Drizzt had been shielded by a telekinetic barrier, absorbing the power, the lightning and fire and physical strikes, of most of Menzoberranzan. He had felt that power growing within him—no, not within, but all about him, sizzling and seething against the magical shield, screaming for destructive release, and threatening that release onto him if he could not hold the shield long enough, or if he could not target it at another. He had done exactly that, blasting Demogorgon in that single mighty stroke, a thousand blows combined into one.

He understood then Kimmuriel's need for the giant bird. If they got into Mez'Barris's chamber to parlay, and Kimmuriel was teeming with the power of such a shield, he would need release.

It would be hard to parlay with Mez'Barris Armgo if that release came in the form of an obliterated drow servant, or one of her noble clan. A magical bird that wouldn't truly be destroyed would be the perfect object of his power.

"We go," Jarlaxle said, grabbing Kimmuriel by the shoulder and taking Dab'nay's hand, and she, in turn, grasped Drizzt's forearm, the warrior with Twinkle and Icingdeath at the ready.

They became insubstantial, Kimmuriel taking them into the realm of thought and sheer willpower. The foursome drifted through the wall of House Barrison Del'Armgo's courtyard, undetected by the soldiers and demons turning their eyes outward at the diversions of the Bregan D'aerthe forces.

To the side of the main house, they went, then through the wall at the spot determined by Kimmuriel. Still in mind alone, they crossed a corridor, another wall, a small room, another wall, and into an alcove in another hallway, and there Kimmuriel showed them back into the material realm, their wandering minds bringing their corporal forms to them.

They appeared just to the side of milling demons, and Drizzt leaped forth, scimitars spinning. He cut down a pair of dretches before they had even turned to look at him, then went up into the air with a spinning kick that drove another into a mane, both falling back and giving Drizzt a clear spot to land and rebalance, his blades going back to work almost immediately on more minor fiends stupidly coming at him.

To the side a line of demons went down under a hail of flying daggers from Jarlaxle.

The horde thinned and Drizzt pressed on, slashing and kicking, leaping past a pair with confidence that Jarlaxle was close behind and would fast dispatch them.

The first real obstacle lay ahead, a vulture-like vrock lifting wide its feathered wings and cackling like a maniacal bird.

Drizzt's thoughts spun, sorting the battlefield, picking a course that would get him through the few dretches between him and vrock in the most favorable manner.

He was interrupted, though, caught by surprise and shock, when Kimmuriel casually strode past him. The seemingly unarmed psionicist pushed through the dretches, not even lifting his arms defensively as they clawed and bit at him.

Drizzt moved in close behind. He winced as a dretch leaped upon Kimmuriel and bit hard at his throat.

No blood appeared, no mark appeared, and Kimmuriel didn't even stagger.

Drizzt's memory of his experience under such a barrier—one then given by the entirety of the illithid hive mind—had him nodding.

Kimmuriel kept walking, calmly, undisturbed. He came up on the dretch, which drove its giant beak down hard atop his head, and despite those recollections, Drizzt couldn't help but grimace.

But the beak did nothing to Kimmuriel, who responded by slapping the vrock, releasing some of the energy he had already built up.

The bird demon shrieked in pain, a bloody hole appearing in its neck.

Drizzt kept his focus, slaughtering the dretches as Kimmuriel passed them by, none even turning back to face him.

Kimmuriel walked past the vrock.

A line of daggers stabbed at the vulture.

Obviously not as unthinking as the minor fiends, the vrock shifted its attention from Kimmuriel and turned to face Drizzt.

It didn't matter. When it tried to batter the ranger, Drizzt ducked and blocked, and when it pecked at him, fast as a viper, Drizzt was faster, dropping low as the blow came down, but with Twinkle and Icingdeath raised, arms locked. Each slid up against the side of the diving beak, guided by the flaring sides right into the eyes of the demon.

The vrock reversed at once, shrieking wildly, and Drizzt retracted and rose fast, stabbing Twinkle under the demon's bill, stabbing Icingdeath, the frostbrand that feasted on creatures of the lower planes, deep into the monster's belly, pushing it through to the hilt as he went up against the demon to avoid its frantically battering wings.

Drizzt bulled ahead. He could feel the resistance lessening by the step, the vrock diminishing, dying, returning to the Abyss.

More daggers flew past him to either side, keeping the minor fiends back.

Drizzt heaved the vrock to the floor and pressed on. Kimmuriel was lost to him in the throng, so many minor fiends between them.

"Catch up to Kimmuriel!" Jarlaxle pleaded from behind.

Drizzt didn't have to be asked twice—and few of the dretches and manes were even looking at him.

He went through in full fury, cutting them apart, the biggest impediment becoming the floor, slick with demon ichor and innards.

With Dab'nay and Jarlaxle close behind, he cleared the way, for surprisingly, there were no demons in the last ten steps of the hallway. He cut down the last ranks just as Kimmuriel turned left around a sharp corner at the hallway's end.

Drizzt started to follow, but fell back, diving low and covering when a fireball erupted around that corner, followed by a blinding blast of lightning that shot out right across the corridor, striking the wall opposite and triggering yet a third trap as the wall's facade crumbled, a distant snap of a spring releasing a square board of dozens of spikes that ripped across the corridor on a guidewire, rushing directly in behind Kimmuriel.

With a distant grumbling of a counterweight, the board of spikes retracted slowly, winding back into place.

Drizzt, Dab'nay, and Jarlaxle held their collective breath

An unharmed Kimmuriel came strolling back around the corner. "Well," he said, "I think they know we are here."

Beyond the corner came the sound of sliding metal. Kimmuriel glanced over his shoulder and shrugged.

"You could have simply requested an audience, Jarlaxle," came the voice of Matron Mez'Barris.

"This is me doing exactly that!" Jarlaxle called back. He rushed past Drizzt and Kimmuriel, Dab'nay close behind. The psionicist followed closely, Drizzt taking up the rear.

They passed through the door and into a long narrow chapel. Some twenty strides away, Matron Mez'Barris stood behind a decorated altar, the hulking Malagdorl behind and to her right, the wizard Kaitain behind and to her left. A line of priestesses, centered by First Priestess Taayrul, stood before the three steps leading up to the altar dais, and just before a low railing, thigh high and thick with webs to the floor.

The figure that held the attention of the newcomers, though, was surely Braelin, hanging upside down just behind Mez'Barris by a thick silken strand, cocooned by webbing from his feet to his neck—and within easy striking distance of the powerful Malagdorl, Drizzt noted.

Stone benches ran down both sides of the chamber from the railing to the main entry doors, just to the left of where the four companions had entered. Jarlaxle led the way to the center aisle between those bench rows, all four glancing about warily at the many statues set about the chamber, of Lolth and of spiders, and even a few of the handmaidens in their natural yochlol form.

Mez'Barris motioned for them to approach, then held up her hand to stop them, still some ten strides away.

"Even for one as brazen as you, this is absurd," she said to Jarlaxle, who was at the end of the four on the left.

"I did not expect you to welcome me formally, as that might compromise your position with whichever side you consider allies," he answered.

"Which side would be compromised? Those who hold true to the Spider Queen, or those who reject her? With which side does your little band of thieves and traders stand?"

"Neither and both," Jarlaxle answered. "I have always found it more profitable to remain an outsider regarding the politics of Menzoberranzan."

"He says that with Drizzt Do'Urden standing at his side," Taayrul remarked.

"It isn't political," Jarlaxle said.

"It is beyond political, and to the very heart of who we are!" Taay-rul retorted.

"Enough," Mez'Barris insisted.

"We took care to enter through a route that put none of your family or soldiers in harm's way. Just demons, who can easily be replaced, though it was unfortunate that there was a vrock among the ranks of the fodder."

"Thank you for only destroying my demons," Mez'Barris snorted as if that meant anything to her. "So here you are."

"Indeed, and it would seem that the reason for this audience is swinging about your head, good matron."

"This worthless murderer?" Mez'Barris scoffed. "He is only here to let you know that I have the upper hand, of course."

"Why would you think you needed it? I come not as an enemy, but as one who can ensure that Matron Mother Mez'Barris, should that come to pass, will have a long reach to the surface world, for valuable trade."

"Why would you think I would want it?"

Jarlaxle shrugged. "Profit?"

Mez'Barris scoffed again, only for her posture and voice to change suddenly, the woman leaning on the altar, both hands slapping hard on the polished stone surface, her eyes narrowing. "You have come, foolishly, and you will hear *my* demands. Your minion here will be made a drider, given to Lolth for his crimes, and I offer you one chance to stop this. Just one."

Drizzt caught the concerned glance Jarlaxle showed to him and the others.

"Pledge your allegiance, to me and to Lolth," the matron ordered. "And give to me Drizzt Do'Urden, whose fate will be determined by the judgment of Lolth."

"You underestimate—" Jarlaxle began, but he stopped when Malagdorl flicked a small black bead from the altar, which sailed down at the foursome.

Drizzt reflexively dove aside, going into a roll, sheathing his scimitars and releasing Taulmaril from its belt-buckle container, and coming up between some benches with an arrow already nocked and leveled, aimed perfectly for Mez'Barris.

On the other side, Jarlaxle, too, reacted quickly, but wasn't quite as fast out of the way as he reached back to grab the surprised Dab'nay. Something blew up from that small bead, not quite catching him, and instead throwing him backward and stumbling toward the wall.

Kimmuriel, so confident in his protective kinetic barrier, didn't even try to avoid it, and Dab'nay barely moved.

And the two of them found themselves inside a globe, a bubble of sorts, although they seemed unharmed.

Across the way, Mez'Barris chuckled gleefully, and the others joined in a mocking chorus.

"Oh, do shoot, heretic!" the matron chided Drizzt. "Do you think me fool enough to sit here open to your barbs?"

"What are you doing?" Jarlaxle demanded. He rushed back for Dab'nay and Kimmuriel, pushing lightly on the bubble encasing them, which sent it rolling easily, tripping both up.

The wizard beside Mez'Barris held forth his hand, palm up, and rolled his fingers skyward, and the bubble floated up into the air, taking Kimmuriel and Dab'nay with it.

"I have changed the calculus, Jarlaxle," Mez'Barris announced. "How long do you suppose Kimmuriel can hold his kinetic barrier intact?"

In response, Drizzt spun and fired Taulmaril up at the globe, but the arrow, as enchanted a missile as any bow might fire, teeming with lightning energy, just skipped off the side of the globe and straight up to blast into the chapel ceiling. The force of the initial impact sent the globe floating across, over Jarlaxle's head, where it hit the wall across from Drizzt and rebounded, shuddering and floating and moving back toward the center.

Mez'Barris laughed all the louder. "Well," she said, "it seems that we have been blessed by fate—or the goddess. Look at your friend, Jarlaxle, teeming, simmering, bursting—soon quite literally—with the energy he gathered in the corridor. Like a lover stopped before the moment of joy, he begs for release, but unlike a lover, he will horribly die if he cannot find it. Perhaps Kimmuriel has found some good fortune here. This was unforeseen, I admit, but so, so delicious. Will he obliterate the priestess?"

"What do you want?" Jarlaxle demanded, trying to keep looking at her, trying to not look at his dear friend trapped above him.

He pulled a rod from under his cloak, aimed it suddenly upward, and cast the command to dispel the globe.

Nothing happened, other than increased laughter from the other end of the room.

"I've told you what I want. You have one play, and judging from the look on the face of your friend up there, you should make it soon," Mez'Barris teased. "You are not in control here, Jarlaxle. All of this was planned, and you followed your role in it perfectly."

Jarlaxle was dismayed. He couldn't deny Mez'Barris's words—Kimmuriel was up there, growing more frantic by the moment. His face was beginning to contort as he fought to hold the kinetic barrier just a bit longer, for if he could not, then all the bites and gouging claws from the dretches and manes, the vrock's brutal attacks, the fireball and lightning bolt and the slam of the spike plate—all of it, other than those few early strikes he had released against the vrock—would burst within him.

"Enough of this!" the matron yelled. "Swear allegiance to me, here and now. Send Drizzt to me here and now—perhaps even he will be spared if Lolth sees hope for him. You will help me defeat that idiotic Quenthel and take down the stain of House Baenre once and for all."

"Free him and we can talk."

"Your answer! Now!"

"Do nothing!" Kimmuriel shouted down from above.

"Oh, so he will obliterate the priestess," Mez'Barris remarked.

"No," Kimmuriel told her. "In the days when Lolth ruled all about me, indeed Dab'nay would already be dead." He turned to Dab'nay and offered a smile. "You have nothing to fear from me, my friend. On my word of honor."

"He will die, Jarlaxle," Mez'Barris warned. "Horribly and before your eyes. And then you and your remaining friends will die. We were prepared for you, do not doubt. Decide!"

Jarlaxle started to speak, but Kimmuriel shouted down again from above, "No! Jarlaxle, no!"

He calmed and smiled down at his dear old friend.

Drizzt shot Taulmaril at the bubble yet again, because he could not stand this moment. This time, he aimed directly at it, no clip shot, taking his chances that the arrow would push through and wound or kill one of the two.

But it didn't. It hit the side of the magical bubble and dissipated in a shower of sparks.

"What guarantee—" Jarlaxle started to say.

No, my friends, Drizzt heard in his mind, and he closed his eyes. *It is all right, more than you can imagine.* Drizzt understood that Kimmuriel was telepathically communicating to Jarlaxle as well, given the way the rogue had bitten off his comment.

He heard Kimmuriel say, "Cover, good woman."

Drizzt opened his eyes and looked up, just in time to see the kinetic barrier waver, to see Kimmuriel's eyes bulging weirdly, almost pressing out of his face. And there were flames behind them, within them! Kimmuriel's white hair began to dance wildly, little sparks clicking off its ends.

"Jarlaxle, don't!" he said in a garbled, stretched manner. "Don't."

His eyeballs flew from their sockets. Dab'nay cried out when one bounced off her, followed by a stream of brain and blood.

Kimmuriel still managed one last gurgling sound before he was blown apart to blood and gore and smoking bits of bones, flesh, and organs.

Dab'nay cried out again, screaming in shock and pain as she was blown aside by the shower of gore and the concussion of Kimmuriel's explosion.

Drizzt lost sight of her, for the bubble was no longer translucent. It was red and black, running streams of blood and viscera.

CHAPTER 24

The Choice of Freedom

The press of attackers outside of House Do'Urden was more than Saribel or Ravel had ever seen.

"They could breach," Saribel had told her brother. "We should begin positioning traps and glyphs and defensive squads in the lower corridors. If we cannot stop them, we make them pay in blood for every corridor. As they push forward, we retreat to the tunnels to House Baenre."

Ravel had nodded his agreement. If the fleeing defenders dispelled the teleport from their lowest chamber to those tunnels, their enemies would not know how to follow them. He rushed away to pass the word to some of his fellow wizards to begin setting up the glyphs.

More Blaspheme and Baenre troops had arrived on the scene, the fighting becoming ever more furious. But still, the enemy forces, mostly demons, continued to pour into the square, continued to press inexorably toward the house.

More magical destruction rained down from the balconies, but the defenders, priest and wizard alike, were exhausting their spells, Ravel and Saribel had understood, and it would not be enough to keep the horde back this time.

But then, from the northeast, there had come another force onto the field, a square of threescore combatants marching in perfect formation, the air about them swirling with spiritual guardians, the area before them teeming with spiritual weapons, floating and striking.

"Who are they?" a nearby priestess asked, the question on everyone's mind.

"Priestesses, clearly," said another. "The guardians, the weapons . . ."

Ravel cast a spell of farseeing to view the new force more clearly. He was taken aback by how steadily they were moving through the demonic hordes swarming in at them, the minor and lesser fiends being torn apart by the spell before they ever reached the ranks!

Priestesses indeed, he thought, and then he saw the truth.

"No," he said to those around him. "Priests. Drow priests, and some priestesses." He saw the man calling out orders. "Led by a man."

"Bregan D'aerthe, then," someone said, but Ravel shook his head. Bregan D'aerthe had a few clerics, but not this many, and almost all the clerics in Jarlaxle's band were women.

Then Ravel saw a man he surely recognized in the front rank.

"Zaknafein Do'Urden," he whispered.

"Then Bregan D'aerthe," said Saribel, repeating the earlier sentiment, but Ravel continued shaking his head.

"These are followers of Eilistraee."

Gasps echoed all around them.

"Powerful allies," Saribel said.

"The battle is not lost yet," Ravel replied, almost to himself. "Renew your fury!" he called to the others on the balcony. "Hold them back! Allies are joining our cause!"

"We have to tell Matron Zeerith," Saribel told him, and she started away, Ravel close behind.

"LOLTH'S WEB," GROMPH ANNOUNCED, LOOKING UP FROM another canyon that rose into the city, a small narrow finger of the great chasm known as the Mistrift. So narrow was the passage that the three had to dismiss their magical mounts. Above them and just to the side stood the stalactite cluster Gromph had named.

Catti-brie had seen it before, but from afar. From this angle, it reminded her of icicles hanging off the roof gutters at the Ivy Mansion, with dozens and dozens of stalactites pointing down from the cavern roof like the rows of teeth of some ancient dragon.

"House Melarn is within those stalactites," the wizard went on. "Up near the cavern roof, mostly, and then within the roof."

"Only commoners and prisoners are in the chambers above the ceiling," Entreri said. "The throne room, the chapels, the war rooms, all are within the down-pointing spires."

Gromph nodded. "I have never been inside, nor did I ever desire to be. Matron Zhindia and her predecessors have always been zealous wretches."

"You are here as our guide," Catti-brie remarked to Entreri.

"More than that," Gromph corrected. "You know why I went to the trouble of bringing you," he said to the assassin.

Entreri drew out his jeweled dagger.

"Nothing terrifies Matron Zhindia Melarn more than that weapon," Gromph explained. "Her daughter was slain with it, and whatever remained of her spirit or mind, if anything, was beyond any hope of resurrection, was even beyond the reach of Lolth. Perhaps she was simply obliterated, erased from the multiverse—it matters not. What matters is that such a fate is something Matron Zhindia greatly fears."

"With good cause, surely," Catti-brie agreed. She looked to Entreri. "But the magic of the dagger is no more, so you said. When you threw it through the web strung by Yvonnel and Quenthel, that curse was stolen."

"It was," Entreri confirmed. "Else I would have fed the blade to the primordial in Gauntlgrym."

"But Zhindia doesn't know that," Gromph said. "When she feels that dagger at her throat, it is likely she will bargain, and that bargain may save the lives of thousands here. *That*, Catti-brie, and not as a simple guide, is why I went to the trouble of bringing Artemis Entreri along."

The woman nodded and somewhat contained her shudder.

"And you understand why I took the trouble to bring you?" Gromph asked Catti-brie.

"I thought you just liked my company," she replied, shaking her head and trying to ignore the condescending insult. Why wouldn't Gromph want her here, after all, for her own powers, both divine and arcane, were truly considerable? She was a chosen of Mielikki.

"You are here to make sure that I stay alive," Gromph told her. "For all that you might well contribute, your most important task is to heal my wounds and keep me in position to do war."

Catti-brie wanted to say something sharp in reply, but she simply nodded. It made sense, she had to admit. This was Gromph's homeland, the city, the enemy, he knew so well, and hopefully one he knew how to defeat.

"You have kept that priestly teleport spell, that trick of recalling you and others back to your home, prepared?"

"For the second time, yes. But understand that *I* came here to do this task with you and then to join with my husband in his fight. I have no intention of putting myself back into the Ivy Mansion without accomplishing those things."

"And you can take him along with you if you go?"

"As long as he is beside me, of course. And you as well."

"I understand your desire to remain, but hear me well, Catti-brie: If I tell you to go, then do not question me. Just go. Both of you. I will only tell you once if the situation so demands, and any delay will certainly cost you your lives. I am not exaggerating or misleading you here in any way. If I tell you to go, be gone." He snapped his fingers in the air and repeated, "Be gone."

"And you?" she asked.

"I told you not to question me. If I say for you to be gone, you both get out with your spell. Are we agreed?"

"Yes," Entreri replied without hesitation, but Catti-brie hedged.

"There is only one answer," Gromph said to Catti-brie.

She stared at him hard, but nodded.

"I will cloak us with invisibility," Gromph explained and began casting. "I will see you, still, but you will not see me or each other."

And then the three vanished.

Gromph took Entreri's hand, then reached for Catti-brie's, but she pulled it away as he tried to grasp it.

"Proving you aren't always right, I see you quite clearly," she told him. A little reminder that she, too, could perform these wizardly dweomers.

"And can you fly?" he returned, and she answered by leaping away, rising up along the chasm wall. With the barest hint of a smile at her pique, Gromph gave the gift of flight to Entreri and himself and guided the assassin up into the air.

"Land on one of the platforms to the southern end," Entreri advised. "The noble chambers are in the north, but the south is far less guarded."

They did just that, coming to a balcony where a single sentry stood guard, leaning against the wall and hardly paying attention.

Entreri dispatched him, coming visible as he struck.

In they went.

"WE ARE RALLYING!" SARIBEL CALLED OUT AS SHE BURST into the private chapel, where Zeerith sat with Tsabrak.

"Disciples of the Dark Maiden have come," Ravel added, rushing in behind his sister. "They are charging through the demon forces, sending them back to the lower planes!"

The two skidded to a stop, still several strides from the seats, where Matron Zeerith turned a sudden scowl upon them.

"They are not all who have come to Menzoberranzan," Archmage Tsabrak replied. He motioned to a mirror laid upon the table between him and Zeerith and waited for the two nobles to get up to where they could look at the images its powers of divination had revealed. "A force of greater demons has come forth from the Fane of the Goddess. Behold, goristro and balors, and all manner of Abyssal carnage."

"How do you think the petty little children of the Dark Maiden will fare against this?" Zeerith hissed at them. "And these great fiends are not all that has come. *She* is here."

"She?" Ravel asked, but when Saribel sucked in her breath suddenly, he understood that Matron Zeerith was referring to Lolth.

"They will surely breach the house," Tsabrak told them. "No magic will hold our doors against the charge of a goristro."

Zeerith nodded.

"Then we flee," Ravel said. "Now. We run to the tunnels and flee to House Baenre."

"To what end?" Tsabrak scolded, waving his hand at the scrying mirror. "Do you think even House Baenre can stand against that?"

"Did you not hear him? *Lolth* is here in the city," Zeerith said. "She is calling to the matrons. I can hear her whispers, as can the others, I am sure."

"Then we fight them as long as we can here, and if we cannot hold, we run for the tunnels—to Lake Donigarten if not to House Baenre, and out the Mantle and into the deep Underdark," Ravel stammered. "We cannot go back, Matron. We cannot!"

"He may be right, I fear," Tsabrak said, taking the comment in an entirely different direction. "We have played the losing side, perhaps too much."

Both Ravel and Saribel expected Zeerith to scold the wizard for such impertinence, but to their surprise and horror, she was simply nodding.

"We must act for forgiveness and not just beg," the matron said after a short pause. "Go, you two, back to the wall. Goad the minions of the Dark Maiden to our sanctuary, and when they near, you, all of you, all of our wizards and priestesses and archers, lay them low. Slaughter them at our gates as an act of contrition to the Spider Queen. Go, and be quick!"

Saribel gasped again, and Ravel shook his head in disbelief. "We saw them," he argued. "The Baenres. Yvonnel and Matron Mother Quenthel! We saw what they did on the overworld. We heard their tale of Menzoberranzan and the true memories—"

Tsabrak clapped his hands together and a burst of lightning slammed Ravel to the ground, taking the words from his mouth as he sat there with his jaw trembling and his hair flying wildly.

"Not another word from you, fool boy," Zeerith scolded. "It is over. It was a delusion, a folly, a great deception, and we fell for it and now must find our way back. The Baenres are doomed. The order of Menzoberranzan will be forever changed, and we can only hope that our actions now bring penance—Matron Zhindia has sent this force against us to remind us, not to destroy us."

"You cannot believe that," Saribel dared to say.

"I told you two to go, so go! Now, and be quick. Slaughter the minions of the Dark Maiden. Kill any Blaspheme and any Baenres that try to join their ranks as they flee the rout that will ensue beyond our walls. And when Matron Zhindia arrives, as she surely will, invite her in and do so with your head properly bowed. Now, go!"

Saribel turned and rushed away, pausing to reach down and help her brother back to his feet, then tugging him along out of the chapel.

"This is madness," Ravel said, his teeth still chattering from the lightning hit.

"We knew it could happen," Saribel said.

"I'm not going back to it," Ravel insisted. "I cannot. I can't go back to that."

"And with Zhindia Melarn as Matron Mother of Menzoberranzan," Saribel said, not disagreeing.

"I can't," Ravel muttered.

Saribel leaned in close to him and whispered, "Tell your friends. Gather them and I will gather mine, if they will come."

"If they will come where?"

"To the tunnels. To gather Dinin Do'Urden and be gone from this place as we just said—to House Baenre, or to Donigarten and out into the open Underdark if we must."

"If Baenre loses, we will be out in the Underdark alone," Ravel said, as if just realizing the truth of the course.

"Are we not already alone? But we don't need to be for long. We will go to Gauntlgrym and King Bruenor," Saribel decided.

"They will hunt us."

"Are we not already hunted?" she asked, once again turning it back on her brother. "Aren't we just the playthings of those above us right now? So we go below them . . . or so they would think."

"And if the dwarves reject our entreaties?"

"Jarlaxle will have us," Saribel insisted. "He will have Dinin."

"Jarlaxle will return to Lolth's bosom or he and his band of idiots will not survive," came a third voice, up ahead, and Archmage Tsabrak turned the corner in the hallway before them.

Ravel and Saribel turned concerned looks to each other.

"I know what you plan," Tsabrak stated bluntly.

The two just stared at him.

"I could stop you," the Archmage of Menzoberranzan said, and neither of the two doubted it.

"Are you telling us to turn around?" Ravel asked.

"We don't want to go back to that," Saribel added.

"You prefer a horrible death? Or an existence in here or in the Abyss as a drider to Lolth?"

"Does it have to come to that? Have we no personal freedom, no choice in the matter at all?" Saribel said, her voice taking on a vicious edge.

Tsabrak scoffed at her. "How long have you lived here? Freedom? You are free to do the best you can, based on your loyalty to Lolth and your inner strengths. On your physical, magical, and intellectual prowess. And, of course, your gender. That you, a noble priestess of a powerful house, daughter to one of the ruling matrons of Menzoberranzan, should—"

"Suppose that is not what I want?" Saribel interrupted. "Perhaps my heart does not condone that which I see all about me."

"Then I would tell you to blink a few times and look again. That it is a matter of survival, not of conscience."

"Is there a point to one without the other?" Ravel interjected.

"Yes!" Tsabrak snapped back. "Ah yes, the ideal of community and empathy, and lifting all others. Idiocy, I say! From the moment you left Matron Zeerith's womb, you have been alone, both of you. You come into this life alone, you survive alone, and you die alone."

"Unless you have Lolth's blessing," Saribel added snidely and with a harder stare at the wizard.

"Lolth's blessing?" Tsabrak nearly choked on that, revealing much to both Saribel and Ravel. "That is a matter for the afterlife, and a great boost in power in the City of Spiders. But you are not wrapped up in a hug of eight legs. She does not walk beside you or guard your sleep. You are *alone*. You do the best you can. You survive."

"Maybe that's exactly what we're trying to do," Ravel replied.

"To House Baenre? Doomed! Out of the city? Nothing but misery and death."

"Drizzt Do'Urden would differ," Ravel retorted.

"Drizzt Do'Urden survives only because he gives great pleasure to Lolth with his subversive antics. He fosters her play. I say again, House Baenre is doomed, and so will you both be if I let you continue along this path."

"Maybe," Saribel replied. "But let it at least be our path to choose."

"If it's doom, then so be it," Ravel agreed. "I would clear my heart at the price of my life."

"Eternal doom?" Tsabrak said to them.

"I don't believe that," Ravel said.

"Nor I," Saribel agreed. "And if I was hearing you right, I'm not sure you do, either. Please, let us choose our own way and suffer the consequences as we may."

"I won't go back to what was before," Ravel steadfastly added.

Tsabrak gave a helpless little laugh. "Matron Zeerith would never forgive me—"

"Would she forgive you killing us?" Ravel interrupted. "Because that is the only way for you to stop us."

Tsabrak snorted and shook his head.

"We never had this conversation," Saribel offered.

"You have no idea of the power you are going against, of the goddess whose memory is longer than those claimed by Yvonnel and Quenthel when they performed the great heresy."

"Matron Mother Quenthel," Ravel corrected as if he had caught Tsabrak in a major breach of Lolthian demands.

But the wizard scoffed again. "For what? Another day? For another hour?"

Ravel wanted to answer, but he found nothing to retort.

"And you," Tsabrak said pointedly to Saribel with another snort of disgust. "You are in line to lead this family. Matron Zeerith is old . . . ancient. You are her prize child, first priestess, destined to rule House Xorlarrin—which is what we *will* be again."

"If I am leading House Xorlarrin, or Do'Urden, or whatever name they next assign to our family, then know that House Xorlarrin will never find the blessing of Lolth. She is no longer in my heart, Archmage Tsabrak. I have seen the truth."

"The truth?"

"I believe it to be that, yes. I have seen it and embraced it. It is not a matter of convenience to me, you see, not like it appears to be to Matron Zeerith, or to you. It is a matter of conscience, of principle. Of choice and of freedom. I have made my choice with all my heart. I cannot change that for my own personal gain, nor even for the welfare of House Xorlarrin, nor can I hide that from Lolth. I reject her, and to stop us, you must kill us. It is that simple."

Tsabrak sighed heavily and stared at the two for a long while in silence. Then he shook his head. "You children think of staying alive as 'convenience.'"

"We think as we think, not as Lolth would have us think."

The wizard snorted.

"We never had this conversation," Saribel said again.

The archmage glared at them, as if trying to instill some final lesson, then snapped his fingers and disappeared.

Both Saribel and Ravel heaved a sigh of relief. Tsabrak would have had little trouble in killing both of them, if he had so chosen, or even in simply catching them in some magical net and dragging them back before Matron Zeerith, their treachery revealed.

"Message your friends, and quickly, and I will do the same," Saribel said a few heartbeats later. "We run straight for the lower rooms, gather Dinin Do'Urden, and use the gate into the deeper tunnels."

Ravel just stood there, shaking his head and staring at where Tsabrak had been.

"Now," Saribel implored him.

"I don't understand," Ravel answered.

"Understand what?"

"Tsabrak hates Lolth, or at least, certainly does not revere and love her. You heard him."

"That surprises you? It is, as he said, for him a mere matter of survival. He is hardly the only one of great power who believes that. Even Matron Zeer . . . even our mother. Do you think her turnabout here is of the heart or of the mind?"

"But she is . . . a she!" Ravel replied. "As are you. The power here is yours to take and hold. Tsabrak has reached the limit of anything he could ever hope for, and still he remains beneath every matron of every house, every high priestess, even. Why would he stay in a society that forever makes of him a lesser class of drow simply because he is a man?"

"His power and his luxury come from the order of the matriarchy," Saribel explained.

"To this level only."

"To this level he might not have achieved without the structures now in place in the city."

"I see no sense in it."

"And yet, it is almost universal in the societies of Faerun, to some extent. It is present in many of the human kingdoms, certainly in the dwarven kingdoms. There is always some reason given by those in power to validate their position, and there are always many who glom on to that reason for the sake of their own advancement, however limited it might be within the order set by those in power. It is the way of things, I fear, and if we somehow get out of this alive, and to the surface, you will see it, my brother. Powerful people use whatever they can to eliminate competition throughout every institution they control. Never forget that.

"Go and gather those who choose to flee. Send your messages and make your way to the lower dining hall, where we will meet shortly, and from there to Dinin and to the gate to the lower tunnels."

"And from there?"

"From there, *we* decide."

Her Precious Grandson

W hat have you done?" Jarlaxle screamed at Mez'Barris, the mercenary leader trembling visibly, shaking his head weirdly as if in utter denial, as his dear friend and co-leader of Bregan D'aerthe had become a giant splatter and nothing more within the bubble floating above him.

Mez'Barris's laughter nearly drowned out the gasping and sobbing of Dab'nay, who was also inside that gore-filled orb, though no one could see her clearly any longer.

"What have I done?" Mez'Barris replied. "What have *you* done, Jarlaxle? Siding with heretics!"

"Bregan D'aerthe did not choose—"

"Stop this ridiculous charade! You did! You chose!" Mez'Barris screamed at him. "And now the last of those fool Oblodrans is dead, and soon so shall you be."

Drizzt aimed his bow at Mez'Barris and called to Dab'nay.

"Throw down your weapons and kneel," Mez'Barris calmly ordered. She thrust a scepter up above her head and a curtain of black smoke fell from the ceiling all about the room, covering every wall and every door. Wisps of flames and sparks of lightning showed within its shadows. "There is no way out."

"No surrender," Drizzt heard Jarlaxle mutter, and it was all he needed to hear. He could feel the tingling energy of the curtain and the heat of the flames within, but he agreed with Jarlaxle.

To the death.

He let fly his arrow, straight for Mez'Barris, but it struck an invisible wall of magical force right before it reached the altar area, again dissipating into a shower of harmless sparks.

The line of priestesses standing before Mez'Barris began casting.

Kaitain lifted his hands to throw his magic.

Matron Mez'Barris began to chant and wave the scepter, and the huge statues, spiders and images of Lolth, lining the chapel walls began to awaken.

There were too many. He and Jarlaxle were too few. They couldn't win.

Still, Drizzt called upon his innermost disciplines, became the Hunter—no, something more—became that combination of the feral warrior and the disciplined monk, as Grandmaster Kane had taught him.

It wouldn't matter. It couldn't matter. Not against this.

They couldn't win.

They would fight, though. Drizzt just hoped that he would die cleanly, and that perhaps he could take Malagdorl or Mez'Barris with him. He wouldn't even look at the statues, no, for those were house guardian constructs and would not go out in the wider battle. His duty now was to inflict as much damage on their living enemies as possible.

The worst thing would be to be captured—that would give them great strength.

He would not let that happen.

To the death, then, and let it be with the knowledge that Cattibrie and Brie, and everyone he loved, would be better off for his effort.

"THE HOUSE LIES MOSTLY WITHIN THE WALL AND CAN BE defended," Zak told Avernil, who rushed up to him as soon as the horde of powerful demons came into view. "The defenders on the balcony see us and know that we share a common foe."

Ahdin Duine overheard the two. "I will go!" she said, and on Avernil's nod, and before Zak could protest, the young woman sprinted off, calling for Galathae to give her a blessing.

A beam of light flew out from Bluccidere to Ahdin Duine and she seemed lighter in her step, and faster. Following in her wake, the square began an organized and calm approach, and Zak was glad that they had at last taken his advice.

To remain out here against the force fast approaching was to be destroyed.

His hopes grew when a group of the defenders of House Do'Urden began throwing their magic at a pack of demons moving to block Ahdin Duine, reducing their numbers considerably with missiles of magical energy and a streaking lightning bolt, followed by a fireball carefully placed so that its flames would not reach the running woman.

A pair of minor fiends managed to escape the carnage and moved before Ahdin Duine to intercept her, but the athletic aevendrow jumped, planted, and leaped over them with a twisting somersault.

Despite the danger, Zak chuckled in admiration, and remembered his match in the half barrel of frozen grapes against this formidable young warrior.

"She will join Biancorso," Azzudonna whispered to him. "Perhaps take the spot I had planned for you."

Zak smiled all the wider.

Ahdin Duine's path to the gates of House Do'Urden was open now; she had free rein to announce the allies.

Until something changed.

More defenders appeared on the balcony. Zak noted some arguing up there, with one man throwing up his hands in seeming disgust and turning away.

The newcomers took up the fight.

A trio of lightning bolts and a swarm of magical missiles swept down from the balcony . . .

All aimed at Ahdin Duine.

She fell from sight as more enemies crowded into the path she had taken, but the last thing Zak saw of the young woman was her lying flat on the ground, bouncing limply as the storm of lightning that scorched her and the ground all about her continued.

"They think us enemies!" one priest yelled from behind the front lines.

Azzudonna and Ayeeda cried out in angry denial.

Galathae turned a scowl at Zak, who had no answers. Had he misread the battle here entirely?

No, that could not be.

"Where now?" the paladin demanded of him.

Zak didn't immediately answer, entranced by the continuing shift in the battle. Across the way, forces he thought allies, carrying the banners of House Baenre, had also turned for House Do'Urden with the arrival of the new and more powerful demonic horde.

Except now they, too, were being assailed from above, from the balconies of the house they had been defending.

"What is happening?" Avernil demanded of Zak, who had no real answers.

"Our enemies have taken House Do'Urden," he said unconvincingly.

"Where for us, then?" he was asked once again.

Zak felt the eyes of all upon him, with enemies drawing near. They were short on time and options—they had come in thinking to join allies in House Do'Urden, and with no fallback. He tried to recall everything Jarlaxle had told him about the fight—which houses were allied and which enemies—and everything he once knew of Menzoberranzan.

"The Qu'ellarz'orl," Zak blurted, pointing to the southeast. "House Baenre. Back to the rift and east alongside it and all the way to the marketplace."

"House Baenre is our ally?" Azzudonna asked.

"If they're not, the battle is already lost. Be quick now!"

The square reversed, moving across the open ground as they backtracked. They had a few moments of reprieve, out of range of the enemies on House Do'Urden's balconies, and with only a few demons to dispatch, but it wouldn't last, Zak knew. Before they reached the end of the Westrift, they would have to punch through the end of the line of the new and more powerful demons that had come onto the battlefield.

He glanced back once, across the way, to see the Baenres and their allies also fleeing from the ground before House Do'Urden.

Something had happened in there only very recently, he realized, and it was nothing good for their cause.

"WE HAVE BROUGHT FRIENDS," YICCARDARIA ANNOUNCED to Matron Zhindia.

Zhindia stared at the handmaiden and at Eskavidne, who stood at Yiccardaria's side, but she hardly registered the words, as she hardly registered the six other yochlols standing behind the pair.

"Ah, sister, she felt the presence," Eskavidne said.

"Was it . . . ?" Zhindia breathlessly asked.

"Do you doubt?" Yiccardaria said, and there was a threat in her tone.

"Of course not . . . I mean, I only doubted that Lolth would think us so worthy as to grace us—"

"Enough," said Yiccardaria. "The Lady is coming here and you are blessed to be the host. We have much to do. Your plans to show Matron Zeerith the truth of her betrayal and the promise of what House Xorlarrin could again become have worked out so very well. Matron Zeerith rejects the call of the heretics now. She has turned her wizards and priestesses upon the Baenre and Blaspheme forces outside of her house and they are fleeing across the city to hide in their hole, an unstoppable army on their heels. The Lady would congratulate you personally."

As she spoke, Eskavidne moved back to the other yochlols and they formed a circle, all seven chanting a common refrain.

Zhindia felt her legs go weak. "Then victory is at hand," she said.

"Did you ever doubt it?" Yiccardaria asked from the circle as she joined in the summoning.

"QUICKLY, WE MUST BE GONE," RAVEL SAID TO DININ WHEN he and Saribel entered the lowest chamber of House Do'Urden. The wizard ran to the center of the room, took a deep and steadying breath, and began opening the gate to the room that led to the tunnels below.

"Are we certain of this?" Saribel asked him, stopping him. "There will be no return."

Ravel paused in his casting. "You sounded quite sure of yourself when we confronted Tsabrak," Ravel replied.

"But now it is so very real."

"It's always been real," Ravel said, but also nodded—he felt the same way. "If we stay, Dinin is doomed and all that we hoped for is lost, likely forevermore."

Both turned to regard the former elderboy of House Do'Urden, who just stood there, unblinking, having moved not at all from where he was when they had entered the room.

"Dinin?" Saribel asked, to no response.

The two stared at him in confusion, until Tsabrak walked into the room.

"I thought we agreed," Ravel said.

"I will allow you to make your own choice, stupid as it is," Tsabrak replied. "I sense that Lolth wishes it this way so she can know the true hearts of those who follow her. She will not be angry with me for letting you go, but him?" He pointed to Dinin. "That is a different matter."

"He gets to choose," Saribel argued.

"I will make of him a perfect gift," Tsabrak said. "If my allowing you to leave is discovered, then this will be my bargain."

"No," Saribel said. "You cannot have him."

"You cannot stop me."

"Perhaps the two of us cannot," Ravel said.

"But we can," said another wizard, entering the room with several of his peers and a trio of priestesses.

Tsabrak stared at the crew for a long while. "A full mutiny when Matron Zeerith needs you most of all?"

"Matron Zeerith's fate is for the Lolthians to decide," Saribel said. "She surrendered to them and their ways."

"But her house will be weaker!"

"Why would she care if she had the blessing of Lolth?" came Ravel's biting response. "Free Dinin Do'Urden of your spell and let us be on our way."

Tsabrak again glanced all around, as if weighing his odds. He knew these wizards and priestesses, and even a small group of warriors who arrived only then.

"Tell Matron Zeerith that you tried to stop us but could not," Saribel offered.

"Or fall now in a blaze of Lolthian glory," Ravel added, drawing a hateful glare from the archmage.

"Be careful your tongue, boy," Tsabrak warned.

Ravel smiled, but was wise enough to let it go at that. He aspired to one day be as strong as Tsabrak and he wasn't ready to take that one on.

"Go and report us, if it will . . ." Saribel started to say, but Tsabrak was already gone, once again in a puff of smoke.

The enchantment on Dinin broke, leaving him confused, but not about to argue when Ravel opened the gate to the lower chamber beyond House Do'Urden. The troupe set off fast through the tunnels, discussing whether their course should be House Baenre or Lake Donigarten.

"YOU FELT IT?" MATRON MOTHER QUENTHEL BAENRE asked Myrineyl and Minolin Fey, who walked the parapets of the great house beside her. Far in the distance to the north and west, they could see the flashes and hear the resounding thunder.

"The vibrations of the thunder? Yes, of course," Minolin Fey replied, and Myrineyl nodded.

Quenthel stared at them in confusion. Of course they had felt the reports of the spell battles raging near House Do'Urden, but in light of that other sensation, that most dire and overwhelming realization that the avatar of Lady Lolth had come to Menzoberranzan, how could they think those thunderous booms even mattered?

Because they had not felt it, Quenthel realized. It had been a message from Lolth, a telepathic announcement to the Matron Mother. To the other matrons, as well, she wondered, or just to her? Had it been a warning perhaps for her to get the City of Spiders back into the fold?

Quenthel didn't know what to make of it, or what to think—except she knew without hesitation that she would not heed whatever call Lolth might be sending.

"Where is Yvonnel?" she asked her companions.

The two looked to each other and shrugged. "With Jarlaxle, I had thought," Minolin Fey replied.

"And where is Jarlaxle?"

This time, the other two could only shake their heads.

"Find him," Quenthel ordered. "Find Yvonnel. I must speak with her immediately."

"I will go," Myrineyl offered and trotted off.

"Set every wizard and priestess who is not otherwise engaged to the task as well," Quenthel called after her.

Quenthel knew that what she had felt was surely the presence of Lolth. That the others hadn't sensed it was perhaps important, perhaps not, but one thing she was fairly certain of: if Lolth was sending her a message, or offering intimidation, she was likely doing the same to Yvonnel.

"Relay word to our guarding force to bring all of House Hunzrin here, through the tunnels," Quenthel added.

"Here?" asked a surprised Minolin Fey.

"Prisoners," Quenthel explained. "Send word far and wide to collect prisoners. As many as we can."

Minolin Fey stared at her for just a few moments. "You think we will need to bargain our way out of this," she said, her tone making it clear that it was an accusation.

Quenthel offered a little smile that was meant to be reassuring, but Minolin Fey's scowl did not diminish.

"You did not feel it," Quenthel offered.

"The battle?"

"Her," explained Quenthel, to a puzzled expression.

"*Her*," she said again, more insistently.

"I don't . . ."

Then she caught on, her eyes going wide.

"Prisoners," Quenthel said. "As many as we can take, and bring them here, fully under our control."

This time, Minolin Fey didn't question.

DRIZZT WORKED HIS SHOTS ALONG THE WALL, ONE END TO the other in a continuing stream, searching for an opening, for some way to get at the Del'Armgo nobles. Blue sparks flew from every impact.

"The statues," Jarlaxle warned, and Drizzt had no choice but to drop the bow and draw his blades.

Jarlaxle looked over at him and shook his head—he had no tricks to play. There was no way out.

Sitting on her throne behind the invisible wall, Matron Mez'Barris looked like a satisfied cat, and Drizzt wondered if she was purring.

"Uthegen . . ." she started to say, but caught herself and giggled with what seemed a bit of embarrassment. "Malagdorl," she corrected, "will kill you now, Drizzt Do'Urden."

He doubted she would allow a fair fight, but however he was slain, she'd make sure her beloved Malagdorl would get all the credit, no doubt.

"Go and kill him, my hero," she said to the large man beside her, and she glanced back at the wizard Kaitain, who nodded.

Malagdorl lifted his arms high and issued a great war cry, Khazid'hea in one hand, that black adamantine trident in the other.

Jarlaxle sent a blob of goo at him from his wand, but it hit the magical wall and could not even find a hold there, sliding down.

"At least kill him," Jarlaxle said to Drizzt, who had every intention of doing just that.

Malagdorl dropped Khazid'hea to the floor, simply let it go. If that action surprised Drizzt, what was even more shocking was when, arms still above his head, he grasped the trident with both hands, then spun down and around, driving the tines right into the face of Matron Mez'Barris!

So sudden and lethal was the blow that she didn't even gurgle, just sat locked in place right there with one tine below her chin into her neck, a second through her cheek beside the base of her nose, and the third through the side of her forehead.

With an extended growl, Malagdorl twisted the weapon shaft, the tines tearing flesh and breaking bone.

The top of Mez'Barris's head flopped over.

The brutal warrior then spun about, whipping his weapon around and launching the missile that was dead Mez'Barris into her daughter and the nearest priestesses lined before the throne. He scooped the scepter from the seat where it had fallen, pointed it at the invisible wall, then flung it ahead—to Jarlaxle, for there was no longer the wall of magical force to stop it!

Then Malagdorl grabbed up Khazid'hea once more and leaped for the stunned priestesses.

Taayrul disappeared in the flash of a recall, clearly wanting no part of this. Behind the throne, an overwhelmed Kaitain, too, wanted nothing to do with this disastrous turn.

And those remaining priestesses, without a magical egress available, scrambled and cried for mercy as Malagdorl fell over them.

Those who did get away from the rampaging man were cut down by Taulmaril.

Drizzt couldn't understand what he was seeing, but he wasn't about to pause and question the inexplicable turn of fate. He turned to shoot the nearest statue, but held up, for it was no longer moving. He turned back to Jarlaxle, holding the scepter up above his head and smiling widely.

"It is Kimmuriel," Jarlaxle explained, a bit of wonder in his voice.

Above them, the bubble burst and Dab'nay tumbled down amid the shower of Kimmuriel's remains.

Before them, the last of the priestesses tried to flee, but Malagdorl was there, cutting them apart with Khazid'hea. And when one neared the rear door, she could not leave, as the magical curtain remained.

A thrown trident skewered her, snapping her backbone. An arrow from Taulmaril finished her as she slumped.

Then it was suddenly quiet, eerily so.

Dab'nay began to sob. She tried to stand, but slipped in the remains of Kimmuriel and fell hard.

Drizzt was by her side, helping her up, while Jarlaxle cut Braelin down from his web bindings. Braelin couldn't begin to stand, but the giant drow warrior walked over and hoisted him easily over his shoulder.

"I cannot hold this much longer," Malagdorl said, and it was obviously Kimmuriel forcing the words out of the mouth of his living marionette.

"We're still trapped," Drizzt said, but as he did, Jarlaxle lifted the scepter and whispered something and the magical curtain fell.

And Jarlaxle's smile widened as he turned to the statues.

"We have new allies."

CHAPTER 26

Tightening the Web

As they rushed back to the east, the Callidaean square met only minor resistance—mostly chasmes and other flying fiends swooping down at them or dropping rocks or even drow bodies from above. However, by the time they got back near the Westrift, they had gained the attention of the right flank of the newest demonic horde. Avernil called for renewed shields of magical guardians and weapons, and ordered the ranks tightened.

A group of demons peeled away, charging for them. Zak thought they would have a chance here, except that centering the demon gang was a goristro, huge and powerful and in full charge. It alone could scatter the square with its seven tons of demonic muscle, flesh, and bone. Standing upright, the behemoth was nearly five times Zak's height, but now it came forward in loping strides on all fours, like some cross between a gigantic rothé bull and a monstrous cave bear.

The litter on its shoulders turned on hinges as it went to all fours, keeping the three drow within upright. Priestesses of the Fane, Zak knew, and they were already casting spells—no doubt, defensive spells to ensure that the goristro would not be slowed or diverted.

"What type of fiend?" Galathae asked him, as Avernil and the others called for the Callidaeans to hold strong, and to slow their pace defensively.

"Goristro."

"Of the Abyss?"

"Yes. What are you thinking?"

"Tighten the rank behind me," Galathae instructed. "When I banish it, I will need you to keep the others from overwhelming me."

"The priestesses . . ." Zak started to warn, but the paladin charged ahead.

"Get them moving!" she called back.

Zak was washed by a great moment of doubt. He knew that he should trust Galathae—she had earned that and more in their previous fight together. But he feared that she, like the others, had underestimated their foes, had seen their victory in the ambush outside the city as validation that their goddess would bring them through.

This was one of the most powerful of demonkind, below just the Abyssal lords themselves. And it had come from the Fane of the Goddess, the heart of Lolth within Menzoberranzan, and so likely summoned by the powerful Sos'Umptu Baenre, who ruled the Fane—perhaps that was even her among the three in the litter!

His hesitation cost him any choice in the matter, though, for Galathae was in a full sprint, Bluccidere bobbing beside her.

"Hurry! Hurry! To Galathae!" he cried.

"Holy Galathae!" came the refrain behind him, and the Callidaeans picked up their pace, though they surely could not match Galathae's speed while holding their formation, or probably not, Zak saw, for she was running with the eager wings of her devotion lifting her feet.

"Hold on, good lady," Zak whispered under his breath many times in those next few moments, sending silent pleas and prayers to the brave paladin leading the way.

He saw the blue-white mist forming around her, with her trailing it like smoke as she ran. She was calling forth the banishment, he knew, as she had done with the eye tyrant. Except, as she had explained it to him, since this goristro wasn't of this plane, the banishment would not be a temporary reprieve. She would send this fiend away for a century.

The monstrous beast gained speed, leaving the other demons behind and closing fast on Galathae. Bolts of energy and fire reached down at her from the priestesses in the litter.

Galathae ran through them.

The paladin was chanting loudly now, falling fully into the trance of Eilistraee, as Zak had witnessed before. He took heart in knowing that even if those spells were inflicting damage, Galathae wasn't feeling any pain.

Her song to the Dark Maiden rang loud and clear and seemed to be bolstering him and everyone around him, like the warmth he had felt from her mere presence when the eye tyrant had thrown its devastating rays at him. Her discipline, power, and inspiration were simply amazing to him, and for that one moment, Zaknafein thought there was nothing this wholehearted follower of Eilistraee could not do. She was a tiny thing indeed, charging into the bulk of the goristro, but she seemed so much more formidable and solid, somehow.

They came together, this strong aevendrow woman and the gigantic demon, with a great blinding flash of blue-white light.

The first thing Zak saw as his eyes adjusted was that the goristro was gone, simply gone, and his heart soared.

But so, too, was Galathae soaring, flying back through the air to tumble down hard to the ground halfway between the charging square and the point of impact.

Zak and Azzudonna sprinted ahead, calling desperately for their friend, who struggled to roll to her back, and trembled as she inched Bluccidere up and across her chest. Then she went still, so very still.

The demons were still coming on, but Zak slid to his knees beside the broken paladin, and indeed she was broken, her hips clearly out of joint, bone showing through one thigh, blood pouring from her nose and mouth and from a dozen other wounds.

"Hold on!" Zak begged her. "Call your healing spell. Galathae!"

She stared at him with eyes that would not blink. She raised her arms, her sword, toward Zaknafein.

"Take it," he heard, though he wasn't sure if he actually heard it with his ears or if it was just something echoing in his mind.

"Galathae, no, the priests are coming."

"Take the sword." This time it was Azzudonna telling him, and in a voice quaking and broken by sniffles.

Zak dropped his ice blade and grasped the hilt of Bluccidere, but not to take it from Galathae, just to support its weight in her trembling arms.

Her arms dropped immediately, though, falling limp across her shattered chest.

"Avernil!" Zak yelled.

"Behind you!" Azzudonna warned.

Zak leapt up and spun about, Bluccidere in his left and calling forth Soliardis in his right hand to meet the charge of a birdlike demon.

Rage filled him as he thought of his friend lying so still behind him. Anger drove his blades in a fast and devastating double-sweep, a backhand with Bluccidere sweeping across, with a forehand slash of Soliardis coming right behind it.

He pushed past the gashed and stumbling vrock and charged ahead, full of rage—and full of something else, he only then understood.

He felt something from the sword of Galathae, something comforting and assuring, telling him that everything was all right. Hardly even thinking of the movement, Zak flipped his blades, putting Bluccidere into his power hand, his right hand.

He called to no goddess, but he, too, fell into a trance, leaping and spinning, slashing and stabbing, running about guided only by whatever enemy was nearest.

Whenever he struck, he didn't pause to follow up, but just kept moving along to the next target, gathering wounded demons in his wake.

He could feel their hatred, but so too their pain as Bluccidere bit hard into demon flesh and the radiance of Soliardis ate at them. Sun and ice. Opposites, and yet with the same effect.

Focused on him, that chasing mass of fiends seemed not to even notice that they were running now within the radius of the spiritual guardians of Avernil's priests, that they were being stung and battered with every stride.

Zak turned on the nearest, a frog-like thing, and cut it down with a series of slashes that removed an arm and nearly its head, even though it had no true neck to sever.

Only then did he come back to the moment at hand fully, as if coming out of a trance lent to him by the spirit of Galathae. He glanced once at her, now being lifted by some Callidaeans, and he knew by the stillness of her body as they did that she was truly gone.

Galathae had given her life to remove the goristro from the field, and now the Callidaeans honored that by finishing this group that had come against them.

When their enemies were dispatched, Avernil called to re-form the square, and for Zaknafein to once again lead it front and center.

Zak looked down at Bluccidere, overwhelmed by it all.

"A paladin presented you her sword as her dying wish," Azzudonna said to him, rushing back to his side. "Wield it well!"

"I am no paladin!"

"Bluccidere chose you, Galathae chose you, else the sword would not now let you hold it," said Azzudonna. "That is a holy blade."

"I am not a disciple of Eilistraee!"

"Who can say? Who can know what is in the heart of Zaknafein?"

"You do."

Azzudonna smiled through her tears. "You declare your beliefs with your actions, not mere words, my love," she said. "Bluccidere knows your heart, as did Galathae, as do I. Now, on we go, to fight, to die, if that is to be."

"Go!" Avernil shouted from behind, and Zak's glance forward explained the desperation in the priest's voice.

For now, many enemies, demon and drow and even the enslaved peoples of Menzoberranzan, were rushing their way, with chasmes flying overhead.

Zak ran on, leading the way, but the enemy line was too far ahead, he knew, and he and the Callidaeans would not break free.

Then he took heart, for they were not alone.

The banners of Baenre showed as those forces ran in retreat, and fought through the nearest enemies to join with the Callidaeans.

"To the Bazaar and south to House Baenre!" Zak called to them as they neared.

"Zaknafein?" came a call of obvious surprise, and Zak recognized the leader of the allied force as Weapon Master Andzrel Baenre.

"Well met!" he called out.

"We shall see," Andzrel replied.

And so began the long and perilous run of the joined forces—Baenre, Blaspheme, and Callidaean—with more than a mile to go along the winding ways before they reached the gates of House Baenre.

Zak was a veteran of many battles, but even if he were not, the answer before him was obvious: many would not make it.

ENTRERI LED THE WAY THROUGH HOUSE MELARN, MOVING far enough ahead of Gromph and Catti-brie to quietly dispatch any wandering guards before his two companions came into view, and relaying back news of larger Melarni forces in side corridors and rooms.

Gromph tapped every door they passed with his staff, placing upon them a magical lock. "Speak the name of the giantess at the Hosttower and the doors will open for you," he whispered to Catti-brie. "Do not, and you will have to batter the door down to get through."

The wizard and Catti-brie came around a corner to find a Melarni woman lying on the floor. Beyond her was an open doorway, and beyond that stood Entreri, signaling to them that the side room was occupied and large.

Gromph cast a spell, creating a disembodied eyeball floating in the air before him. It seemed solid at first, but then faded to become translucent, and even though they watched its initial movements, the other two could barely track it as Gromph sent it ahead to peer into the room's open door.

The wizard closed his eyes for a moment, then gave a shrug that seemed almost bored, almost as if he thought this a trivial matter as he moved near to the door. Casting again, he created a small ball of flame in his hand. He tossed it into the room, enacted a simple cantrip to bring the door swinging shut, then walked past, tapping the door with his staff to seal it and noting not at all the shudder from within as his fireball exploded, nor the licks of flames that came from around the door in its frame, from underneath the opening at the bottom with such intensity that they singed his boots.

There came some agonized screaming from within, the fires devouring drow. Catti-brie and Entreri exchanged looks, even the assassin clearly taken aback by the sheer brutality and mercilessness of Gromph.

But that was how it had to be, Catti-brie understood, nodding to Entreri, her expression grim. They weren't here to parlay—the time for that seemed long past.

Clearly unperturbed, Gromph motioned for Entreri to hurry on his way and guide them to Matron Zhindia.

Entreri showed Gromph his dagger once more. "I will find her," he promised. "And I will convince her that she should speak with you." He nodded back toward the sealed door. "How do you know that all in there are de . . . no longer a threat?"

Gromph chortled.

"Stupid question," Catti-brie noted.

"Apparently," said Entreri. "We are nearing the side of the compound which houses the noble family. Let us hope Zhindia is at home."

"Your task is her alone now," Gromph reminded him, and once more, the wizard covered Entreri with a cloak of invisibility. "Ignore any guards you can quietly pass. Stay as well concealed as you can manage even with the enchantment I have placed upon you," Gromph warned. "No simple spell of invisibility will get you through the corridors about the chambers of one as strong and cunning as Zhindia Melarn."

"I'm aware," Entreri said, and with a shake of his head at the patronizing archmage, off he went, into the shadows, the other two moving more cautiously and quite conspicuously behind.

As he crept along, he thought of how Gromph could have made

them both invisible as well, as could Catti-brie, for that matter, and for a moment, Entreri was confused.

Then he nodded as he came to understand. His companions weren't shying from any fights from this point on. They would welcome the attention so that he could get to Zhindia while her minions were otherwise engaged with them. Whether that mattered wasn't clear—Gromph's plan still seemed unlikely to him. Would one as zealous as Matron Zhindia Melarn simply throw aside that loyalty to Lolth and surrender her lofty ambitions?

The assassin felt his dagger hilt and wondered if the deception would be enough.

Yes, Zhindia knew what it had done to her daughter. And it made sense to surmise that it would do her no good to hang on to her loyalty to Lolth if she was going to be sent beyond the Spider Queen's grasp into the void of obliteration.

Except, of course, that was an empty threat, and that gave Enteri pause.

What other choice did they have, though? And maybe the subterfuge would work. The mere fact that Gromph was so determined to try ignited a thousand more questions in the assassin's mind, but those were questions for another day, for now the present demanded his every attention.

No matter what, he thought, he'd have a knife to the matron's neck, and even if he didn't destroy her soul, he *could* spill her blood.

He found that his memory of the house layout was correct, as he passed by many more sentries in short order, too alert and too close together for him to surreptitiously clear the way for his two partners.

That wasn't his job, though. And besides, Gromph and Catti-brie hardly needed him to deal with some minor house guards.

He came upon a door he recognized, and knew beyond it lay Zhindia's war room. He recalled a fight in there from his last visit to House Melarn, and pictured the layout and large table.

He cracked open the door and peered in, then pulled away immediately to find that the table was ringed not by Melarni priestesses, but by ugly demonic creatures. Yochlols, he knew, the Handmaidens of Lolth.

He peeked in once more.

Zhindia wasn't there.

He listened to the chatter of the demons, though he didn't know their language well enough to decipher much.

He peeked in once more when he heard a woman's voice addressing the yochlols, and in common Drow, a language Entreri knew well.

"Matron Zhindia will join you shortly," the priestess told them. "She remains in her private quarters in preparation."

How convenient, Entreri thought, but he wasn't about to question his luck. Unless the layout of the house had been changed, he knew the way.

He neared Zhindia's door soon after, but stopped and ducked to the side when the two guards before it perked up suddenly. They hadn't seen him, though, he realized a moment later, when the jolting report of a lightning bolt echoed somewhere behind him.

Gromph and Catti-brie, he understood—just as he understood they didn't know about the handmaidens!

One of the guards pushed open Zhindia's door and called inside. A sharp response came from within and the guard fell back, then gathered up her peer and the two ran off to join the fight, drawing their swords as they went.

Entreri knew that he had to trust his friends—even with the yochlols, should those demons even join the fight, he had to believe that Gromph and Catti-brie could handle it.

His job lay before him.

He went to the door and glanced in.

Zhindia was at her desk across the way, her back to him.

Silent as death, Artemis Entreri entered her chamber.

CATTI-BRIE AND GROMPH CROUCHED ON OPPOSITE SIDES of an intersection of two corridors. Behind them, the Melarni guards had scattered under the thunder of a Gromph lightning bolt, but there remained commotion down there and they both knew that they would soon be assailed from behind once again.

Catti-brie worked hard, delving into her spell repertoire to put as many wards and fortifications as she could upon herself and on her partner, as he, too, worked.

Before them, the resistance was heavier, with priestesses and a pair of wizards returning magical destruction. A fireball went off right above and between the two, filling the corridors about them.

Catti-brie's skin reddened under the heat, but her spells fended the brunt of the blast. She renewed them, as Gromph returned the fireball in kind, only with one many times more powerful.

Screams from ahead in the corridor told Catti-brie that their enemies were not as well warded.

"Keep moving forward," Gromph instructed, putting action to his words and stepping into the main corridor, inviting her to fall in right behind him.

A hail of crossbow bolts and javelins flew at him, but he had enacted a magical shield and that first volley of missiles was fully blocked.

A lightning bolt followed, sizzling down the hallway, a swarm of missiles of magical energy on the lightning's heels.

But Gromph held up his staff and the lightning bolt struck its tip and was absorbed. The missiles, too, went into that powerful item, as if it simply ate them—only to regurgitate them, flinging them back down the corridor the way they had come. One unfortunate guard took that moment to stand and level his crossbow.

The swarm blew him from his feet—literally. Catti-brie tried not to grimace at the sight of a pair of boots left standing where the guard once was.

"Keep moving," Gromph said.

ZHINDIA SEEMED IN NO HURRY TO JOIN THE YOCHLOLS, nor was she showing any urgency in this room, even though the report of the lightning strikes could be heard not so far away. She sat in meditation, seemingly, her back to the door, hands folded before her, at a desk in front of a mirror.

Entreri looked for some clue that he had been seen when he entered the room. He was invisible, yes, but was Zhindia aware of him? Of anything?

It didn't really matter. His companions were waging a fight down there, one he could stop fast by arriving with this particular prisoner.

Her eyes were closed, he noted from the reflection in the mirror as he slowly and silently approached.

Then he was there, at her side, with a sudden rush, and he drew out his dagger and put it against her throat, coming visible as he nicked her, just a bit.

Zhindia's eyes popped open wide and she made a little hissing sound.

"You dare to enter my chamber? To threaten *me*, the Chosen of Lolth?"

"Now you are *my* chosen. And I choose to do with you whatever I will."

"You believe you can do anything to me?"

"I do. You do not recognize me, it seems," Entreri whispered to her, moving his lips right beside her ear. He saw himself in the mirror and admired the job he had done in disguising himself as a drow.

"Do you recognize this, perhaps?" He called forth the magic of the jeweled dagger, drawing a bit of her life force through its vampiric blade. The blade could still do that much, even though its soul-destroying curse had been removed.

Zhindia stiffened in her chair. She had felt the former and clearly did not know about the latter.

"Yes, look at it closely, Zhindia Melarn," Entreri whispered. "You have seen this dagger before. It took from you your daughter. It took your daughter from Lolth."

"What do you want? Are you mad? The tortures that await—"

"Shut up," Entreri said, and he scraped the blade against her skin. "You think you can possibly be in a god's favor when you don't even *exist?* What good is the service you've shown to Lolth if you are forever taken from her? You understand that, don't you?"

"I don't know that there have been many human driders."

"You can avoid the fate," Entreri said, ignoring her threat, or at least, making it seem like he was ignoring her threat—he had to admit he was a little impressed at the drow's bravado. "We want this war ended and you can do that. And if you do that, I will not take from you your soul."

"Is that why you have come to this house with Gromph Baenre and Catti-brie Do'Urden, Artemis Entreri?" she replied calmly. "To threaten my eternal soul?"

He started to respond, but got caught by the notion that she not only knew his name, but the names of his companions. He asked the question with his expression in the mirror.

"And with a dagger that is no longer even capable of such a feat."

And Zhindia, who was much more than Zhindia Melarn, gave him his answer. She didn't change position, but she grew, suddenly and violently, sprouting eight legs from her two, gaining in size to dwarf the man, her sheer increase in bulk sending him flying backward.

Entreri hopped back to his feet and reached for his sword.

But he knew . . .

He knew the futility of *any* weapon—cursed or not—in this chamber, and he reached instead for the door, bursting out of the room with the avatar of Lolth close behind.

THE TWO OF THEM FELL INTO A BEAUTIFUL AND HARMO-nious rhythm, Gromph filling the corridor behind with fireball after fireball, knowing that the doors had all been magically sealed, and thus offering the attackers few places to hide from the biting flames. To the right—as he was on the right-hand side of the intersection—he favored lightning bolts, launching a devastating and blinding flash when an enemy appeared.

And before him, where the corridor widened considerably into an interior courtyard before the section housing the nobles, and the defenders had cover in the form of strategic barricades and unsealed doors, Gromph chased them with psychic attacks, from which they could not hide.

For Catti-brie, the course of spells depended more on the actions of the enemy. Whenever an attack of some various elemental magic came in, she countered with protections. Her healing spells flew constantly, minor ones, to keep both herself and her companion free of pain so that they could better concentrate on the task at hand.

When a priestess leaped out in the left-hand corridor, not too far from Catti-brie, she stole the spell right from the woman's mouth with a countering chant, then hit her hard with a jolt of wind that sent her flying backward.

She turned her attention back to healing and protective spells when a fireball exploded above the intersection, then felt her hair fly wildly from the tingling of a lightning bolt that began right beside her, one thrown from Gromph down the hall at the priestess she had been battling.

When the flames cleared, Catti-brie looked that way to see the priestess crumbled and smoking before the charred door at the end of that corridor.

I believe we two could level half the city! she heard in her mind, and she glanced over to see a wink from the archmage.

Their coordination was so instinctive, so seamless, that Catti-brie wasn't sure she doubted him.

She dared to hope.

And that hope only grew when the corridors about their position quieted.

"Entreri?" she whispered across the hall to Gromph, who stood ready but was not in the act of spellcasting.

She looked down the hall beyond the wizard, then back behind them both, and then forward again, toward the region known to house the Melarni nobles. Their enemies were still all about, she noted, but not a whisper could be heard.

Ahead and to the right, a door opened, and a parade of yochlols came through.

"Gromph?" Catti-brie whispered with some urgency, and heard in her head in response, *Hold . . . Entreri is persuasive. Yochlols are not formidable in battle.*

"But where is he?" she asked, and the wizard shook his head. She wanted to trust in Entreri's abilities—she had seen them personally over the course of many years and knew that there was none better at the art of assassination than Artemis Entreri.

Still, the hairs on the back of her neck were standing up. Had he neutralized House Melarn?

Unlike the quiet entrance of the handmaidens, a door across the courtyard before them to the left burst open suddenly, and Artemis Entreri came running through, darting left and right and diving repeatedly as if expecting a rain of missiles.

He headed straight for Gromph and Catti-brie, yelling, "Run!"

But the word elongated, stretched weirdly as Artemis Entreri stretched weirdly, caught by some shadowy arms that confused Catti-brie for just a moment—until she saw the giant drider that was obviously much more than a drider coming through the same door, bursting the jamb and the wall about it as it simply plowed through with godlike power.

Or with goddess-like power.

And her hope faded to nothing.

CHAPTER 27

Lolth's Warrior

Quickly, then," said Drizzt. "Before Kimmuriel loses control of Malagdorl." He started to lead the way, but Jarlaxle held up his hand to stop him.

"*They* will lead," the rogue corrected, and again put the scepter to use.

Now the statues, of spiders and of Lolth, moved to his commands, pushing through the doors at the front of the chapel, into the main house of Barrison Del'Armgo.

"Hold on," Drizzt heard Jarlaxle telling Kimmuriel as they moved swiftly behind their wall of living stone.

"I . . . I have him," Kimmuriel said through Malagdorl, a voice shaky at first, but steadying as the psionicist strengthened his mental hold on the warrior.

"Throw him into battle," a still-shaken, still-mortified Dab'nay suggested. "Let him kill more of them, then let him die by their hands!"

"Keep him!" Jarlaxle quickly countered.

"Just . . . move," Kimmuriel gritted out.

They were out of the main house, rushing down a wide stairway for the courtyard leading to the primary compound gate. Stone spiders flanked them and protected their rear, while the statue of Lolth led the way, chasing off any Armgo guards that stood before them.

There was no resistance, however, those outside clearly too confused to even attempt to slow the run, and the troupe made it almost all the way across before a voice magnified by magic finally rang out: "It is Drizzt the heretic! Kill them!"

Kaitain, they knew.

Jarlaxle sent the statue of Lolth in full charge at the gate guards. He lifted a wand and sent a ball of sticky goo up to seal the door of the guard tower on one side, then the other.

But now crossbow bolts began to fly at them, chipping the animated spider statues, which Jarlaxle kept closely huddled about them like some monstrous moving battlement.

Drizzt brought out Taulmaril once more and returned fire, arrows sparking with magic flashing around the compound with streaks of lightning.

"Go," Kimmuriel told them when they reached the gate. "I will fight and let Malagdorl feel the pain and the chill of creeping death."

"No," Jarlaxle answered, not in a plaintive and desperate plea, but in the tone of one hatching a scheme. "No, we need him. Hold a bit longer and let us be gone."

Jarlaxle started through the gate, but stopped fast and jumped back in, looking down at the scepter as if deceived.

"By Lolth's Skitter!" he cursed.

"What?" Dab'nay asked, stumbling out from the compound.

"Mez'Barris's scepter won't work beyond this gate."

THE SHADOWY ARMS LIFTED ENTRERI UP INTO THE AIR, then slammed him back to the floor. He tried to crawl for his friends, again trying to tell them to run.

Nothing came out, though—it was hard to yell when the air was being knocked out of you—and up he went again, then back down hard, and this time, he just lay there on the floor.

The shadowy arms began to drag him backward. The giant half drow, half spider glared at Catti-brie and Gromph, as if daring them to intervene.

So they did.

Catti-brie reached out with a spell of healing, bringing Entreri back to consciousness, and Gromph did her one better, throwing a line of strange magical energy at Entreri, one that became a twisting swirl about him, bending the shadowy arms, bending the man, bending, it seemed, the very nature of the Material Plane.

Entreri spun and twisted and wrapped in on himself, and then was gone—or not gone, reappearing right beside Catti-brie.

"Kill them," she heard, or felt in her head—she couldn't be sure— from the great creature, and the drow arm reached out with a clawed hand, and from that came a bolt of dark energy, crackling across the room at Gromph.

The wizard presented his staff before him, and as with the earlier spells, it caught the witch bolt and trapped it, absorbing the power.

But now all the others in the hall were casting, too, and Catti-brie understood that she and her companions were likely doomed. She launched into her own spell, ignoring the incoming firepower and hoping her wards would hold it back enough.

Even standing a couple of steps from the archmage, she could feel Gromph's staff vibrating with power!

The flash of fire bit at her, at Gromph, at Entreri, who lay writhing on the ground beside her.

But she kept her concentration and brought forth a globe of protection, a shield against all but the most powerful spells. Even the dark energy aimed at Gromph was halted by it.

She was surprised, then, when Gromph turned an angry scowl upon her.

JARLAXLE EXCLAIMED, "GO, YOU THREE! I'LL HOLD THE fight as long as I can."

"We fight as one," Drizzt argued, and Dab'nay seconded him.

Jarlaxle started to protest, but Drizzt wouldn't hear of it. He hadn't wanted to bring in Guen, as the panther had been used extensively in his time here patrolling the Braeryn and needed rest, but he wasn't about to let Jarlaxle try to hold the ground alone. He produced the onyx figurine and called to the panther.

"Farewell, then, my oldest friend," the voice of Malagdorl, the spirit of Kimmuriel, said. "My time runs short."

"No, hold on!" Jarlaxle implored him. "We will find a way."

Be quick, Jarlaxle, for I cannot hold much longer, came the telepathic reply to Drizzt, to Jarlaxle, and to Dab'nay, who was then struggling to get out of the huge warrior's grasp.

A fireball went off nearby, close enough to tell them that their time in the compound was over.

"Get out," Jarlaxle ordered.

"All of us or none!" Dab'nay demanded.

"I have no intention of dying in here," Jarlaxle told her, told them all.

Drizzt, bow in hand and arrows now flying out at the closing Armgo forces, looked to his friend.

"I'm touched that you'd think I'd die for you," Jarlaxle told him. "But get out now!" As he spoke, he was removing his hat. Drizzt knew what was in there and suspected that Jarlaxle had the escape all planned out.

"Go," he told Dab'nay, rushing past her toward the gates.

"We go together or not at all!" Dab'nay continued to protest to Jarlaxle, but Malagdorl picked her up, tucked her under one arm as if she were no more than a child, and went out of the compound behind Drizzt, carrying both her and Braelin. He and Drizzt paused and turned back to regard Jarlaxle.

Despite the dire situation, despite knowing this might be the last time he looked upon a good friend, Drizzt almost laughed helplessly as he sorted out the moves by Jarlaxle.

"Trust in him," he told himself, reminded himself, for how many times had he seen Jarlaxle escape what had seemed like certain death?

Of course, the same could have been said about Kimmuriel.

The Lolth-like statue was closing the gates, which opened into the courtyard, while the spiders were huddling and following close behind. Jarlaxle would press them against those gates, then deactivate them and make his escape, leaving the Armgos to figure out how they might get their gates opened again without destroying their own constructs.

A crossbow quarrel from above reminded him that they could not wait. He leveled Taulmaril and returned fire, a line of lightning arrows that put the Armgo defenders back down behind their parapet. Then he turned and fled behind Malagdorl and Dab'nay, down the short entry walkway and out onto the main boulevard of the raised area filled with noble houses. There, at the street know as Highcastle Lane, the fleeing companions were given pause once more, for coming from the north was the retreat of the Baenres and their allies, fleeing for the great house across the way on the eastern end of the Qu'ellarz'orl.

Behind the routed forces came the demon horde and the soldiers of the enemy houses.

"Keep going!" Drizzt heard Jarlaxle's voice from behind, and he turned to see the rogue coming through the gate of Barrison Del'Armgo, though it was surely still closed. Jarlaxle pulled his portable hole from the barrier and tucked it away, sprinting toward his friend—and still holding the scepter of Matron Mez'Barris, Drizzt noted.

Drizzt laid down cover fire as Jarlaxle caught up to his friend, and they turned as one for House Baenre, which was not far away. It seemed like they could beat the incoming horde to the gates of that last sanctuary. And perhaps even offer help to those retreating under the banner of House Baenre.

Drizzt! the ranger heard in his head, and he knew it to be Kimmuriel. *Farewell!*

Jarlaxle's gasp told him that he wasn't the only one who had heard the dire pronouncement.

He turned about just in time to see Malagdorl—and it was indeed Malagdorl once more—drop Dab'nay to the ground, flip the weak Braelin over his shoulder, and draw out Khazid'hea.

LIGHTNING AND FIRE, A STORM OF POUNDING SLEET AND a barrage of magical missiles, pounded the dome covering the three companions. Melarni attackers showed in all four corridors, bolstered, no doubt, by the presence, the overwhelming presence, that had come onto the battlefield.

The yochlols were chanting, the avatar—Catti-brie was certain it was indeed the avatar of Lolth—stood tall and smug, smiling and mocking the trio.

"Go," Gromph told Catti-brie. "Go now."

"Come with us."

Gromph snarled at her, his feral disapproval and his scowl reminding her of their deal, of the promise he made her swear.

He turned back to the wider area, to the avatar and the Melarni nobles and the yochlols. Presenting his staff, he walked out of the globe.

"You cannot beat them!" Catti-brie yelled.

"I will settle for a draw," came the reply.

MALAGDORL TURNED FOR THE STUNNED BRAELIN, LIFTing the deadly Khazid'hea, but Drizzt was there in an eyeblink, intercepting the stroke with Icingdeath and batting it wide, then driving Malagdorl back with a rolling flurry of his scimitars, one over the other so rapidly that Malagdorl had no chance of picking off every cut and so was forced back, away from Braelin.

"Jarlaxle!" Drizzt called. "Get her to House Baenre."

"Don't kill him," Jarlaxle replied. "We need this one."

Drizzt wasn't quite sure that was going to be an option, but he grunted in assent as Jarlaxle gathered Dab'nay up behind the ranger and the two of them went to Braelin. Drizzt heard them shuffling off.

Malagdorl started to Drizzt's right, moving to cut them off, and Drizzt spun that way, blades spinning and stabbing, trying to force the brutish man back.

But the intercept was a feint, Malagdorl using Drizzt's compassion against him, and he changed his angle even as Drizzt rolled in front of him, and sidestepped back the way he had come, just a single step, but enough to give Malagdorl a bit of an opening.

So he thought.

Indeed, Drizzt's blades were farther over, and the drow was leaning that way, but taking that as an indication of Drizzt being overbalanced proved folly, for as Malagdorl stabbed out with his trident, Drizzt leaned farther to his right, bent straight over, and lifted his left leg, driving the tip of his boot up into Malagdorl's left armpit.

Drizzt got his leg down before Khazid'hea came slashing across, and he turned, now facing up against the man and wasting no time in going after him, after the lowered trident and arm as the man recovered from the shock and sting of the kick.

A lesser warrior would have been finished against the superbly trained and viper-quick Drizzt, but Malagdorl had more than brute strength.

Much more, Drizzt realized.

He threw back his left shoulder, trident going behind him as he half turned, Khazid'hea cutting hard across, then in a backhand the other way. And now Malagdorl kicked high and hard for Drizzt's chest as Drizzt leaned backward to avoid the cutting sword.

But the kick didn't hit, for Drizzt just kept going backward, bending at the knees, falling so low that he seemed as if surely to topple over to the ground.

Malagdorl recovered from both his missed kick and the wild backhand and leaped up and ahead to try to stomp the prostrated ranger.

Except Drizzt was not lying flat. His shoulders lightly touched down and in that instant of contact with the stone, he reversed the move, stomach tightening, calves and hamstrings locking, pulling, and he came back upright, ducking to get under the leaping Malagdorl, turning as he did and driving his forearm and shoulder against the back of the big man's legs, upending him.

Malagdorl crashed down hard and Drizzt went for the cripple, driving Twinkle down hard on the big man's thigh.

Malagdorl's black plate mail rejected the blow, wholly.

Now Drizzt was surprised—there wasn't much that his scimitar could not cut through—and in that instant of shock, Malagdorl rolled and kicked him hard, sending him flying backward, stumbling.

JARLAXLE'S EYES WIDENED INDEED WHEN HE CAME TO recognize some of the fleeing Baenre allies.

"Zaknafein," he breathed.

"Callidaeans," Dab'nay said at his side.

The group was still far to the north and turning east for House Baenre.

But they, too, were watching the fight of the titans before the entryway of House Barrison Del'Armgo.

"The heretic!" someone cried from the back of one of the pursuing Melarni groups.

"Lolth's Warrior!" many shouted together.

And then came Zak's voice: "Drizzt!"

The flight for House Baenre and the pursuit of those retreating forces all seemed to stop then, as this clash of Drizzt and Malagdorl was called all about.

Not the demons, though. The frenzied beasts just kept charging, forcing the Baenre group to take up their run once more.

Jarlaxle looked back at his friend and the weapon master. "Finish the fight fast," he whispered.

He wondered what effect the defeat of Malagdorl, of Lolth's Warrior, in front of the Lolthian forces might have.

This was an outcome Jarlaxle began to doubt when a familiar figure appeared on the wall of the Barrison Del'Armgo compound, not so far from the battling warriors.

Kaitain, powerful and deadly, and taking aim for Drizzt.

MALAGDORL CAME ON WITH SEEMING ABANDON, Khazid'hea flashing across with wild slashes, the trident following, sometimes a slash, sometimes a stab.

Drizzt kept moving, left, right, and back, looking for openings, confident he could keep ahead of the purely straightforward barrage. He was surprised by the brutish and unsophisticated tactics, but understood that Malagdorl's sheer power would overwhelm most fighters, after all.

Perhaps the weapon master had abandoned all finesse in his supreme confidence.

Or maybe it was just a feint, a lure to force Drizzt into a more prosaic response, to get him in close. Time was on the hulking man's side, after all, as the demon hordes and Lolthians were coming fast up to the Qu'ellarz'orl.

In any case, he was overswinging, and even with his great strength allowing him to halt a strike or reverse a sidelong cut, he was offering openings.

Drizzt took them—always alert to any subterfuge—coming in behind the cuts, stabbing with his scimitars, scoring in Malagdorl's belly, his chest, even a double-low thrust that got the man on the legs and nearly tripped him up.

But didn't hurt him. None of them hurt him!

The wild flurry continued, Malagdorl bulling ahead, pursuing to the side, blade and trident always in motion, always prodding, cutting, anything to score a hit—and giving up many strikes in return.

Futile strikes.

"Your weapons will not get through," Malagdorl taunted, skidding to a sudden stop. "But ask yourself: Do you think *your* meager armor will hold back *these?*" He presented the trident and Khazid'hea and charged, only to pull up short, looking up and past Drizzt.

That one moment registered clearly in Drizzt's thoughts and he reacted by simply throwing himself aside—right as a lightning bolt struck the ground where he had been standing with thunderous force, chipping the very stone.

Drizzt spun and rolled, kicking the ground hard, ignoring the burn of the near miss, the tingling numbness in his limbs. He came up to find Malagdorl laughing and stalking in.

But again, Malagdorl paused and glanced to the side, leading Drizzt's gaze to the wall of House Barrison Del'Armgo and the lone figure up there, the wizard Kaitain, waving his arms for another assault.

"Have you met my protector?" Malagdorl taunted and laughed again—or started to, until a ball of flying blackness rose up behind the wizard, slammed into the wizard, and drove him over the wall and crashing to the ground, six hundred pounds of feline fury landing atop him.

"I have," Drizzt said. "Have you met mine?"

Malagdorl howled in rage and leaped ahead, as Drizzt had hoped. His strikes were heavy, too powerful to block, and an opponent who tried to do so would have felt the barbed tines of the trident and the fine edge of Khazid'hea blasting through and finishing the fight.

So Drizzt didn't try to block. His hands, speed magnified by his enchanted bracers, moved his blades expertly enough to redirect the attacks, just a tiny bit, over to his right.

A tiny bit was all the fast warrior needed.

To further disorient Malagdorl, Drizzt flipped Icingdeath straight up between the trident and sword.

Looking at the blade, slapping it aside, Malagdorl could not comprehend that Drizzt had ghost-stepped, a single, sudden stride, to put him behind and to the side.

Drizzt turned fast, thinking to strike with Twinkle . . . and he might have gotten his blade far enough around with his left hand to score a hit on the exposed flesh of the back of Malagdorl's neck.

But he changed his mind and struck out with his bare hand—his closer hand—instead, his open palm clapping hard against the enchanted armor.

And so strong was that strike that it sent Malagdorl stumbling forward. The armor, of course, prevented any serious physical injury.

But it did mean he could do something to the hulking warrior.

With that knowledge, Drizzt calmed . . . and smiled.

CATTI-BRIE MOVED AS NEAR TO GROMPH AS SHE COULD without leaving the globe of protection, peering through the splashes of flames and lightning bolts the enemy was raining upon them.

She yelled to the archmage repeatedly, but he paid her no heed, and probably could barely hear her through the din of magical explosions and chanting from every direction. She saw him, though, standing there so very vulnerable, his robes trailing wisps of smoke from the bits of fireballs that got around the wards he and Catti-brie had placed, his hair dancing wildly under the shock of lightning.

But he stood there, staff presented, and he was not casting.

As one shower of lightning sparks flew aside, Catti-brie saw clearly Gromph's staff, glowing with energy now, absorbing more.

Then it hit her. She knew of such rare staves that could hold great magical power. Overcharged or otherwise broken and they would release it all, all at once, a single, devastating blast.

She thought of Gromph's other items, the helm and the necklace, which could also be triggered in such a cataclysm.

No, she mouthed.

"Go!" Gromph ordered for the last time, and he was shaking and he was burning, and he took the staff up in both hands, top and bottom, and held it horizontally before him, falling to one knee, the other foot braced before him as he brought the staff down across his knee.

With no further hesitation, Catti-brie grabbed Entreri's shoulder and voiced her word of recall, but she saw, just for an instant, the flash of the breaking staff, felt, just for an instant, the sudden roll of pure magic released.

Her sight was taken from her in that instant. She felt disembodied, just for a moment, as she was thrown through the blast, through the miles of rock and soil, and she felt some tassels tickling her nose as she lay on the ground.

On the rug in her room in the Ivy Mansion.

SEEMING MORE PERTURBED THAN HURT, MALAGDORL caught himself a few strides later, straightened, and turned slowly to face Drizzt.

"And now you have but one blade," he said, looking to the side and the fallen scimitar.

"And now . . ." he started to add, raising his weapons. But he stopped the sentence and the movement, a curious expression coming over his face.

"Do you feel them?" Drizzt asked, reaching out with his free hand. "The vibrations?"

"What?" Malagdorl asked as Drizzt snapped his hand shut, releasing the brutal monk strike, the quivering palm.

Malagdorl's next attempt to curse came out as a gush of blood, and he wavered and stumbled, trying to orient his weapons as Drizzt charged in.

Malagdorl swung—too high!—as Drizzt fell into a skid past him, then planted one foot to lock himself in place and send him spinning around and up in a circle kick that buckled his leg and dropped him to one knee. Stubbornly, Malagdorl came around with a cut of Khazid'hea, but Drizzt hadn't stopped moving, continuing his spin like an unwinding coil, rising and kicking Malagdorl again, right in the face—one of the few unarmored parts of his body—laying him low on the ground.

Drizzt started away, motioning to Jarlaxle, but barely had he gone a few steps when he heard a growl from behind. He turned about, blinking in surprise, to see Malagdorl stubbornly rising and growling. Drizzt had exchanged quivering palm strikes with Grandmaster Kane, blows that had left both of them ragged. He had executed this one with clear and full force against Malagdorl, a man who had no knowledge or understanding of it, and to see him fighting through the debilitating effects was truly startling.

Drizzt stared at him, shaking his head in disbelief, and forcing from himself a new and higher level of respect for this hulking weapon master's sheer toughness.

He watched to see if Malagdorl would sway as he straightened, and he did seem off-balance for just a moment. But then he steadied, and, amazingly, he charged, roaring and stabbing and slashing with unbridled ferocity.

Drizzt wanted no part of that weapon-leading bull rush, and he started right, then darted left, spinning out of Khazid'hea's reach just barely, and snapping off a backhand to slap the sword farther ahead of Malagdorl, to keep the big man moving forward and thus, farther past him.

Drizzt didn't pursue, though he might have been able to land some hit or another. Nothing that would finish Malagdorl, he knew, and he decided that such inconsequential strikes weren't the way at this point.

He was there when Malagdorl turned about, though, meeting the big man's next flurry with the deft and perfectly angled parries of Twinkle.

Ahead stabbed the adamantine trident, and a quick down-and-out block moved it harmlessly wide.

Across came Khazid'hea, brutally, right behind, but Drizzt ducked, got his blade up fast enough to intercept Malagdorl's sudden attempt to reverse the sword's route, then down again fast enough to block the trident as the weapon master tried to slash it across.

Drizzt sprang into a backflip, landing farther from the big man, breaking the flow.

He had learned something on the deflection of Khazid'hea. He had felt the residual weakness within Malagdorl from the quivering palm. His opponent was running on pure determination now, Drizzt understood, simply denying the damage.

On Malagdorl came, stabbing with the trident, slashing the sword, once and again, then reversing and stabbing Khazid'hea while locking the trident under his arm, then leaping forward to close the gap and swinging about violently to send that three-tined killer sweeping for the side of Drizzt's chest.

Drizzt had seen the arm lock, though, a commitment to that very strike, and as Malagdorl began his turn, Drizzt knew that it was one he could not reverse, could not stop.

Up went Drizzt, high into the air, the trident cutting below him, and as he rose, Drizzt twisted and inverted, coming back down from on high, twisting and turning again to take full advantage of the weight of his descent, lying almost flat out so that his full force gathered in that single downward punch against the side of Malagdorl's face, violently snapping the man's head to the side.

Drizzt landed almost flat, but lightly, springing right back up, ready to retreat or strike again.

He needed to do neither, though. Malagdorl's head came back

around so that he was facing Drizzt, though whether he was staring incredulously at Drizzt or off into nothingness, Drizzt could not tell.

"I am Lolth's Warrior!" Malagdorl roared in denial.

Then he simply fell over to the side.

"That should tell you something about Lolth," Drizzt replied. He sheathed Twinkle and took a step for Icingdeath.

GROMPH FELT THE POWER GROWING BEYOND THE LIMITS of his powerful stave. The tingling energy rolled up his arm as surely as the licking flames from fireballs that could not be caught by the implement.

He knew that just letting it swallow a few more spells would cause it to burst, but that didn't seem satisfying enough to him in this moment of ultimate defiance.

He didn't know if Catti-brie and Entreri had left—but if not, it was their own fault, and so he didn't care.

He only cared about this moment before him, when he could punch Lolth—her avatar, at least—in the face.

He brought the staff down across his knee knowing that it would be the end of his physical body, that the released energies of the retributive strike would turn him to ash. Sometimes such a fate could be avoided, so said the old texts he had read when researching the item, but Gromph didn't even try.

He watched the staff crack over his knee, saw the blinding burst of brilliance, felt the concussive heat wave roll out, roll through him.

And then he felt out of body, as if the very consciousness and being of the udadrow known as Gromph Baenre had simply ceased to exist, and nothing mattered, past or future, because there was no present—just this thought, his seemingly last experience and expression of . . . nothingness.

Blackness. So deep he no longer knew it was blackness.

Quiet. So quiet he no longer knew it was silent.

He just no longer knew.

CHAPTER 28

The Disbursement

Drizzt started to move toward the fallen weapon master, but then came such a roar, such a thunderous retort, such a brilliant white light, then such an overwhelming line of concussion, that Drizzt was thrown from his feet—many were thrown from their feet.

Drizzt managed to catch himself and spin about to see the source, a washing, widening circle of force in the west, in the stalactite maze known as Lolth's Web, in House Melarn. Like a heavy shovel cracking sidelong across the icicles on a roof overhang, the force shattered and splintered those stalactites.

A host of fireballs exploded in the tumbling stone. A series of multicolored beams flashed every which way, adding to the destruction and the sheer power of the blast.

The entire cavern that housed Menzoberranzan groaned in protest. The earthquakes continued as spire after spire of House Melarn fell from on high, great chunks of the ceiling above Lolth's Web following their descent.

"Drizzt!" Dab'nay shouted, drawing the ranger from his shock, turning about to see Malagdorl standing once more.

Up came his scimitars, but the hulking warrior dropped his weapons and held up his hands.

"It's me, Kimmuriel. You sent his mind away and so I found a last grip here. But quickly, run, all of us, to House Baenre. The enemy is come!"

Relieved his friend was—somehow—still here, Drizzt watched as the body of the weapon master sprinted past him over to Dab'nay and Jarlaxle, scooping Braelin from them easily and rushing for House Baenre.

Drizzt paused only long enough to grab the trident and Khazid'hea.

Wield me! the sentient sword rang in his mind. *Oh, true warrior, I have returned to you!*

"Oh, shut up," Drizzt replied and slid the silly thing into one of his scabbards, caring not at all for the awkward fit in a sheath meant for a scimitar.

They ran for the house, getting to the gates along with the hundreds fleeing from the battle before House Do'Urden.

Baenre guards lined the walls there and the entry path to the courtyard, weapons ready. Those on the wall sent out missiles, physical and magical, at the pursuing demon horde, while those by the gates closely watched those entering—and a great pause indeed was given them when Malagdorl Del'Armgo arrived.

"He is with me," Jarlaxle said.

"And with me," Drizzt added.

"A fine prisoner!" Jarlaxle told them.

A team of Baenres immediately ran to the huge man, magical cords going out to bind him tightly, wrists and ankles. They were not careful with him and they brought him hard to the ground to finish fully incapacitating him.

"Do you feel that pain?" Jarlaxle asked.

"A bit," Kimmuriel conceded. "But this one does so deserve it."

"I will tell Yvonnel who you really are and she will free—"

"No," Kimmuriel interrupted. "He is already waking. He will push me out."

"Then find another, a weaker one, and—"

"No!" Kimmuriel said flatly. "I can think of little less moral."

"A body, then," Jarlaxle offered. "One freshly killed, and physically healed by the priestesses as you enter and take control."

The big man, hoisted back to his feet, laughed at the absurd notion.

"Then how?" Jarlaxle demanded.

Drizzt came over in support of his friend.

"Where will you go?" Jarlaxle pleaded when Kimmuriel didn't answer.

"You know," the hulking possessed man replied audibly.

"No," Jarlaxle breathed. "I won't let you!"

Drizzt saw that Jarlaxle was fighting back tears.

"Take another—a weaker one, and hold on," Jarlaxle ordered.

"My time is ending," the voice of Malagdorl repeated. "There is nothing to be done."

"Except to say farewell," Drizzt said. "I will remember our talks on the road to the monastery, my friend. May you find oneness with the hive mind and peace in eternity."

"And you, warrior. Survive, I beg."

"There is an emptiness . . . I will miss you, Kimmuriel," Jarlaxle said, as quiet as Drizzt had ever heard the rogue.

It was followed by a growl, a roar of defiance, as Malagdorl, helplessly bound, again took control of his mind.

The moment of pain was cut short by Dab'nay's cry of "Zaknafein!"

Drizzt and Jarlaxle spun about to see Zak and Azzudonna running toward them, the four and Dab'nay falling into a much needed hug.

CATTI-BRIE TRIED TO MOVE OFF THE RUG SHE WAS LYING on. She ached profoundly in every joint. She felt as if she had been thrown into the sun itself.

But she felt.

She was alive.

In sudden panic, she pushed up to her elbows and spun about.

Artemis Entreri sat on the floor beside her bed, leaning heavily against it.

"I fear that I have bled on your bed coverings," he said and gave a helpless little laugh.

Catti-brie rolled about, calling for help, for she feared that she hadn't any magical energy left to heal the sorely wounded man.

"I showed her the dagger," Entreri said, his tone subdued. "Zhindia, I mean. Or I thought it was Zhindia. She became something a bit more than that, I fear."

"The spirit of Lolth entered her body," Catti-brie told him.

"Transformed her body." The man paused and looked up at Catti-brie. "Gromph?"

She shook her head.

The room's door banged open and Penelope Harpell burst in, and knowing they were in good hands, Catti-brie let her eyes close once again.

MENZOBERRANZAN WAS FULL OF DROW WITH LONG MEMO-ries, but none of them, other than those of Yvonnel the Eternal, which were offered to Quenthel, reached back to a time when the full defensive might of House Baenre was forced out on display.

Soon after the retreating forces flowed into the Baenre compound, the demons assaulted the great house at the eastern end of the Qu'ellarz'orl, and for three straight days, those fiends were turned to smoking husks before the walls, and the only demons who breached those walls were dying chasmes falling from the sky after being shot dead by ballistae or crossbows, lightning bolts or Taulmaril, for indeed Drizzt killed many.

Only a couple of the defenders were lost, with those others who fell grievously wounded quickly revived by waiting priestesses. But among the attackers destroyed, only a handful were demons who could not be easily replaced.

As the battle finally ebbed, Jarlaxle found the opportunity to at last confer with the Baenre powers.

"Who are they?" Matron Mother Quenthel demanded of him.

"Allies," he replied. "Minions of the Dark Maiden."

"I know that, but from where?"

"There are many such enclaves on the surface," Jarlaxle replied. He wasn't about to give up Callidae, of course, and the Callidaeans had remained among their own, along with Dab'nay and Jarlaxle and Drizzt, and in an area they had been assigned to defend in the first wave of demons—and one they defended quite brilliantly

Quenthel stared at him hard. She obviously knew he was hiding something, but to her credit, she didn't press the issue. They had bigger things to worry about.

"Matron Zeerith has turned against us," Quenthel remarked. "I reached out to her through my divination and she rejected me, us. She has thrown in with Lolth once more."

"House Do'Urden was doomed," Andzrel Baenre put in. "If she had not, her entire family would have been trapped within and murdered. The demons that came upon the field . . ." The weapon master shook his head.

"The whispers say that the avatar of Lolth appeared in the Fane and graced Sos'Umptu with a great magical circle for such summoning," said Minolin Fey. "One of the priestesses of the Fane was taken in the fighting, in the retreat to House Baenre. She quite willingly boasted that Lolth herself had come to them."

"What else?" Jarlaxle asked, but Minolin Fey merely shrugged. There really hadn't been much time for interrogation or magical spellcasting unrelated to the ferocious battle.

"Lolth was here," Quenthel confirmed. "I sensed her clearly."

"Was?" Jarlaxle noted.

Quenthel looked at them all carefully, licking her lips, seeming almost afraid to speak her thoughts. "She let us know, the matrons at least. She was here, along with a host of handmaidens. I felt it, keenly. And then I did not."

"When did you not?"

"The moment House Melarn blew apart."

That brought gasps all about.

"Dare we hope that Lolth was in there?" Jarlaxle asked. "Or perhaps it was Lolth who created that cataclysm."

"Against Zhindia Melarn?" Quenthel replied incredulously.

"Perhaps it was Lolth's way of telling us that we are not damned," Myrineyl put in eagerly. "Perhaps we have been wrong in rejecting *Her*, or that the web on the surface was a heresy against *Her*. Maybe it was *Her* will all along, and we are—"

"Stop!" Quenthel told her daughter. "Do not be a fool."

"The Spider Queen came here, so you claim, and House Melarn was obliterated," Myrineyl pressed.

The others in the room just glared at her, except for Andzrel, who said, "Let us hope that Lolth has rejected Matron Zhindia, then, and will recognize House Baenre as the true leader once more."

"Hope?" Quenthel asked him. "Would you put all of this as it was?"

"There are thousands dead," Andzrel replied. "House Fey-Branche is destroyed. House Hunzrin gutted, House Barrison Del'Armgo decapitated! Even if things revert to the days before the events on the surface, it will hardly be the same. Our greatest rivals are no more. Zhindia is no more, so it seems. Bregan D'aerthe, our allies, alone hold the grounds beyond the city now, their rivals in our dungeons. If this war is ended, the position of House Baenre will hold supreme, more so than at any time in . . ."

He stopped in the face of Quenthel's iron scowl. "You really do not understand any of this, do you?"

"Who will challenge us?" the weapon master replied.

"Challenge us for what? The Lolthians will fight us forever, and for all of your claims of supremacy, all of our power is here within this compound."

"Almost four thousand drow are in here!" Andzrel replied.

"And twenty thousand out there, with tens of thousands of minor fiends and hundreds of major demons as well," Jarlaxle reminded.

"And yet, they cannot breach!" Andzrel yelled at him.

"Would you like to lead the charge out of the gates?" Jarlaxle invited him. "Do you think you'd even get off the Qu'ellarz'orl?"

"Have you a better plan?"

Jarlaxle ignored him, other than to offer a disgusted shake of his head as he turned back to Quenthel.

"You have scouts out and about the city?" Quenthel asked him.

"Huddled, mostly, I would expect," Jarlaxle replied. "But yes. I believe so. The one most intent on destroying them was Matron Zhindia, and if she is truly removed from the field, as it seems likely, then my network should remain."

"We can prepare the scrying pool—"

"We don't work like that," Jarlaxle stopped her.

"Because you had Kimmuriel. Alas, you have him no more."

But Jarlaxle kept shaking his head. "Braelin Janquay is recovered. He and I will go out and learn what we may."

"But not Drizzt nor Zaknafein," Quenthel told him, and he agreed, and not only for the reasons Quenthel was implying. Jarlaxle had spoken at length with Braelin. He knew the story of a certain drow returned with the advent of the Blaspheme, one who had been in House Melarn, but likely was not when it exploded.

IN ANOTHER BUILDING IN THE BAENRE COMPOUND, DRIZZT and Zaknafein considered their course.

"How long would we stay, then?" Zaknafein asked.

"Can we even get out?"

"I have the wizard Allefaero working on that. They must get away, at least, though priest Avernil is a stubborn one. Jarlaxle has covered up well for them, but they risk much by remaining here, and not just to themselves."

"I am surprised they came here in the first place."

"They did so without permission, indeed against the edicts, of the Temporal Convocation," Zak said. "Only Galathae and I were given permission."

Drizzt didn't quite know how to take that, didn't know how to feel about any of this.

"Are you glad that I have come?" Zak asked, and Drizzt knew that he was wearing his emotions plainly on his face.

"I am," he decided. "Though I will feel better when we are all out of here."

"You have given up on conquering the city, then?"

"It was never about conquest. We've seen the truth of it now, and that truth is not what I had hoped. I take no pleasure in this fighting. In destroying demons, of course there is satisfaction, but the forces behind those demons are drow, battling for Lolth, and many more than I had hoped."

"She has ruled this city for millennia," Zak reminded. "Surely you didn't doubt the resolve of her priestesses to hold on to the source of their power."

"It is hardly just the matrons and their priestesses, though. As this has sorted, there seem many more against our revolution than for it."

"For many reasons, though," Zak reminded. "Fear of their matrons and of Lolth, of course. Or simply fear of this unknown future the Baenres have offered. They know the way it's been, for the entirety of their lives, even for those whose lives have spanned centuries. They know their place within that truth. They know the boundaries, the lines not to cross, the acts that give them gain and those that offer only pain. What do they know of this promised world beyond Lolth, particularly when it, too, from their perspective at least, will be under the designs of House Baenre?"

"But it won't."

"But they cannot know that. I've been gone for a long time, but I was here for a long time before that. Few who are not Baenre hold any love for this house, and certainly no trust for the Matron Mother and her entourage."

"So where does that leave us?"

"You came here thinking of this as a war against Lolth and all that she stood for," Zak offered. "Perhaps we think of it instead as a rescue mission to get those who would abandon Lolth out of this prison she has built within this cavern."

Drizzt mulled on that for a bit and at last came to nod and smile. That would have to do. And it was something, at least, and something, he came to believe, that was worth the fight.

There came a knock on the door and Jarlaxle entered, followed by a healthier Braelin Janquay.

"Well met again, Braelin," Drizzt said.

"Braelin has news that you should hear, Drizzt," Jarlaxle said. "And you as well," he added to Zaknafein. "I think it will shock you, but given all that we have seen in these last years since the Spellplague, will anything truly do that?"

"We're not easily shocked," Zak remarked.

"You know of the Blaspheme, of course, of how they were once living driders in Menzoberranzan, then went in death to serve as drider lackeys to Lolth and her handmaidens. And now, of course, they have been returned to their living drow bodies through the web woven by Yvonnel and Quenthel."

Drizzt and Zak looked to each other. Of course they knew, as that action was why they were here in the first place.

Jarlaxle turned to Braelin.

"When I escaped House Melarn, I did so with another who was imprisoned there, one that Matron Zhindia had kept aside for special treatment. She had planned to turn him into a drider very publicly, and mostly to discredit you and all that you represent." He looked at Drizzt as he said that, and Drizzt stared back hard, beginning to see the possibilities of the forthcoming revelation.

"It was—" Braelin started.

"Dinin, my brother," Drizzt finished for him, and the scout nodded, confused and surprised.

"I was wrong," said Zak. "I can still be shocked." He looked to Drizzt. "Dinin?"

"He was cursed into the abomination of a drider by Vierna," Drizzt said, and Zak's expression suggested he was more upset to hear that than any of the news about Dinin. "And killed by King Bruenor, almost a hundred and fifty years ago."

"And now he is back?" Zak asked Jarlaxle.

"He escaped House Melarn, perhaps, and was said to be heading to House Do'Urden, but we know not his fate."

Drizzt and Zak looked to each other again, and it was clear that neither of them knew how to even feel regarding this information. Their relationships with Dinin had been complicated, and not very familial. There had been a lot between Zak and Dinin as teacher and student, and Drizzt had grown up in the house as secondboy to Dinin's elderboy (and only because Dinin had murdered their oldest brother), but as with Zak and Dinin, there had never been any real brotherly or family love between the two.

"I thought you should know," Jarlaxle said.

Drizzt nodded.

"If I can learn more, I will relay it."

Drizzt wanted to think that he didn't care.

But, like Zak, he found he could be surprised.

Because he did care.

THE SIEGE OF HOUSE BAENRE CONTINUED. THE DEMONS came at them every day—minor fiends almost exclusively, for their enemies had obviously come to understand that attrition would not favor their demon army, given the sparseness of casualties within House Baenre.

Now it was more a matter of keeping the heretics too busy to form any counterattack, obviously, giving the Lolthians time to shore up their defenses across the city outside the great house.

And likely to murder any who did not fall in line with them.

"We only have one card to play," Jarlaxle told Quenthel and the other leaders on the fifth day of the battle. "Prisoners, and many of them valuable. Whoever leads the Lolthians—"

"I think we know who now leads the Lolthians," Quenthel interrupted.

"Not necessarily. Zhindia may still be alive. We don't know that she was in her house when it fell. Four other matrons of the Ruling Council are out there, perhaps. Only Mez'Barris is known to be dead, and Byrtyn Fey now cursed. One will make a play . . ."

"It is Sos'Umptu," Quenthel said definitively. "You saw the power of the horde that came forth from the Fane. I suspect that it was always going to be Sos'Umptu—who else could sit in command of the city from this house and restore what once was."

"Zhindia was just Lolth's pawn," Minolin Fey added. "Someone she would have no issue sacrificing if it came to that. Even the manner of this battle at our walls makes me see the truth of that. Sos'Umptu, on the other hand, understands above all others out there the importance of keeping us engaged here, instead of out there, where we might turn some, like Zeerith, back to our cause."

"Our position is untenable," Jarlaxle declared. "As I've said, we have one play. Let me go and make it."

"To Sos'Umptu?"

"That would seem to be the course, unless I learn differently from my agents in the Braeryn."

"She'll kill you," said Quenthel.

"She'll have to be quick," Jarlaxle replied. "Many have tried, you might recall. And I have ways to get far, far away from her."

"Like you did in the chapel at House Barrison Del'Armgo?" Drizzt reminded sourly. "If Matron Mez'Barris had her house prepared like that, why would you think the Fane is less so?"

"I see no choice in the matter," Jarlaxle answered, and seemed perturbed. "I'm going out to the Braeryn to learn what I can, as only I can. We have bargaining chips—we have Malagdorl, and that is no small thing!—and I must learn what they are worth to whoever it is that leads these demons against us. We cannot just stay here and let them plot their assaults while their demons keep us engaged."

"But to the Fane?" Quenthel asked doubtfully.

"If the information I gain can prevent the visit, then so be it," Jarlaxle promised. "But we both doubt that to be the case. Braelin Janquay will come with me through our secret ways, and he will return to you with all that we have learned from our agents, perhaps with me by his side, perhaps not—that's not what really matters."

"It matters to me," Drizzt said.

"I appreciate it, but we are speaking of Jarlaxle, remember?" he said with a smile. "I will be okay. Now, let us discuss our demands. We have the Hunzrins, and that is no small thing to any of our enemies. Cut off from Bregan D'aerthe, the Hunzrins are their only real ties to anything beyond Menzoberranzan. And as I said, we have Malagdorl, Lolth's Warrior. Lady Lolth herself named him as such, and what a prize that will be to the next determined Matron Mother, or if not to her, then to those who will take control of House Barrison Del'Armgo. Taayrul, I expect. And we have the scepter of Barrison Del'Armgo, whose statues are still in the courtyard blocking their gate, from all that we can see."

"We have over four hundred Lolthians in our jails," Minolin Fey added.

"So we have to decide what all of that is worth to them and to us," Jarlaxle said. "What do we want?"

Jarlaxle could see the pain on Quenthel's face as she struggled to come to terms with their reality—one that was far less than the vision she had created after denying Lolth and freeing the Blaspheme.

"We cannot win the city," he said flatly to her.

"And thus, we cannot stay in the city," said Minolin Fey, to which both Andzrel and Myrineyl chortled, Quenthel's daughter storming away.

"Go, Jarlaxle," Quenthel agreed, and that was all the confirmation he needed. "Be quick, I beg."

JARLAXLE AND BRAELIN WERE OUT OF HOUSE BAENRE within the hour, traveling the tunnels and secret ways back to the Braeryn and the Oozing Myconid.

Braelin hesitated as they approached. The last time he had seen Azleah, he had seen four versions of her, three of them succubi.

"I was betrayed the last time I came here," he said to Jarlaxle's stare at his hesitation.

"I know all about it. Poor Azleah was trapped under the sorcery of the succubus."

Braelin nodded.

"It is difficult," Jarlaxle told him. "But now is not the time to work through the conflicts within you. Too much isn't at stake—*all* is at stake."

He led the way into the tavern, and once over the threshold, Braelin paused again, this time fully stopping, his eyes going wide as he stared at the woman he loved, one eye grayed over and badly scarred.

"Azleah betrayed more than Braelin Janquay," Jarlaxle explained.

"You said it was not her fault," Braelin stammered.

"Not against you."

Braelin shook his head.

"She is forgiven," Jarlaxle assured him.

"He finds me hideous," Azleah said from behind the bar, the weakness in her voice assaulting Braelin's very heart.

He hesitated no more, sprinting across the room toward her, rolling over the bar to land beside her where he swept her up into his arms for a passionate kiss.

"You might be wrong," a grinning Jarlaxle said to the woman.

"Never could I," Braelin told Azleah when they broke the clench. "Never, never, could I. I had feared you dead."

"As I, you," Azleah said, and Braelin kissed her again, pressing against her.

"I hope the succubi were within House Melarn when it was obliterated," Braelin whispered to her. "I hope they felt all the pain of that blast to their very soulless core. I hope they are no more, simply forever gone, the fiends."

"For what they did to you," Azleah added, but Braelin shook his head.

"I was caught, but you were stolen," he said, and he kissed her again, simply because he couldn't help himself.

"Let us hope there will be a time soon for this lovely reunion to properly take its course," Jarlaxle said, pulling Braelin back from the woman. "But for now . . ."

Braelin nodded nervously, overwhelmed by his emotions, but his face grew serious as he collected himself.

"If we survive this, we will find a priestess who can properly restore your eye," Jarlaxle promised them both. "Catti-brie will oblige, I am sure."

"It doesn't matter to me," Braelin said. "She is no less beautiful."

"Shut your mouth," Azleah told him, and slapped him across the shoulder. "It matters to me, and don't you doubt that!"

Jarlaxle laughed at that, but only for a brief moment before repeating, "But for now . . ."

With a nod, Azleah took them to her room behind the bar and to a closet that held a secret, extra-dimensional room where she could relay the whispers she had heard from the streets.

House Do'Urden had not been breached in the battle, she told them, the goristro and other powerful fiends stopping short of their gates on the orders of Sos'Umptu Baenre, and on the word that Matron Zeerith, as they had suspected, had indeed reversed and rejoined with the Lolthians.

"Matron Zeerith Xorlarrin," Azleah emphasized. "She will no longer use the name Do'Urden, and has cursed it from her balconies for all to hear."

"Drizzt and Zaknefein will be so disappointed to hear that," Jarlaxle drolled.

She went on to relay that no one had seen or heard from Zhindia since the explosion in her house, and all the whispers said that she had been consumed, something which was then confirmed by another drow Azleah let into the room.

"I left the house only a short while before the explosion," Kyrnill Kenafin told Jarlaxle and Braelin, and to Braelin, she added, "I am glad that you found your way out."

"And Zhindia was in there, and remained in there?" Jarlaxle asked.

"She was in there with a Lolthian coven of yochlols."

"And the explosion itself?"

Kyrnill shrugged. "I was out of the house, going to House Do'Urden to confirm the change of Matron Zeerith's heart. At least, that is what I had been instructed to do. I was wandering, and wondering, trying to figure my course. When Lolth's Web was shattered, I came here instead."

"You deny Lolth?" Jarlaxle asked bluntly.

"She knows that Lolth's priestesses will not forgive her if they learn the truth of her dealings," Braelin vouched for her. "She saved me, or tried to before the succubi dragged me back. I will be forever grateful."

Jarlaxle nodded. "As will I. And we will get you to House Baenre, if you wish, and hopefully beyond. Another escaped with Braelin."

"Dinin Do'Urden," Kyrnill replied. "That was part of the reason I was sent to speak with Matron Zeerith, as word was that he had gone into House Do'Urden."

"And?"

"I did not go to Matron Zeerith. I know nothing of it."

Jarlaxle looked to Azleah, who shook her head and shrugged.

"What of Yvonnel Baenre?" Jarlaxle asked them both, but again, neither had any word of the missing woman.

Kyrnill was dismissed then, and Azleah went on to explain that there was some not insignificant support for the heretics on the streets of the city, particularly in the Braeryn, but when Jarlaxle asked if she thought that enough to turn the fight, she shook her head without hesitation.

Thus, barely an hour later, Jarlaxle stood hat in hand, literally and figuratively, in the nave of the Fane of the Goddess before the altar and throne of Sos'Umptu Baenre.

"We can hold out forever," he blithely answered the priestess's opening salvo when she demanded a surrender and the gates of *her* house thrown open wide. "How long until your greater demons are found out and destroyed? Your fodder ranks will be diminished then, of course."

He expected Sos'Umptu to lash out at him with that, but she did not. He studied her carefully, and had done so since he had been allowed in to parlay with her. He thought she would be more confident, more forceful and demanding.

But she was stung, and badly.

The fall of Lolth's Web had wounded many beyond House Melarn, it seemed.

"Your mother . . . my mother, Matron Mother Yvonnel the Eternal, put up with me, embraced me and my ways, though they were not in accord with Lolth's designs—her demanded rituals, at least," Jarlaxle said.

"You were ever a heretic."

"But a useful one. Matron Mother Baenre valued me because she knew I acted out of the notion of mutual benefit. She was stronger with me and Bregan D'aerthe in her court. I come here in that belief of practicality. The streets of Menzoberranzan run with drow blood and stink of smoking demon husks. It makes me wonder who rules here: drow or demon."

"Lolth rules here!"

"In that chaos rules, yes, I suppose that is undeniable, but we know that her actual presence here is fleeting, as the destruction of House Melarn has shown us. So let's not focus on the abstract and rather on what we can do for each other. That is the question we should both be exploring."

"Your words offend me and your game bores me, Jarlaxle. I will have the throne of House Baenre and will rule this city under the blessing of Lolth!"

"Granted, and in return . . ."

"In return? I will make driders of you and all the rest. Does that bargain sound fair enough to you?"

Jarlaxle couldn't suppress his smile. "Dear sister—"

"Do not *ever* call me that."

Jarlaxle put his hat upon his bald pate and tipped it to her. "Dear First Priestess of the Fane," he said formally. "You are hurt, and you are weakened. She was in there, wasn't she? Her handmaidens were, and so their material bodies were surely destroyed in the cataclysm and are now banished for a hundred years."

"You cannot banish a goddess for long!" Sos'Umptu snapped back.

There it was, and Sos'Umptu slumped back a bit an instant later, knowing that she had given Jarlaxle all the confirmation that he needed.

"But she *is* gone—for now. And without her, without her handmaidens, you are vulnerable," Jarlaxle said.

"I could destroy you here and now."

"Possibly—I'd give you maybe two-to-one odds on that. But where does that leave you? House Barrison Del'Armgo is greatly weakened, their weapon master in our custody, I have control of the magical constructs that defend their keep, and Mez'Barris is dead—but all that should give you little comfort in this moment. To win this fight, you need to destroy those within House Baenre, and where is Sos'Umptu left in that event, especially with Matron Vadalma Faen Tlabbar, her powerful house fully intact, seeing a clear ascent, particularly with her hated enemy, Zhindia, out of the way? And what of Matron Zeerith? Zeerith Xorlarrin once more, I am told. A powerful matron with powerful allies, and a ruling matron, like Vadalma Faen Tlabbar, Miz'ri Mizzrym, and Asha Vandree, who resented your ninth seat at that table meant for eight. Those will be the only ruling matrons left if you defeat Quenthel, and where does that leave you?"

"I have the blessing of Lolth. They witnessed the power of the force that came forth from the Fane."

"And they witnessed her being banished," Jarlaxle corrected. "Even for a short while to us drow, one hundred years is still a good bit of time for the politics of this city. Can you stand against them long enough?"

"House Barrison Del'Armgo remains formidable," Sos'Umptu stated. "Kaitain survived the attack at the wall, and a capable priestess, Taayrul, will take their throne."

"They will if they ever get the scepter back. That's not really what's important, though, because you are Baenre, and the Armgos hate the Baenres more than any other!"

"Not if I promise her the Second House and a seat at my side."

"You cannot promise her anything the four remaining ruling matrons will offer." He put on a sly look. "Or perhaps you can."

"You are boring me."

"You already said that. And no, I'm not. I am *worrying* you, and you should be worried. Believe me when I tell you, for my own selfish reasons, that I would have Sos'Umptu become the ruling Matron Mother above all other possibilities—if you even win this war, I mean, against the current Matron Mother.

"And what of Yvonnel?" Jarlaxle teased. "She could have taken the throne before, and now who could stand before her?"

"Yvonnel is gone," Sos'Umptu stated.

"Gone?" He did all he could to keep the shock out of his voice and face.

"Gone. She made the mistake of challenging me here in this place.

She lost. She is gone, hurled through the planes to an eternal prison from which she cannot escape, and one where you will never find her. She is gone."

Jarlaxle looked at her suspiciously.

"Why would I lie about that? She is gone."

Jarlaxle licked his lips.

"You thought it Yvonnel who destroyed Lolth's Web," Sos'Umptu reasoned, and indeed he had thought exactly that.

"Who else could . . ."

"It was my brother. Your brother."

"Gromph?"

"Gromph. His final act. I watched it from here, in a scrying pool, as I was witnessing again the beauty of Lolth's avatar, this time hosted by Matron Zhindia. Gromph did it. He blew it up, all of it, and himself as well."

Jarlaxle wasn't sure how to digest that. Kimmuriel gone, Gromph gone.

So many gone.

"And, Jarlaxle," she said slyly, "*should* I allow you back to House Baenre, do tell Drizzt Do'Urden that Catti-brie was in there with Gromph. And Artemis Entreri, as well. So tell me again how badly I am hurt, would you please?"

Jarlaxle swallowed it all and tucked it far away. For the sake of those left alive, he had to do that, had to resolve this here and now. This was a war, after all, and losses—even ones as devastating as what she was suggesting—were a part of war.

But still . . .

"Let us end this for both our sakes," he told Sos'Umptu. "I have what you need and you have what I need. Together, we both survive and thrive, while apart, we are both diminished."

"I must be confused: What do you have that I need?"

"I have House Hunzrin."

"And?"

"And you're not so naïve to not know what that means. You bringing them from the dungeons of House Baenre gives you stature in the eyes of your rivals, and Matron Shakti will surely sit on the new Ruling Council and will know that it was you who saved her and her family."

"Do go on."

"I also have Bregan D'aerthe. You know me and my value. Your eyes will be turned inward to the city for now, no doubt. But that will not be enough as time passes, and you know what I can bring to your table."

She said nothing to that.

"I have Malagdorl Armgo, Lolth's Warrior," Jarlaxle announced.

"You have Lolth's Warrior, all right, but it is not Malagdorl, I dare-say. She does love that heretic who bested him—quite embarrassingly, I am told—and who has caused so much chaos in this city for nearly two centuries."

That put Jarlaxle off-balance, but he recovered quickly. "And so, you do not wish to destroy him," he said flippantly, and Sos'Umptu didn't argue the point, other than to say, "Catti-brie was in House Melarn. He is already destroyed."

"We have over four hundred Lolthian prisoners," Jarlaxle replied, ignoring that jibe. "Many valuable. And we have House Baenre itself, which you now covet."

"I will win House Baenre," she said. "Four hundred are not so great a loss. More than three thousand drow have already been killed in this war our sister began."

"What good is House Baenre if there's nothing of value in it?"

"How do you mean?"

"We will destroy everything you desire in House Baenre, I prom-ise, should it come to that. But it should not! You will have Matron Shakti Hunzrin at your side. And with Malagdorl freed by you, House Barrison Del'Armgo will not oppose you. Make of him your patron and your weapon master in House Baenre! The play is so obvious, and with Houses Baenre and Barrison Del'Armgo joined, who will argue? You will have the peace you need to rebuild."

"And what do you get in return?" Sos'Umptu asked.

"We leave."

"Leave?"

He hid the smile he felt at her bemusement.

"We leave. All who will go. We leave Menzoberranzan, the City of Spiders, the City of Lolth. We leave never to return, and with your word that you will not pursue us."

"I cannot give you that word. I serve Lolth."

"Then just let us leave, and we will do what we must if it comes to that."

"The Blaspheme remains."

"You would not want that and I cannot offer that."

Sos'Umptu sat back for a bit and considered her reply, seeming to agree with the former part, at least.

"Quenthel is doomed. She stays and pays for her great heresy."

"No."

"No?"

"No. As I said: all who want to must be allowed to go. Besides, I cannot make decisions for her. Do you not understand that? Do you not understand what this is all about, what it has been about since the beginning? It is about individual choice and freedom. Personal agency to determine life and faith—yes, faith! Mostly faith! How can you demand fealty to a goddess from those who do not worship her? Why would she even want them? Why would you want them causing only unrest in your city? That's what we fought for, Sos'Umptu. Lolth was a symbol of the oppression, nothing more."

Sos'Umptu laughed at him. "You were always an idiot, Jarlaxle, believing that others carried such pride as you have within your heart. You never saw Lolth as your great mother and so you are arrogant enough to believe that all others feel as you do."

"Not all. Not you, clearly."

"Not hardly all," Sos'Umptu said.

"Then prove it. I call your dare!"

"What does that even mean?"

"As I've said: let those who wish to leave go. Obviously, those will be of heart similar to my own and not yours. If you have such confidence that so many others see the beauty of the Spider Queen, then let them prove it.

"Or are you afraid?"

She stared at him hatefully.

"The more who go, the stronger you will be," Jarlaxle slyly answered that look. "Think about it. The Armgos will certainly remain, as they will move so near to that which they have always desired, particularly when you join the families with Malagdorl as your patron. And I will be honest with you here: Under this agreement, it is likely that many will remain in House Baenre. The temptation of ascending the ladder of power will be too great for many of the Baenre nobles."

"Because what is out there for you who will leave," she said, seeming to finally accept his premise.

"Freedom," he pushed, not wanting her to lose the thread. "Just that, Sos'Umptu."

"Power is freedom."

Jarlaxle shrugged.

Sos'Umptu sat staring at him for a long while, and every passing second gave him hope. She was hurt so very badly. With Lolth gone, it was likely that the priestesses who had seen such an amplification of their power were now greatly diminished. Even though she knew that House Baenre could not defeat the combined power of Menzoberranzan, she feared this fight and its implications for her, and yes, for that physical house itself, one she only now had come to realize how much she coveted.

"Get out of my city, all of you," she said at length. "I will march into House Baenre at Narbondel's first light. Those among the heretics who wish to recant and beg for mercy will be saved—and Jarlaxle, on your word, you will tell the Blaspheme that they will be spared any punishment if they beg the mercy of Lolth."

"On your word?"

"On my word. They will serve House Baenre, and House Baenre will serve Lady Lolth," Sos'Umptu told him convincingly. "And when you are gone, yes, you will forever look over your shoulders, because your crimes will not be forgotten or forgiven. None may return. Ever."

Jarlaxle bowed.

"Except, perhaps, unless Bregan D'aerthe and I come to an agreement in the future that is of mutual benefit, brother."

Jarlaxle's returning smile fit the moment perfectly, but behind it wasn't Sos'Umptu's offer, but rather his proof that even with her, even with this most loyal servant of Lolth, it was all about selfish gain.

It was always all about selfish gain, he thought, but then corrected himself, and reminded himself why he loved Drizzt and Drizzt's friends, and why, in a most profound way, knowing them had given him so much more than any promises Sos'Umptu or any other Matron Mother of Menzoberranzan could ever offer.

A TRIUMPHANT SOS'UMPTU DID WALK THROUGH THE gates of House Baenre the next morning, to find, as Jarlaxle had predicted, many of the Baenre nobles and foot soldiers and nearly half the Blaspheme waiting to greet and serve her. Among those ranks were Andzrel, who had little idea that he would soon be replaced by Malagdorl Armgo. And to her surprise—and to the utter shock of Quenthel and Minolin Fey—beside Andzrel stood Quenthel's daughter, Myrineyl.

FROM THE STENCHSTREETS, THEY CAME. FROM MANY OF the lower houses, they came, accepting the invitation to make their own path from the soon-to-be Matron Mother Sos'Umptu of Menzoberranzan. Along with the refugees of House Baenre, the contingent of outsiders of the Dark Maiden, and the soldiers of Bregan D'aerthe, nearly three thousand udadrow had left Menzoberranzan, past Donigarten and through the little-used Wanderways.

It wasn't until they were long out of the city, moving fast along the trails that would bring them to the lower gates of Gauntlgrym, that Jarlaxle assembled his closest friends and told them of the loss of Yvonnel.

And told them of Gromph's great sacrifice.

And looked Drizzt right in the eye as he revealed, "Catti-brie and Artemis Entreri were in House Melarn when Gromph destroyed it. They were with him."

Malagdorl Armgo had not been able to knock the legs out from under Drizzt.

Grandmaster Kane had not been able to knock the legs out from under Drizzt.

A pair of dragon sisters had not been able to knock the legs out from under Drizzt.

Ygorl, the slaadi god, had not been able to knock the legs out from under Drizzt.

But now his legs would not hold him, and he fell to the ground, gasping, then sobbing. He tried to tell himself that it had all been worth it, that this battle, which had become a rescue mission of sorts, had saved so many from the damnation of Lolth.

But he couldn't hold that thought. Not then. Not with his heart torn asunder in his chest.

Zak was there with him, crying. Jarlaxle was there, crying for Drizzt's pain and for his own. The three huddled closely, two whispering comfort when they could get words out past their own pain, the third lost in pure emotional agony.

It was only when Zak mentioned Brie that Drizzt found some measure of calm.

He felt empty in that moment, but he was not empty. He had their legacy. He had his responsibility.

The pain didn't ease. The questions—*why had she been there?*—didn't go silent. The sense of loss, of helplessness, didn't abate.

He stood up and went on, silently, playing the role he had to play in their march.

The next day, Allefaero and Nvisi came to him and Zak and Jarlaxle. Allefaero told them that Nvisi had discovered a small group of drow moving parallel to them.

"Saribel?" Allefaero asked. "Ravel? Do these names mean anything to you? They flee the city, and Nvisi says they left before we did."

"Xorlarrins," Jarlaxle said to the others. "Perhaps not all of them agreed with Zeerith's choice. We should go find them."

"Be quick," Allefaero told him. "Nvisi has seen others, too, coming fast from Menzoberranzan and they are not our allies."

"You should get back to Callidae," Jarlaxle told him. "Prepare your spells and fly off as soon as you can."

"In time," Allefaero said. "Do you think we could pry Zaknafein away from you now? We came to see this through, and so we shall." Jarlaxle nodded. He wasn't surprised by the latter information. Sos'Umptu would try to hurt them badly, of course, to chase those who survived on their way. He organized a group to find the Xorlarrins and bring them in, and remained unsurprised to find a certain member of that renegade group who was not Xorlarrin.

"SO IT IS TRUE," ZAKNAFEIN SAID TO HIM WHEN HE AP-proached.

"You are no more stunned than I," Dinin replied.

Drizzt, sitting beside Zaknafein, said nothing.

"I . . . we," Dinin said, looking around and spotting some of his fellow Blaspheme warriors taking their meal. "We served as driders in the Abyss, every day in torment. We were freed of the curse outside of the dwarven kingdom, and now we fight Lolth with everything we can muster."

"Not all," Zak answered. "Nearly half remained to serve Matron Mother Sos'Umptu Baenre."

"Because they fear Lolth profoundly. You cannot understand the pain, eternal and unrelenting. If they were given pardons for remaining, I understand."

"If you wish to go back . . ." Drizzt said.

"Brother?" Dinin replied.

"Don't," Drizzt warned.

Dinin really didn't know what to make of Drizzt in that moment. He hadn't expected warmth, certainly, from either. He didn't know what to make of Zak being back from the dead, even, and he remained well aware that he had been sent to the Abyss in a fight with one of Drizzt's friends.

But even with all that, he couldn't quite parse Drizzt's statement. Finally, he simply said, "Fear of Lolth makes us all do things we regret."

"Is that what you told our brother Nalfein?"

Drizzt's words even drew a gasp from Zak.

"You think I have forgotten all that was before?" Drizzt went on.

"I do not, nor would I expect you to, nor can I," Dinin replied. He paused and lowered his gaze, wanting them to see that he was struggling with how to finish his response. "I ask nothing of you, brother."

"You get nothing from me."

"Of course not. I understand. Perhaps with time, I can show you that which I have learned, about myself, about Lolth. There is no greater torment—"

"Where will you go if you survive this journey?" Drizzt asked.

The mere fact he had asked that gave Dinin a bit of hope his brother did indeed care, a bit, at least.

"They are coming after us, even now," Zak added.

"Perhaps Jarlaxle will have me back in Bregan D'aerthe," Dinin said after a while.

"I think he will," said Zaknafein. He winked at the former drider, then stood, walked over, and patted Dinin on the shoulder. "We have all been through much, so much, in a life journey that winds unpredictably."

"Thank you."

"Welcome back," Zak told him.

Drizzt took a deep breath and nodded, just a bit, but said no more.

Dinin didn't really know what to think when he left them. Whispers said that Zhindia was dead, but his pact hadn't been forged with her, after all, but only through her.

His pact was with Lolth.

Lolth was eternal.

Lolth was merciless.

He had time, that much had been made clear, and so he would bide that time, through the months and years.

But he wouldn't waver on the course and the culmination until he had some tangible evidence that Lolth had forgotten him.

No matter the circumstance, the one truth that guided Dinin

Do'Urden at that time was that he would not again become a drider, whatever the cost to anyone else, including Zaknafein and Drizzt.

Including Drizzt's daughter.

THE FORCE PURSUING THEM WAS CONSIDERABLE, NVISI and other diviners discerned over the next two days, and they would be in for a terrific fight before they ever got to Gauntlgrym, it seemed, unless they could somehow manage to keep ahead of the pursuit.

They feared that battle upon them—though Drizzt, still full of helpless rage, was almost glad that he would put his blades back to work—when the lead scouts informed Jarlaxle and the others that there was another force *before* them, blocking their way. They started making plans to either veer down a side passage or fight their way through, but in the middle of the debate, Avernil and Allefaero begged an audience with their friends of Bregan D'aerthe.

"Weal," Avernil told them when he caught up to Jarlaxle

"Weal?"

"Weal to go forward," Avernil explained.

"Nvisi has seen them," Allefaero added. "These are not enemies in the tunnels between us and your destination. It is a large army come to meet us, led by a dwarven king."

"Send word to Quenthel and all the others," Jarlaxle told Braelin. "Be quick and be glad. If King Bruenor is there, then our pursuers will fast retreat!"

Braelin called for other couriers to spread the word, then ran off.

"You said to our destination and not your own," Jarlaxle said then, catching the subtle distinction the wizard had made.

"We will go and meet this dwarf king," Avernil said. "Perhaps a bit further. But it is time for us to bring our dead home."

"I know that Zaknafein can return," Jarlaxle replied. "And I know they will welcome the body of Holy Galathae. But didn't you come here against the wishes of the Temporal Convocation?"

Avernil shrugged. "They will not be pleased with us. There may even be a penance to pay. But no matter. We are loyal to Callidae, second only to the Dark Maiden, and we will return to our home and properly bury the fallen heroes we are able to retrieve from the battlefield."

"I suppose you will be able to convince Valrissa and the others," Jarlaxle offered.

"How many udadrow escaped Lolth's tyranny?" Avernil asked. "Two thousand? Twenty-five hundred?"

Jarlaxle nodded. They hadn't done an exact count, but the number seemed close.

"For the lives of thirty Callidaeans, more than two thousand prisoners of Lolth are now free," Avernil stated flatly. "The price is no minor thing, but the cost was worth the gain, both in the eyes of Eilistraee, surely, and in the hearts of Mona Valrissa and the rest of Callidae. We will be welcomed back."

Jarlaxle let it go at that, dropping a friendly hand on Avernil's shoulder and offering a sincere nod of appreciation for all that they had lost. Then he looked to the two men standing beside him, both Drizzt and Zak shifting eagerly.

"Bruenor," Jarlaxle said. "He covers his heart with gruff, but will be there when—"

"I have to tell him," Drizzt said solemnly, and he started on his way.

Jarlaxle looked at Zak, but both understood Drizzt's reference. Bruenor had lost a daughter, so they believed.

Moving ahead of the main force, Drizzt, Jarlaxle, and Zaknafein trotted quickly through the tunnels and finally into a large chamber that had been prepared for battle, with war machines and grim-faced dwarves in metal armor and carrying mayhem.

They were recognized, of course, and so by the time they got past the outer sentries, they found King Bruenor flanked by Regis and Wulfgar on one side, Thibbledorf Pwent and Athrogate on the other, rushing to meet them.

And two others, as well, and quite unexpectedly, one of whom, an auburn-haired woman with deep blue eyes that had so long ago stolen his heart, had Drizzt once more crumbling to the floor in tears, but this time of joy.

EPILOGUE

I t had been a moment of exhilaration and the purest power he had ever felt flowing through him.

Just an instant, a flash, a burst of cataclysmic proportions.

Sometimes the inciter of a retributive strike could avoid the devastation, could turn the power of the release into propulsion to another plane of existence, and thereafter return.

But Gromph Baenre hadn't even tried to avoid the breaking of the staff. He welcomed it. He basked in it for just that moment before his physical coil was turned to flying ash.

And now there was silence, and blackness. Just blackness.

He reached up and felt the tangible lid, and pushed open the coffin in the room of his extra-dimensional mansion.

And then, in the clone he had prepared—and through the magics that had been revealed in ancient tomes and the collected wisdom of the Hosttower of the Arcane, and clarified and refined for him by the necromancer Ethan Sin'dalay—a younger specimen of Gromph Baenre sat up and took his first deep breath.

It had worked!

Gromph had beaten death.

And he had beaten Lolth, though he knew that was likely a temporary thing.

He decided to get back to work.

If he did it once, he could do it again.

Lord Parise Ulfbinder came into the room, apparently hearing the noise as Gromph was exiting the coffin.

"Is it?" he asked tentatively. "Did it . . . did it work?"

Gromph smiled at him. "You may join me for dinner—I am surprisingly hungry. But then I ask that you leave my home for the night. I have much to do."

"I should continue my preparations, then?"

Gromph smiled at him. "Don't you also want to live forever?"

"SOS'UMPTU HAS CONSOLIDATED HER POWER," JARLAXLE told Entreri, Dab'nay, Braelin, and Zak one morning in One-Eyed Jax, the Bregan D'aerthe tavern, as they sat having breakfast a tenday after returning to Luskan.

"You have spies already at work in the new Menzoberranzan?" Dab'nay asked in surprise.

"I have spies that span the multiverse," was all Jarlaxle would answer to that, but his grin told them that something was going on he had not yet shared.

"Consolidating what power?" Braelin asked, though he was looking over at Azleah, who had gone to the bar to find them some good morning libations. He threw his beloved a wink and got a wide smile in return. "What is left of that city?"

"What is not?" Jarlaxle replied.

"Much of the great powers of Menzoberranzan were killed."

Jarlaxle scoffed at the notion, and Dab'nay answered for him perfectly: "People who have found power and wealth always think they are special, that there is some divine blessing upon them, when in truth, they are imminently replaceable," she said. "Menzoberranzan will survive, and, more than likely, thrive."

"A strange thing for a priestess to be claiming," Braelin noted.

"Not so strange," said Zak, who had known Dab'nay for centuries, and had known even those centuries before that the woman truly hated Lolth and yet couldn't understand her own power, which was supposedly coming to her through the blessing of the Demon Queen of Spiders.

"Well, no matter," said Jarlaxle. "We have much to do." He looked to Zak. "When are you leaving for Cal . . . for your home?"

"As soon as Azzudonna and Allefaero return from their last walk about Luskan."

"They are considering my idea?" Jarlaxle asked. "Cattisola is being reclaimed and there will be room."

"They're not about to let thousands of refugees in," Zak answered, and Jarlaxle knew that, of course.

Or at least, he knew they wouldn't do it all at once. His proposal to High Priest Avernil had been for a gradual immigration to Callidae, allowing for full vetting of anyone accepted, and for the Callidaeans to watch over them until trust was fully gained.

He knew the rules of the Callidaeans and how seriously they took their security, but he had to try, particularly for those, like his sister Quenthel, who had given up so much and had put herself at great risk. In truth, he didn't even know how many of those who had abandoned Menzoberranzan would want to go. Some had joined with Bregan D'aerthe, including Dinin—though Jarlaxle hadn't told Drizzt yet— and Kyrnill Kenafin, and the refugees from House Xorlarrin. Saribel and Dab'nay had already become fast friends, and Ravel was serving as Gromph's understudy at the Hosttower, and as liaison between Gromph and Bregan D'aerthe.

Others had dispersed to the winds, some going to Icewind Dale, despite the season, others to Baldur's Gate, others to who knew where? Three hundred had purchased ships with the gold they had brought from home, and were learning to sail in Luskan Harbor when the weather and the winter waves permitted, intent on seeing the wide world when the season turned.

They were all finding more acceptance than they had anticipated, it seemed, and Jarlaxle took great pride in that. For he and Kimmuriel, Beniago and Braelin and all the others who had taken command of Luskan, had ruled well, had broken barriers and erased prejudice with experience.

What he found in Callidae was Jarlaxle's happiest dream, and perhaps he would someday go there and live it, as Zak was doing.

Or maybe he could make that dream come true here.

He wasn't kidding himself, though. The Realms were not suddenly becoming more inviting to drow or to anyone else.

Power was the only true measure of security in this world, and Jarlaxle's power was knowledge.

"We will meet again," Jarlaxle told Zak, as he had several times before in the process of saying his goodbyes to his oldest friend.

"We will."

"I hope Allefaero's magical aim is good," Braelin said. "It's freezing out here, I can only imagine . . ."

He stopped there, with Jarlaxle hushing him. Callidae was not to be even hinted at openly.

Jarlaxle left them, then, and went to his private room. He sat down before a table and pulled a cloth off the circular object resting in a tri-pronged stand atop it. He closed his eyes and reached out, hoping.

A familiar image appeared in the ball a long while later, and Jarlaxle breathed a sigh of relief.

"I am glad you are floating about this day," Jarlaxle said. "You miss me."

This day, he heard in his mind, a most familiar voice. *And perhaps again, now and then.*

Jarlaxle understood the unsaid part: Kimmuriel would not come to him at his beckon.

Less so, came the thought in his mind. *There is so much. So much.*

"And so much I still need from you."

You will be disappointed.

"Yvonnel," Jarlaxle begged. "Surely you felt a connection to her in life, a friendship with one worthy of your time. Sos'Umptu hinted that she wasn't destroyed, but rather banished, thrown away to . . . somewhere."

Then hope.

"No, more than hope," Jarlaxle insisted. "I need help. Sos'Umptu claimed I could never find her, but she could not have known of you. You can find her, and must, I beg."

He felt something from Kimmuriel. Perhaps some sympathy, or agreement, but it was thin.

"Sos'Umptu's words made me think she remains alive, but imprisoned."

What is alive, really?

"No, don't play like that," Jarlaxle ordered. "Perhaps this is all meaningless to you now in the glorious truth you see, but to us . . ."

Donjon, the ghost of Kimmuriel imparted through the crystal ball. *She drew from the Deck.*

"The Deck?"

Relay it to Gromph, he will know.

"He will know where to find her?"

He may figure out where to begin looking.

Jarlaxle let that float around in his thoughts for a few moments, then begged, "Give me more."

There is no more.

He felt no possibility of debate in that response. And so he closed his eyes and took a deep breath, grateful that perhaps he had a starting point, at least.

"I am lesser without you, my friend," Jarlaxle told the image. "Both practically and in my heart."

It is the way of things.

And that was it, and the spirit of Kimmuriel departed once more. Perhaps for the last time, Jarlaxle knew, though he desperately hoped that wouldn't be the case.

He felt a profound sense of loss, as had happened after every one of these seances.

But the sadness ebbed, replaced by memories of the grand adventures he had found beside Kimmuriel.

And replaced by the more practical matters at hand. Kimmuriel had been a huge boon to Bregan D'aerthe and to Jarlaxle in particular. The man's talents were outside the understanding of potential enemies and business associates alike. The advantage had been invaluable.

Now he had to look for more avenues, like the one he had been cultivating in the Hosttower of the Arcane. At his request, a surprisingly amiable Gromph had agreed to extend an invitation to Nvisi of the Ulutiuns to study and practice there.

Jarlaxle hadn't quite figured Nvisi out yet, but if that was the case with him, he knew that all others would be totally perplexed by the strange little man's magic.

Divination was foresight.

Power was knowledge.

Advantage, Jarlaxle.

THE LAUGHTER OUTSIDE THE IVY MANSION REACHED thunderous proportions when King Bruenor Battlehammer, weighing more than he had admitted to, went airborne over the bank Pikel had fashioned along the ice slide.

The snow was deep and so the landing was soft enough, and Bruenor came up covered in snow, his beard and hair more white than orange.

Off to the side of the course, Ivan Bouldershoulder argued with Thibbledorf Pwent, telling him over and over again that his armor would ruin the ice, so if he wanted a run, he should be out of it, while down at the bottom of the slide, Regis plunked Wulfgar in the back of the head with a snowball and would have been buried by the charging man had not Penelope Harpell thrown a spell of grease before him, sending him tumbling into a snowbank before he reached the halfling.

Drizzt was next down the slide, chased by Catti-brie and Breezy, with the little girl barely able to see under the brim of the one-horned helm she had stolen from her grandfather.

It was all so simple, so gloriously play, just play.

These were the moments, Drizzt realized then, as Catti-brie had come to know on a day very similar to this one. And as with his wife, for Drizzt, it was a reminder, not an epiphany. This simple little play was what made life worth it. Not Bruenor's gold or Jarlaxle's network, and not some adventure or war—those were fortunate luxuries and painful necessities—but this, this simple, childish, joyful play, was what truly made it all worth it to Drizzt Do'Urden. Because this was love, this was friendship, this was family.

Winter gave way to spring, spring turned to summer, and that notion of family came shining through again one fine morning when Jarlaxle came to visit Drizzt and Catti-brie in the Ivy Mansion, bearing exciting news.

"You three," Jarlaxle explained, his grin nearly taking in his ears. "Wulfgar and Penelope, Regis and Donnola, Bruenor, of course, and one or both of his wives."

"What of us?" Drizzt asked.

"And myself, of course, and a few others."

Drizzt looked to Catti-brie, both shrugging cluelessly, then turning back to Jarlaxle.

"Of course," Catti-brie agreed with the grinning rogue, though she had no idea of what he was talking about.

"We have been invited on a grand excursion," Jarlaxle finally explained. "On the day of the autumnal equinox, Zaknafein will battle beside Azzudonna for Biancorso in cazzcalci. We are invited to visit, to watch, and to sing with the Callidaeans by Mona Valrissa herself."

"Pops Zak!" Breezy said, and Drizzt laughed with joy.

"Oh, by the gods," Catti-brie lamented.

"What?" Drizzt and Jarlaxle asked in unison.

"When this one witnesses cazzcalci," she said, looking pointedly at Drizzt, "we'll never get him back home."

"Maybe he'll already be at home," Jarlaxle offered.

"I take my home with me," Drizzt said, ending the debate.

Catti-brie hugged him, their daughter wrapping her arms around them both, completing the circle.

The simple little joys.

Acknowledgments

With great thanks to my agent, Paul Lucas of Janklow&Nesbit, to Paul Morissey and all the folks at Wizards of the Coast for helping me to keep Drizzt alive and growing, and to David Pomerico and the folks at Harper Voyager for making me do the best I can do.

Dramatis Personae

Along the streets of Menzoberranzan . . . the drow.

Matron Mother Yvonnel Baenre: Also known as Yvonnel the Eternal. Ruled the house and the city for two thousand years. Killed by King Bruenor Battlehammer when she led the city against Mithral Hall more than a century ago.

Quenthel Baenre: Daughter of Yvonnel the Eternal and current Matron Mother of Menzoberranzan, ruling from the seat of House Baenre. Gifted with the memories of Yvonnel the Eternal by the illithids so viscerally that they are as much a part of her as they were her mother. Through them, she discovered the deception of Lloth and helped create the Great Heresy against the Spider Queen.

Sos'Umptu Baenre: Yvonnel the Eternal's daughter, mistress of Arach-Tinilith, former first priestess of House Baenre and current high priestess of the Fane of the Goddess. Remains fervently loyal to Lloth, putting her at odds with Matron Mother Quenthel and House Baenre.

Yvonnel Baenre: Daughter of Gromph and Minolin Fey Branche. Like Quenthel, she was gifted the memories of her grandmother, Yvonnel the Eternal, only for her, it was performed in utero. She is only a few years old, but was born with full consciousness and two thousand years of memory. Perhaps the most powerful drow in Menzoberranzan, she used magic to age herself into a young drow woman. She admires Drizzt, secretly loves him, and, with Matron Mother Quenthel, facilitated the Great Heresy, leaving the city of Menzoberranzan on the verge of civil war.

Matron Zhindia Melarn: Zealot of Lloth, led the assault of the Sword Coast of Faerun against Luskan, Gauntlgrym, and Bleeding Vines, and seemed on the verge of victory until the Great Heresy of Quenthel and Yvonnel stole her drider army out from under her.

Matron Zeerith Xorlarrin: The matron of the powerful House Xorlarrin, known for its practitioners of the arcane magic, lost much of her status when her house struck out to create a sister city to Menzoberranzan, only to be rudely evicted by King Bruenor and his armies when he reclaimed Gauntlgrym. Her friends, the Baenres, gave to her the abandoned House Do'Urden, a name she never wore comfortably. Ever the diplomat, the old matron wishes to avoid war in Menzoberranzan and also wishes to restore her proper family name.

Saribel Xorlarrin: Saribel once carried the surname of Baenre, after marrying the brash young weaponmaster Tiago of the First Family. Practical and clever, Saribel is the sole remaining daughter of Matron Zeerith and serves as First Priestess of the new House Do'Urden.

Ravel Xorlarrin: Son of Zeerith, Ravel is a blossoming young wizard. Events have slowed his studies in the arcane arts, but have shown a side of him both cunning and diplomatic. Never enamored of Lolth, he welcomes the changes sought by the Baenres.

Tsabrak Xorlarrin: The powerful wizard of Zeerith's house ascended to the rank of Archmage of Menzoberranzan after the abdication of the position by Gromph Baenre. He came to glory among the udadrow in the War of the Silver Marches, when he channeled the power of Lolth to blot out the sun in an event called the great Darkening.

The Blaspheme: An army of some eight hundred driders returned to life on the Material Plane to serve Matron Zhindia Melarne in her surface war. But when Yvonnel and Quenthel fashioned the magical web to remove all curses, even the Curse of Abomination that eternally tormented them in their half-drow/half-spider form, they rushed through to become again true drow, now following House Baenre in opposition to Lloth.

Mal'a'Voselle "Voselly" Amvas Tol: Mighty warrior from another age, the long-dead House Amvas Tol, where she ranked as weapon master. The powerful, broad-shouldered woman serves as Blaspheme field commander.

Aleandra: Another of the Blaspheme, and friend of Voselly since their days fighting side by side in House Amvas Tol in ancient Menzoberranzan.

Dininae: Another of the Blaspheme, and one of the few who lived in recent years in Menzoberranzan. His true identity is Dinin Do'Urden, elder brother of Drizzt. He was turned into a drider by his sister, Vierna, and met his end at the end of King Bruenor Battlehammer's many-notched axe.

Malagdorl: The Weapon Master of powerful House Barrison Del'Armgo, Malagdorl has been turned into the image of his ancestor, the great Uthegentel. Considered the greatest warrior in Menzoberranzan, he is prized and beloved by his grandmother, the Matron Mez'Barris. He wants nothing more than to battle and kill Drizzt Do'Urden.

Along the streets of Callidae . . . the aevendrow and other.

Nvisi: A human of the Ulutiun culture, Nvisi is short and hunched with a face wrinkled and ruddy, bright and round, and with one eye flashing amber, the other crystal blue. He is a seer, a wizard of the school of divination . . . maybe. The other wizards of Callidae don't understand him and don't trust his ways, his magic, or his visions, with the notable exception of Allefaero, who has come to recognize that Nvisi might be among the best seers of the city. Nvisi doesn't care. As long as he has his casting bones and his loyal glacial lemming familiar, Doodles, all is well.

Azzudonna: A young aevendrow woman, proud warrior of the Biancorso cazzcalci team, hero in the most recent match. A fierce fighter, Azzudonna has found a strong bond with Zaknafein.

Holy Galathae: Paladin of Eilistraee, Galathae is a leader in the defenses of Callidae and was instrumental in accepting the four strangers—Jarlaxle, Catti-brie, Artemis Entreri, and Zaknafein—who happened upon the city.

Aida "Ayeeda" Umptu: The innkeeper of Ibilsitato in the borough of Scellobel. With unusual blue eyes, mostly blue hair, and a perpetual smile and joy of life, she became friends with the four strangers, particularly Jarlaxle, who spent their nights in Callidae in her establishment. She is very close with Azzudonna, Ilina, and Alvinessy.

Allefaero: A young bookworm and wizard, this mage-scholar is the city's expert on much of the flora and fauna of the region. Preferring to spend his days in the library, Allefaero is nervous that his understanding of the dangerous environ will almost certainly put him on the front lines of a great struggle.

Ilina: Priestess Ilina was one of the earliest to accept the four strangers, as her god is quite similar to that of Catti-brie, Mielikki. With an indisputable reputation, Ilina's vouching for the outsiders was an important voice in their acceptance.

Alvinessy "Vessi": Best friend of Azzudonna, the short wiry man plays dasher for Biancorso. Like Azzudonna, he is young and full of life and hope and dreams.

Doum'wielle Armgo: Daughter of a drow man and a moon elf woman, Doum'wielle found her way to Menzoberranzan and a place as a noble in Barrison Del'Armgo, the city's Second House. She ran afoul of Gromph Baenre and was thrown through a portal to the far north. Jarlaxle convinced his three companions to go north primarily to find her, and learned that she, too, had stumbled upon Callidae, and had been accepted by the aevendrow, but now, alas, was seemingly lost forever.

Mona Valrissa Zhamboule: The current *mona,* or governor, of Callidae, Valrissa carries the weight of great responsibility on her shoulders. A savvy politician and decent woman, she balances the responsibilities of office in leading the Temporal Convocation with the responsibilities to her heart, and that which she knows is right.

From the Sword Coast . . .

Gromph Baenre: Yvonnel the Eternal's oldest child, former archmage of Menzoberranzan, and now the archmage of Luskan's Hosttower of the Arcane. Considered among the most powerful wizards in the world.

Kimmuriel: Co-leader of Bregan D'aerthe with Jarlaxle, Kimmuriel has ever been an enigma to his roguish counterpart. For Kimmuriel is a powerful psionicist, a master of mind magic who spends quite a bit of time with the strange illithids at their hive mind. He is older now, and more introspective, asking the larger questions of his life.

Dab'nay: The drow priestess has served Jarlaxle in Bregan D'aerthe for many decades. Once a lover of Zaknafein, always a friend to him and to Jarlaxle, she often questioned why Lloth was seemingly granting her divine spells, since she has no love for the evil Spider Queen. Her prominence within Bregan D'aerthe had grown in recent years as she had become integral to their handling of their rule in the city of Luskan.

Jarlaxle: A houseless rogue who began Bregan D'aerthe, a mercenary band quietly serving the needs of many drow houses, but mostly serving their own needs.

Drizzt Do'Urden: Born in Menzoberranzan and fled the evil ways of the city. Drow warrior, hero of the north, and Companion of the Hall, along with his four dear friends.

Catti-brie: Human wife of Drizzt, chosen of the goddess Mielikki, skilled in both arcane and divine magic. Companion of the Hall.

Regis (Spider Parrafin): Halfling husband of Donnola Topolino, leader of the halfling community of Bleeding Vines. Companion of the Hall.

King Bruenor Battlehammer: Eighth king of Mithral Hall, tenth king of Mithral Hall, now king of Gauntlgrym, an ancient dwarven city he reclaimed with his dwarven kin. Adoptive father of both Wulfgar and Catti-brie. Companion of the Hall.

Wulfgar: Born to the Tribe of the Elk in Icewind Dale, the giant human was captured by Bruenor in battle and became the adopted son of the dwarf king. Companion of the Hall.

Artemis Entreri: Former nemesis of Drizzt, the human assassin is the drow warrior's near equal or equal in battle. Now he runs with Jarlaxle's Bregan D'aerthe band, and considers Drizzt and the other Companions of the Hall friends.

Guenhwyvar: Magical panther, companion of Drizzt, summoned to his side from the Astral Plane.

Andahar: Drizzt's summoned steed, a magical unicorn. Unlike the living Guenhwyvar, Andahar is a purely magical construct.

Penelope Harpell: The leader of the eccentric wizards known as the Harpells, who oversee the town of Longsaddle from their estate, the Ivy Mansion. Penelope is a powerful wizard, mentoring Catti-brie, and has dated Wulfgar on occasion.

Grandmaster Kane: A human monk who has transcended his mortal coil and become a being beyond the Material Plane, Kane was the Grandmaster of Flowers of the Monastery of the Yellow Rose in far-off Damara. He was friend and mentor to Drizzt as the drow learned to find peace at last along a turbulent road.

Thibbledorf Pwent: A walking weapon in his spiked and sharp-ridged armor, Pwent is a battle-hardened dwarf whose loyalty is as strong as the aroma emanating from him. He led every seemingly suicidal charge with a cry of "Me King!" and gave his life saving King Bruenor in the bowels of Gauntlgrym. His death was not the end of Pwent, though, for he was slain by a vampire, and now continues as one—a cursed and miserable thing, haunting the lowest tunnels of Gauntlgrym and satisfying his insatiable hunger by feeding on the goblins beyond the dwarven realm.

The Brothers Bouldershoulder, Ivan and Pikel: Ivan Bouldershoulder is a grizzled old veteran of many battles, mundane and magical. He's risen to a position of great trust as a commander in Bruenor's Gauntlgrym guard. More eccentric and extreme than Ivan, the green-haired Pikel fancies himself a druid, or "doo-dad," and helped Donnola Topolino create wonderful vineyards in Bleeding Vines. His limited and stilted vocabulary only adds to the deceptive innocence of this quite powerful dwarf.

Eternal Beings

Lolth, the Lady of Chaos, the Demon Queen of Spiders, the Queen of the Demonweb Pits: The mighty demon Lolth reigns as the most influential goddess of the drow, particularly in the greatest drow city, Menzoberranzan, known as the City of Spiders for the devotion of its inhabitants. True to her name, the Lady of Chaos constantly shocks her followers, keeping her true plans buried beneath the webbing of other more obvious and understandable schemes. Her end goal, above all, is chaos.

Eskavidne and Yiccardaria: Lesser demons known as yochlol, they serve as two of the handmaidens of Lolth. The pair have proven so resourceful and skilled that Lolth gives them great rein in walking the ways of the drow and making a glorious mess of everything.

Eilistraee: The Dark Maiden is the drow goddess of beauty, song, dance, freedom, moonlight, swordwork, and hunting. For the udadrow, she is the anti-Lolth, giving hope and purpose to those who have escaped the deceits of the Spider Queen.

Qadeej: One of the Vaati, or Wind Dukes of Aaqa, a group of godlike beings opposing chaos in the cosmos. The legend of Qadeej claims that he lay down on the north pole of Toril and there died, and that the great glacier that now houses Callidae on one end, and the frost giant and slaad castle on the other, arose from the magic of his body.

About the Author

More than thirty-five years ago, R. A. Salvatore created the character of Drizzt Do'Urden, the dark elf who has withstood the test of time to stand today as an icon in the fantasy genre. With his work in the Forgotten Realms, the Crimson Shadow, the DemonWars Saga, and other series, Salvatore has sold more than thirty million books worldwide and has appeared on the *New York Times* bestseller list more than two dozen times. He considers writing to be his personal journey, but still, he's quite pleased that so many are walking the road beside him! R. A. lives in Massachusetts with his wife, Diane, and their two dogs, Dexter and Pikel. He still plays softball for his team, Clan Battlehammer, and enjoys his weekly *DemonWars: Reformation* RPG and *Dungeons & Dragons* 5e games. Salvatore can be found at rasalvatore.com.